DRY COUNTRY

RICH TOMMASO

IMAGE COMICS
PORTLAND, OR

IMAGE COMICS, INC.
Robert Kirkman—Chief Operating Officer
Erik Larsen—Chief Financial Officer
Todd McFarlane—President
Marc Silvestri—Chief Executive Officer
Jim Valentino—Vice President

Eric Stephenson—Publisher / Chief Creative Officer
Corey Hart—Director of Sales
Jeff Boison—Director of Publishing Planning
& Book Trade Sales
Chris Ross—Director of Digital Sales
Jeff Stang—Director of Specialty Sales
Kat Salazar—Director of PR & Marketing
Drew Gill—Art Director
Heather Doornink—Production Director
Nicole Lapalme—Controller
IMAGECOMICS.COM

RY COUNTY, Complete TP. First printing. September 2018. Published by Image Comics, Inc. Office of publication: 2701 NW Vaughn St., Suite 780, Portland, OR 97210.
pyright © 2018 Rich Tommaso. All rights reserved. Contains material originally published in single magazine form as DRY COUNTY #1-5. "Dry County," its logos, and the
enesses of all characters herein are trademarks of Rich Tommaso, unless otherwise noted. "Image" and the Image Comics logos are registered trademarks of Image Comics, Inc.
part of this publication may be reproduced or transmitted, in any form or by any means (except for short excerpts for journalistic or review purposes), without the express
itten permission of Rich Tommaso, or Image Comics, Inc. All names, characters, events, and locales in this publication are entirely fictional. Any resemblance to actual persons
ving or dead), events, or places, without satiric intent, is coincidental. Printed in the USA. For information regarding the CPSIA on this printed material call: 203-595-3636 and
ovide reference #RICH—812003. For international rights, contact: foreignlicensing@imagecomics.com. ISBN: 978-1-5343-0830-5.

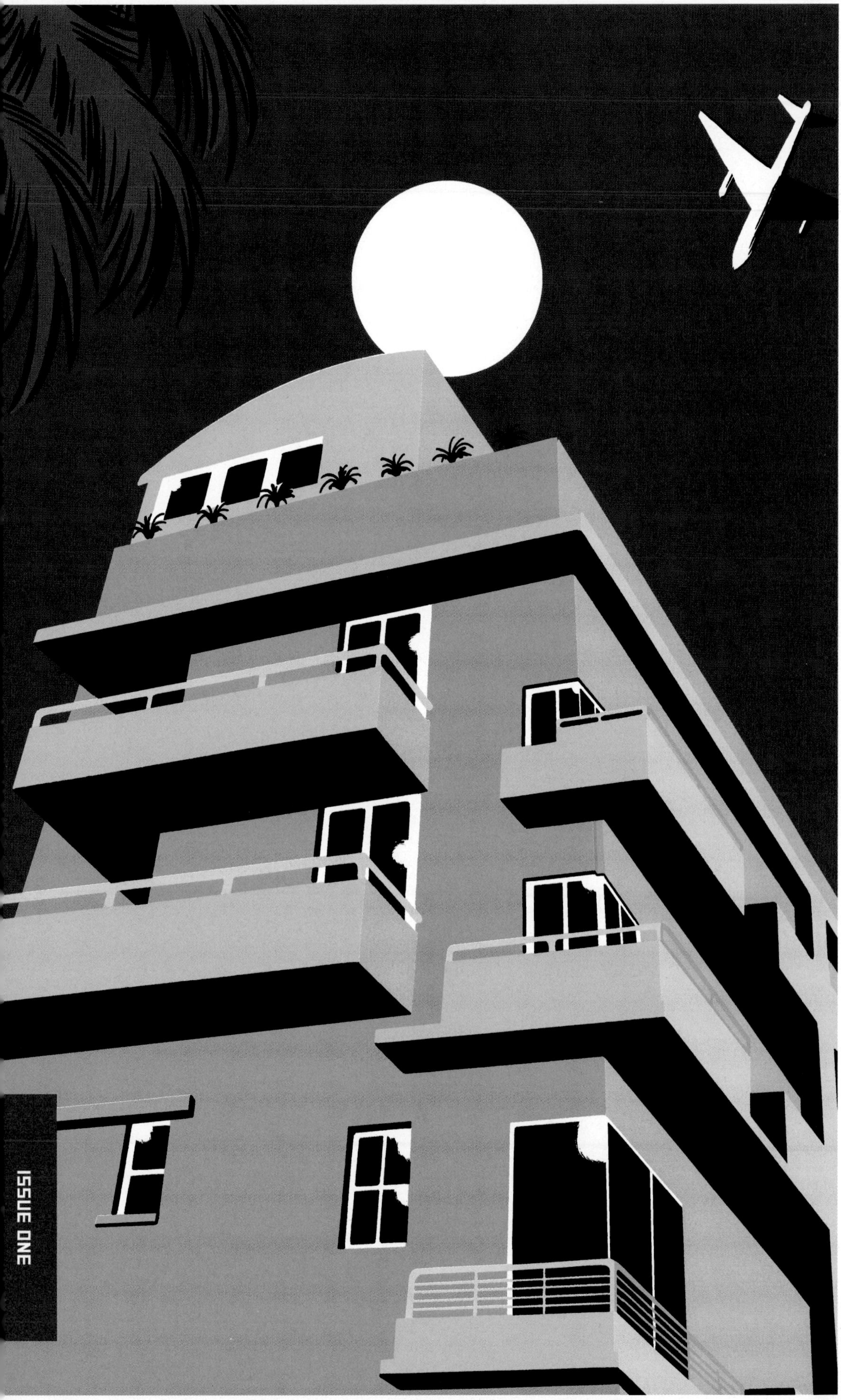
ISSUE ONE

1

MIAMI NIGHT LIFE ~ DANCE CLUBS BLARING HOUSE MUSIC, RAVES GOING ON UNTIL 6 THE NEXT MORNING, HORDES OF PEOPLE, TWISTING AND SHAKING, DRINKING AND LAUGHING ~ CHRIST, HOW I HATED IT...

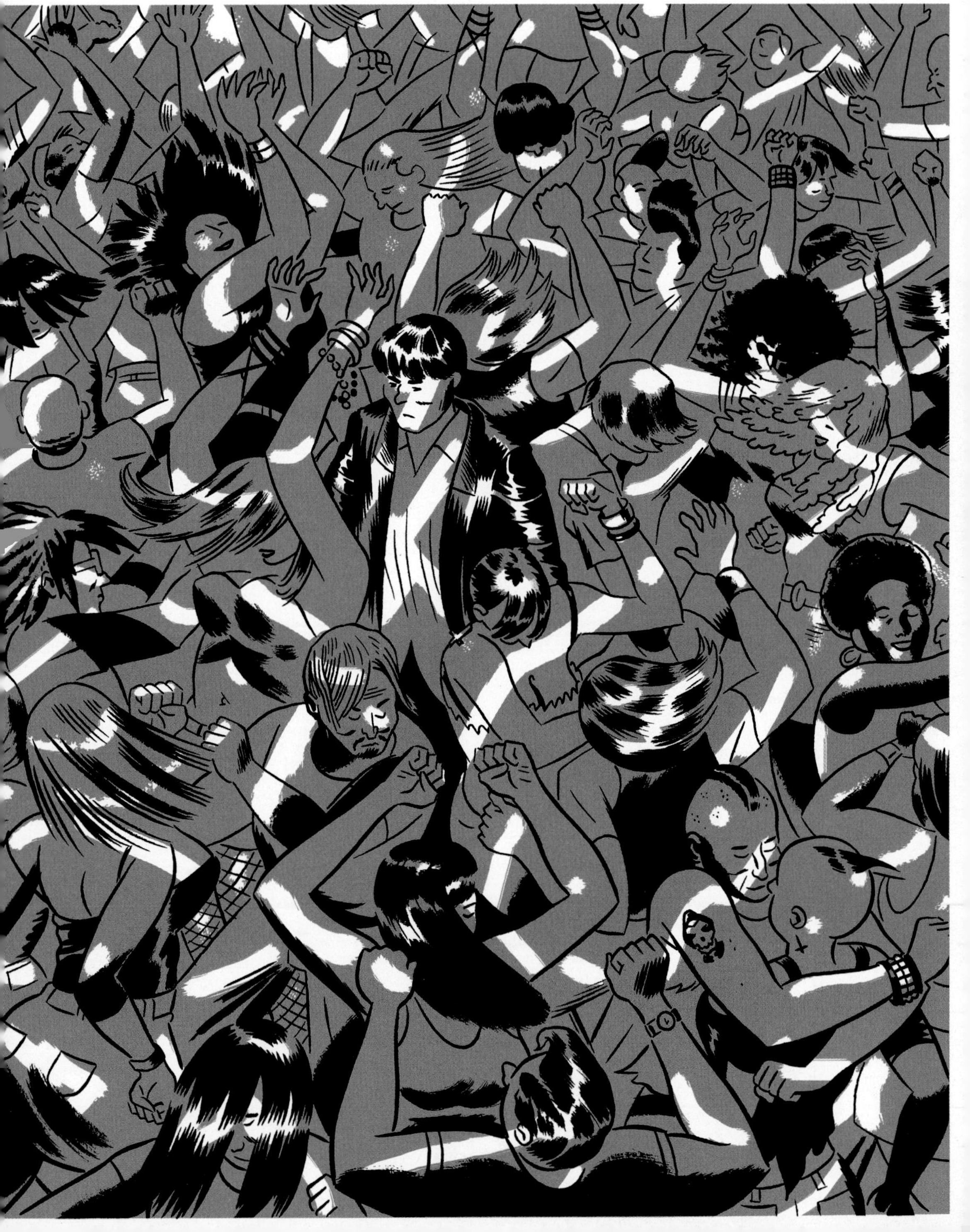

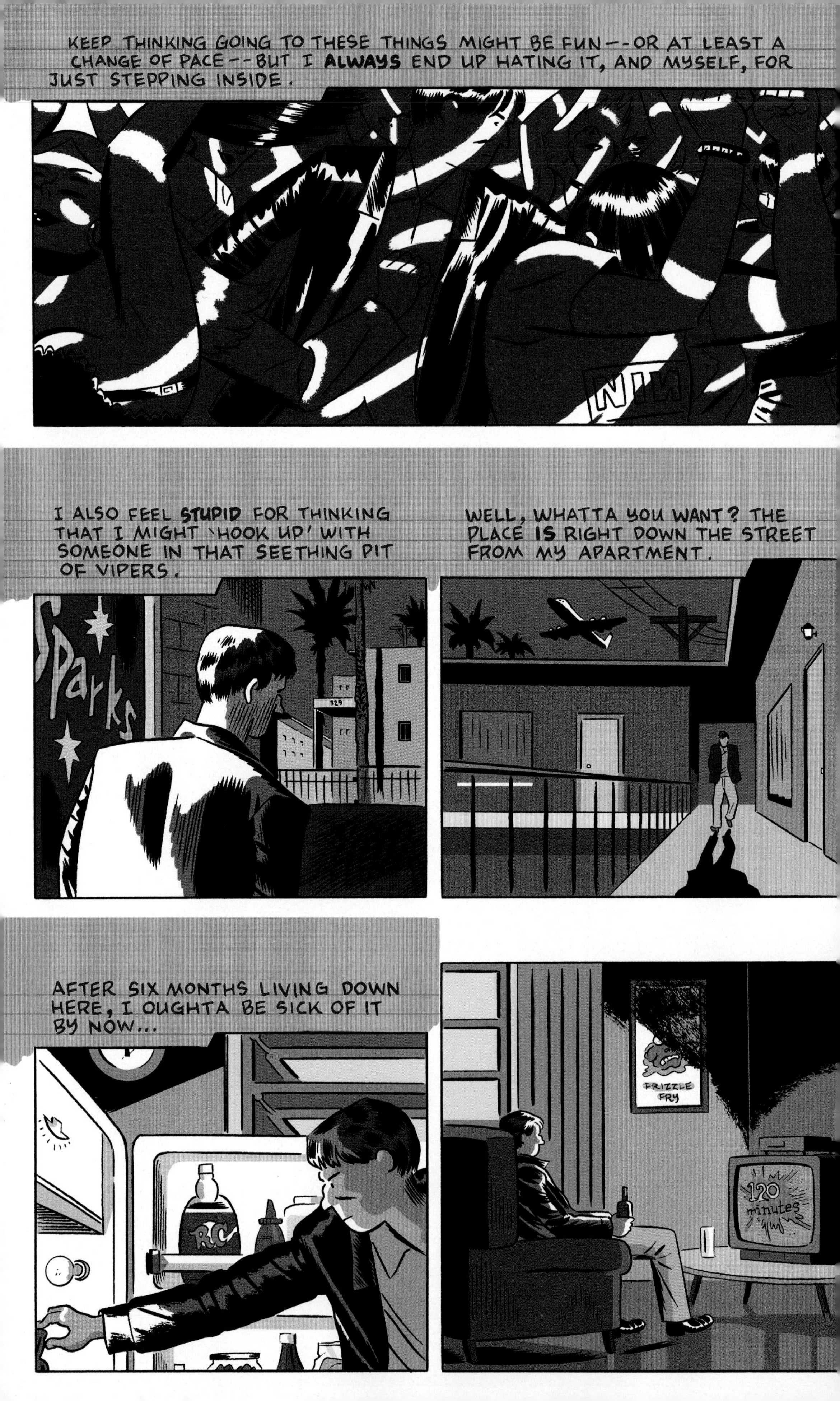
KEEP THINKING GOING TO THESE THINGS MIGHT BE FUN--OR AT LEAST A CHANGE OF PACE--BUT I **ALWAYS** END UP HATING IT, AND MYSELF, FOR JUST STEPPING INSIDE.
NIN
I ALSO FEEL **STUPID** FOR THINKING THAT I MIGHT 'HOOK UP' WITH SOMEONE IN THAT SEETHING PIT OF VIPERS.
Sparks
329
WELL, WHATTA YOU WANT? THE PLACE **IS** RIGHT DOWN THE STREET FROM MY APARTMENT.
AFTER SIX MONTHS LIVING DOWN HERE, I OUGHTA BE SICK OF IT BY NOW...
RC
FRIZZLE FRY
120 minutes

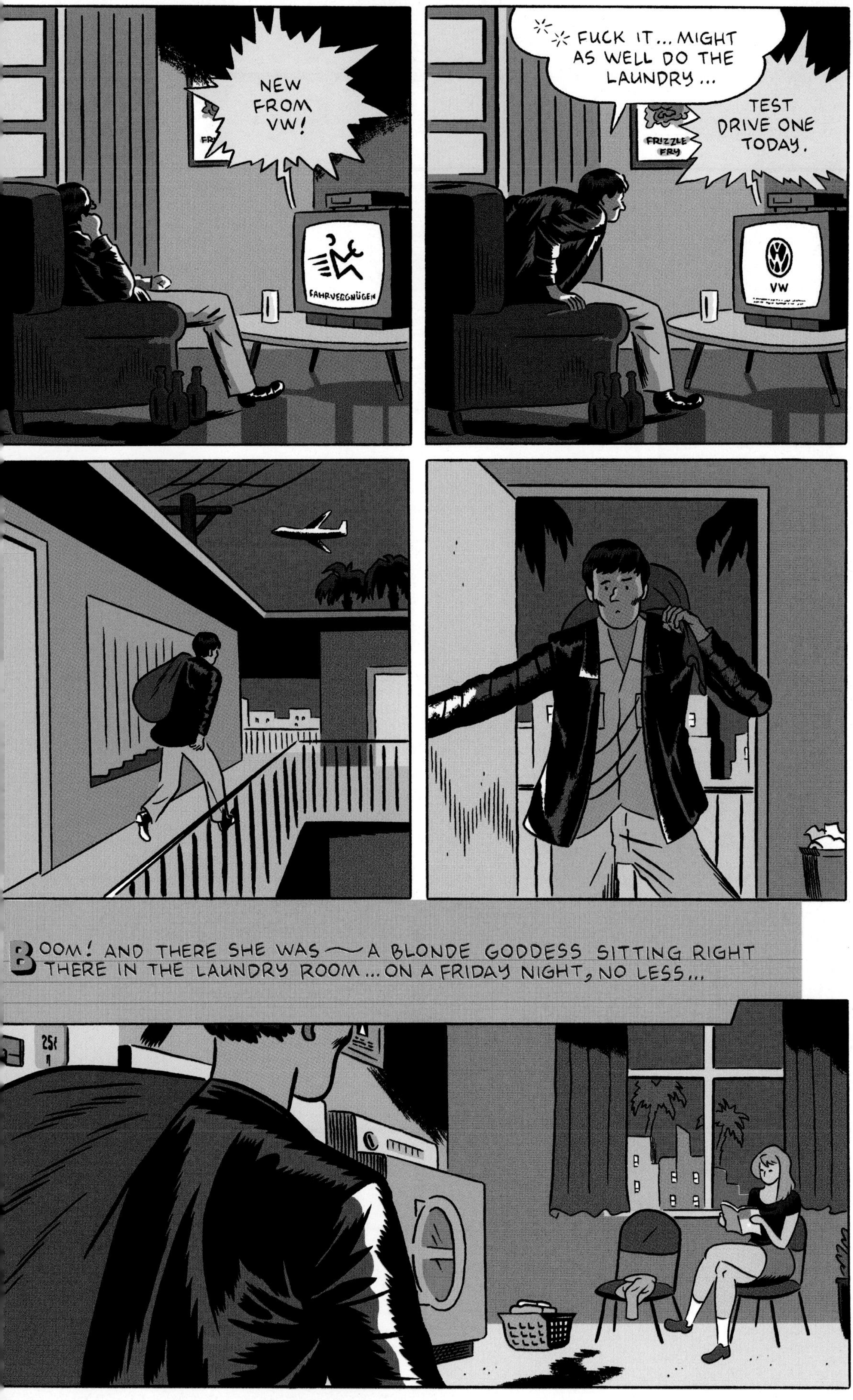
NEW FROM VW!
FAHRVERGNÜGEN
FUCK IT... MIGHT AS WELL DO THE LAUNDRY...
FRIZZLE FRY
TEST DRIVE ONE TODAY.
VW
BOOM! AND THERE SHE WAS — A BLONDE GODDESS SITTING RIGHT THERE IN THE LAUNDRY ROOM... ON A FRIDAY NIGHT, NO LESS...
25¢

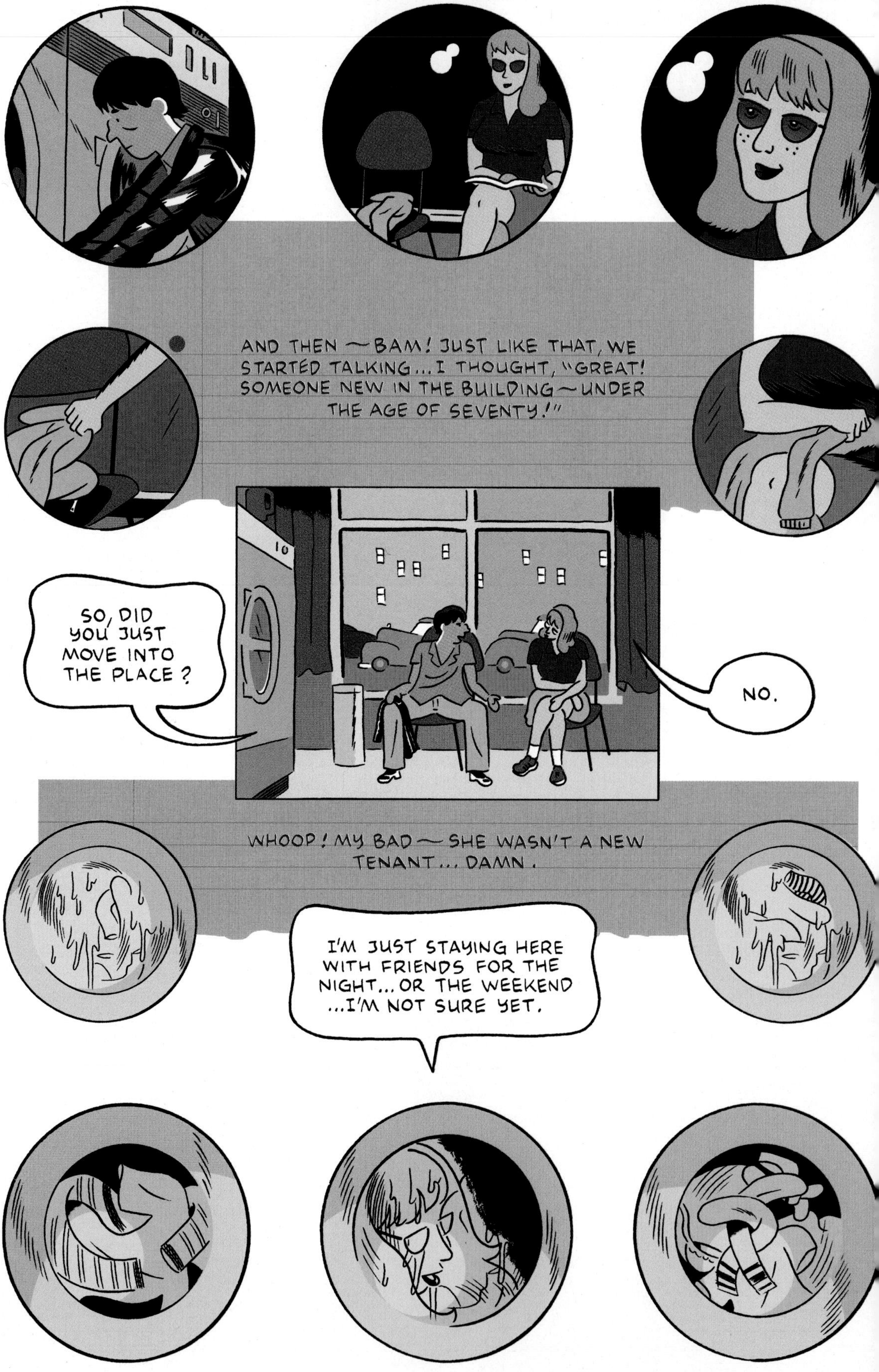

AND THEN — BAM! JUST LIKE THAT, WE STARTED TALKING... I THOUGHT, "GREAT! SOMEONE NEW IN THE BUILDING — UNDER THE AGE OF SEVENTY!"
SO, DID YOU JUST MOVE INTO THE PLACE?
NO.
WHOOP! MY BAD — SHE WASN'T A NEW TENANT... DAMN.
I'M JUST STAYING HERE WITH FRIENDS FOR THE NIGHT... OR THE WEEKEND ...I'M NOT SURE YET.

SHE AND I SEEMED TO BE HITTING IT OFF PRETTY QUICKLY. I TRIED TO KEEP MY EYES ON HERS, BUT I COULDN'T HELP THEM FROM OCCASIONALLY TRAVELING AROUND TO OTHER PARTS OF HER BODY ...

WHEN YOU CAN TELL THAT SOMEONE LIKES YOU, YOU FEEL IT'S PROBABLY OKAY IF THEY CATCH YOU LOOKING THEM UP AND DOWN A BIT... WHENEVER SHE DID CATCH MY EYES WANDERING AROUND, IT ONLY SEEMED TO MAKE HER SMILE AND BLUSH A LITTLE.

WE TALKED ON AND ON, BACK AND FORTH, EXCHANGING PERSONAL INFORMATION AS OUR PERSONAL ITEMS WRESTLED EACH OTHER IN THE DRYER (THERE WAS ONLY ONE DRYER THAT WAS ANY GOOD IN THIS DUMP, SO WE SHARED IT)...

WHILE WE WAITED FOR THEM TO FINISH, I RAN BACK TO MY APARTMENT AND BROUGHT BACK A COUPLE OF BEERS AS A WAY TO CELEBRATE HER LITTLE VISIT TO THE FLEUR DE LIS.

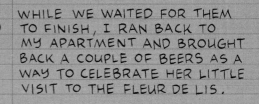

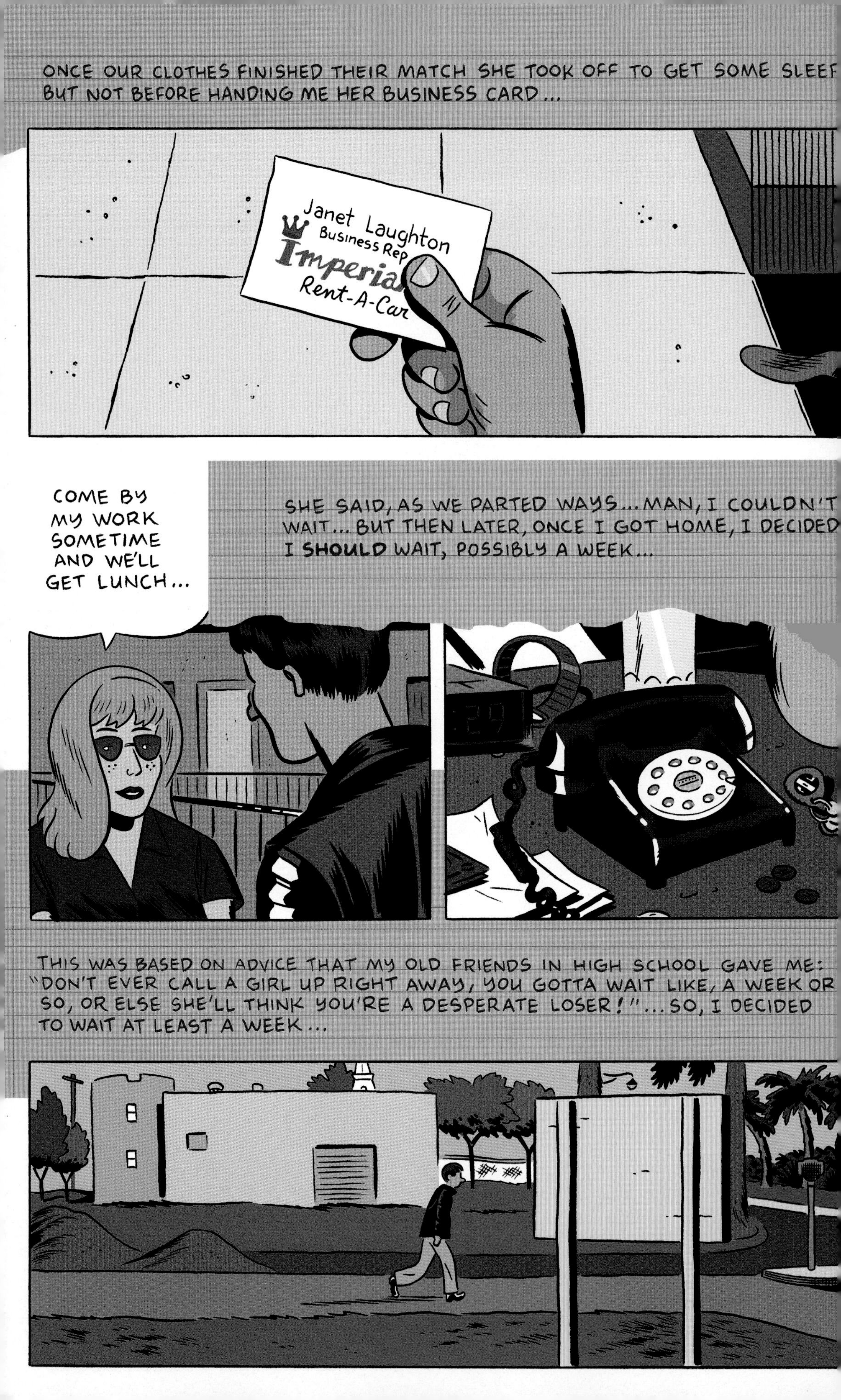
ONCE OUR CLOTHES FINISHED THEIR MATCH SHE TOOK OFF TO GET SOME SLEEP BUT NOT BEFORE HANDING ME HER BUSINESS CARD...
Janet Laughton
Business Rep
Imperia
Rent-A-Car
COME BY MY WORK SOMETIME AND WE'LL GET LUNCH...
SHE SAID, AS WE PARTED WAYS... MAN, I COULDN'T WAIT... BUT THEN LATER, ONCE I GOT HOME, I DECIDED I **SHOULD** WAIT, POSSIBLY A WEEK...
THIS WAS BASED ON ADVICE THAT MY OLD FRIENDS IN HIGH SCHOOL GAVE ME: "DON'T EVER CALL A GIRL UP RIGHT AWAY, YOU GOTTA WAIT LIKE, A WEEK OR SO, OR ELSE SHE'LL THINK YOU'RE A DESPERATE LOSER!"... SO, I DECIDED TO WAIT AT LEAST A WEEK...

2

TWO DAYS LATER, I CALLED UP JANET--I **COULDN'T** WAIT. SHE WAS HAPPY TO HEAR FROM ME AND WE MADE A DATE TO HAVE LUNCH THAT VERY SAME AFTERNOON.

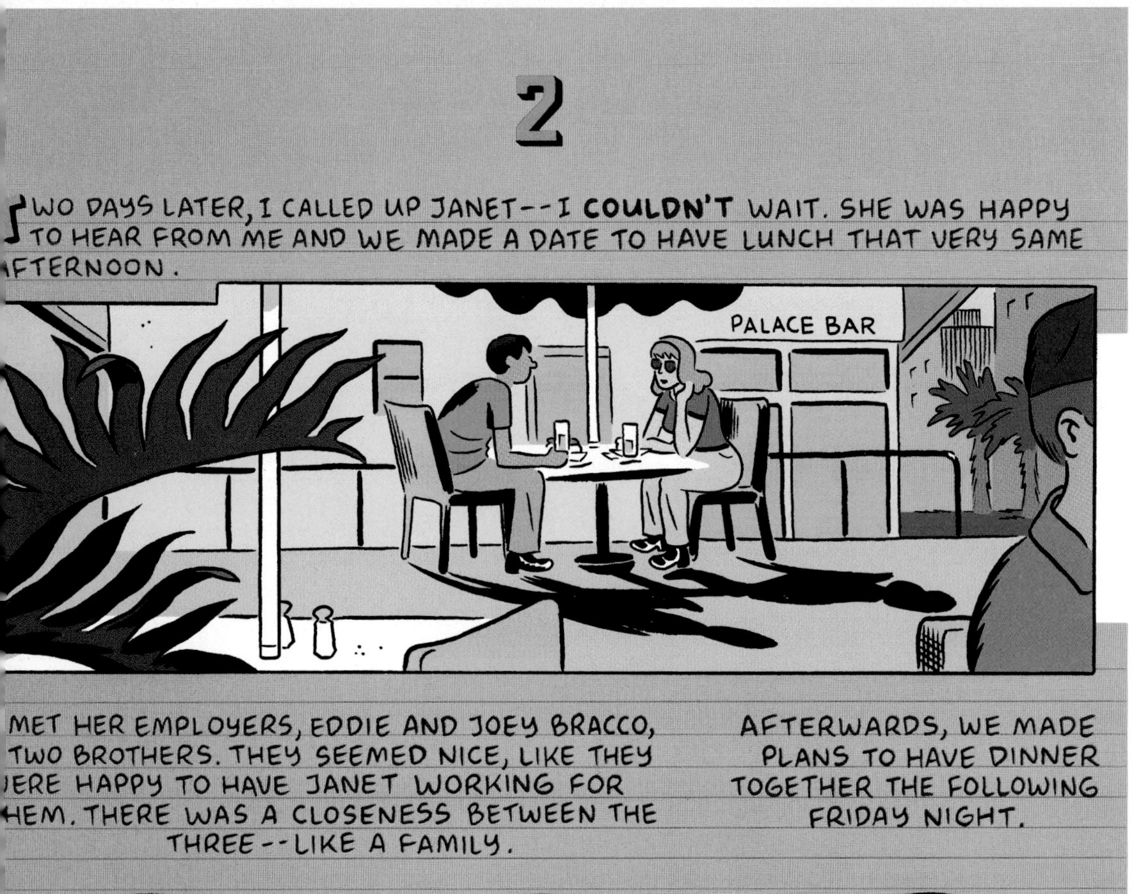
PALACE BAR

I MET HER EMPLOYERS, EDDIE AND JOEY BRACCO, TWO BROTHERS. THEY SEEMED NICE, LIKE THEY WERE HAPPY TO HAVE JANET WORKING FOR THEM. THERE WAS A CLOSENESS BETWEEN THE THREE--LIKE A FAMILY.

AFTERWARDS, WE MADE PLANS TO HAVE DINNER TOGETHER THE FOLLOWING FRIDAY NIGHT.

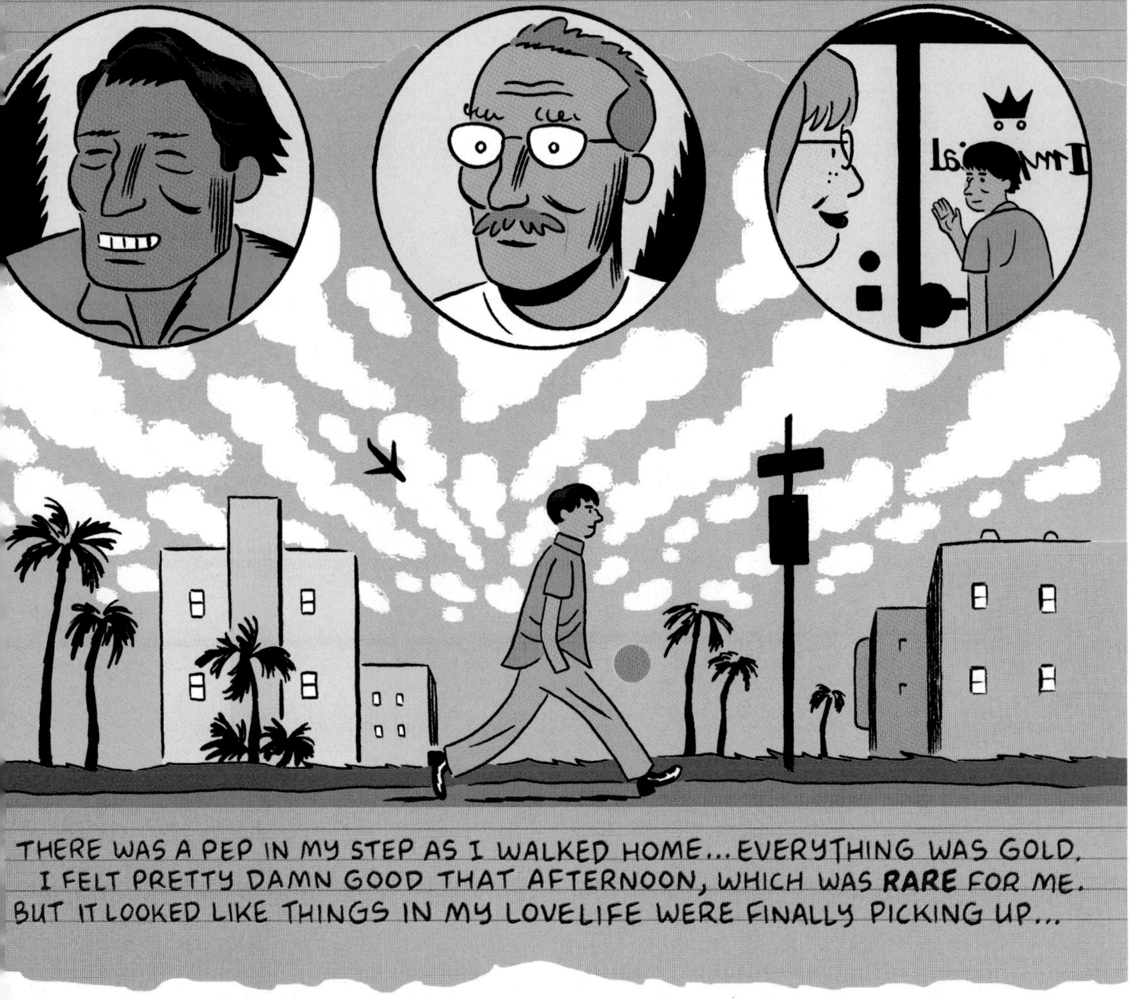

THERE WAS A PEP IN MY STEP AS I WALKED HOME... EVERYTHING WAS GOLD. I FELT PRETTY DAMN GOOD THAT AFTERNOON, WHICH WAS **RARE** FOR ME. BUT IT LOOKED LIKE THINGS IN MY LOVELIFE WERE FINALLY PICKING UP...

3

IT WAS MONDAY AND MY WORK ONCE AGAIN WAS FINISHED FOR THE DAY. IT WAS JUST AFTER 2:30 WHEN SHE CAME RUMBLING INTO THE OFFICE LIKE A DUST DEVIL RIPPING INTO A SILO.

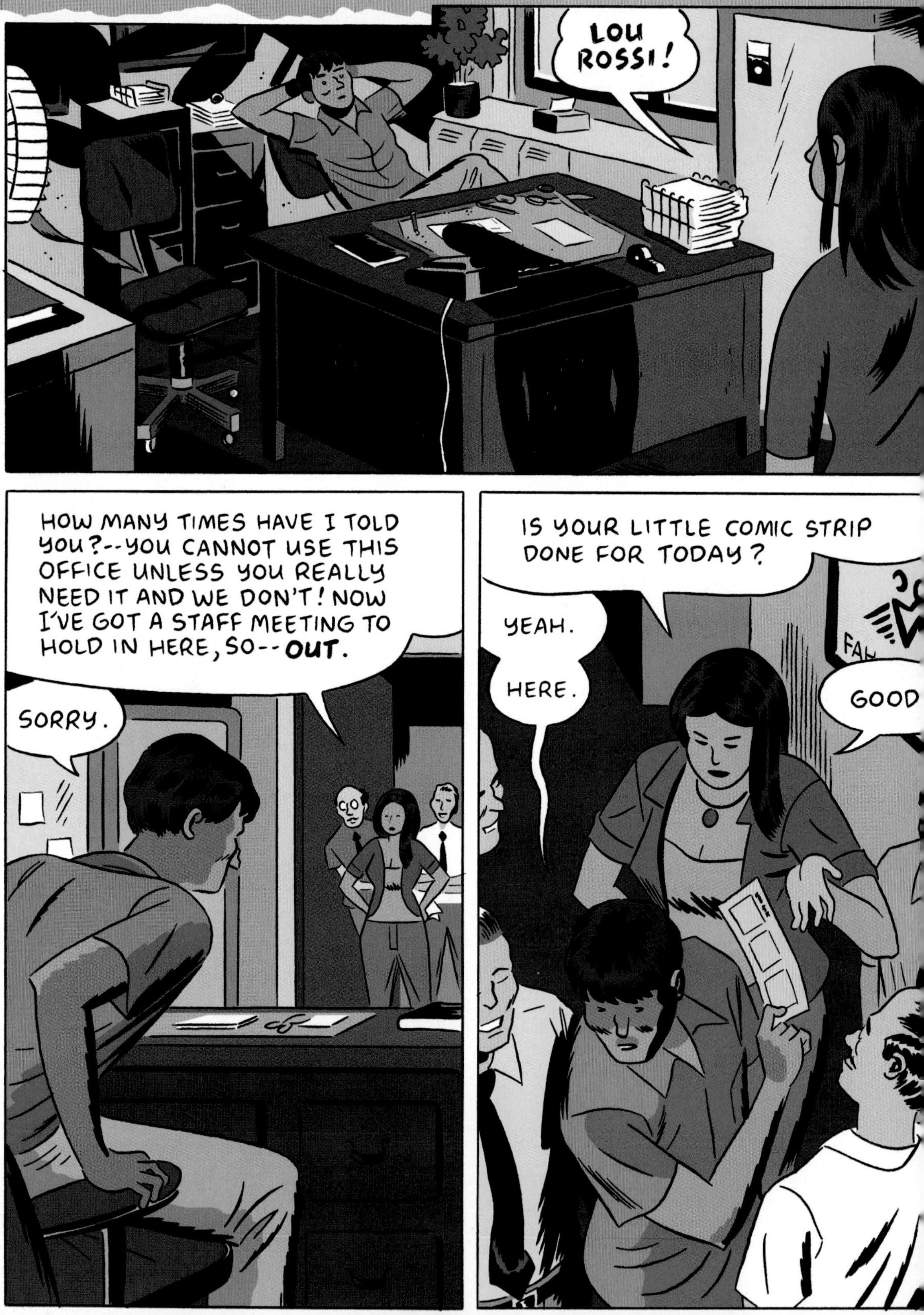
LOU ROSSI!
HOW MANY TIMES HAVE I TOLD YOU?--YOU CANNOT USE THIS OFFICE UNLESS YOU REALLY NEED IT AND WE DON'T! NOW I'VE GOT A STAFF MEETING TO HOLD IN HERE, SO--**OUT**.
SORRY.
IS YOUR LITTLE COMIC STRIP DONE FOR TODAY?
YEAH.
HERE.
GOOD

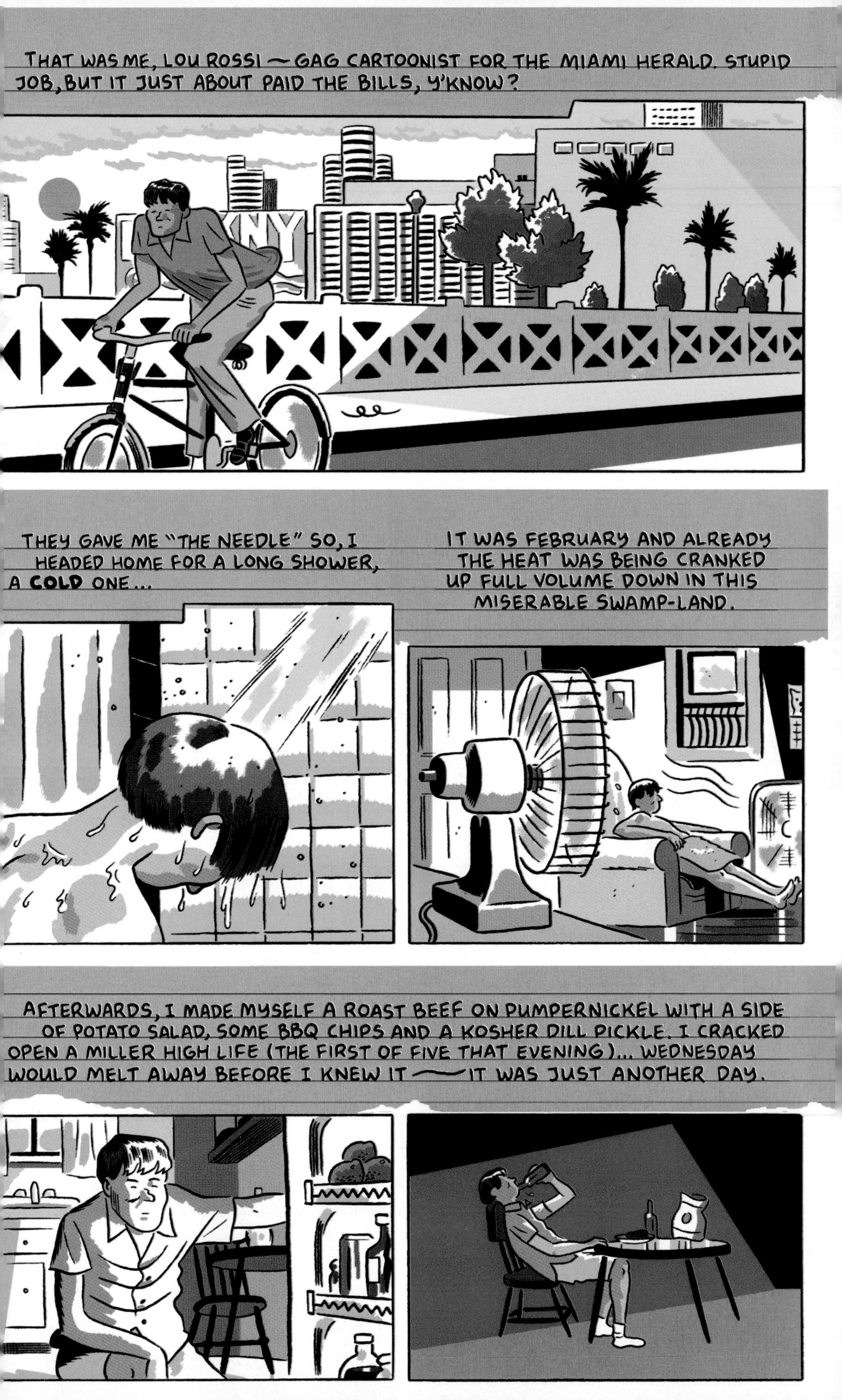
THAT WAS ME, LOU ROSSI — GAG CARTOONIST FOR THE MIAMI HERALD. STUPID JOB, BUT IT JUST ABOUT PAID THE BILLS, Y'KNOW?
THEY GAVE ME "THE NEEDLE" SO, I HEADED HOME FOR A LONG SHOWER, A **COLD** ONE...
IT WAS FEBRUARY AND ALREADY THE HEAT WAS BEING CRANKED UP FULL VOLUME DOWN IN THIS MISERABLE SWAMP-LAND.
AFTERWARDS, I MADE MYSELF A ROAST BEEF ON PUMPERNICKEL WITH A SIDE OF POTATO SALAD, SOME BBQ CHIPS AND A KOSHER DILL PICKLE. I CRACKED OPEN A MILLER HIGH LIFE (THE FIRST OF FIVE THAT EVENING)... WEDNESDAY WOULD MELT AWAY BEFORE I KNEW IT — IT WAS JUST ANOTHER DAY.

4

SO, LET'S GET TO IT, HUH? FRIDAY HAD ARRIVED AND I'D SPENT ABOUT TWO HOURS GETTING READY FOR MY DATE WITH JANET... YES I WAS PROBABLY TRYING TOO HARD TO MAKE A GOOD IMPRESSION, BUT I LIKED TO LOOK GOOD WHEN I WENT OUT ON A DATE ~ I DIDN'T WANT TO LOOK LIKE SOME DIRTY HIPPY...

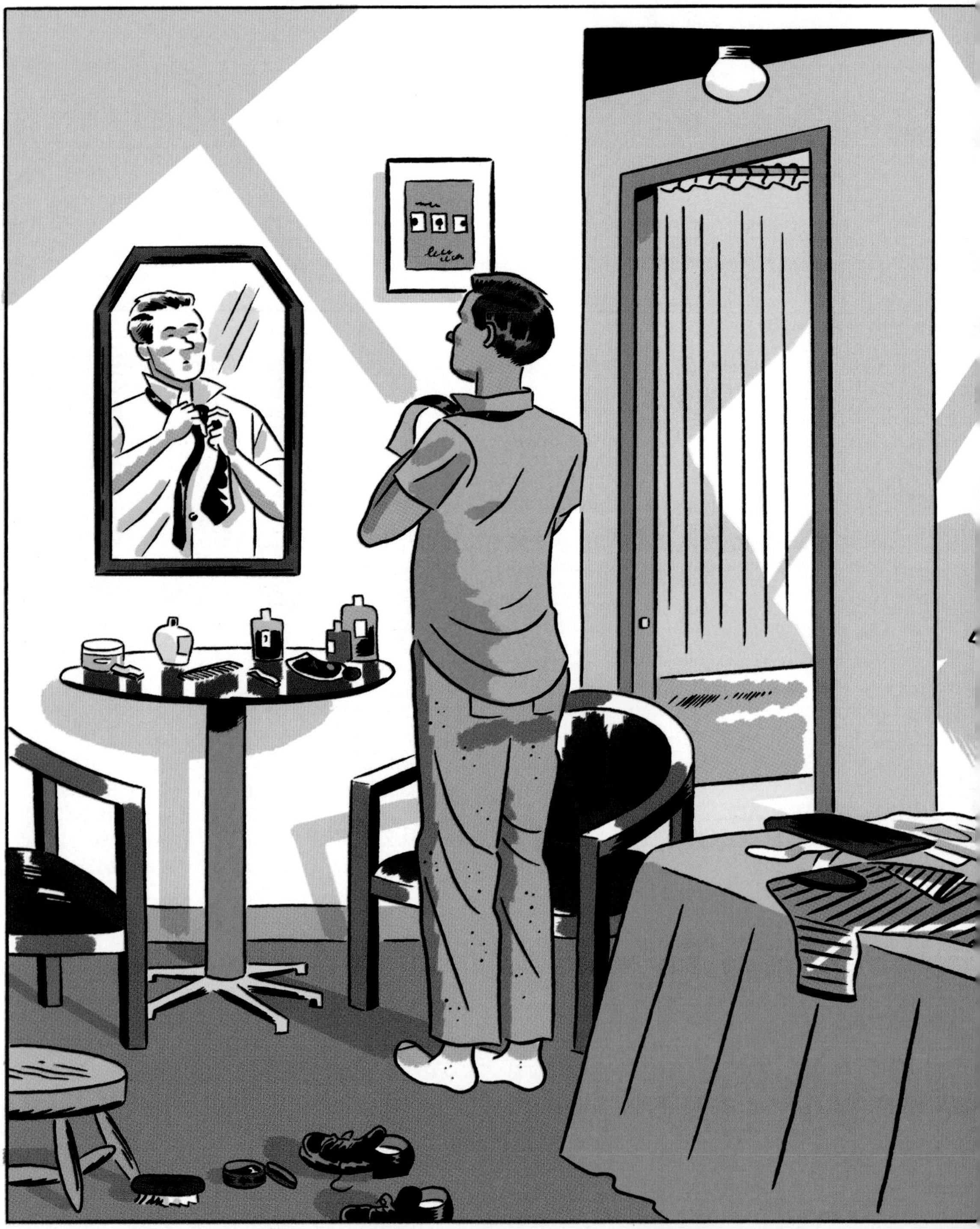

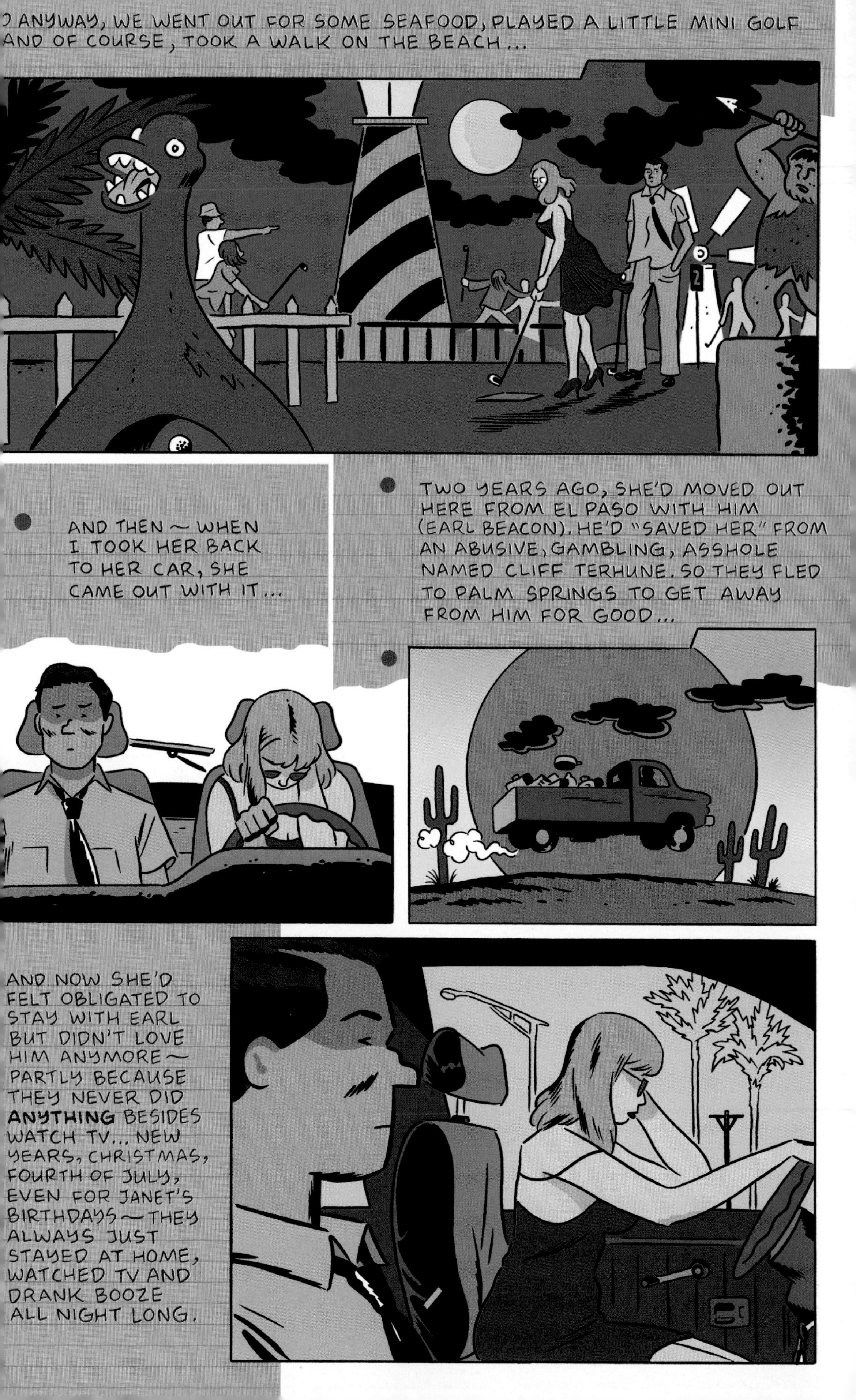
O ANYWAY, WE WENT OUT FOR SOME SEAFOOD, PLAYED A LITTLE MINI GOLF AND OF COURSE, TOOK A WALK ON THE BEACH...
2
AND THEN ~ WHEN I TOOK HER BACK TO HER CAR, SHE CAME OUT WITH IT...
TWO YEARS AGO, SHE'D MOVED OUT HERE FROM EL PASO WITH HIM (EARL BEACON). HE'D "SAVED HER" FROM AN ABUSIVE, GAMBLING, ASSHOLE NAMED CLIFF TERHUNE. SO THEY FLED TO PALM SPRINGS TO GET AWAY FROM HIM FOR GOOD...
AND NOW SHE'D FELT OBLIGATED TO STAY WITH EARL BUT DIDN'T LOVE HIM ANYMORE ~ PARTLY BECAUSE THEY NEVER DID **ANYTHING** BESIDES WATCH TV... NEW YEARS, CHRISTMAS, FOURTH OF JULY, EVEN FOR JANET'S BIRTHDAYS ~ THEY ALWAYS JUST STAYED AT HOME, WATCHED TV AND DRANK BOOZE ALL NIGHT LONG.

NOW THAT SHE'D FOUND A GOOD JOB AND SOME FRIENDS HERE, NATURALLY HE WANTED TO MOVE AWAY AGAIN ~ THIS TIME TO FORT MYERS ~ ALL THE WAY ON THE OTHER SIDE OF SOUTH FLORIDA, OFF THE WEST COAST. I FELT MY HEART SINK WHEN I HEARD THAT...

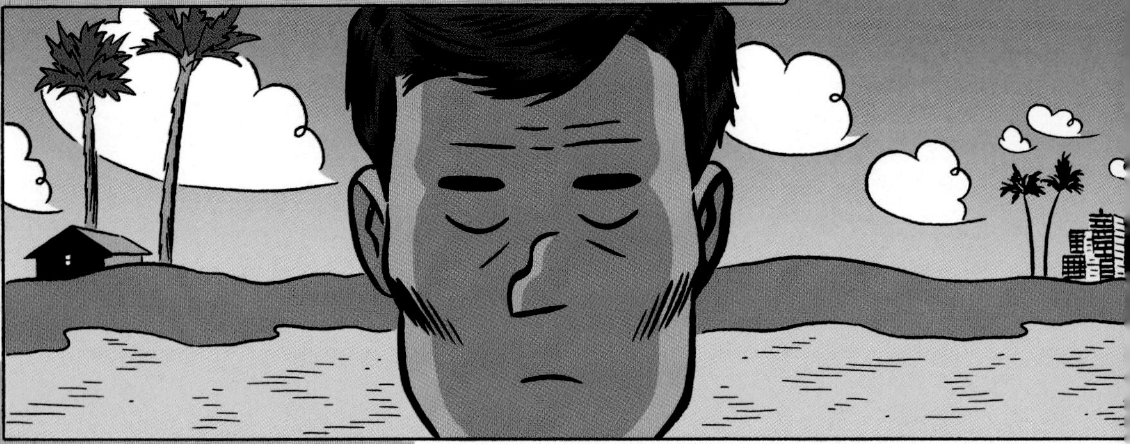

JANET DIDN'T LIKE THIS IDEA EITHER, WHICH WAS WHY SHE WAS IN MY NEIGHBORHOOD LAST WEEKEND; SHE'D HAD A BIG FIGHT WITH HIM ABOUT IT AND STORMED OUT OF THEIR HOME TO GET AWAY FROM HIM FOR A WHILE... NOW SHE WAS VERY CONFUSED AND AFRAID AND DIDN'T KNOW WHAT TO DO...

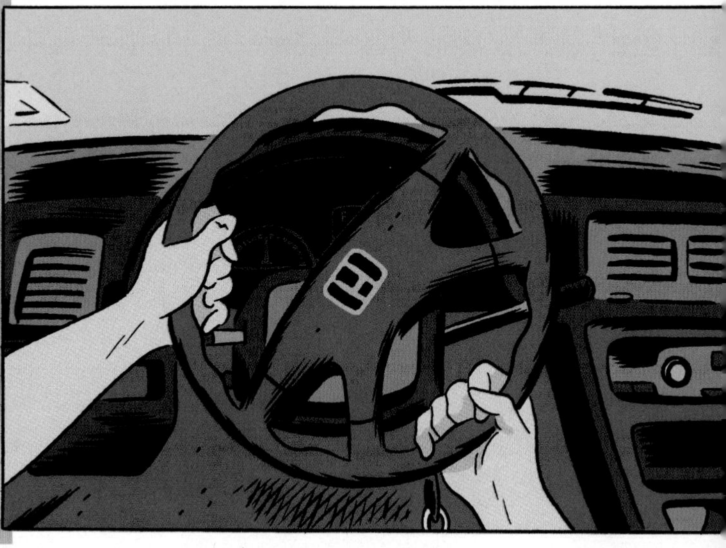

I WAS PRETTY DRUNK AT THIS POINT (AND UPSET) SO I WAS BLUNT. I TOLD HER SHE SHOULD DUMP THE JOKER BECAUSE TO MY MIND, STASHING SOMEONE IN YOUR HOME AND PRETENDING THEY WEREN'T THERE WHEN THE WRONG PARTY CAME AROUND LOOKIN' FOR THEM WASN'T MY IDEA OF "SAVING" THEM... I TOLD HER SHE OWED HIM NOTHING AND THAT SHE SHOULD DO WHATEVER SHE WANTED WITH HER LIFE AND BLAH, BLAH, BLAH...

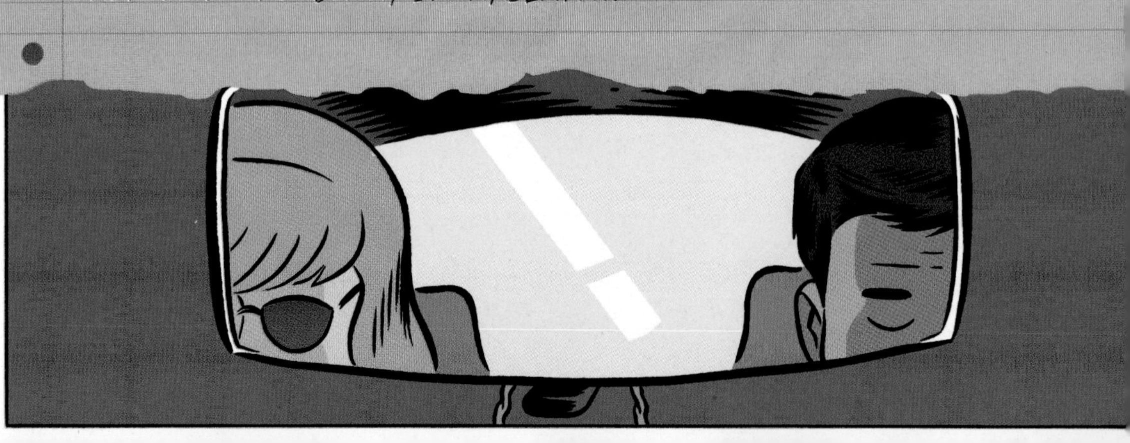

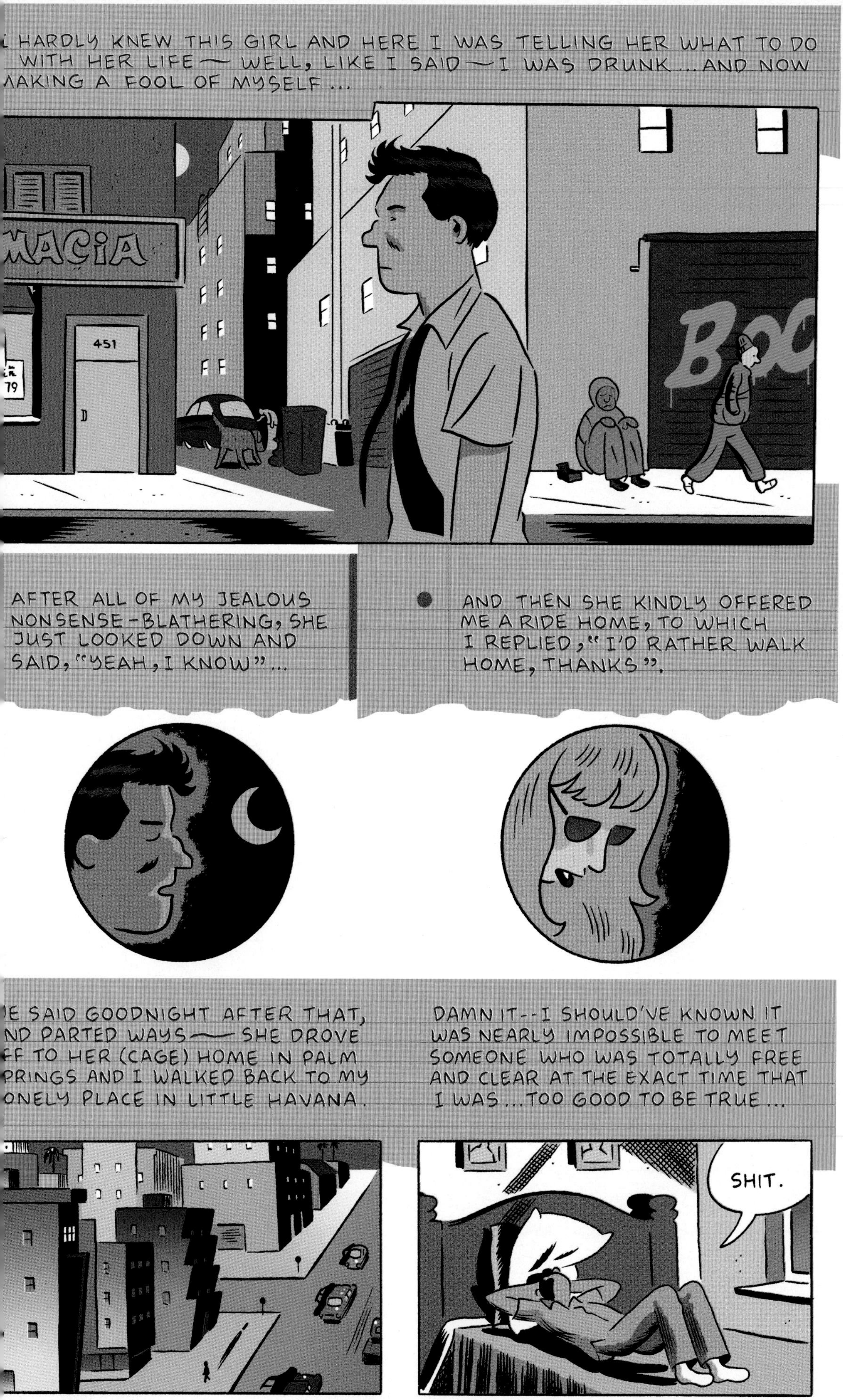
HARDLY KNEW THIS GIRL AND HERE I WAS TELLING HER WHAT TO DO WITH HER LIFE — WELL, LIKE I SAID — I WAS DRUNK ... AND NOW AKING A FOOL OF MYSELF ...
MACIA
451
AFTER ALL OF MY JEALOUS NONSENSE-BLATHERING, SHE JUST LOOKED DOWN AND SAID, "YEAH, I KNOW"...
AND THEN SHE KINDLY OFFERED ME A RIDE HOME, TO WHICH I REPLIED, "I'D RATHER WALK HOME, THANKS".
E SAID GOODNIGHT AFTER THAT, ND PARTED WAYS — SHE DROVE FF TO HER (CAGE) HOME IN PALM PRINGS AND I WALKED BACK TO MY ONELY PLACE IN LITTLE HAVANA.
DAMN IT--I SHOULD'VE KNOWN IT WAS NEARLY IMPOSSIBLE TO MEET SOMEONE WHO WAS TOTALLY FREE AND CLEAR AT THE EXACT TIME THAT I WAS ... TOO GOOD TO BE TRUE ...
SHIT.

5

THE FOLLOWING WEEK I WAS MISERABLE—I COULDN'T STOP THINKIN ABOUT HOW EASILY I'D BLOWN IT WITH JANET. HERE I'D FINALLY CAUGHT A BREAK IN LIFE AND MANAGED TO SCREW IT UP WITHIN DAYS... I WASN'T EVEN ENJOYING MY WORK...

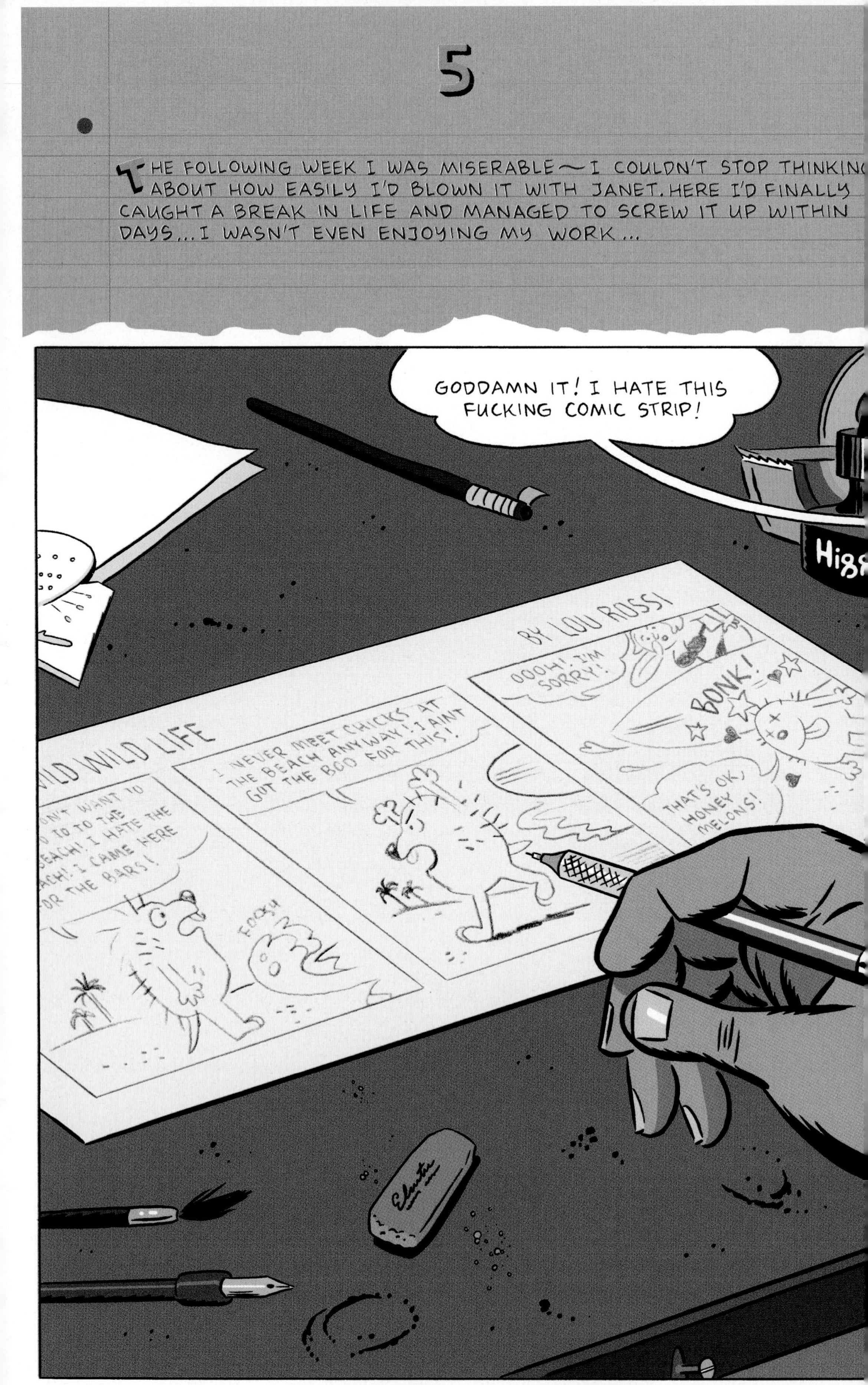

GODDAMN IT! I HATE THIS FUCKING COMIC STRIP!
BY LOU ROSSI
I NEVER MEET CHICKS AT THE BEACH ANYWAY! I AIN'T GOT THE BOD FOR THIS!
OOOH! I'M SORRY!
BONK!
THAT'S OK, HONEY MELONS!

FRIDAY AFTERNOON ~ AFTER WORK ~ I WANDERED AROUND MY NEIGHBORHOOD FOR A WHILE, BEFORE HEADING HOME... MY MIND WAS BUZZING AND SWIRLING IN A CESSPOOL OF UTTER FRUSTRATION...

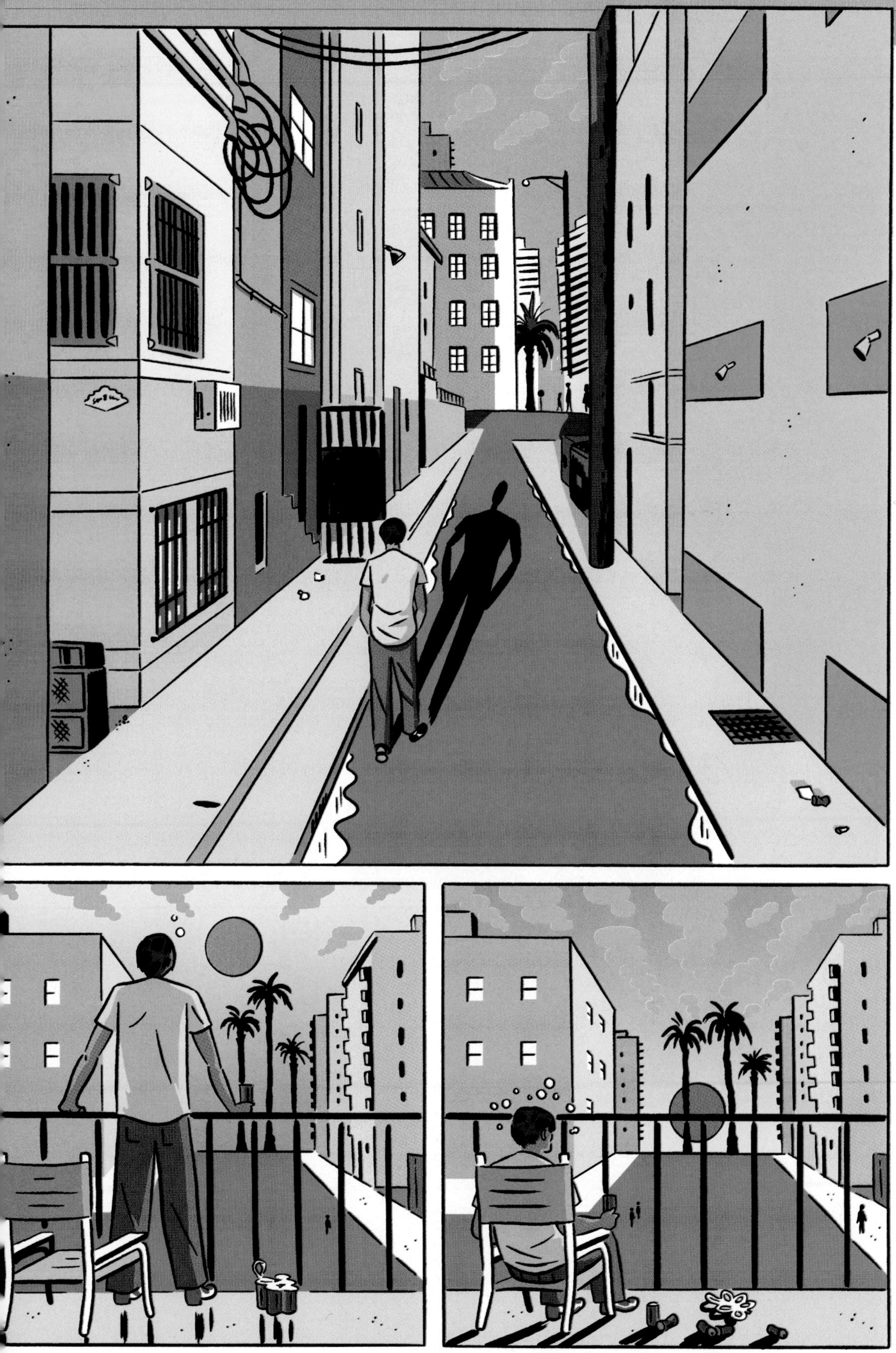

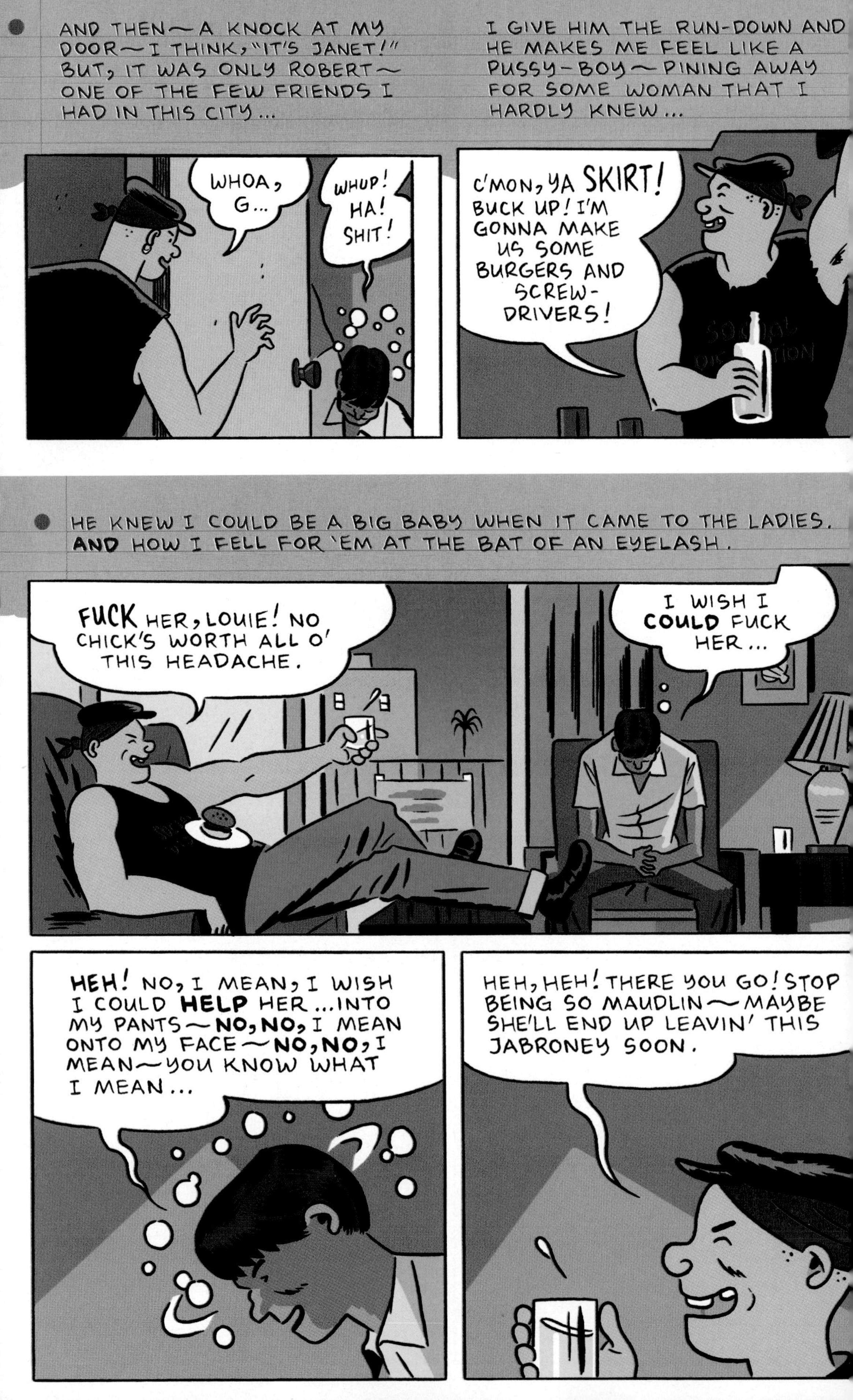
AND THEN—A KNOCK AT MY DOOR—I THINK, "IT'S JANET!" BUT, IT WAS ONLY ROBERT—ONE OF THE FEW FRIENDS I HAD IN THIS CITY...
WHOA, G...
WHUP! HA! SHIT!
I GIVE HIM THE RUN-DOWN AND HE MAKES ME FEEL LIKE A PUSSY-BOY—PINING AWAY FOR SOME WOMAN THAT I HARDLY KNEW...
C'MON, YA SKIRT! BUCK UP! I'M GONNA MAKE US SOME BURGERS AND SCREW-DRIVERS!
HE KNEW I COULD BE A BIG BABY WHEN IT CAME TO THE LADIES. AND HOW I FELL FOR 'EM AT THE BAT OF AN EYELASH.
FUCK HER, LOUIE! NO CHICK'S WORTH ALL O' THIS HEADACHE.
I WISH I COULD FUCK HER...
HEH! NO, I MEAN, I WISH I COULD HELP HER...INTO MY PANTS—NO, NO, I MEAN ONTO MY FACE—NO, NO, I MEAN—YOU KNOW WHAT I MEAN...
HEH, HEH! THERE YOU GO! STOP BEING SO MAUDLIN—MAYBE SHE'LL END UP LEAVIN' THIS JABRONEY SOON.

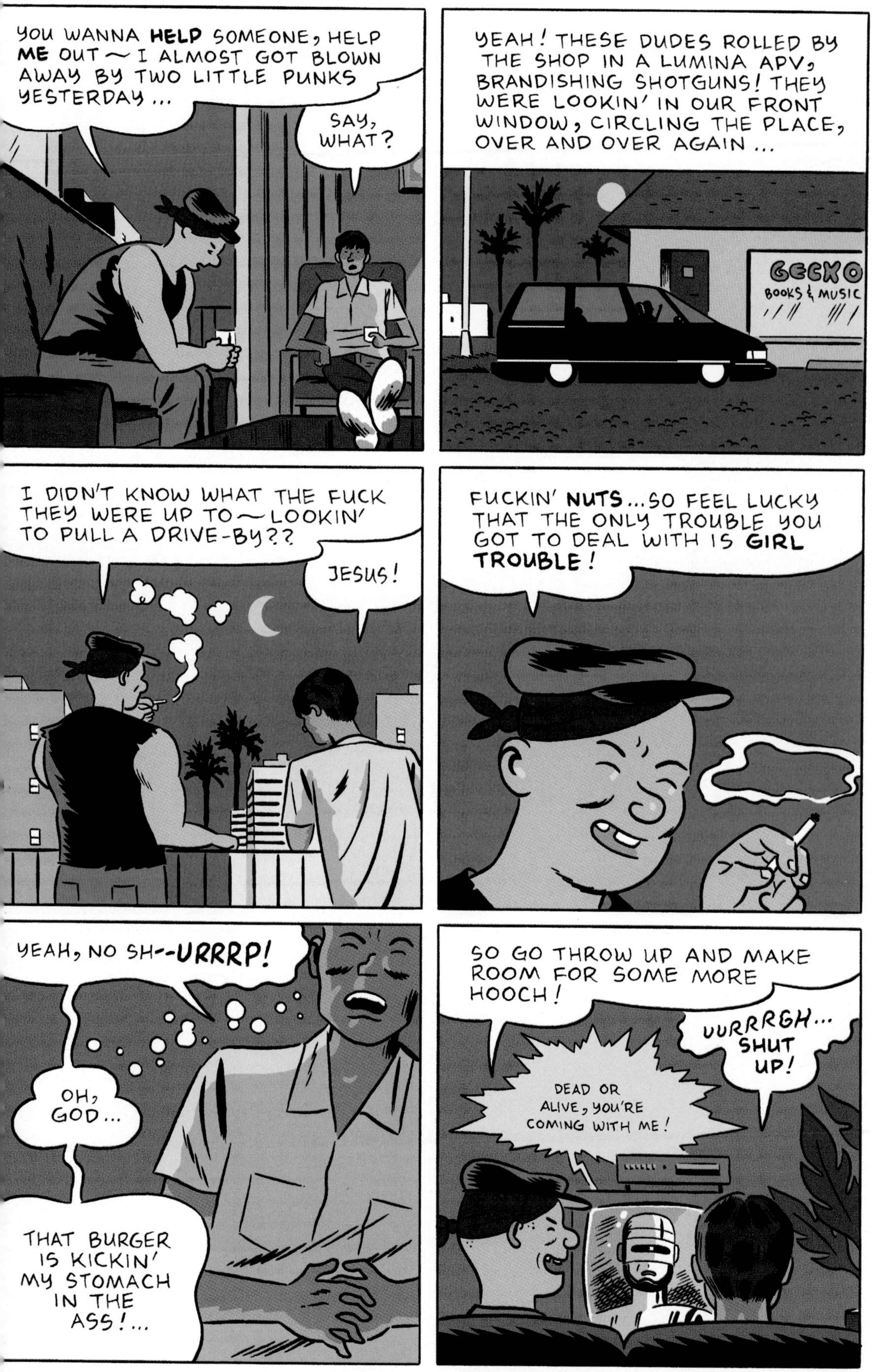

YOU WANNA HELP SOMEONE, HELP ME OUT — I ALMOST GOT BLOWN AWAY BY TWO LITTLE PUNKS YESTERDAY...
SAY, WHAT?
YEAH! THESE DUDES ROLLED BY THE SHOP IN A LUMINA APV, BRANDISHING SHOTGUNS! THEY WERE LOOKIN' IN OUR FRONT WINDOW, CIRCLING THE PLACE, OVER AND OVER AGAIN...
GECKO
BOOKS & MUSIC
I DIDN'T KNOW WHAT THE FUCK THEY WERE UP TO — LOOKIN' TO PULL A DRIVE-BY??
JESUS!
FUCKIN' NUTS...SO FEEL LUCKY THAT THE ONLY TROUBLE YOU GOT TO DEAL WITH IS GIRL TROUBLE!
YEAH, NO SH--URRRP!
OH, GOD...
THAT BURGER IS KICKIN' MY STOMACH IN THE ASS!...
SO GO THROW UP AND MAKE ROOM FOR SOME MORE HOOCH!
UURRRGH... SHUT UP!
DEAD OR ALIVE, YOU'RE COMING WITH ME!

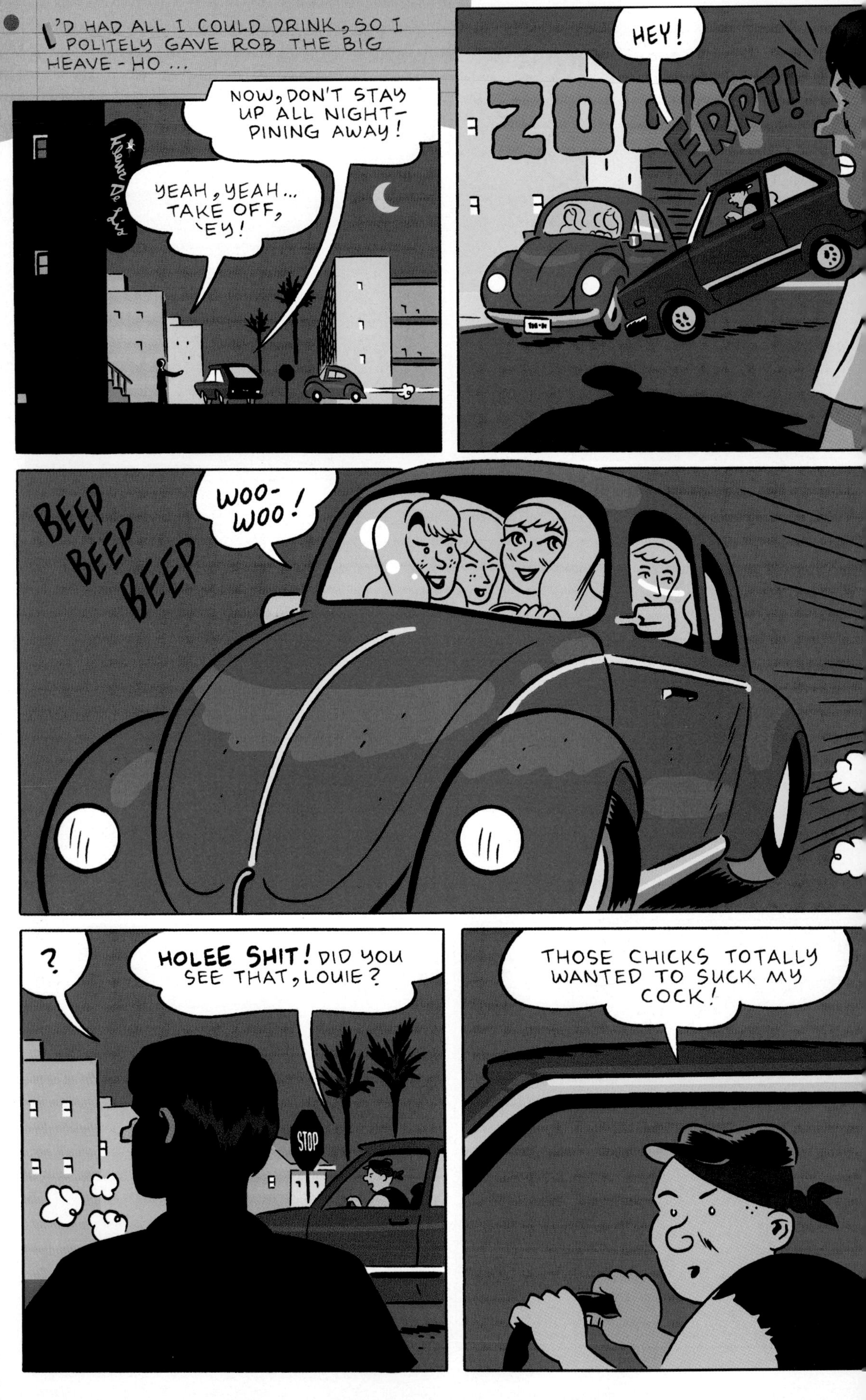
I'D HAD ALL I COULD DRINK, SO I POLITELY GAVE ROB THE BIG HEAVE-HO ...
NOW, DON'T STAY UP ALL NIGHT-PINING AWAY!
YEAH, YEAH... TAKE OFF, 'EY!
HEY!
ZO
ERRT!
BEEP BEEP BEEP
WOO-WOO!
?
HOLEE SHIT! DID YOU SEE THAT, LOUIE?
STOP
THOSE CHICKS TOTALLY WANTED TO SUCK MY COCK!

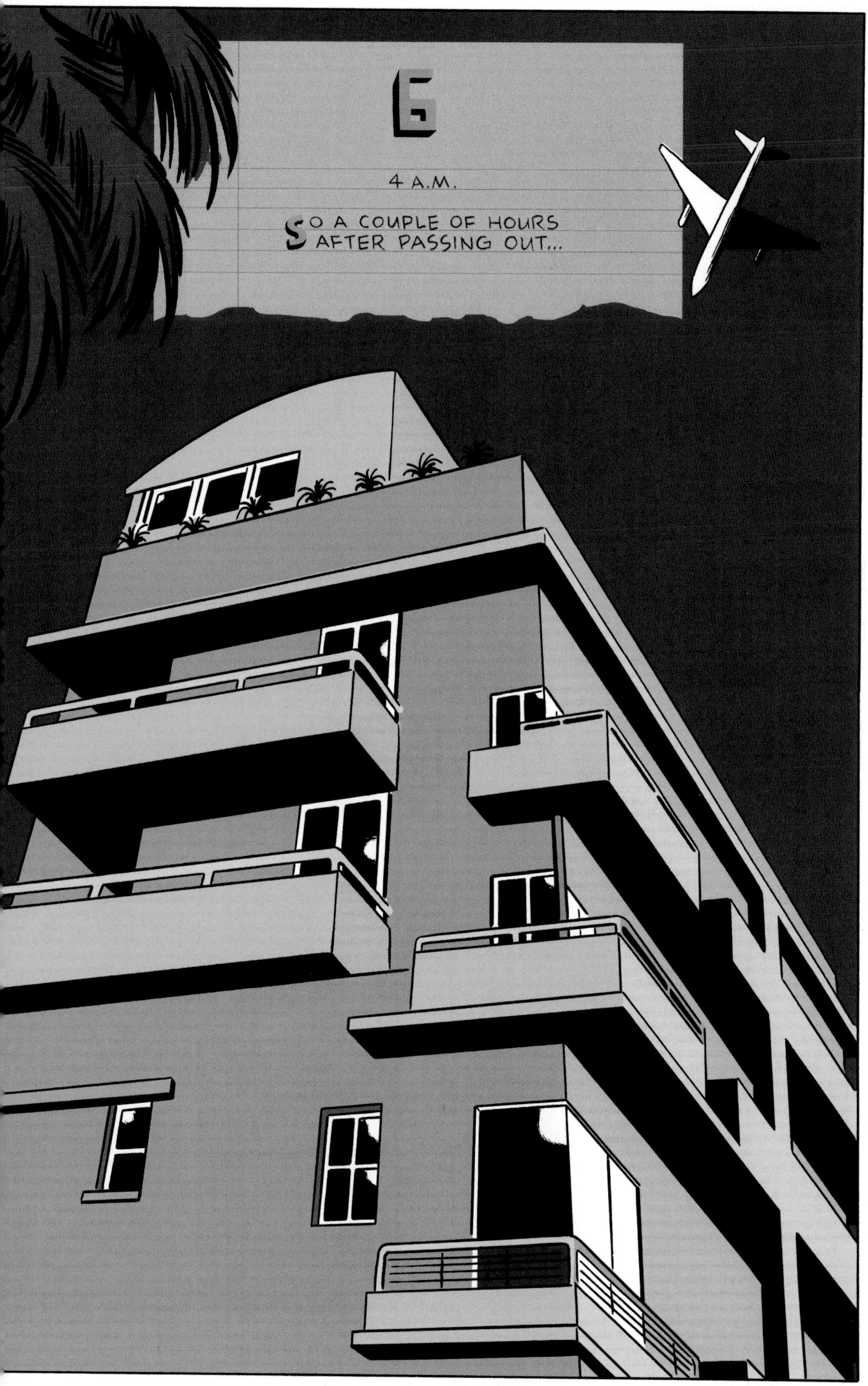
6
4 A.M.
SO A COUPLE OF HOURS AFTER PASSING OUT...

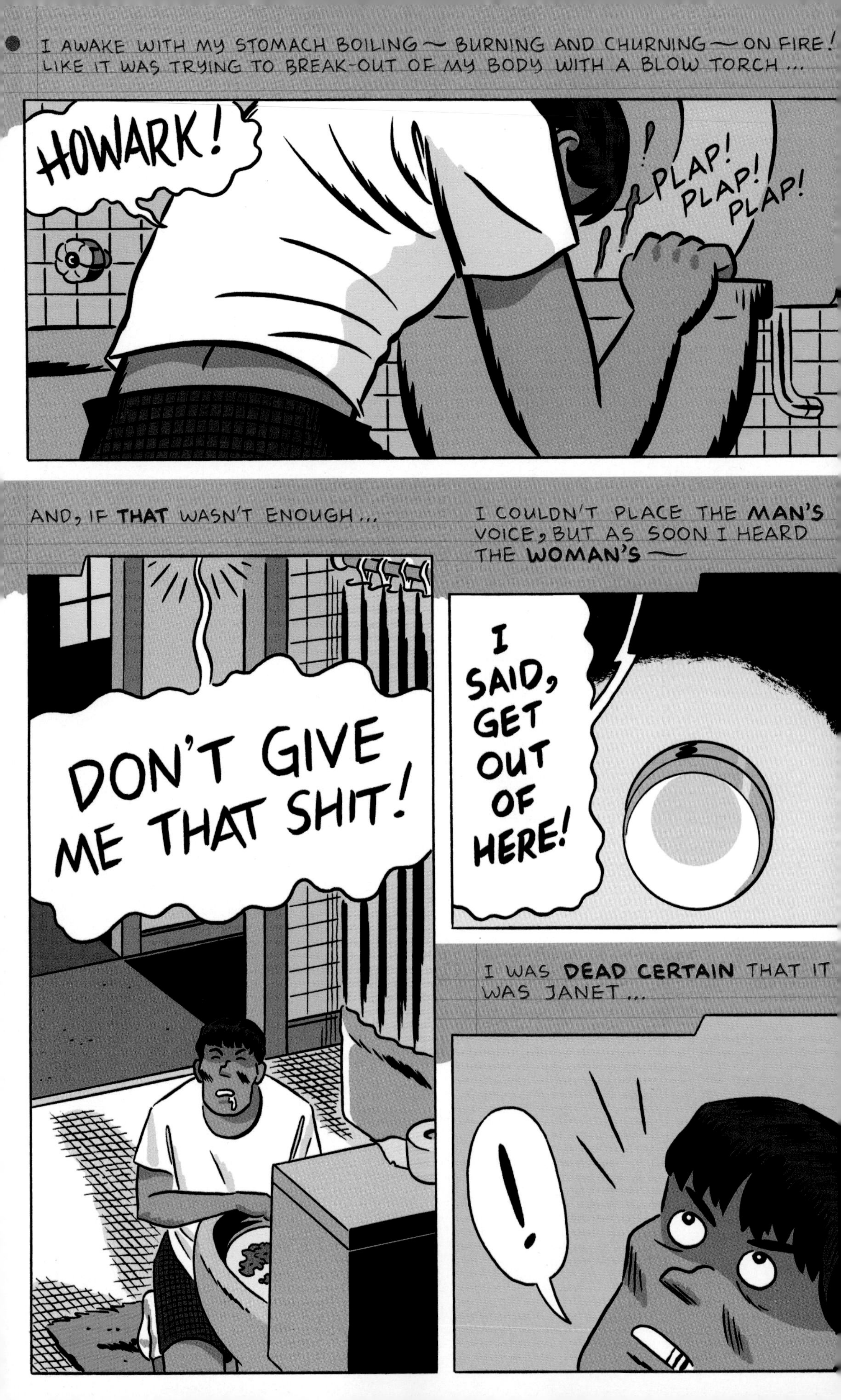
I AWAKE WITH MY STOMACH BOILING ~ BURNING AND CHURNING ~ ON FIRE! LIKE IT WAS TRYING TO BREAK-OUT OF MY BODY WITH A BLOW TORCH...
HOWARK!
PLAP! PLAP! PLAP!
AND, IF THAT WASN'T ENOUGH...
DON'T GIVE ME THAT SHIT!
I COULDN'T PLACE THE MAN'S VOICE, BUT AS SOON I HEARD THE WOMAN'S ~
I SAID, GET OUT OF HERE!
I WAS DEAD CERTAIN THAT IT WAS JANET...
!

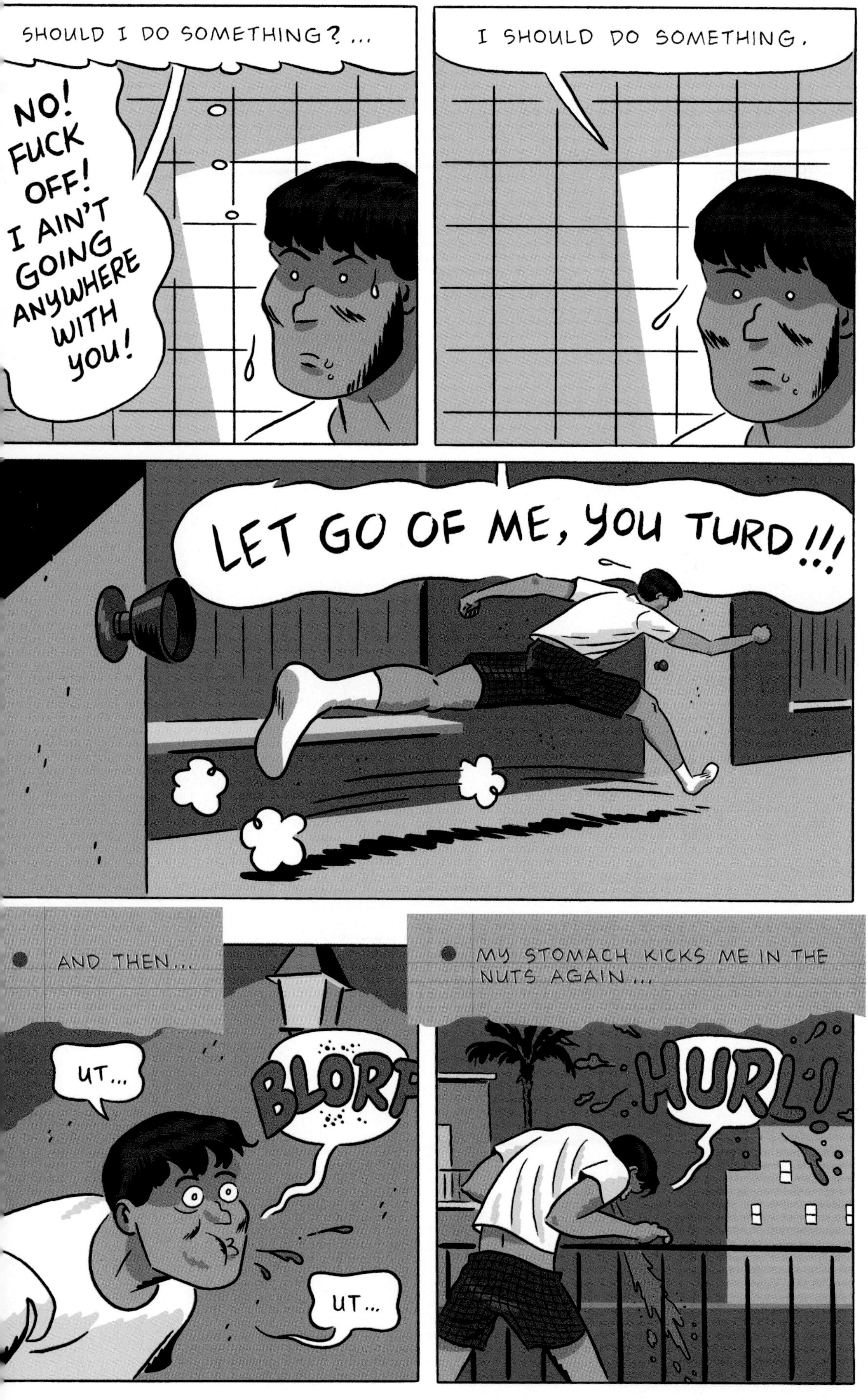
SHOULD I DO SOMETHING? ...
NO! FUCK OFF! I AIN'T GOING ANYWHERE WITH YOU!
I SHOULD DO SOMETHING.
LET GO OF ME, YOU TURD!!!
AND THEN...
UT...
BLORF
UT...
MY STOMACH KICKS ME IN THE NUTS AGAIN...
HURL!

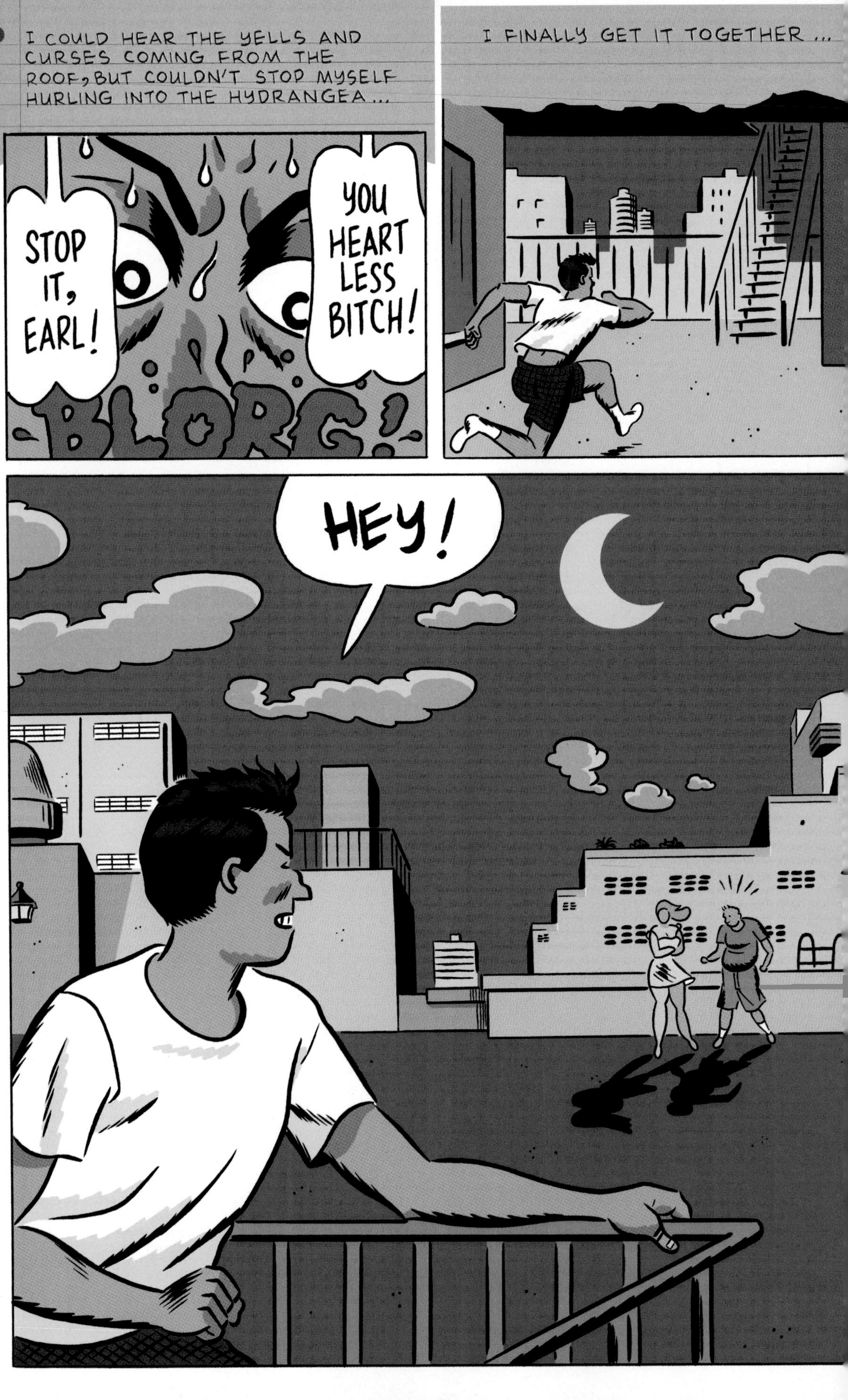
I COULD HEAR THE YELLS AND CURSES COMING FROM THE ROOF, BUT COULDN'T STOP MYSELF HURLING INTO THE HYDRANGEA...
STOP IT, EARL!
YOU HEARTLESS BITCH!
BLORG!
I FINALLY GET IT TOGETHER...
HEY!

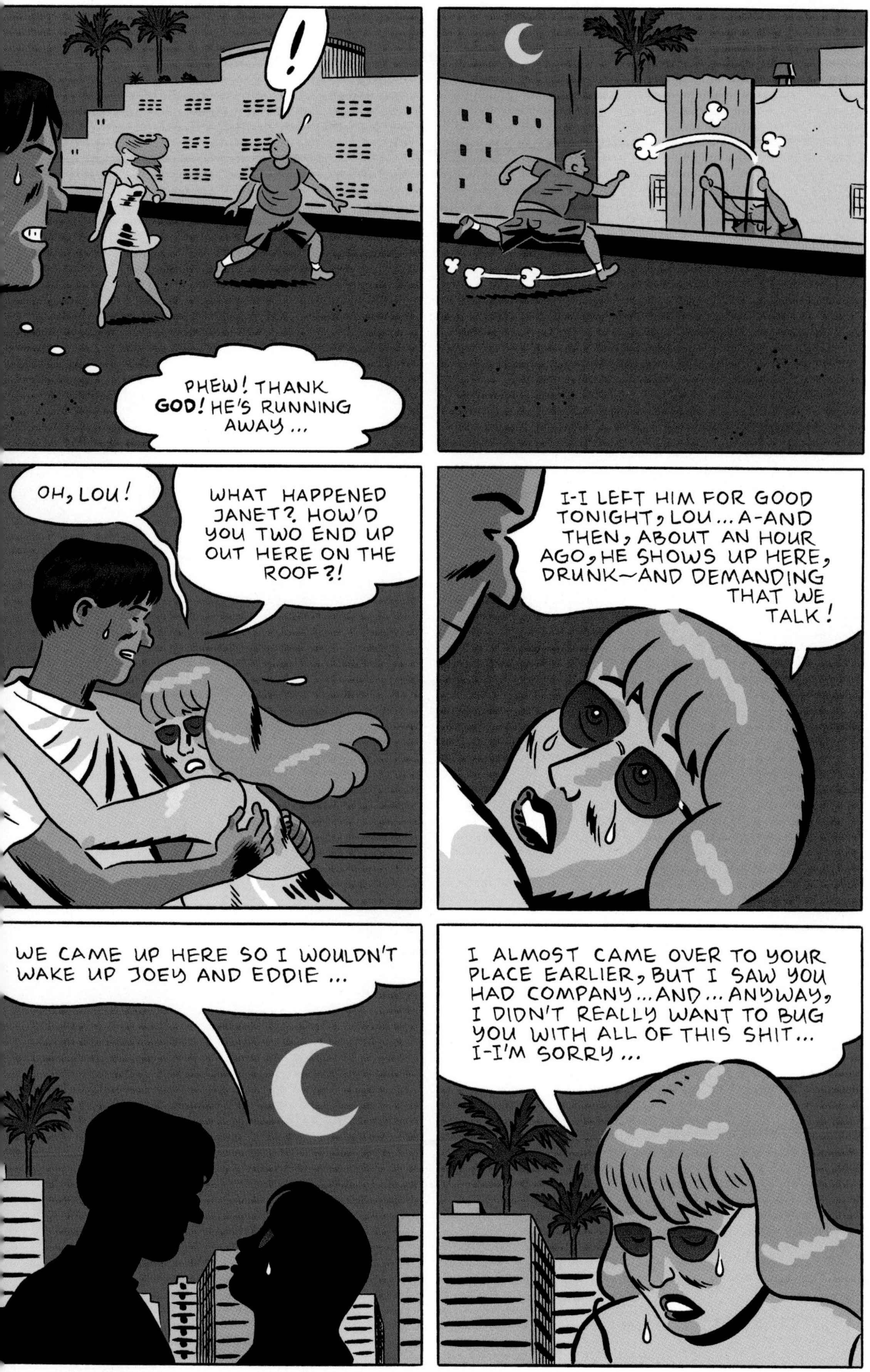
!
PHEW! THANK **GOD!** HE'S RUNNING AWAY...
OH, LOU!
WHAT HAPPENED JANET? HOW'D YOU TWO END UP OUT HERE ON THE ROOF?!
I-I LEFT HIM FOR GOOD TONIGHT, LOU... A-AND THEN, ABOUT AN HOUR AGO, HE SHOWS UP HERE, DRUNK~AND DEMANDING THAT WE TALK!
WE CAME UP HERE SO I WOULDN'T WAKE UP JOEY AND EDDIE...
I ALMOST CAME OVER TO YOUR PLACE EARLIER, BUT I SAW YOU HAD COMPANY... AND... ANYWAY, I DIDN'T REALLY WANT TO BUG YOU WITH ALL OF THIS SHIT... I-I'M SORRY...

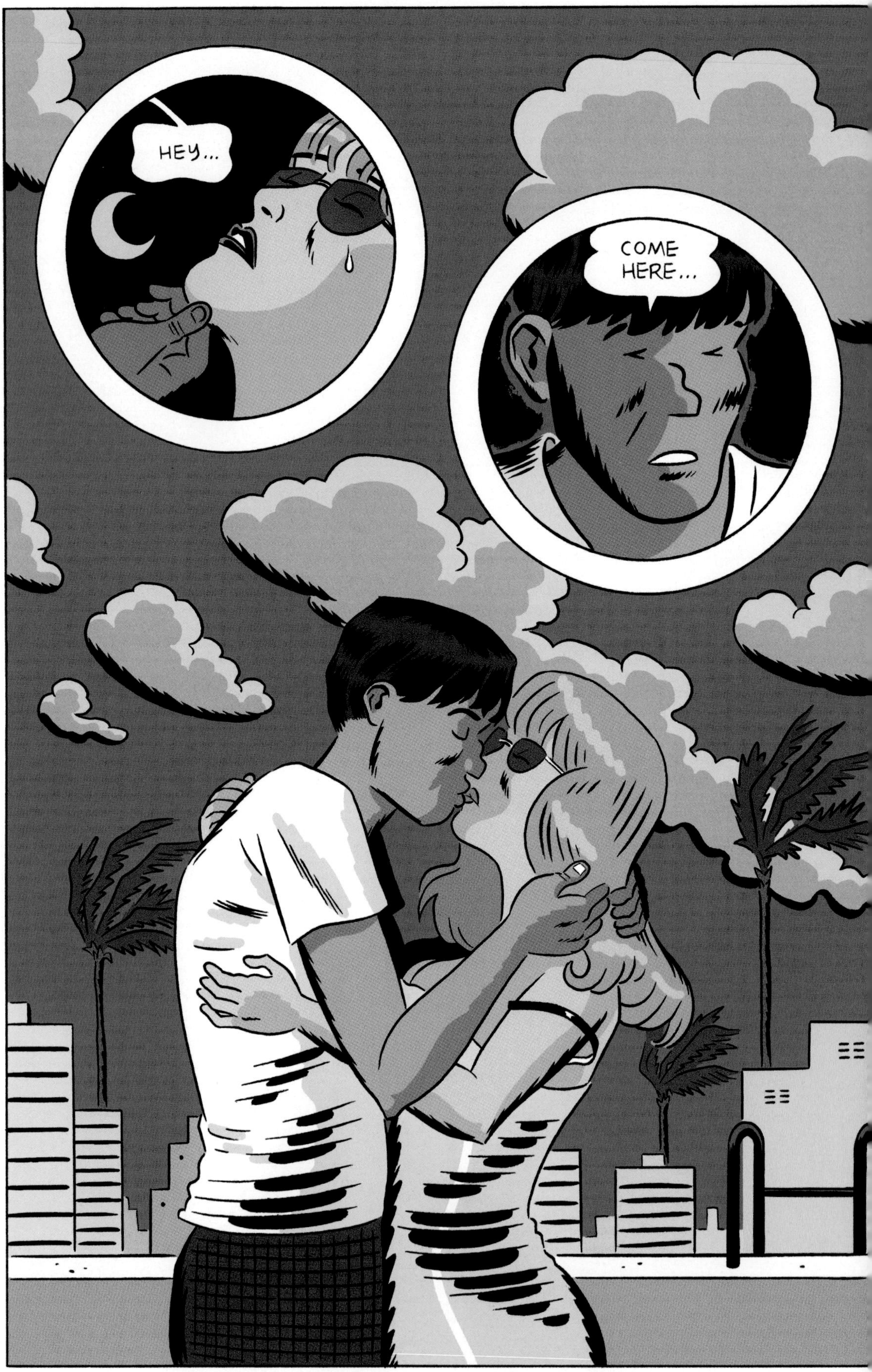
HEY...
COME HERE...

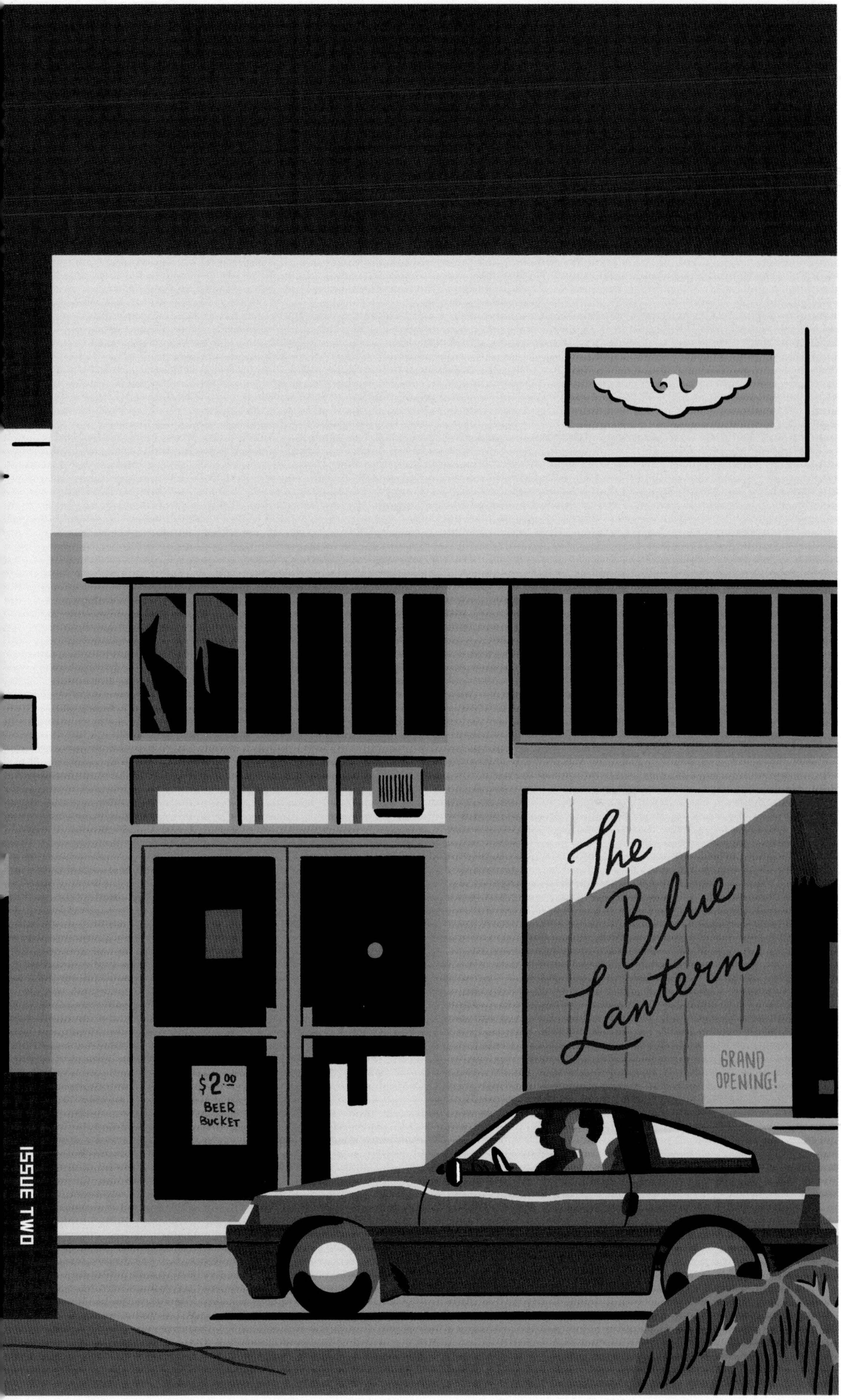
The Blue Lantern
GRAND OPENING!
$2.00 BEER BUCKET
ISSUE TWO

7

IT WAS OFFICIAL ~ JANET HAD COMPLETELY BROKEN FREE OF EARL AND HAD RAT-PACKED ALL OF HER BELONGINGS AT JOE AND EDDIE'S PLACE...

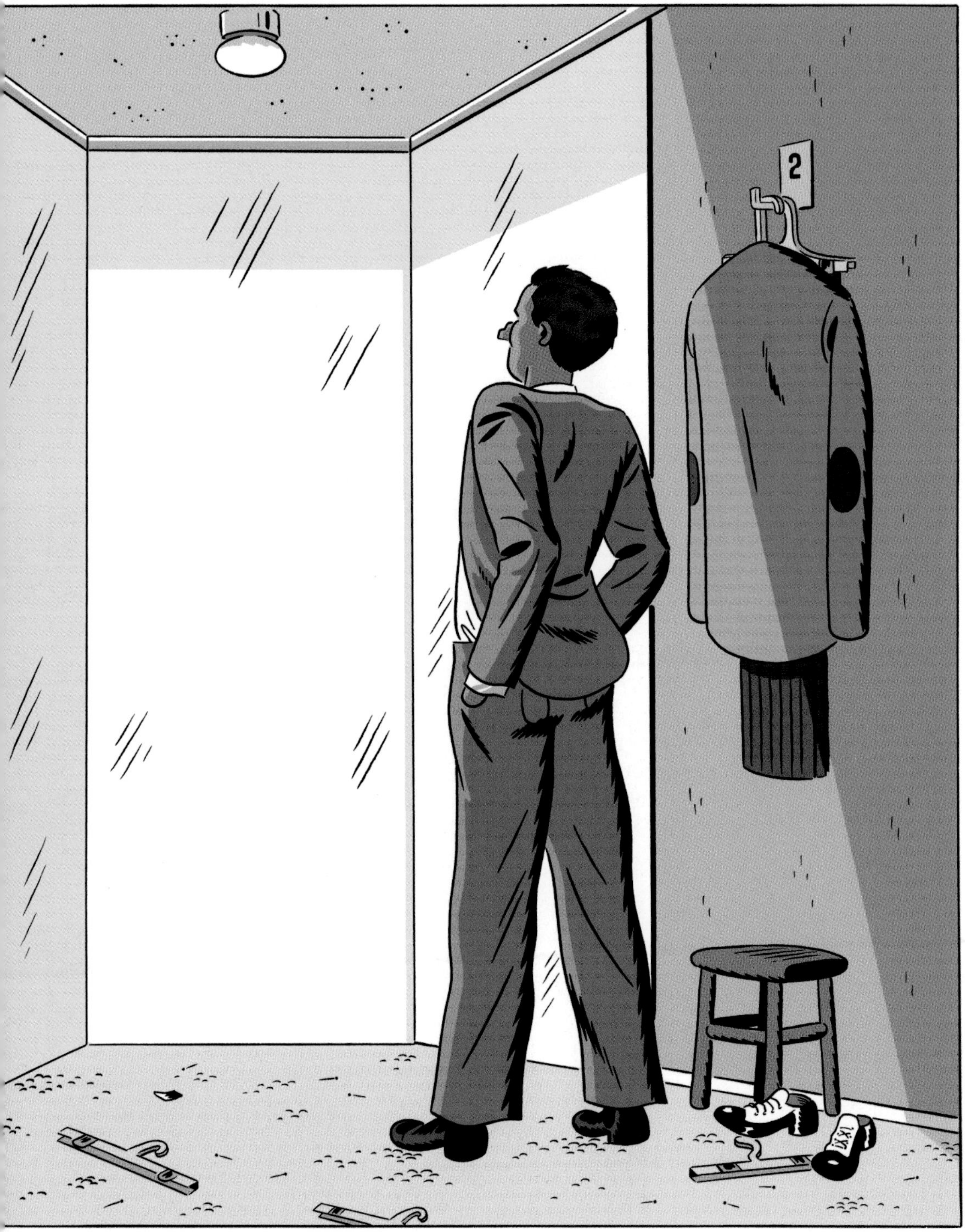

2

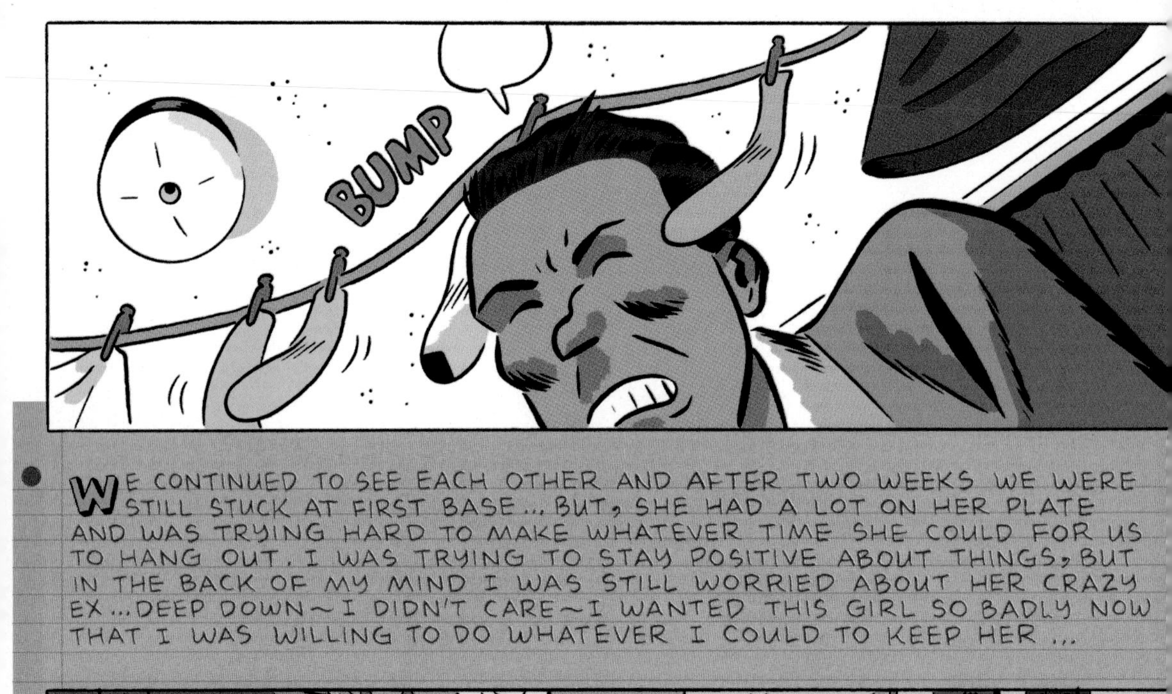
BUMP

WE CONTINUED TO SEE EACH OTHER AND AFTER TWO WEEKS WE WERE STILL STUCK AT FIRST BASE... BUT, SHE HAD A LOT ON HER PLATE AND WAS TRYING HARD TO MAKE WHATEVER TIME SHE COULD FOR US TO HANG OUT. I WAS TRYING TO STAY POSITIVE ABOUT THINGS, BUT IN THE BACK OF MY MIND I WAS STILL WORRIED ABOUT HER CRAZY EX... DEEP DOWN ~ I DIDN'T CARE ~ I WANTED THIS GIRL SO BADLY NOW THAT I WAS WILLING TO DO WHATEVER I COULD TO KEEP HER...

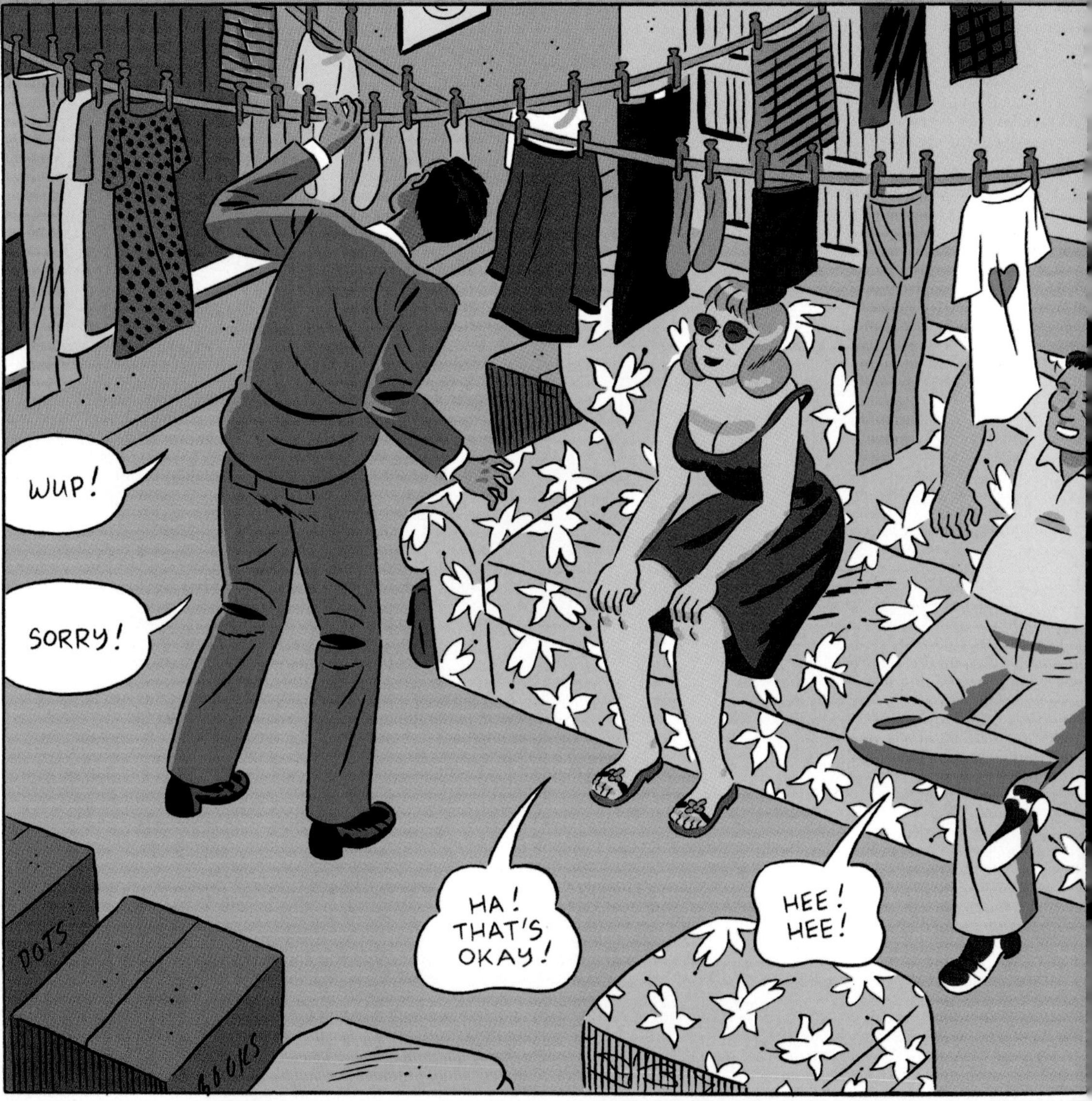
WUP!
SORRY!
HA! THAT'S OKAY!
HEE! HEE!
POTS
BOOKS

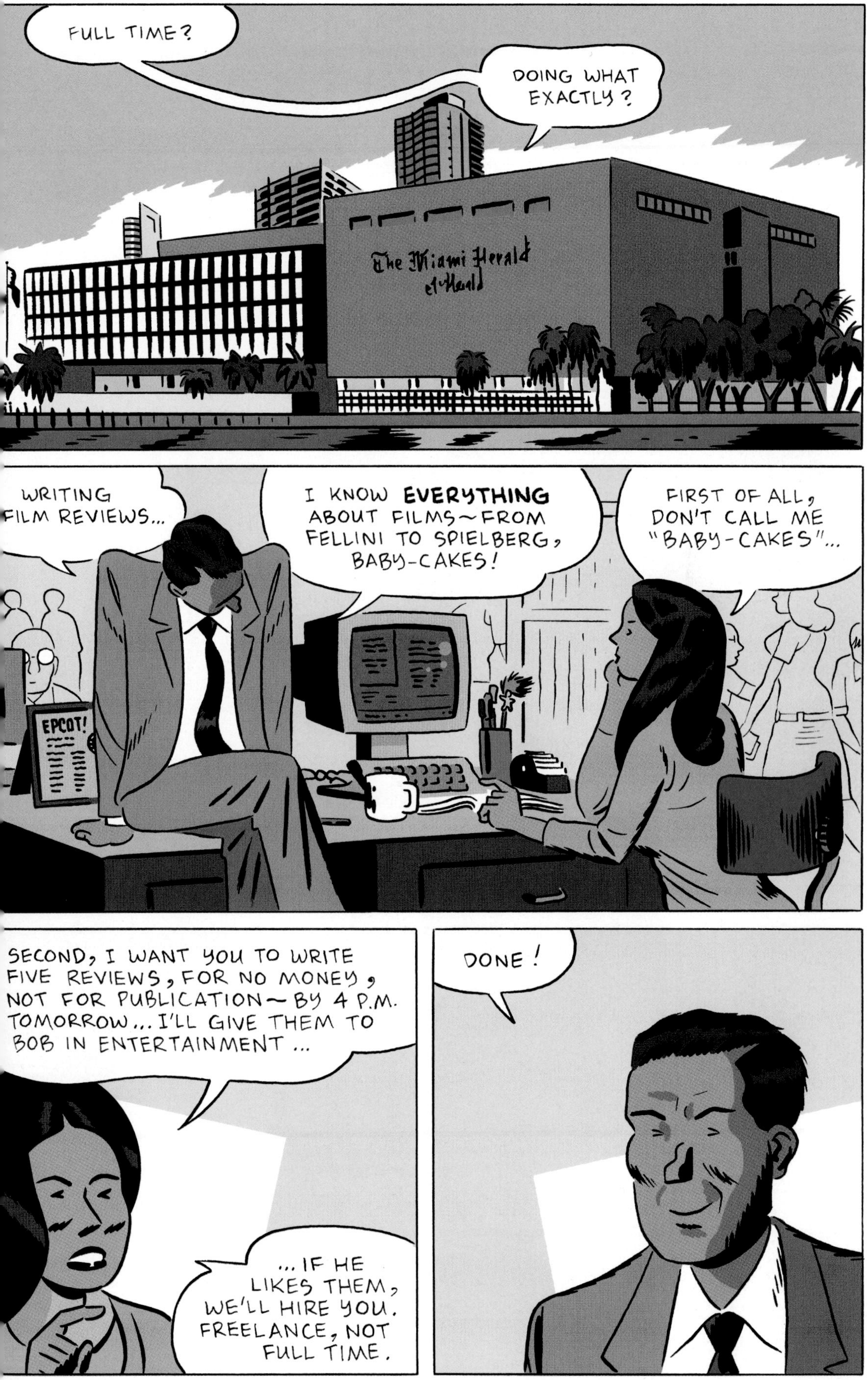
FULL TIME?
DOING WHAT EXACTLY?
The Miami Herald
WRITING FILM REVIEWS...
I KNOW **EVERYTHING** ABOUT FILMS~FROM FELLINI TO SPIELBERG, BABY-CAKES!
FIRST OF ALL, DON'T CALL ME "BABY-CAKES"...
EPCOT!
SECOND, I WANT YOU TO WRITE FIVE REVIEWS, FOR NO MONEY, NOT FOR PUBLICATION~BY 4 P.M. TOMORROW... I'LL GIVE THEM TO BOB IN ENTERTAINMENT...
...IF HE LIKES THEM, WE'LL HIRE YOU. FREELANCE, NOT FULL TIME.
DONE!

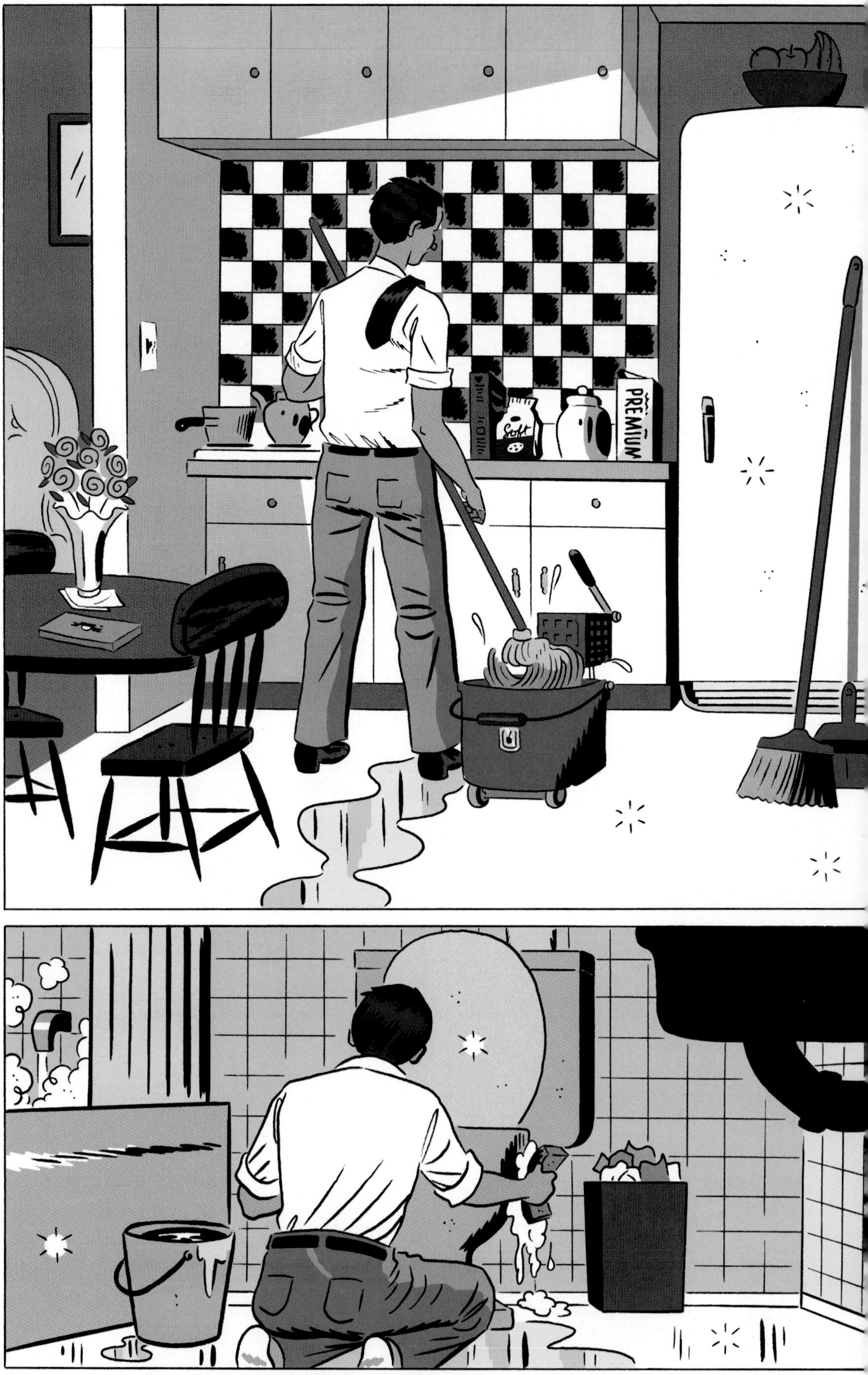
Soft
PREMIUM

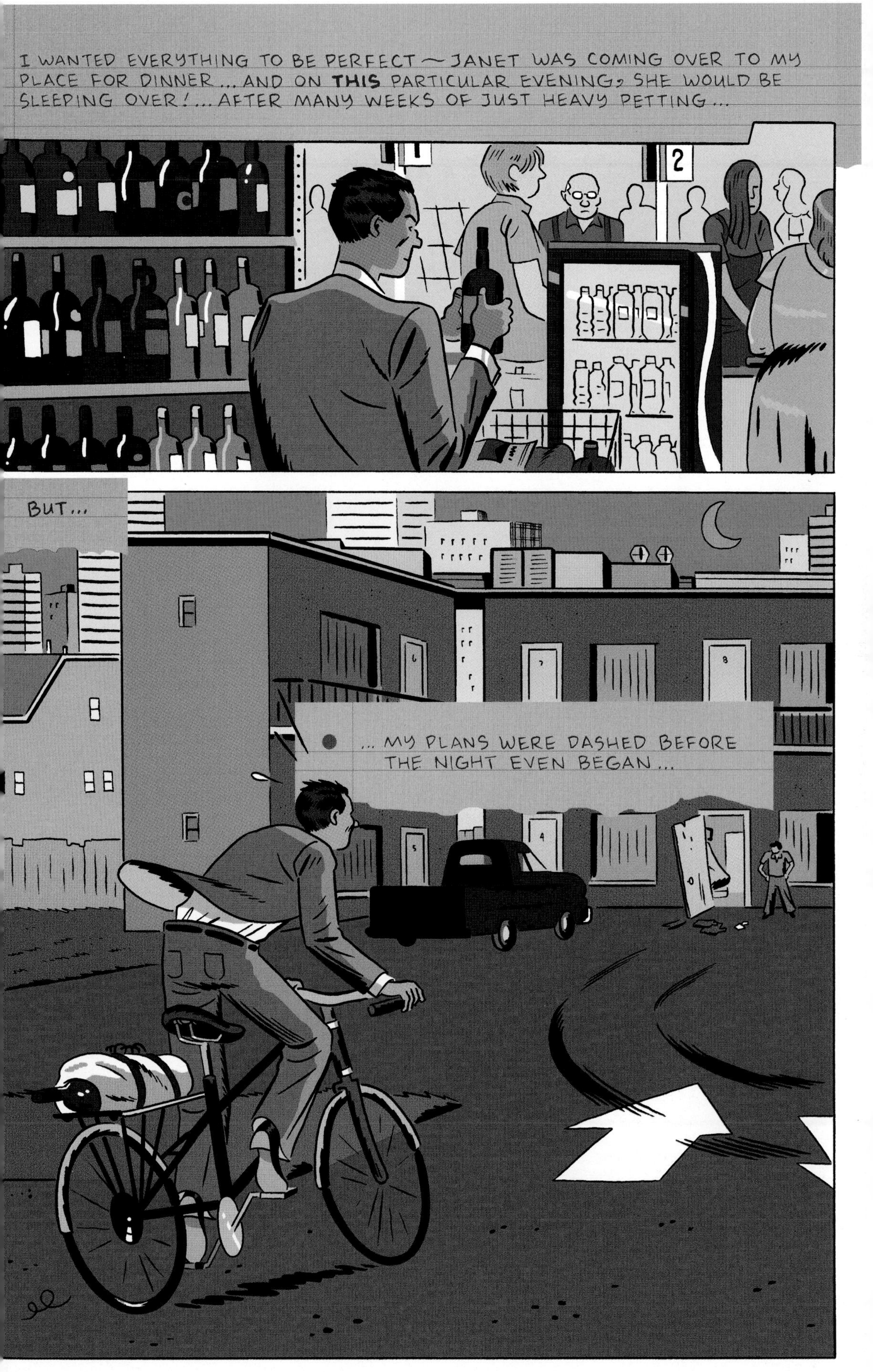
I WANTED EVERYTHING TO BE PERFECT ~ JANET WAS COMING OVER TO MY PLACE FOR DINNER ... AND ON **THIS** PARTICULAR EVENING, SHE WOULD BE SLEEPING OVER! ... AFTER MANY WEEKS OF JUST HEAVY PETTING ...
2
BUT...
... MY PLANS WERE DASHED BEFORE THE NIGHT EVEN BEGAN ...

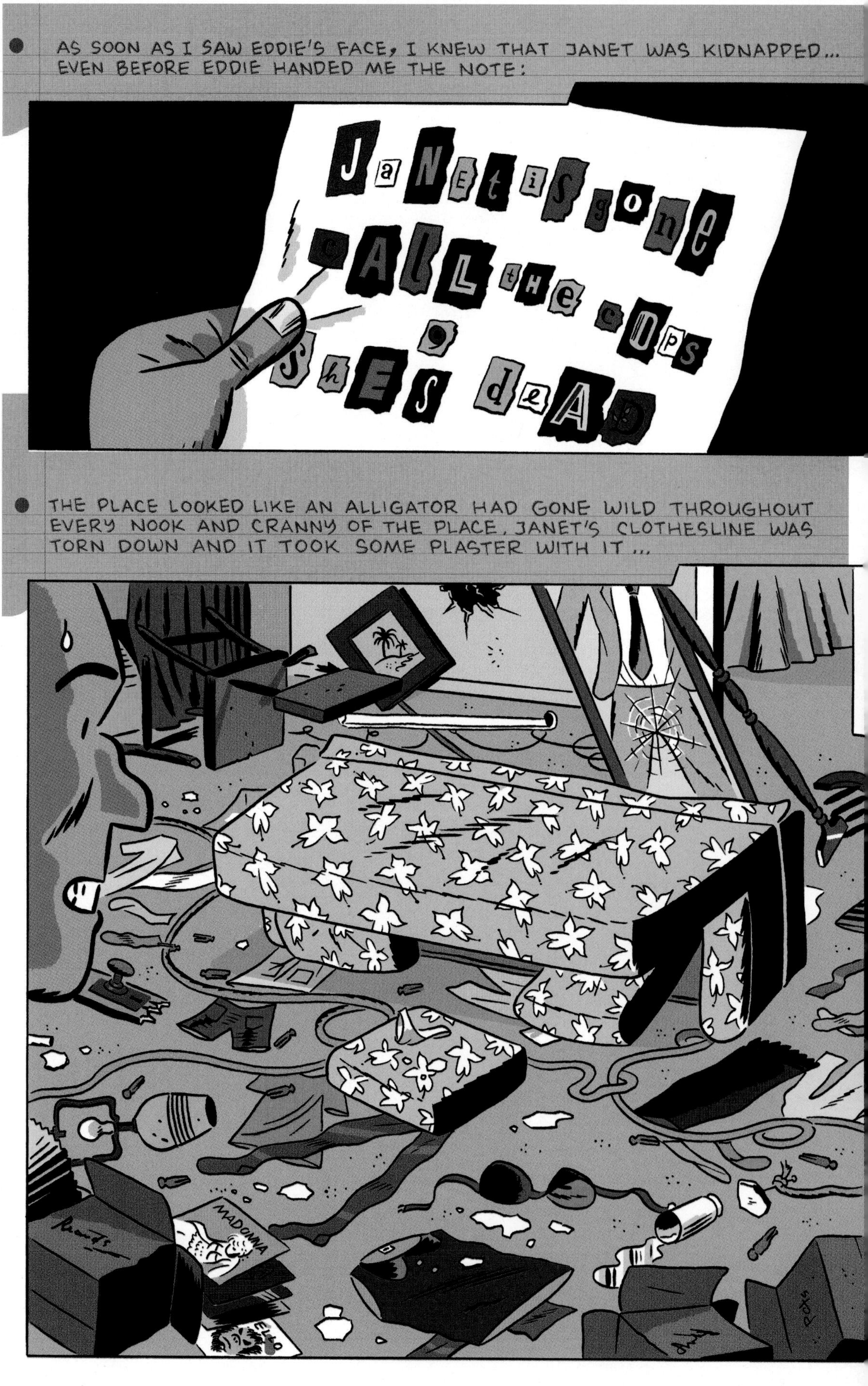
AS SOON AS I SAW EDDIE'S FACE, I KNEW THAT JANET WAS KIDNAPPED... EVEN BEFORE EDDIE HANDED ME THE NOTE:
JaNEt iS gone
cALL the cOps
ShES deAD
THE PLACE LOOKED LIKE AN ALLIGATOR HAD GONE WILD THROUGHOUT EVERY NOOK AND CRANNY OF THE PLACE. JANET'S CLOTHESLINE WAS TORN DOWN AND IT TOOK SOME PLASTER WITH IT...
MADONNA

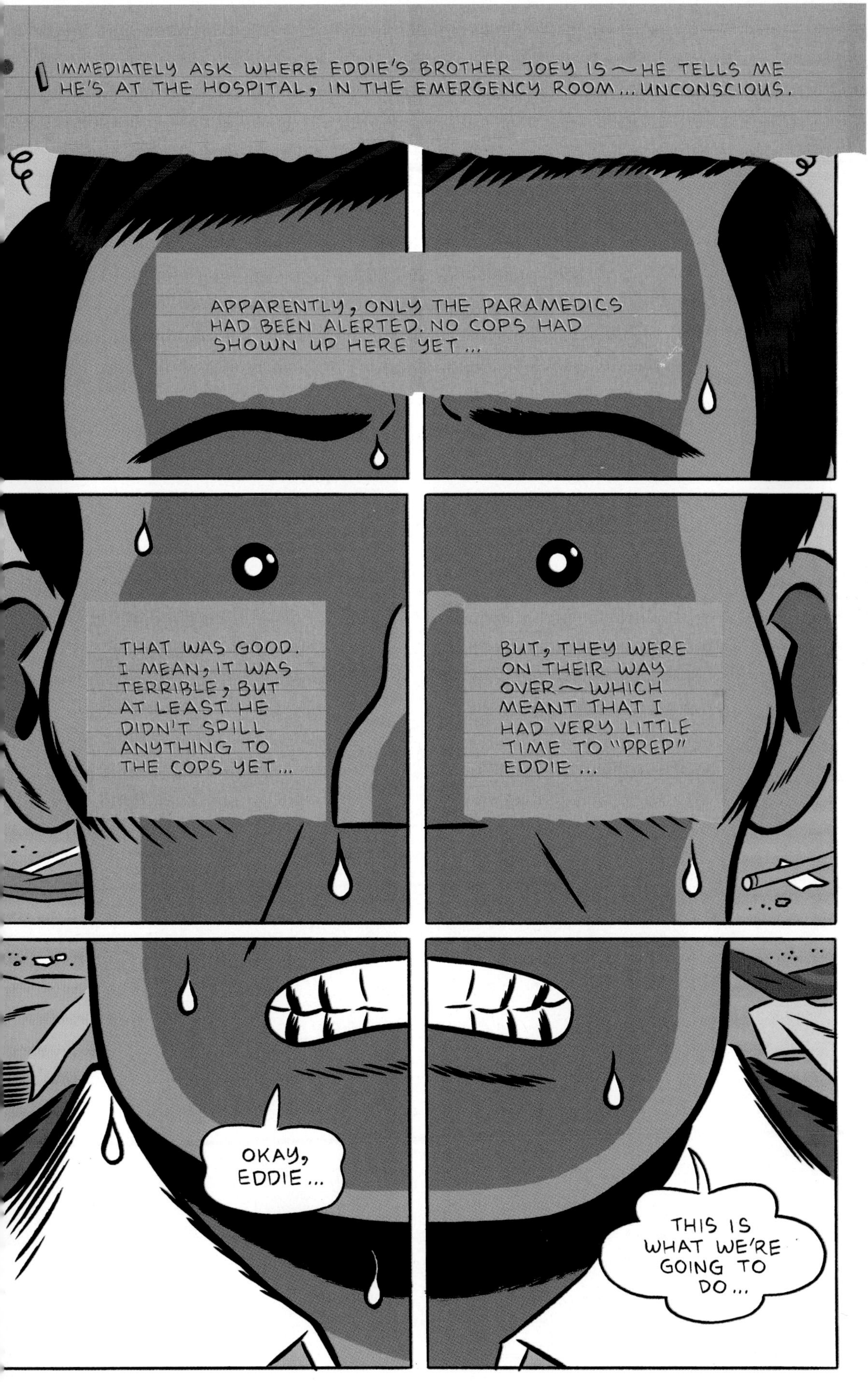
I IMMEDIATELY ASK WHERE EDDIE'S BROTHER JOEY IS ~ HE TELLS ME HE'S AT THE HOSPITAL, IN THE EMERGENCY ROOM... UNCONSCIOUS.
APPARENTLY, ONLY THE PARAMEDICS HAD BEEN ALERTED. NO COPS HAD SHOWN UP HERE YET...
THAT WAS GOOD. I MEAN, IT WAS TERRIBLE, BUT AT LEAST HE DIDN'T SPILL ANYTHING TO THE COPS YET...
BUT, THEY WERE ON THEIR WAY OVER ~ WHICH MEANT THAT I HAD VERY LITTLE TIME TO "PREP" EDDIE...
OKAY, EDDIE...
THIS IS WHAT WE'RE GOING TO DO...

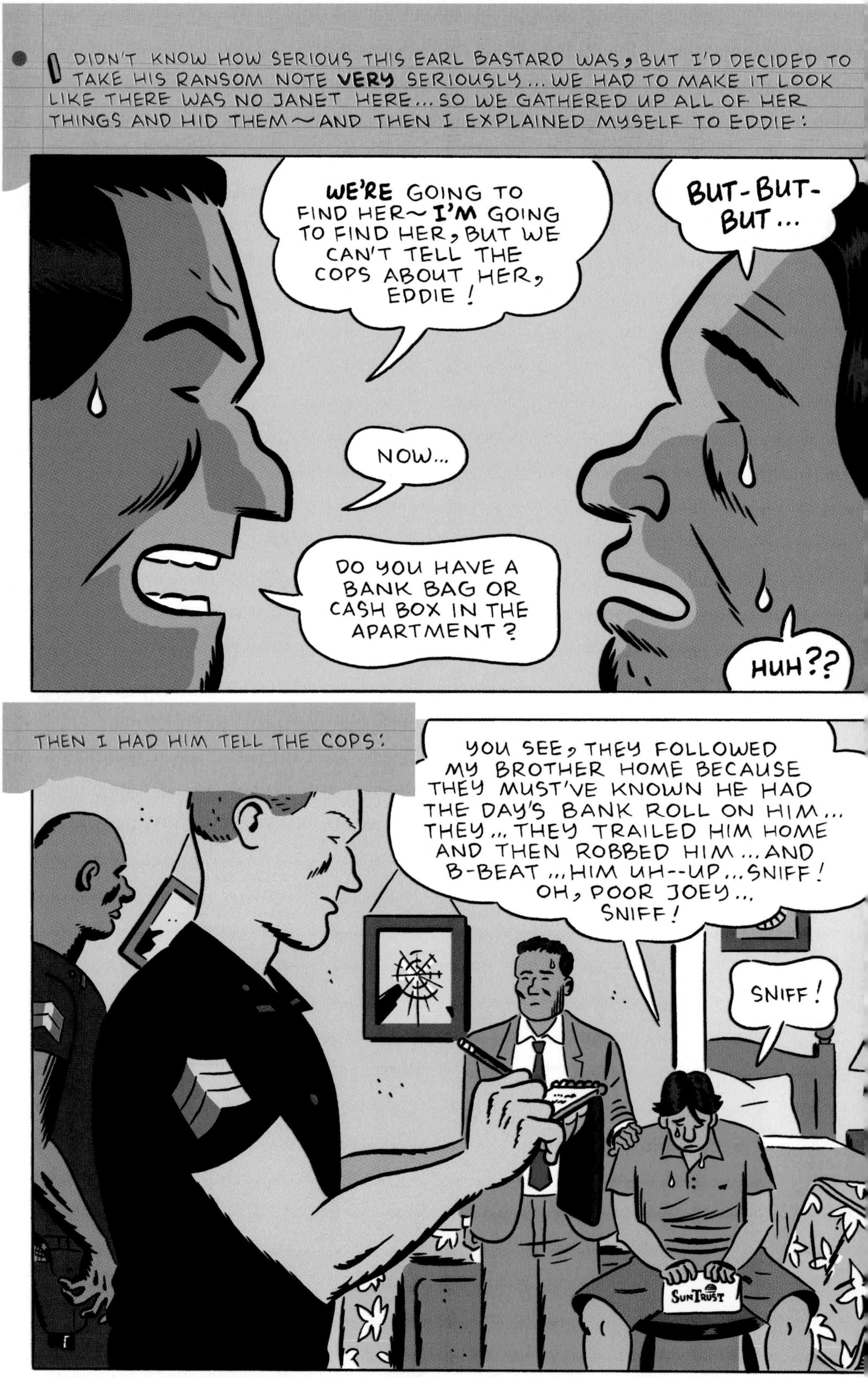
I DIDN'T KNOW HOW SERIOUS THIS EARL BASTARD WAS, BUT I'D DECIDED TO TAKE HIS RANSOM NOTE **VERY** SERIOUSLY... WE HAD TO MAKE IT LOOK LIKE THERE WAS NO JANET HERE... SO WE GATHERED UP ALL OF HER THINGS AND HID THEM ~ AND THEN I EXPLAINED MYSELF TO EDDIE:
WE'RE GOING TO FIND HER ~ **I'M** GOING TO FIND HER, BUT WE CAN'T TELL THE COPS ABOUT HER, EDDIE!
BUT-BUT-BUT...
NOW...
DO YOU HAVE A BANK BAG OR CASH BOX IN THE APARTMENT?
HUH??
THEN I HAD HIM TELL THE COPS:
YOU SEE, THEY FOLLOWED MY BROTHER HOME BECAUSE THEY MUST'VE KNOWN HE HAD THE DAY'S BANK ROLL ON HIM... THEY... THEY TRAILED HIM HOME AND THEN ROBBED HIM... AND B-BEAT... HIM UH--UP... SNIFF! OH, POOR JOEY... SNIFF!
SNIFF!
SunTrust

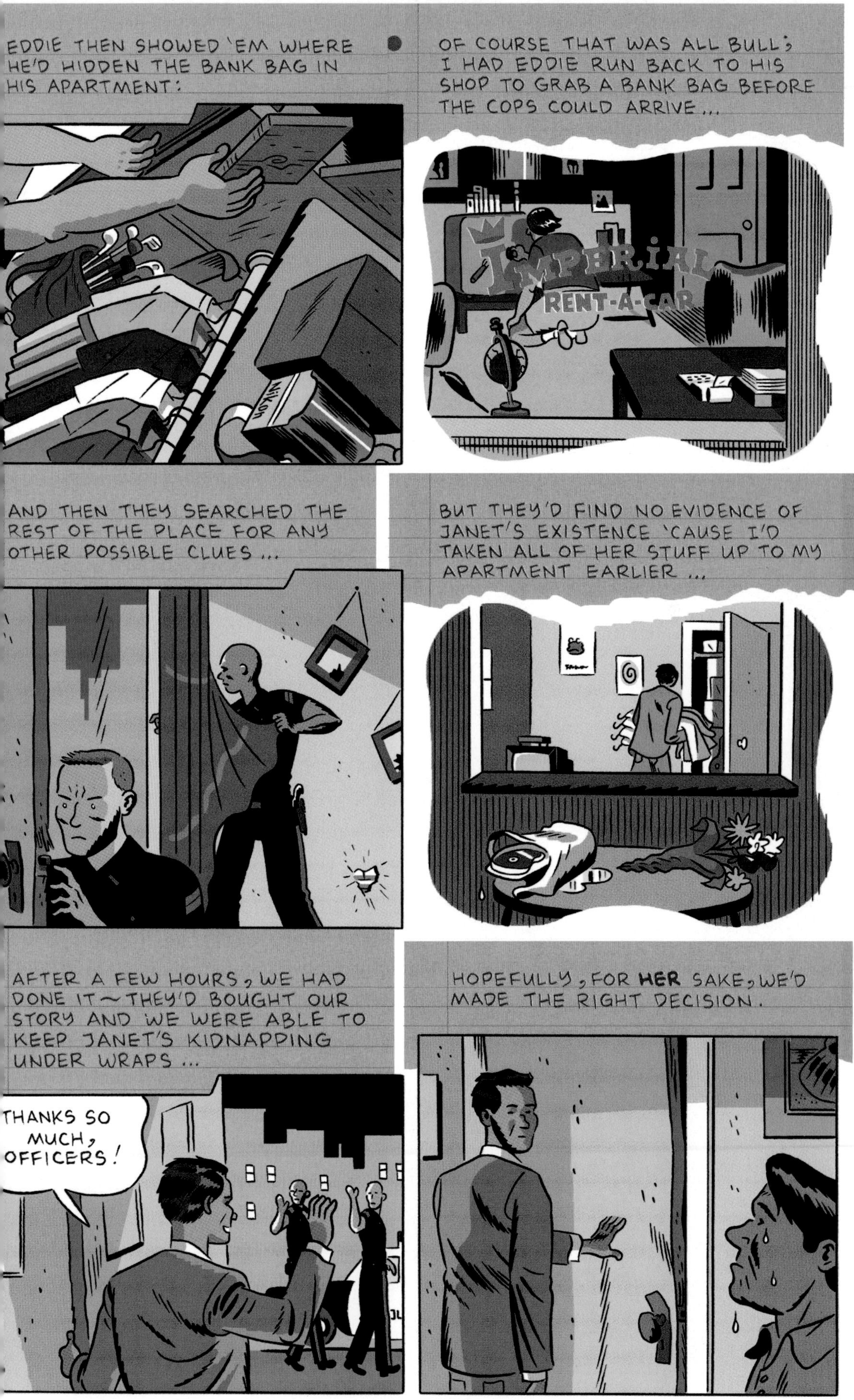
EDDIE THEN SHOWED 'EM WHERE HE'D HIDDEN THE BANK BAG IN HIS APARTMENT:
Nikon
OF COURSE THAT WAS ALL BULL; I HAD EDDIE RUN BACK TO HIS SHOP TO GRAB A BANK BAG BEFORE THE COPS COULD ARRIVE...
IMPERIAL RENT-A-CAR
AND THEN THEY SEARCHED THE REST OF THE PLACE FOR ANY OTHER POSSIBLE CLUES...
BUT THEY'D FIND NO EVIDENCE OF JANET'S EXISTENCE 'CAUSE I'D TAKEN ALL OF HER STUFF UP TO MY APARTMENT EARLIER...
AFTER A FEW HOURS, WE HAD DONE IT~THEY'D BOUGHT OUR STORY AND WE WERE ABLE TO KEEP JANET'S KIDNAPPING UNDER WRAPS...
THANKS SO MUCH, OFFICERS!
HOPEFULLY, FOR HER SAKE, WE'D MADE THE RIGHT DECISION.

8

I WAS GETTING CAUGHT UP FOR THE WEEK ON MY COMIC STRIP SO I COULD RUN OUT TO FORT MYERS, ASAP ~ I BELIEVED THAT'S WHERE JANET WAS BEING HELD ~ MOST LIKELY, AT EARL'S NEW PLACE... JUST AS I WAS WRAPPING EVERYTHING UP, SWEET LI'L SIXTEEN-YEAR-OLD MICHELLE DROPPED BY TO SLOW ME DOWN...

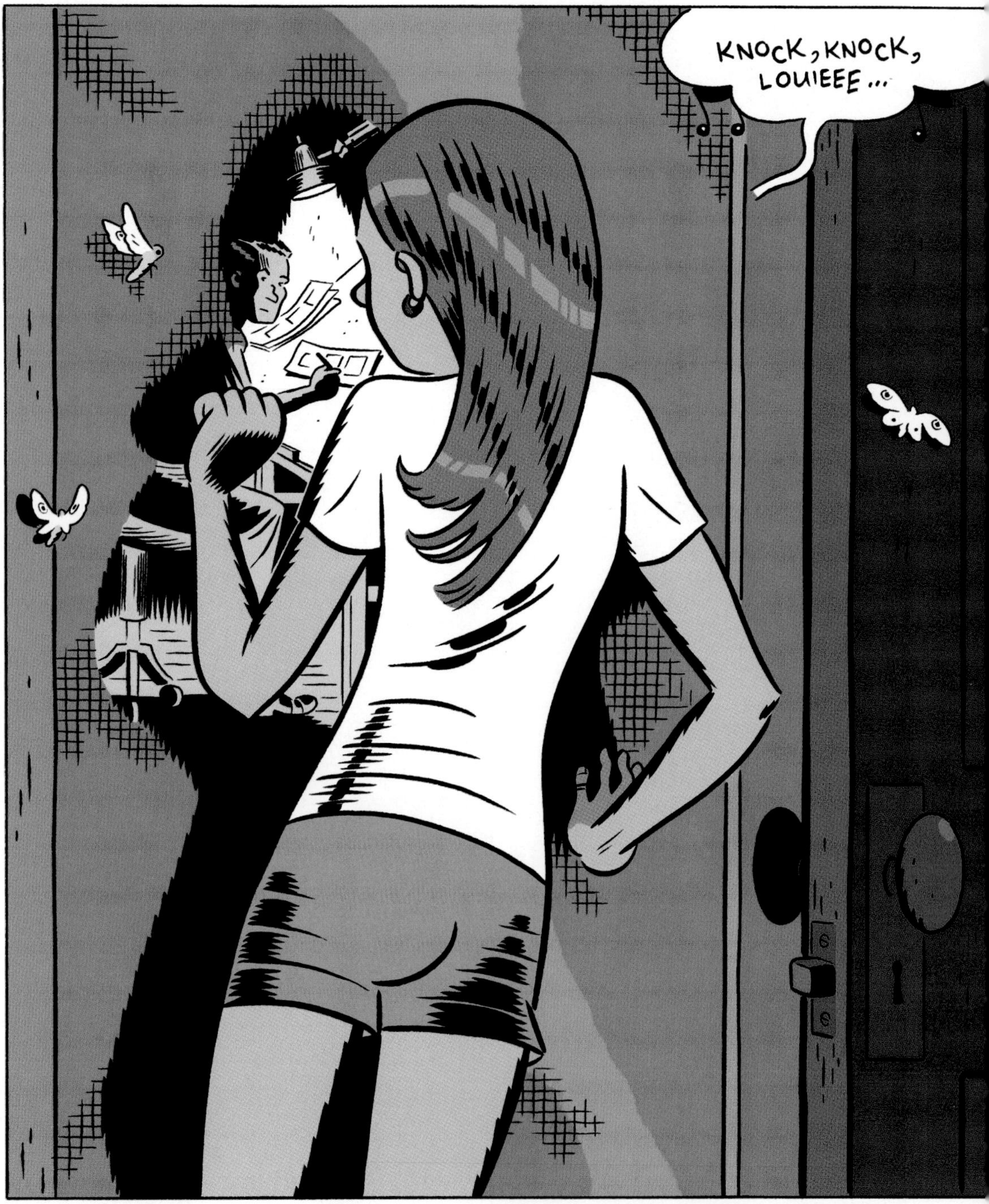

KNOCK, KNOCK, LOUIEEE...

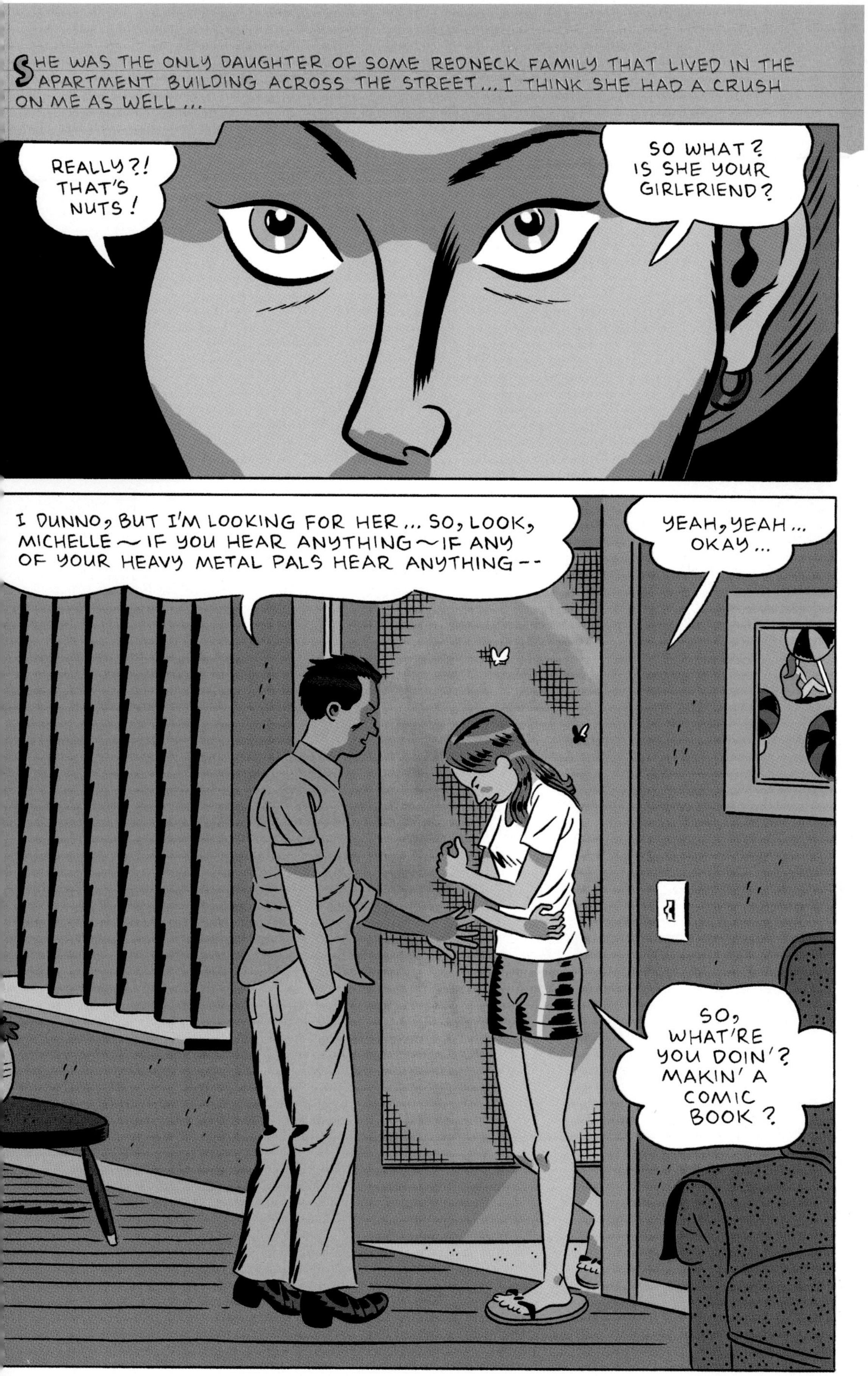
SHE WAS THE ONLY DAUGHTER OF SOME REDNECK FAMILY THAT LIVED IN THE APARTMENT BUILDING ACROSS THE STREET... I THINK SHE HAD A CRUSH ON ME AS WELL...
REALLY?! THAT'S NUTS!
SO WHAT? IS SHE YOUR GIRLFRIEND?
I DUNNO, BUT I'M LOOKING FOR HER... SO, LOOK, MICHELLE ~ IF YOU HEAR ANYTHING ~ IF ANY OF YOUR HEAVY METAL PALS HEAR ANYTHING --
YEAH, YEAH... OKAY...
SO, WHAT'RE YOU DOIN'? MAKIN' A COMIC BOOK?

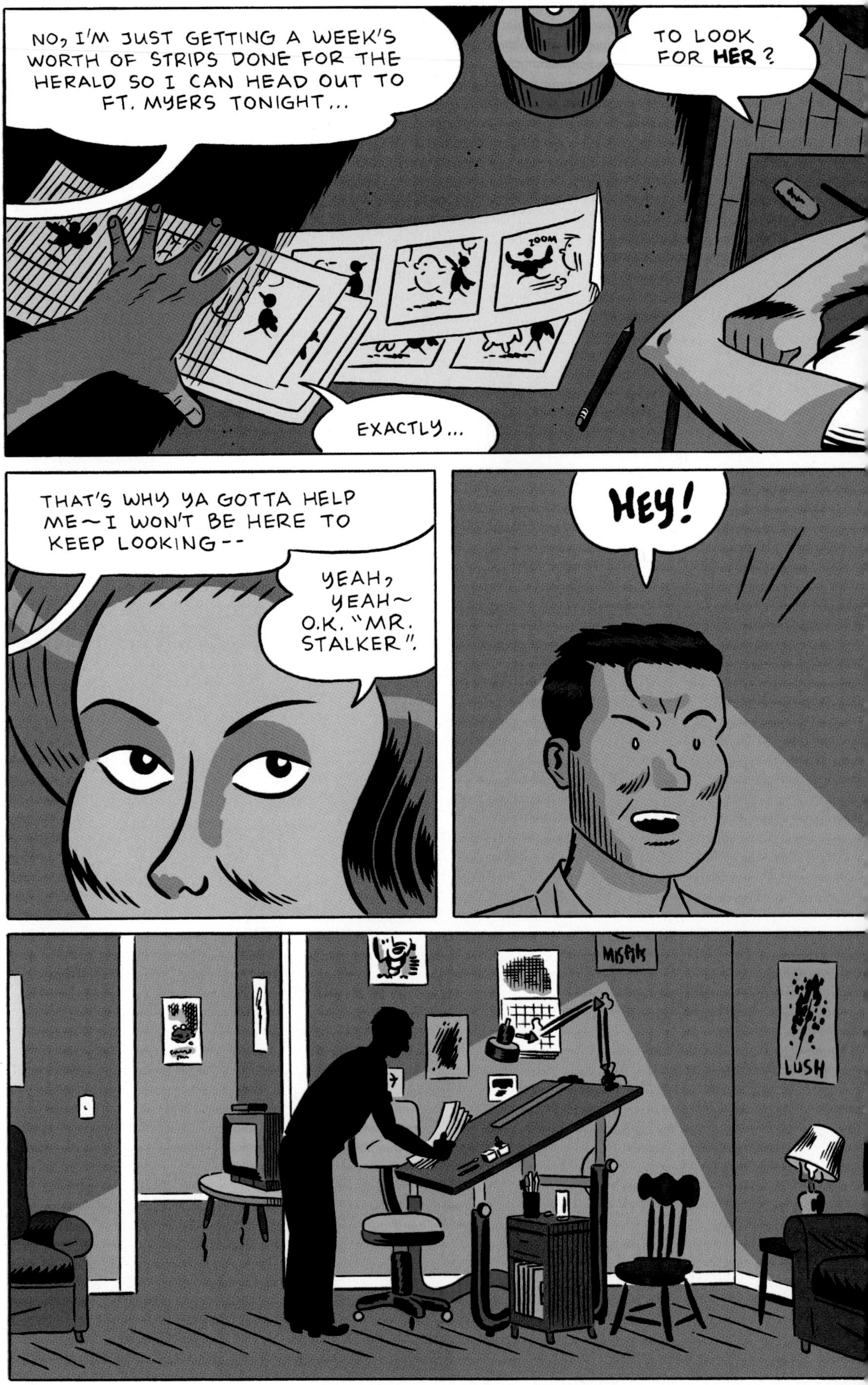

NO, I'M JUST GETTING A WEEK'S WORTH OF STRIPS DONE FOR THE HERALD SO I CAN HEAD OUT TO FT. MYERS TONIGHT...
TO LOOK FOR **HER**?
ZOOM
EXACTLY...
THAT'S WHY YA GOTTA HELP ME~I WON'T BE HERE TO KEEP LOOKING--
YEAH, YEAH~ O.K. "MR. STALKER".
HEY!
MISFITS
LUSH

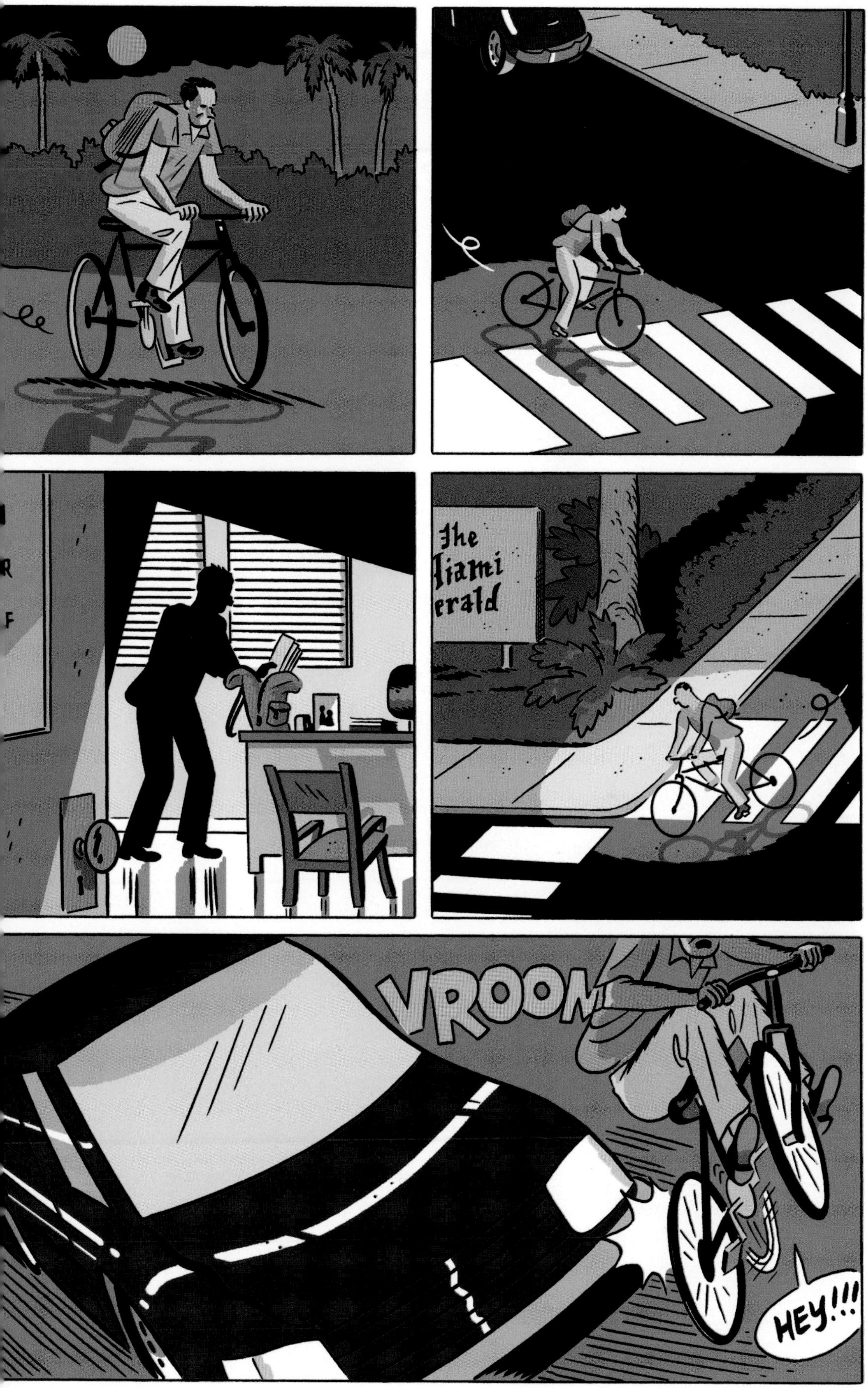
The
iami
erald
VROOM
HEY!!!

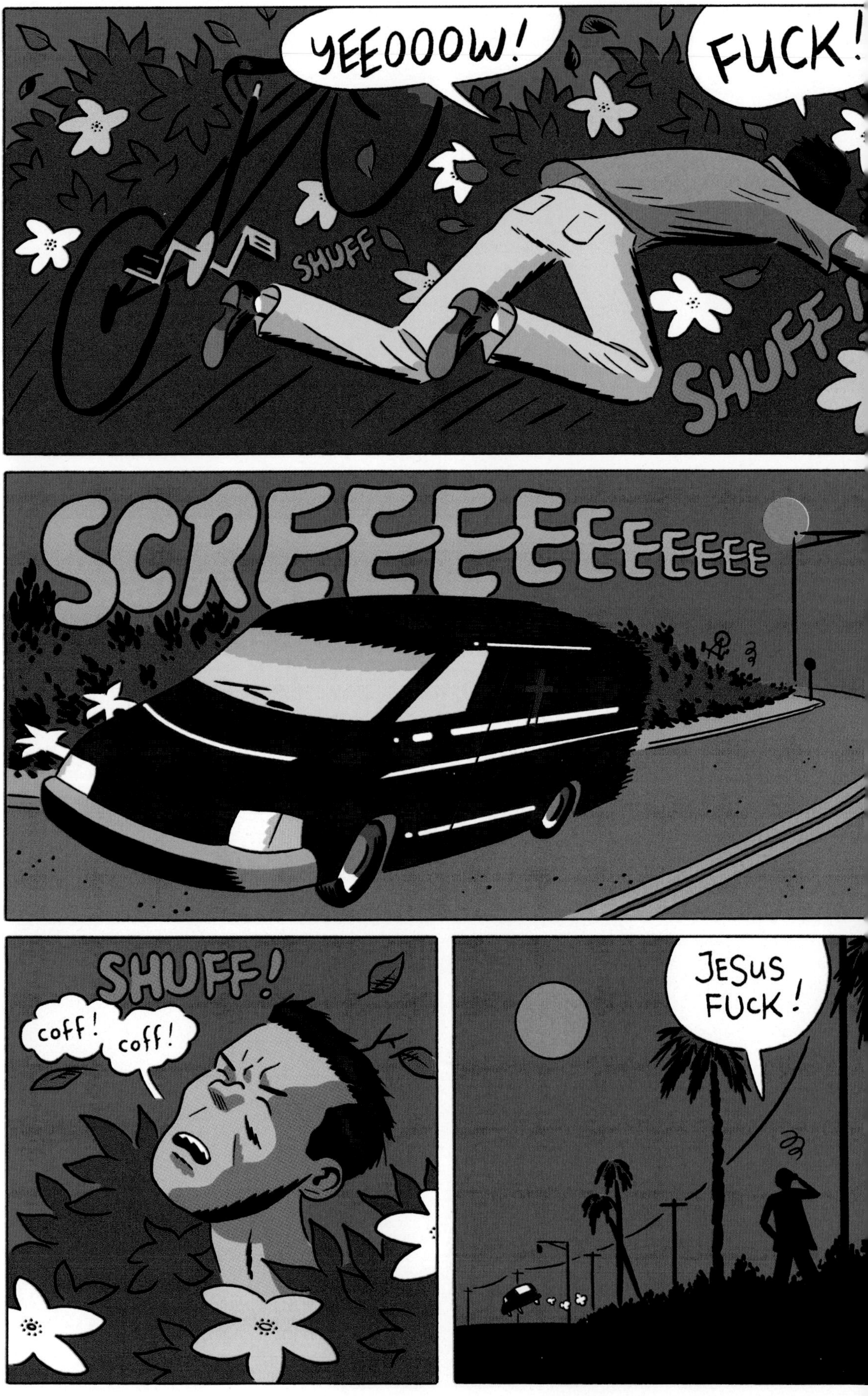
YEEOOOW!
FUCK!
SHUFF
SHUFF!
SCREEEEEEEEEEE
SHUFF!
coff!
coff!
JESUS FUCK!

9

THERE WERE TWO ROUTES FROM MIAMI TO FORT MYERS ~ ROUTE 41 (OR TAMIAMI TRAIL) AND ROUTE 75, THE FREEWAY (OR ALLIGATOR ALLEY). ROUTE 41 WAS CLOSER TO MY NEIGHBORHOOD, SO I TOOK THAT... NOT A FUN DRIVE ~ A TWO-LANE BLACKTOP ROAD THAT RAN STRAIGHT THROUGH THE SWAMP ~ WITH VERY FEW GAS STATIONS (OR ANYTHING ELSE) ALONG THE WAY... ANYWAY, WE ARRIVED IN FORT MYERS AROUND MIDNIGHT ~ THAT'S RIGHT, I TOOK ROB ALONG WITH ME...

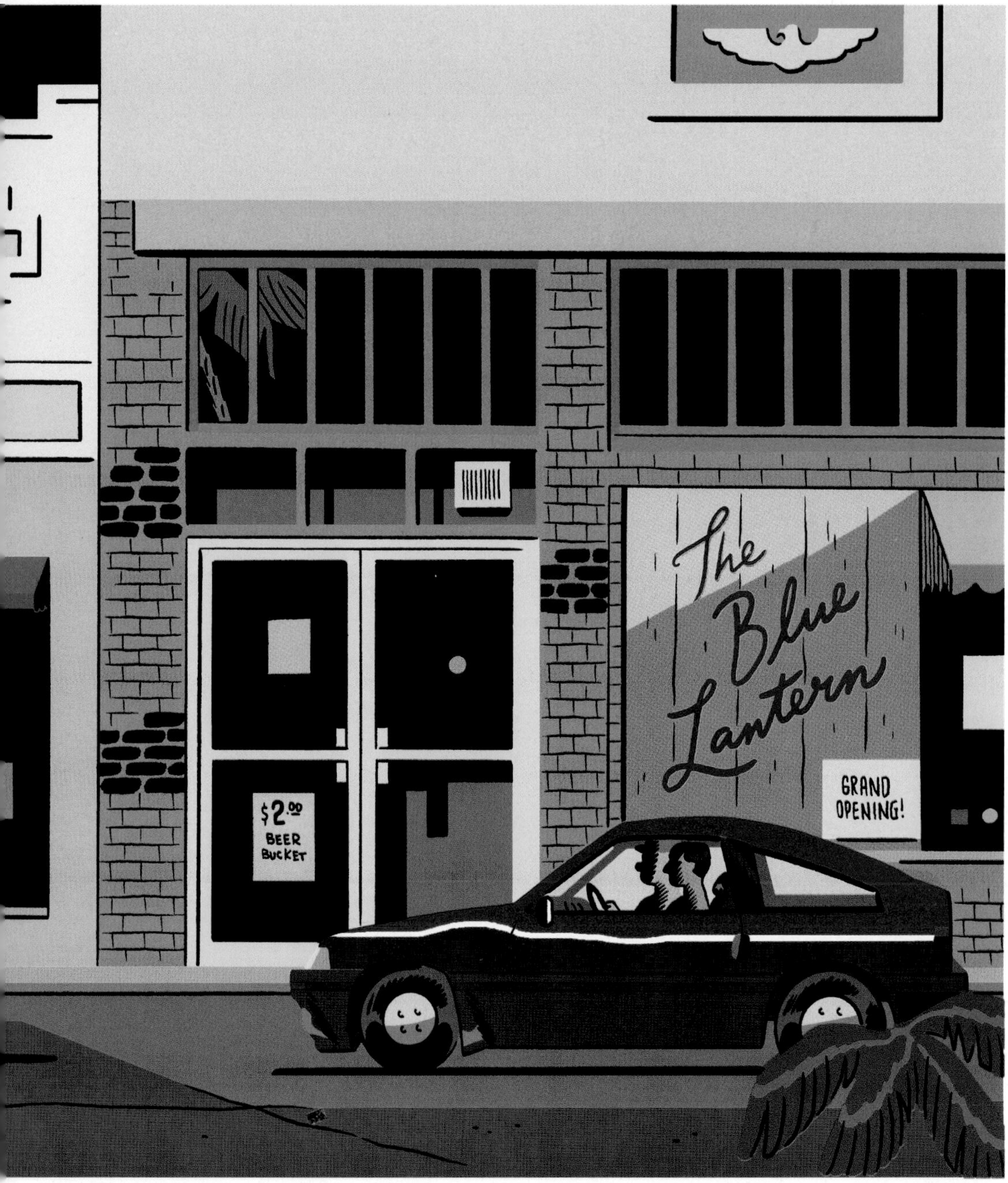

The Blue Lantern
GRAND OPENING!
$2.00 BEER BUCKET

WE FOUND THE BLUE LANTERN GRILL EASILY ENOUGH — THIS WAS EARL'S REASON FOR MOVING TO FORT MYERS — TO OPEN THIS DUMP OF A TAVERN...

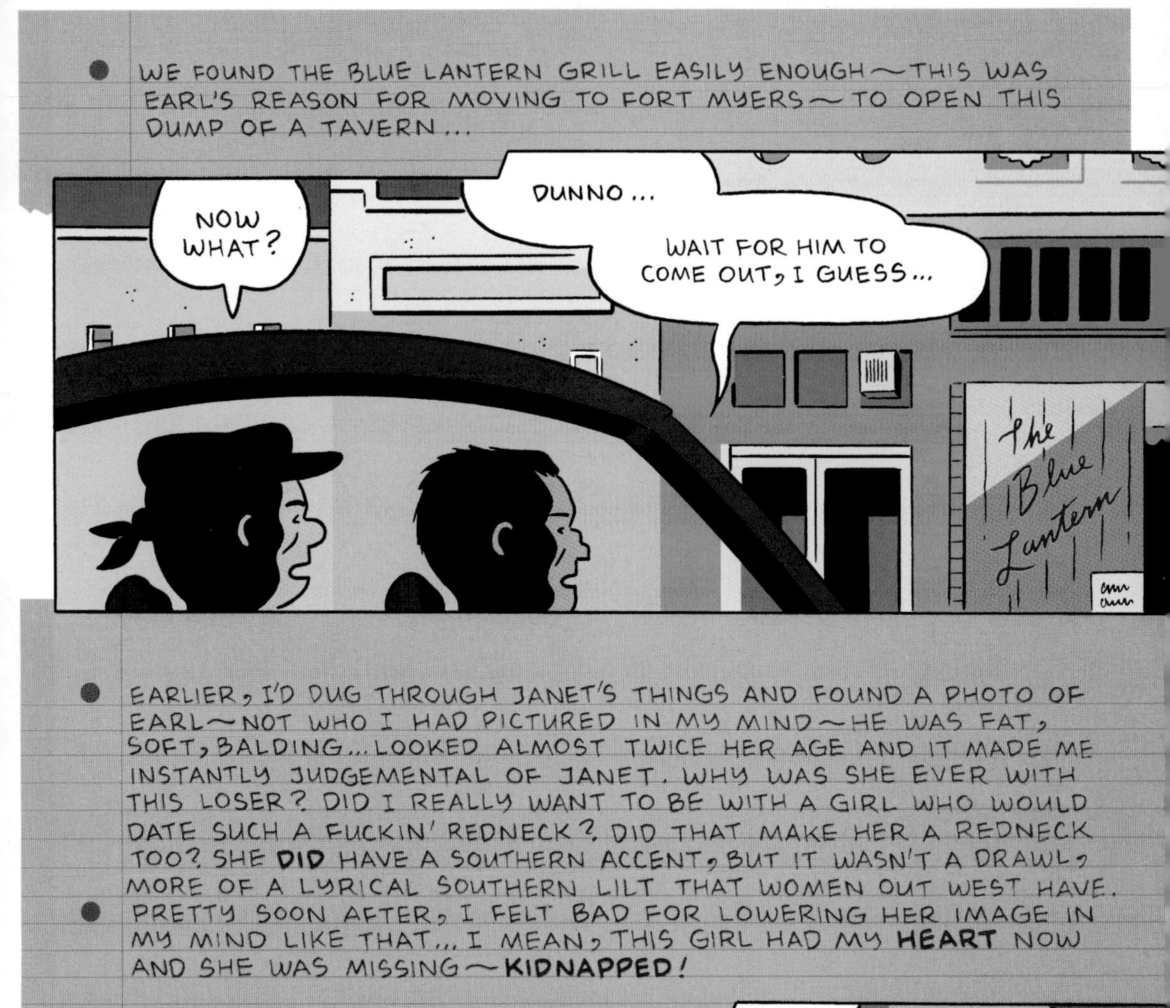
NOW WHAT?
DUNNO...
WAIT FOR HIM TO COME OUT, I GUESS...
The Blue Lantern

EARLIER, I'D DUG THROUGH JANET'S THINGS AND FOUND A PHOTO OF EARL — NOT WHO I HAD PICTURED IN MY MIND — HE WAS FAT, SOFT, BALDING... LOOKED ALMOST TWICE HER AGE AND IT MADE ME INSTANTLY JUDGEMENTAL OF JANET. WHY WAS SHE EVER WITH THIS LOSER? DID I REALLY WANT TO BE WITH A GIRL WHO WOULD DATE SUCH A FUCKIN' REDNECK? DID THAT MAKE HER A REDNECK TOO? SHE **DID** HAVE A SOUTHERN ACCENT, BUT IT WASN'T A DRAWL, MORE OF A LYRICAL SOUTHERN LILT THAT WOMEN OUT WEST HAVE.

PRETTY SOON AFTER, I FELT BAD FOR LOWERING HER IMAGE IN MY MIND LIKE THAT... I MEAN, THIS GIRL HAD MY **HEART** NOW AND SHE WAS MISSING — **KIDNAPPED**!

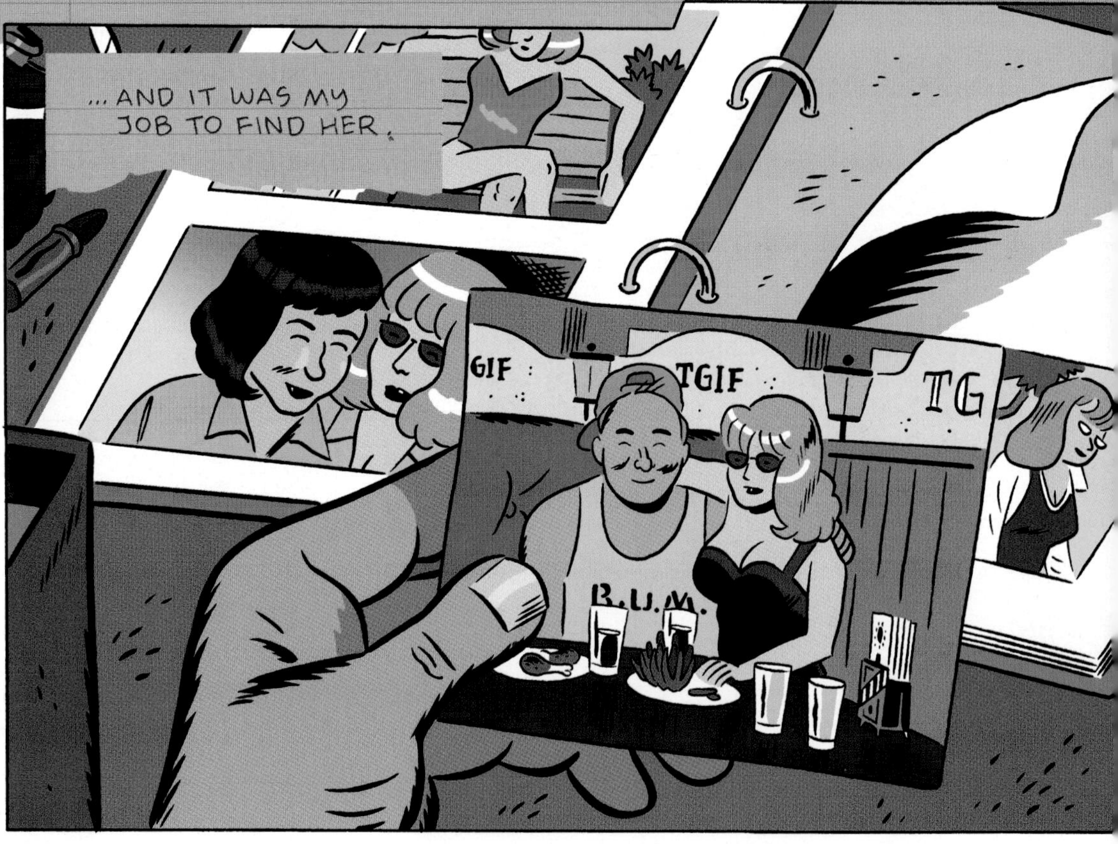
...AND IT WAS MY JOB TO FIND HER.
GIF
TGIF
TG
B.U.M.

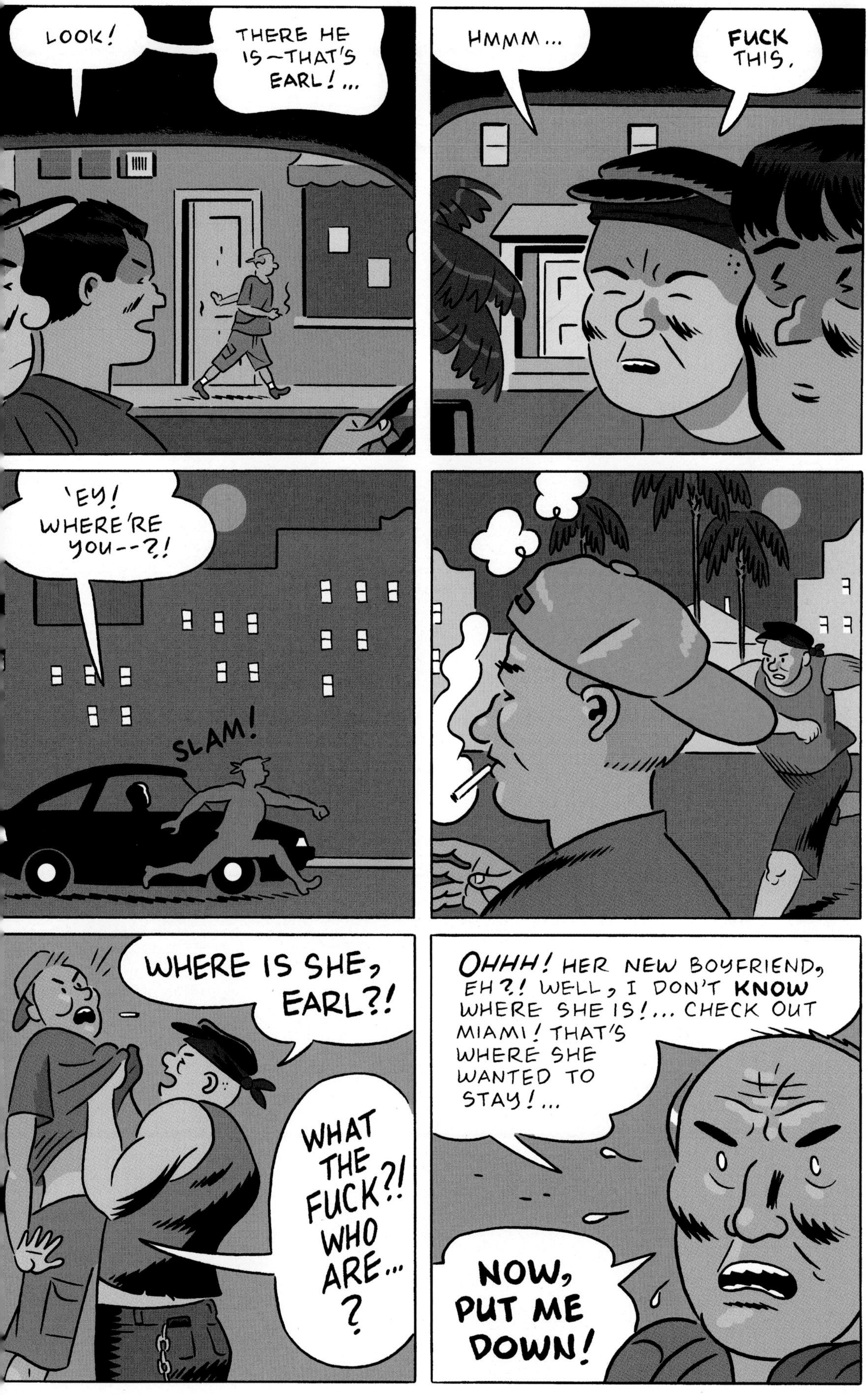
LOOK!
THERE HE IS—THAT'S EARL!...
HMMM...
FUCK THIS.
'EY! WHERE'RE YOU--?!
SLAM!
WHERE IS SHE, EARL?!
WHAT THE FUCK?! WHO ARE... ?
OHHH! HER NEW BOYFRIEND, EH?! WELL, I DON'T KNOW WHERE SHE IS!... CHECK OUT MIAMI! THAT'S WHERE SHE WANTED TO STAY!...
NOW, PUT ME DOWN!

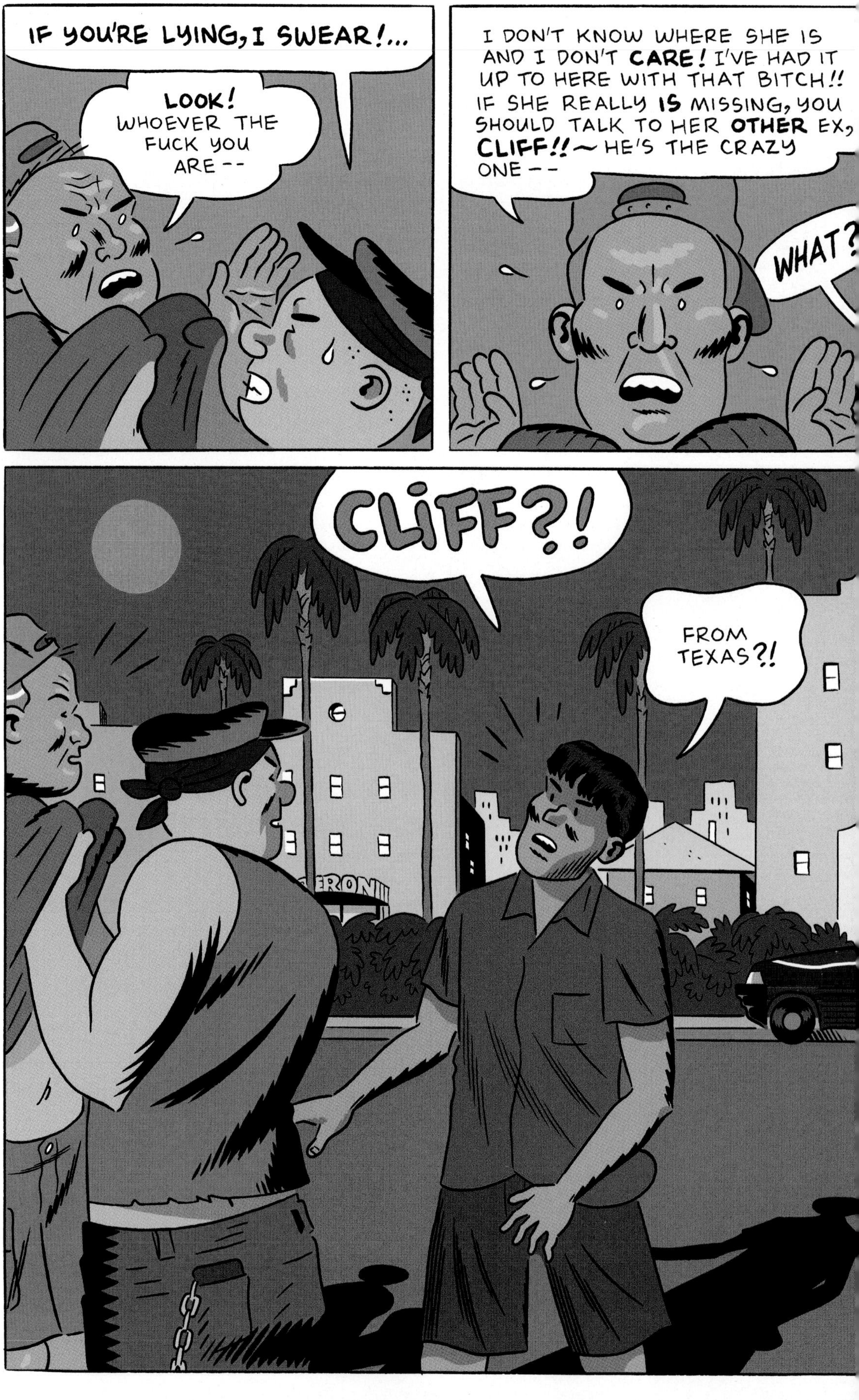
IF YOU'RE LYING, I SWEAR!...
LOOK! WHOEVER THE FUCK YOU ARE --
I DON'T KNOW WHERE SHE IS AND I DON'T CARE! I'VE HAD IT UP TO HERE WITH THAT BITCH!! IF SHE REALLY IS MISSING, YOU SHOULD TALK TO HER OTHER EX, CLIFF!! ~ HE'S THE CRAZY ONE --
WHAT?
CLIFF?!
FROM TEXAS?!

10

I COULDN'T BELIEVE IT... COULD IT ACTUALLY BE TRUE THAT THIS CLIFF CHARACTER WAS BEHIND JANET'S KIDNAPPING? OR WAS EARL JUST TRYING TO AVOID A BEATING? ROB AND I MADE OUR WAY BACK TO MIAMI... THE NEXT NIGHT WE HIT UP SOME CLUBS IN CORAL GABLES ~ JANET'S OLD NECK OF THE WOODS...

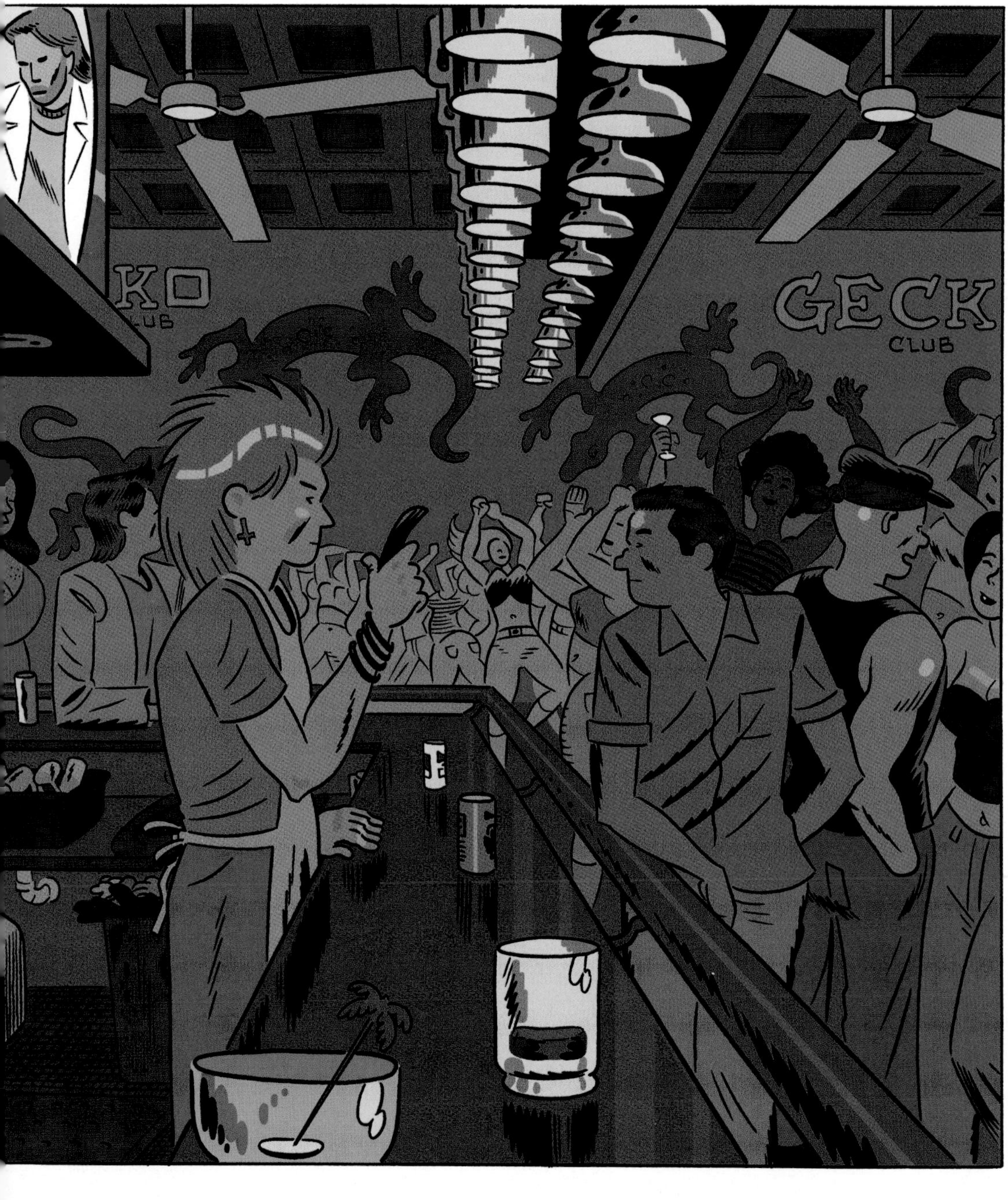

KO
CLUB
GECK
CLUB

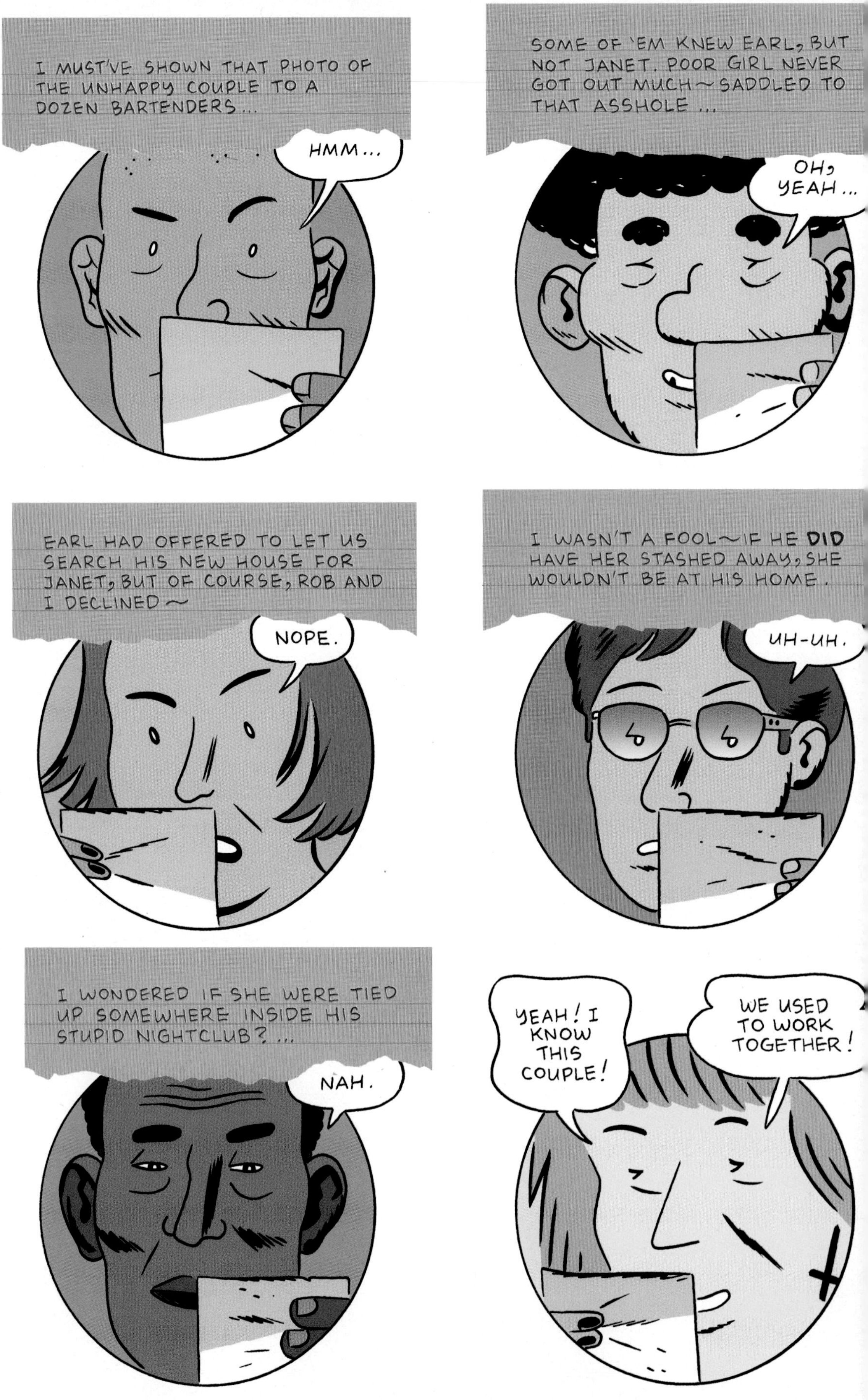
I MUST'VE SHOWN THAT PHOTO OF THE UNHAPPY COUPLE TO A DOZEN BARTENDERS...
HMM...
SOME OF 'EM KNEW EARL, BUT NOT JANET. POOR GIRL NEVER GOT OUT MUCH ~ SADDLED TO THAT ASSHOLE...
OH, YEAH...
EARL HAD OFFERED TO LET US SEARCH HIS NEW HOUSE FOR JANET, BUT OF COURSE, ROB AND I DECLINED ~
NOPE.
I WASN'T A FOOL ~ IF HE **DID** HAVE HER STASHED AWAY, SHE WOULDN'T BE AT HIS HOME.
UH-UH.
I WONDERED IF SHE WERE TIED UP SOMEWHERE INSIDE HIS STUPID NIGHTCLUB?...
NAH.
YEAH! I KNOW THIS COUPLE!
WE USED TO WORK TOGETHER!

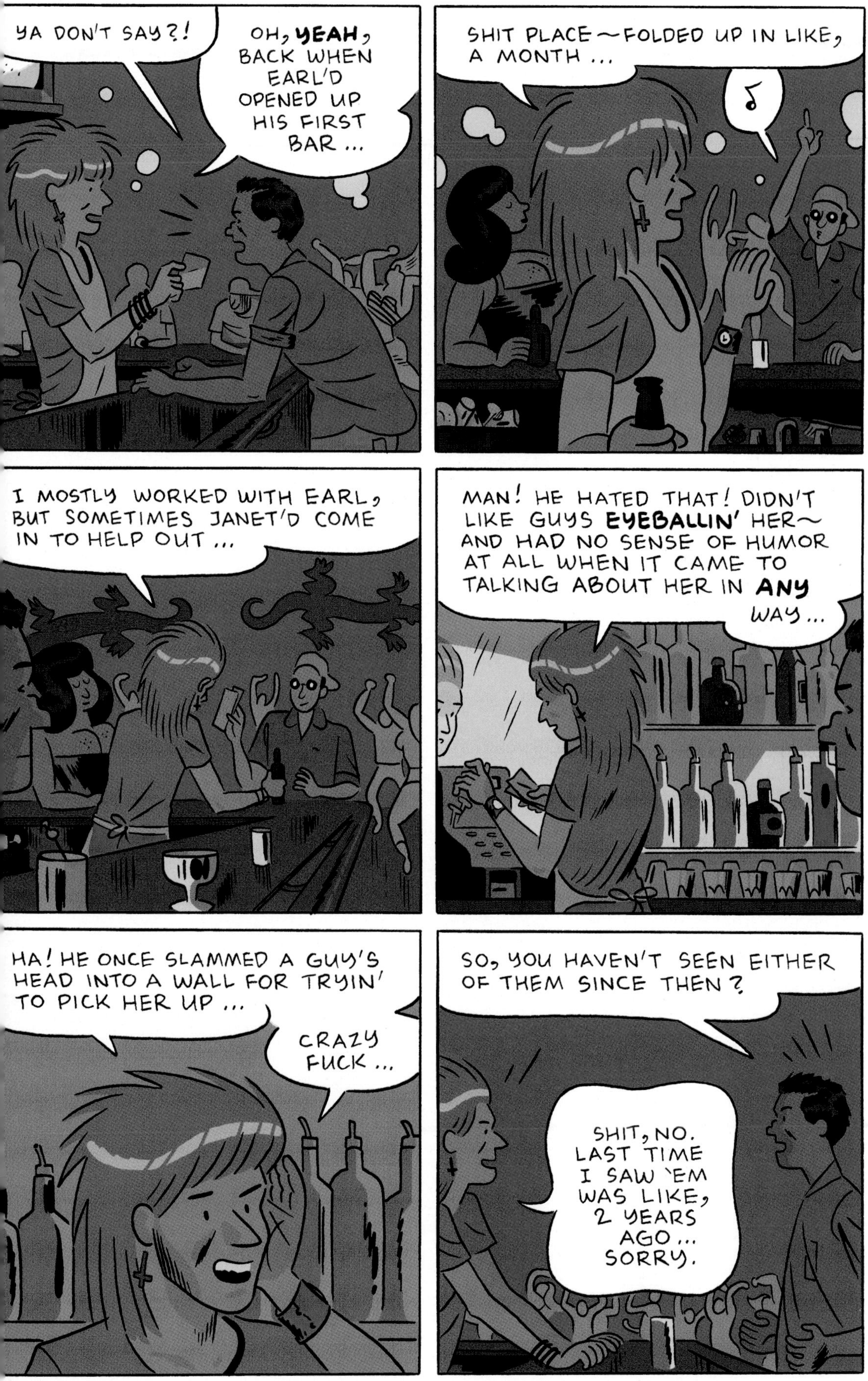
YA DON'T SAY?!
OH, YEAH, BACK WHEN EARL'D OPENED UP HIS FIRST BAR ...
SHIT PLACE ~ FOLDED UP IN LIKE, A MONTH ...
I MOSTLY WORKED WITH EARL, BUT SOMETIMES JANET'D COME IN TO HELP OUT ...
MAN! HE HATED THAT! DIDN'T LIKE GUYS EYEBALLIN' HER ~ AND HAD NO SENSE OF HUMOR AT ALL WHEN IT CAME TO TALKING ABOUT HER IN ANY WAY ...
HA! HE ONCE SLAMMED A GUY'S HEAD INTO A WALL FOR TRYIN' TO PICK HER UP ...
CRAZY FUCK ...
SO, YOU HAVEN'T SEEN EITHER OF THEM SINCE THEN?
SHIT, NO. LAST TIME I SAW 'EM WAS LIKE, 2 YEARS AGO ... SORRY.

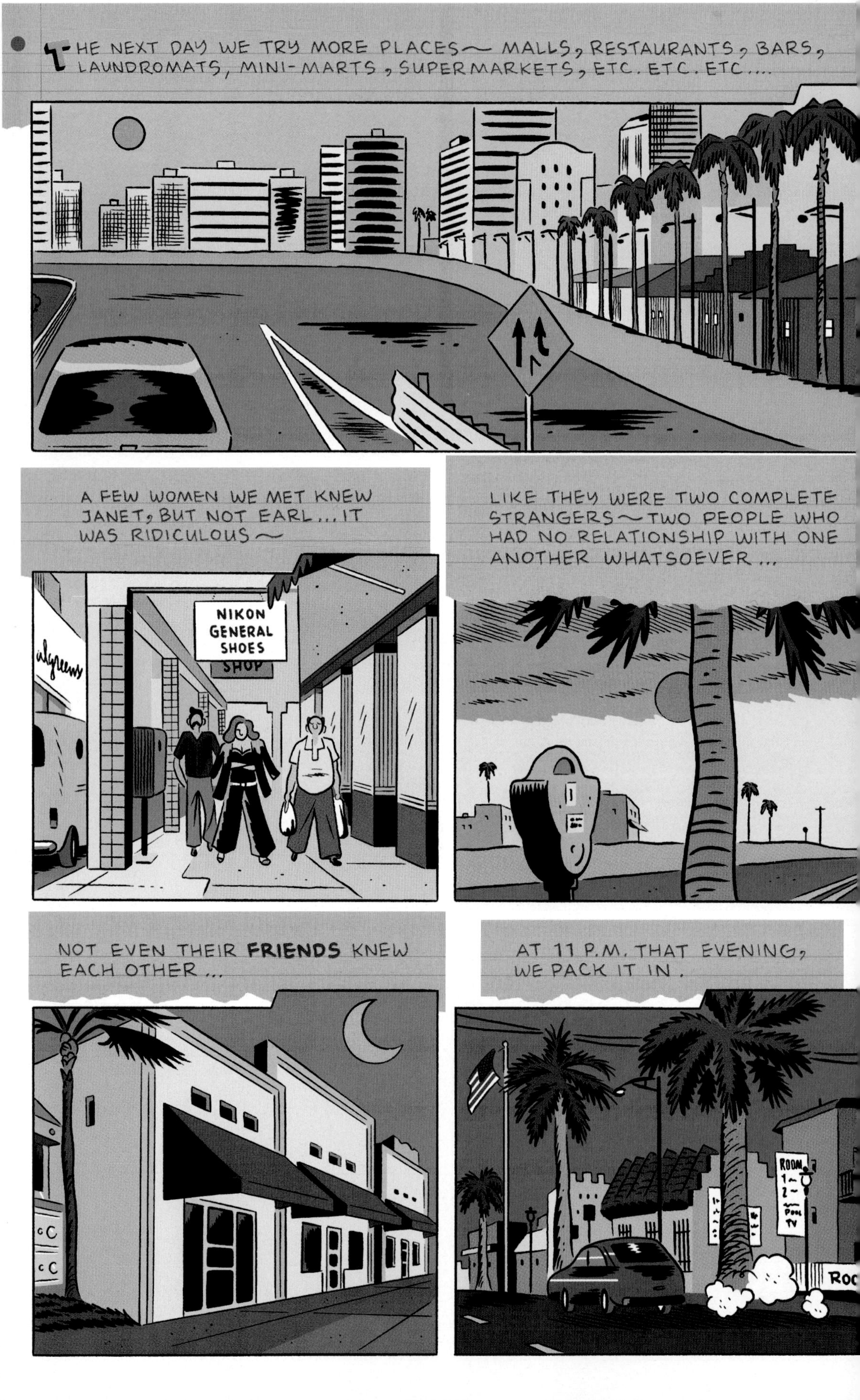

THE NEXT DAY WE TRY MORE PLACES — MALLS, RESTAURANTS, BARS, LAUNDROMATS, MINI-MARTS, SUPERMARKETS, ETC. ETC. ETC....
A FEW WOMEN WE MET KNEW JANET, BUT NOT EARL... IT WAS RIDICULOUS —
NIKON GENERAL SHOES
SHOP
LIKE THEY WERE TWO COMPLETE STRANGERS — TWO PEOPLE WHO HAD NO RELATIONSHIP WITH ONE ANOTHER WHATSOEVER...
NOT EVEN THEIR **FRIENDS** KNEW EACH OTHER...
AT 11 P.M. THAT EVENING, WE PACK IT IN.
ROOM
POOL
TV

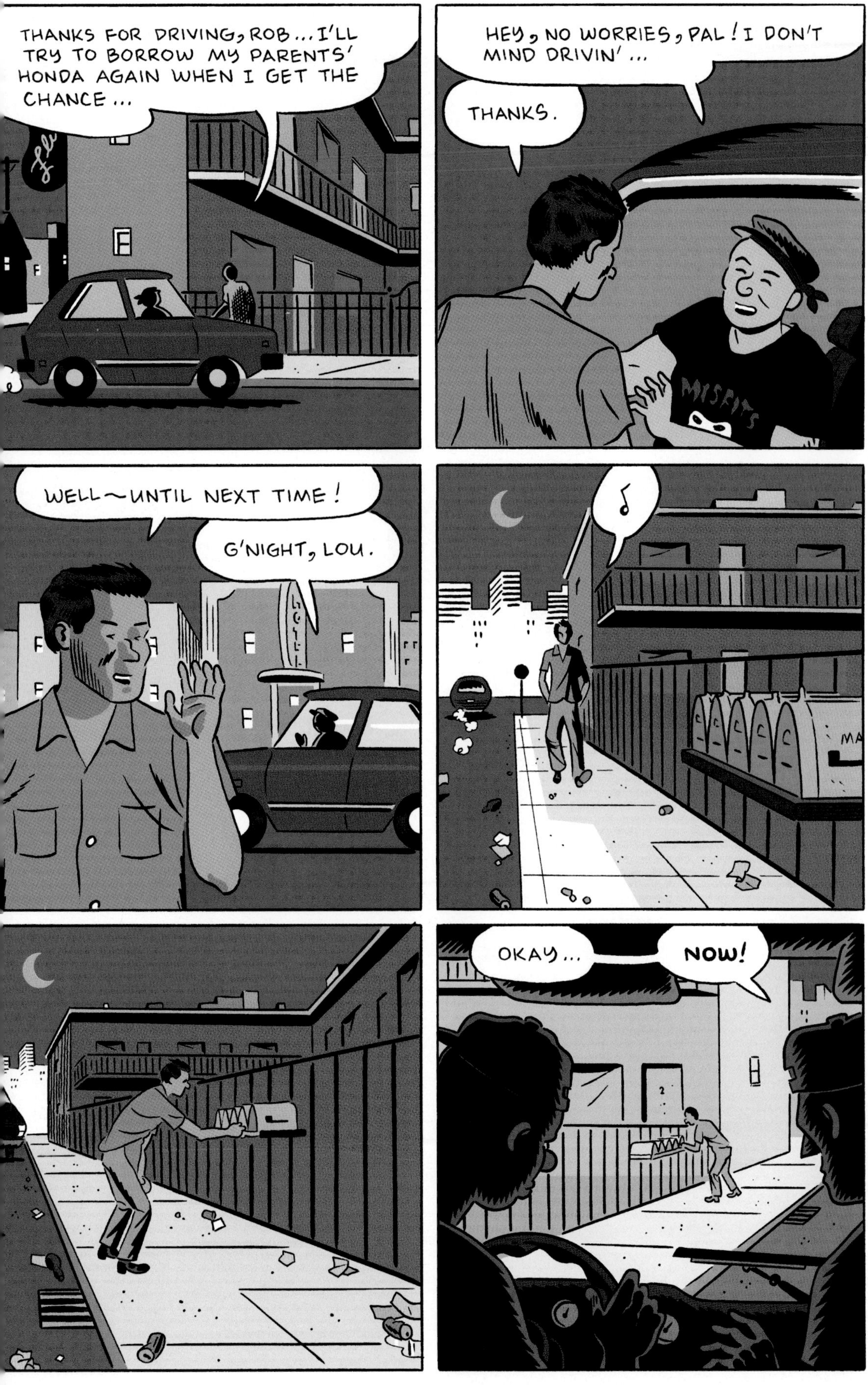
THANKS FOR DRIVING, ROB... I'LL TRY TO BORROW MY PARENTS' HONDA AGAIN WHEN I GET THE CHANCE...
HEY, NO WORRIES, PAL! I DON'T MIND DRIVIN'...
THANKS.
MISFITS
WELL~UNTIL NEXT TIME!
G'NIGHT, LOU.
HOTEL
OKAY...
NOW!

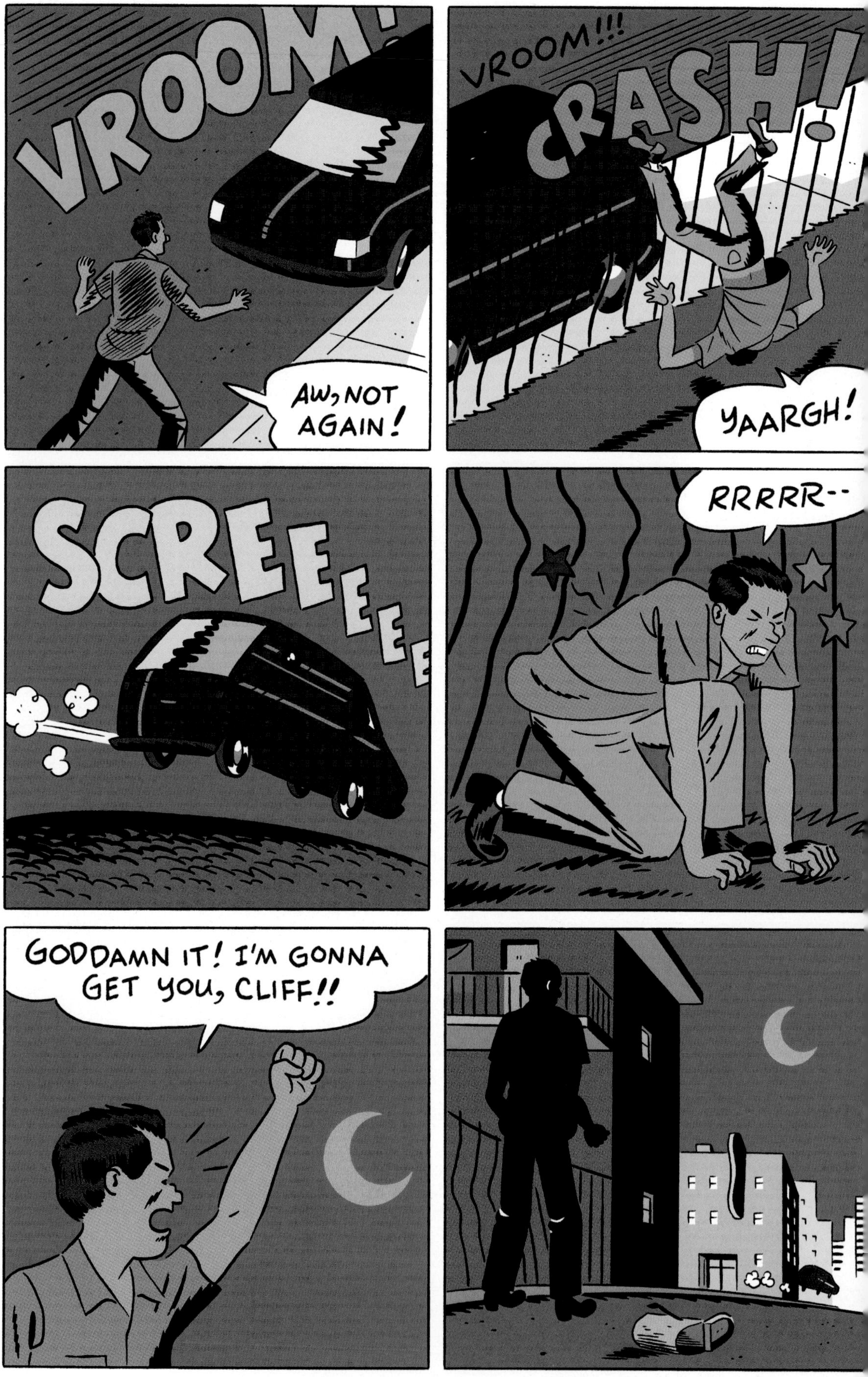
VROOM!
AW, NOT AGAIN!
VROOM!!!
CRASH!
YAARGH!
SCREEEEE
RRRRR--
GODDAMN IT! I'M GONNA GET YOU, CLIFF!!

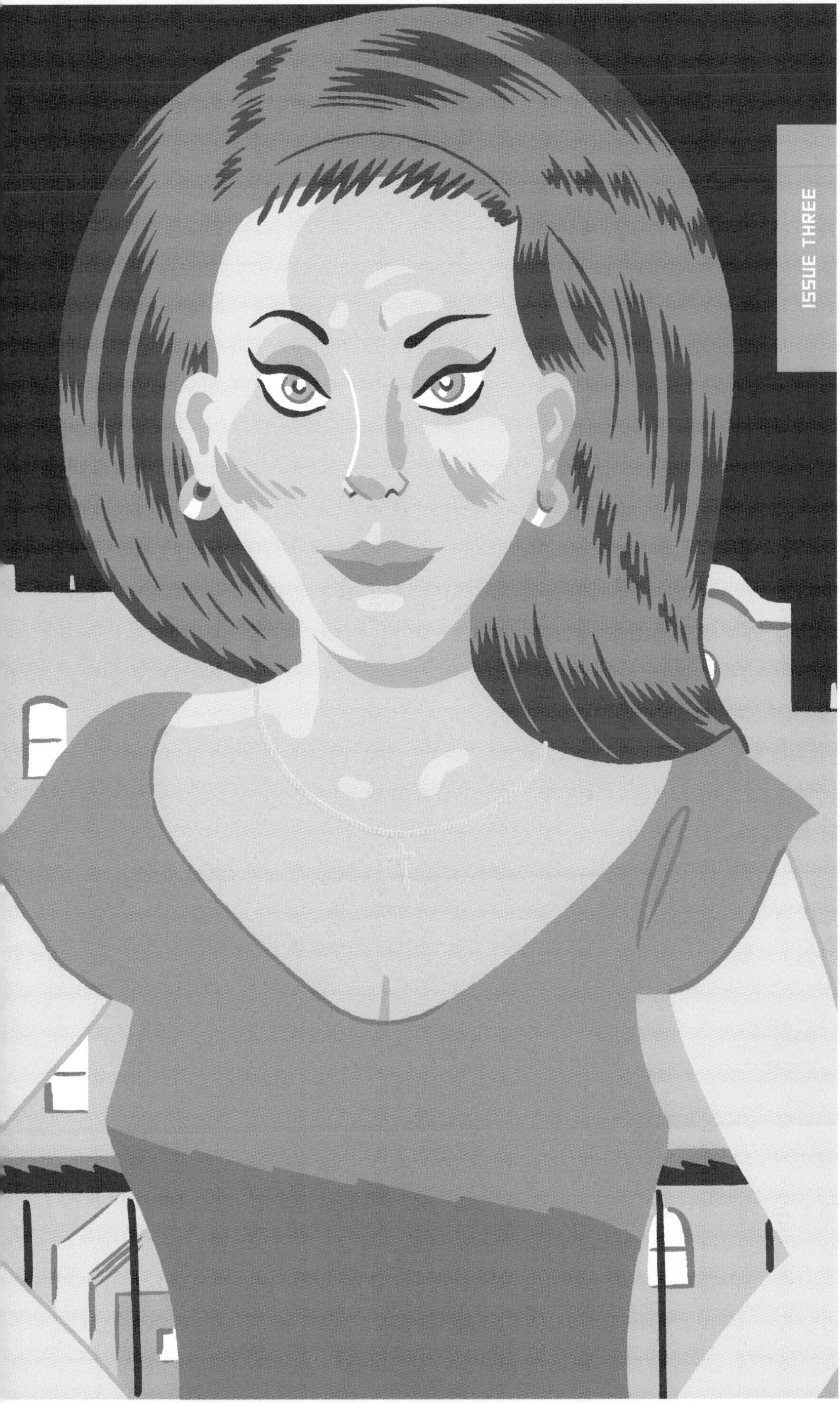

ISSUE THREE

11

ON THURSDAY, I CAME UP WITH A BRILLIANT PLAN ~ I WAS GOING TO TRY TO SEND MESSAGES TO JANET THROUGH MY COMIC STRIP...

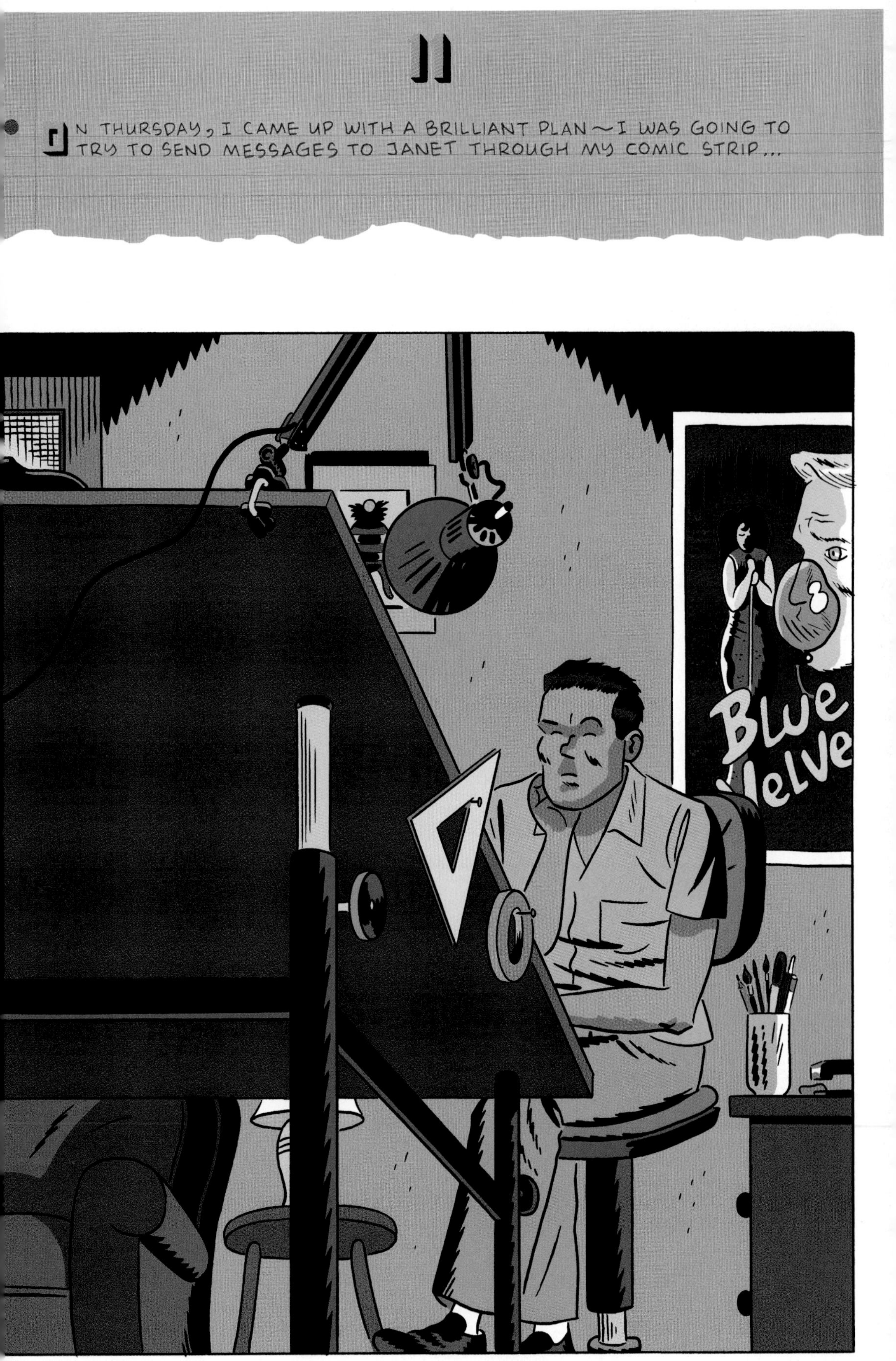

Blue

I'D HOLD A READERS CONTEST WHERE PEOPLE WOULD HAVE TO PROVIDE THE PUNCHLINE FOR EACH FRIDAY'S STRIP...

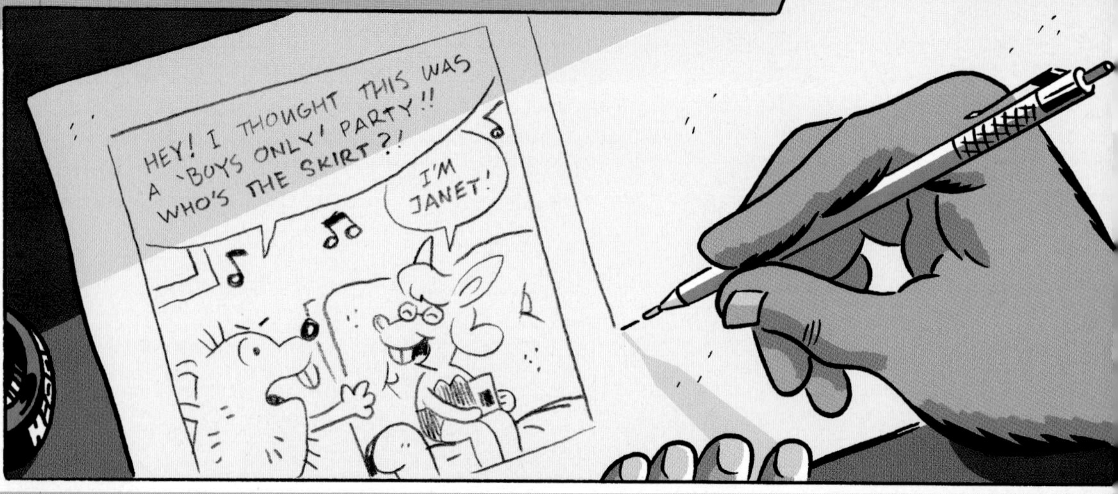
HEY! I THOUGHT THIS WAS A 'BOYS ONLY' PARTY!! WHO'S THE SKIRT?!
I'M JANET!

I KNEW SHE READ THE HERALD AND THAT SHE ENJOYED MY STRIP... EVEN THOUGH IT WAS KIDS STUFF TO ME, SHE SAID IT WAS COOL TO KNOW SOMEONE WHO MADE COMICS FOR THE PAPER... DORKY THING TO FIND COOL, HUH? ...

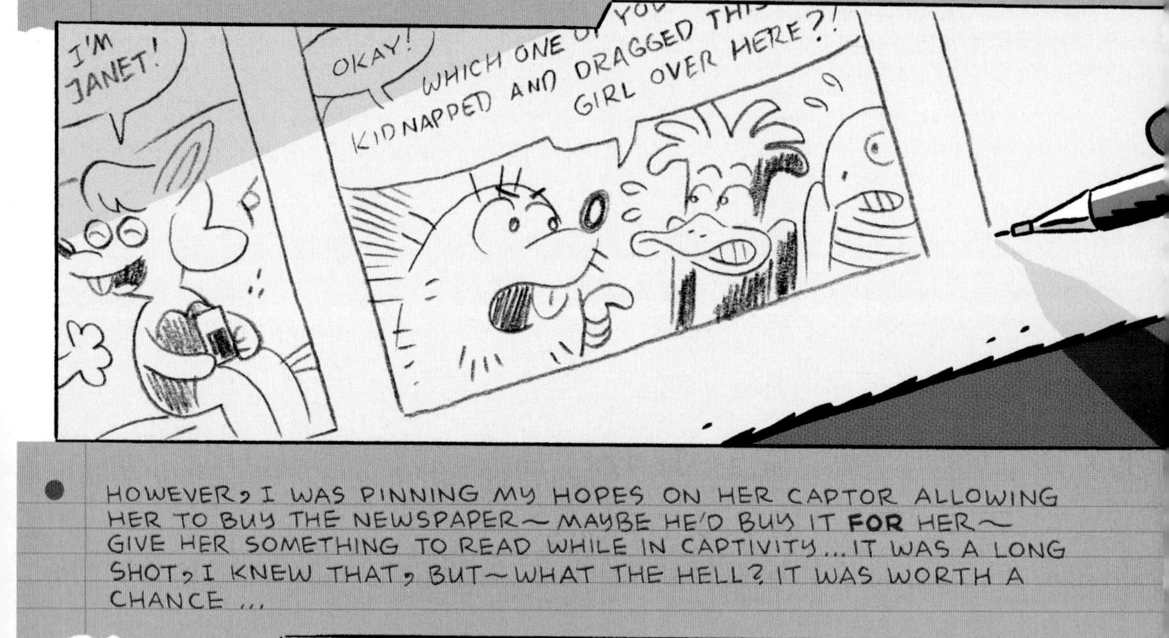
I'M JANET!
OKAY!
WHICH ONE OF YOU KIDNAPPED AND DRAGGED THIS GIRL OVER HERE?!

HOWEVER, I WAS PINNING MY HOPES ON HER CAPTOR ALLOWING HER TO BUY THE NEWSPAPER~ MAYBE HE'D BUY IT **FOR** HER~ GIVE HER SOMETHING TO READ WHILE IN CAPTIVITY... IT WAS A LONG SHOT, I KNEW THAT, BUT~ WHAT THE HELL? IT WAS WORTH A CHANCE...

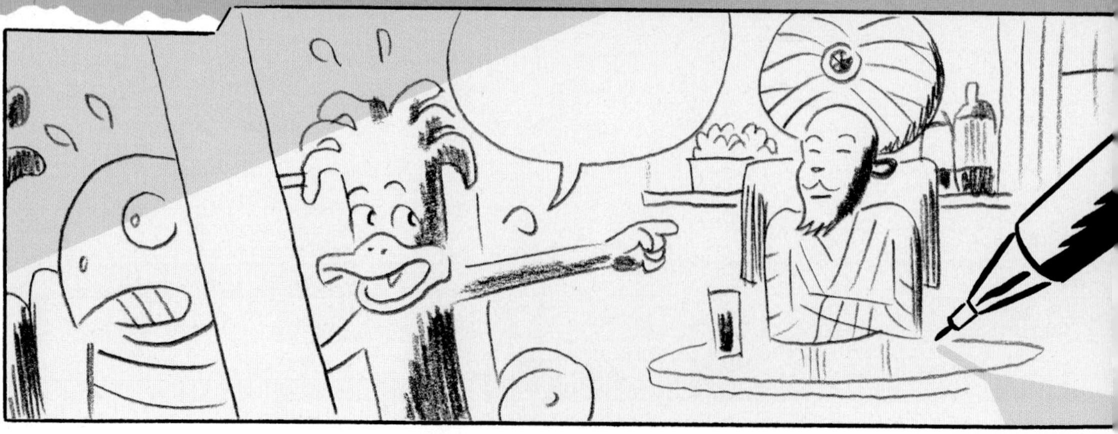

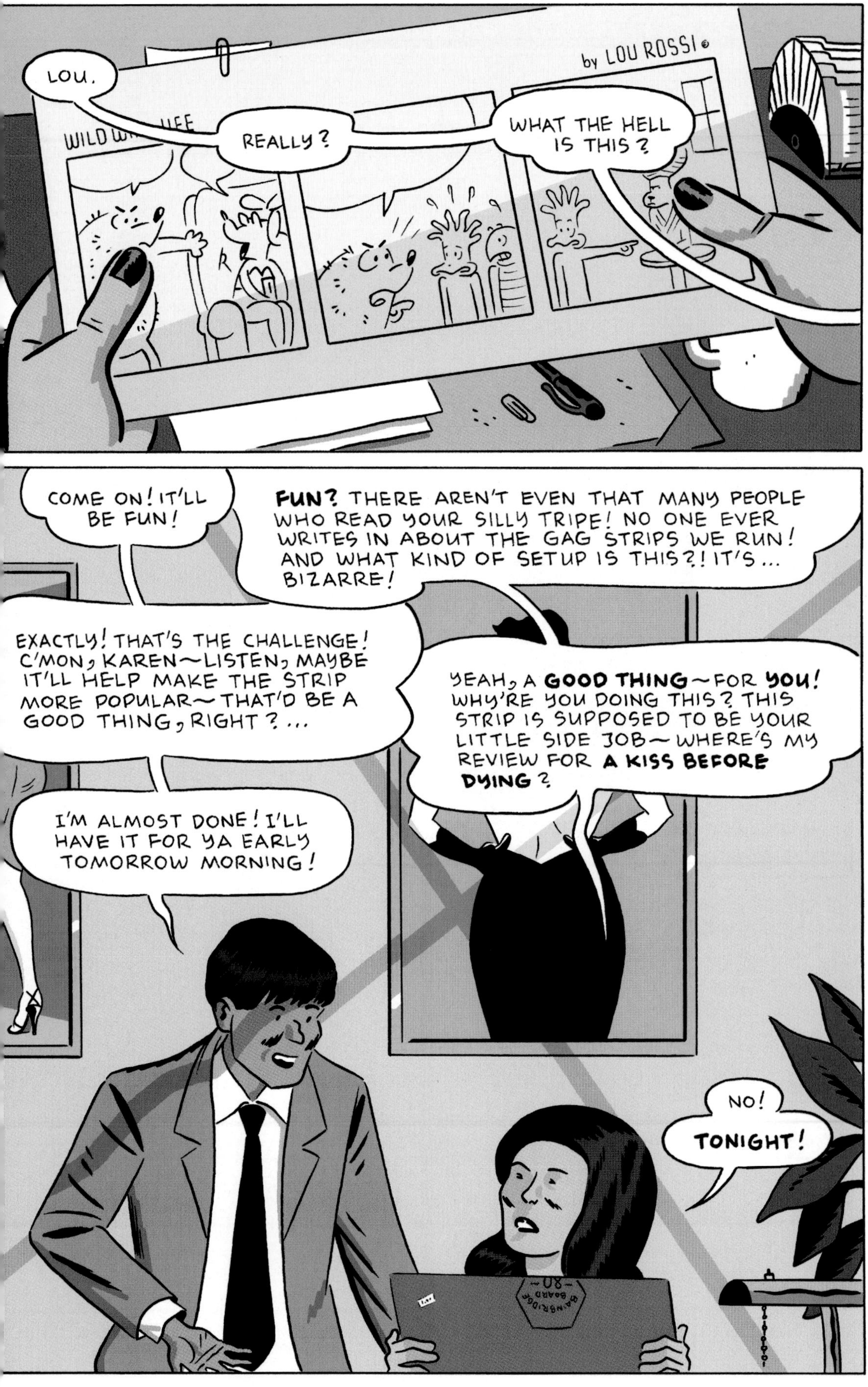
by LOU ROSSI ©
LOU.
REALLY?
WHAT THE HELL IS THIS?
COME ON! IT'LL BE FUN!
FUN? THERE AREN'T EVEN THAT MANY PEOPLE WHO READ YOUR SILLY TRIPE! NO ONE EVER WRITES IN ABOUT THE GAG STRIPS WE RUN! AND WHAT KIND OF SETUP IS THIS?! IT'S... BIZARRE!
EXACTLY! THAT'S THE CHALLENGE! C'MON, KAREN~LISTEN, MAYBE IT'LL HELP MAKE THE STRIP MORE POPULAR~THAT'D BE A GOOD THING, RIGHT?...
YEAH, A GOOD THING~FOR YOU! WHY'RE YOU DOING THIS? THIS STRIP IS SUPPOSED TO BE YOUR LITTLE SIDE JOB~WHERE'S MY REVIEW FOR A KISS BEFORE DYING?
I'M ALMOST DONE! I'LL HAVE IT FOR YA EARLY TOMORROW MORNING!
NO!
TONIGHT!

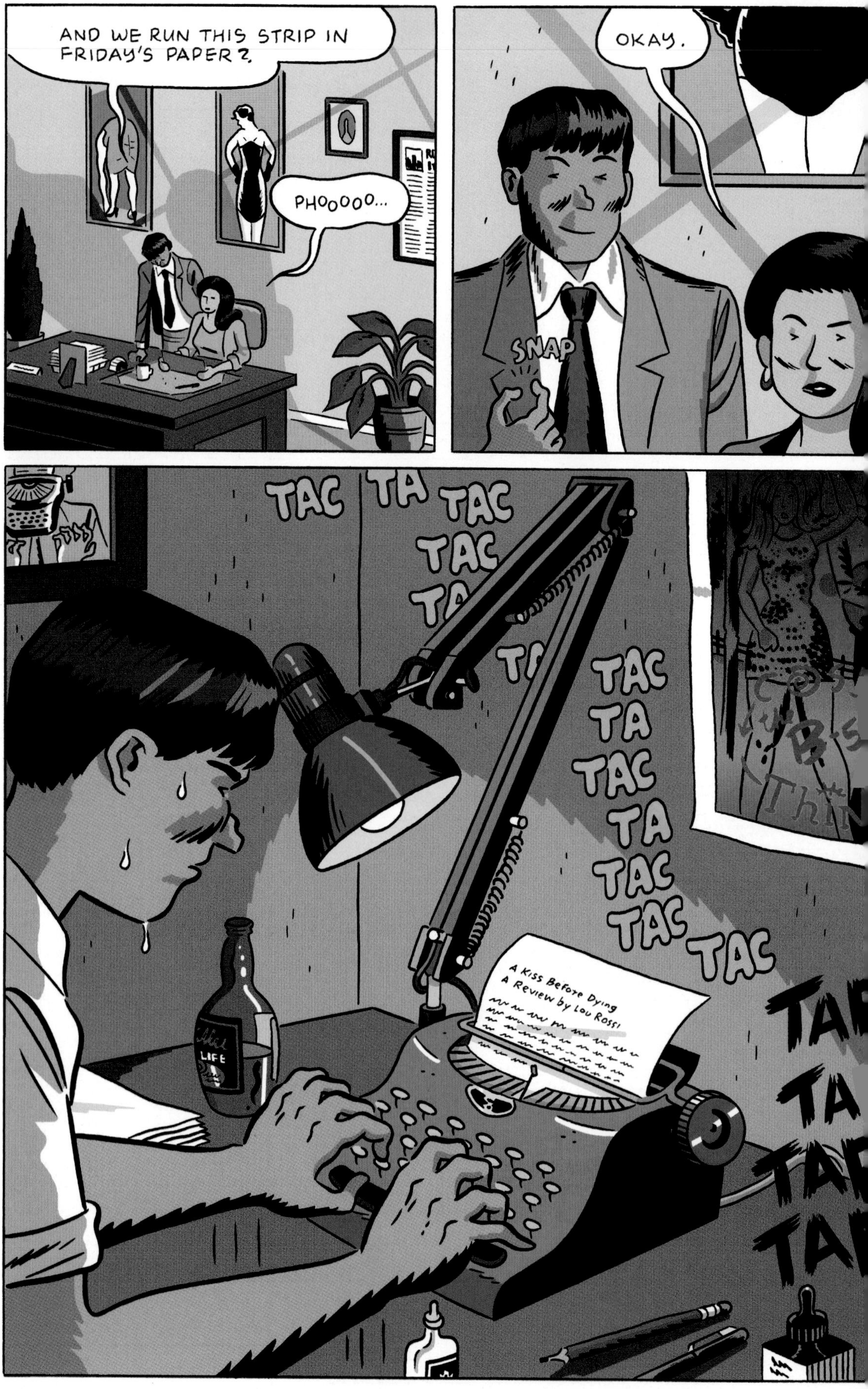

AND WE RUN THIS STRIP IN FRIDAY'S PAPER?
PHOOOOO...
OKAY.
SNAP
TAC TA TAC TAC
TAC TA TAC TA TAC TAC TAC
A Kiss Before Dying
A Review by Lou Rossi

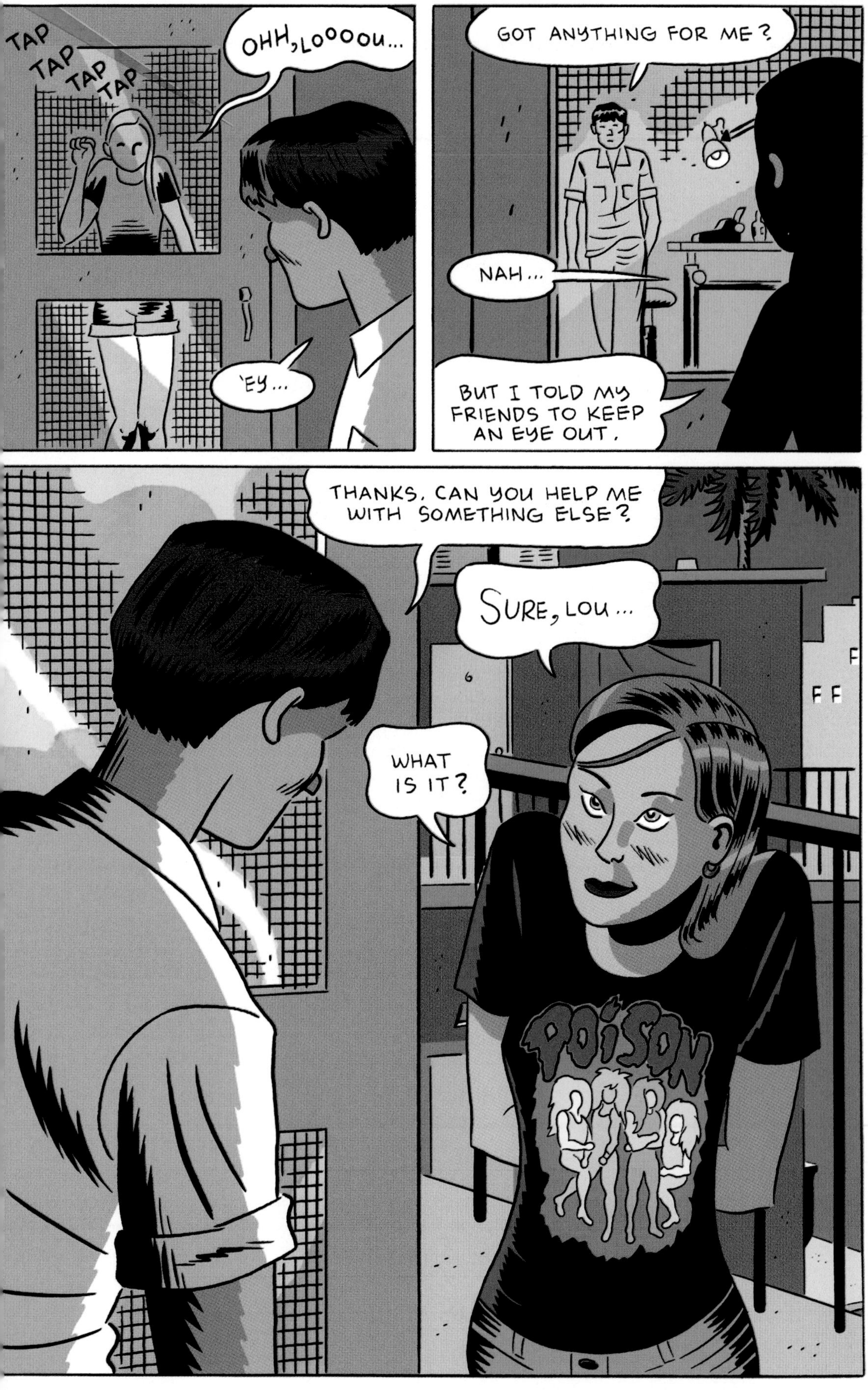
TAP TAP TAP TAP
OHH, LOOOOU...
'EY...
GOT ANYTHING FOR ME?
NAH...
BUT I TOLD MY FRIENDS TO KEEP AN EYE OUT.
THANKS. CAN YOU HELP ME WITH SOMETHING ELSE?
SURE, LOU...
WHAT IS IT?
POISON

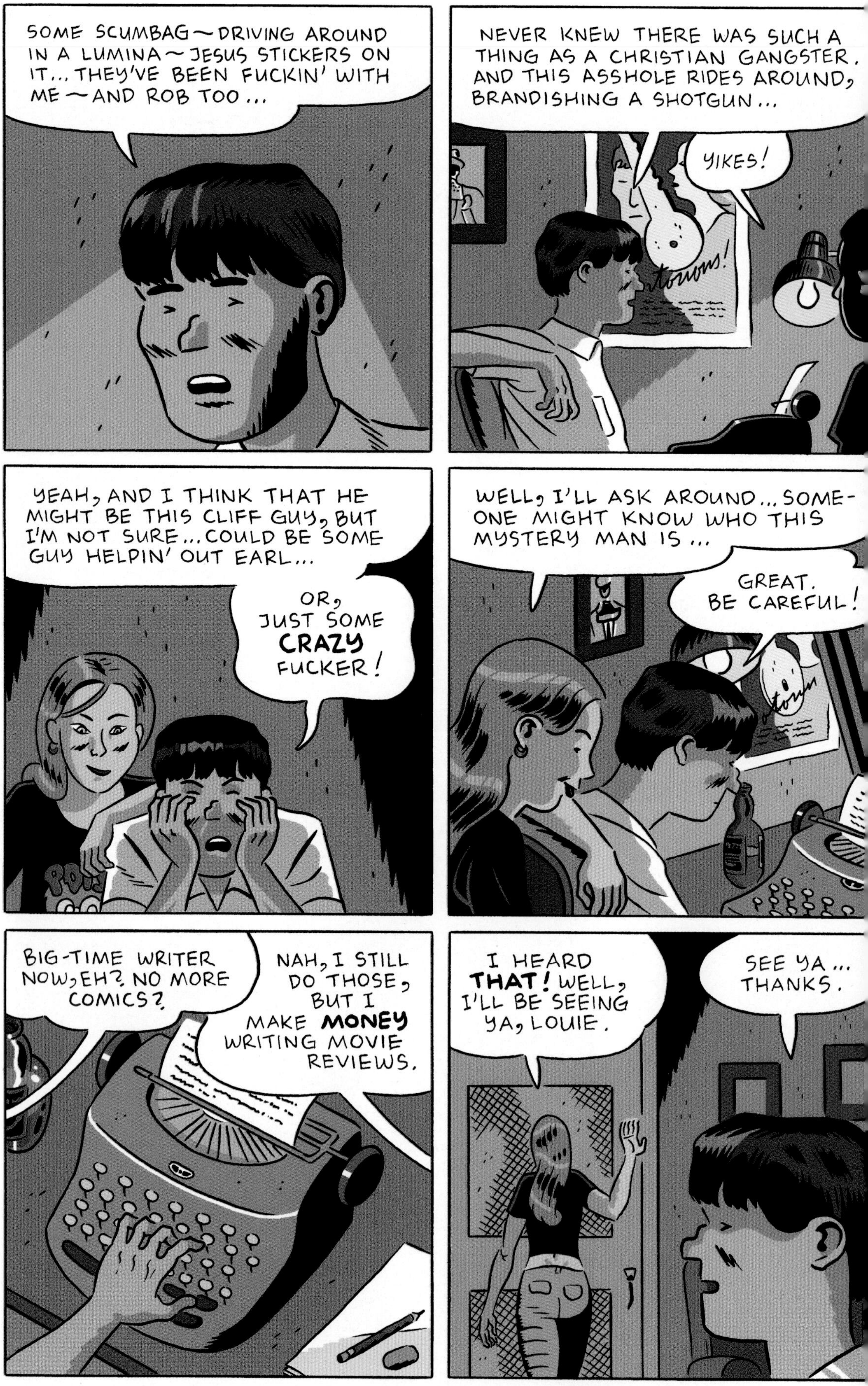
SOME SCUMBAG ~ DRIVING AROUND IN A LUMINA ~ JESUS STICKERS ON IT... THEY'VE BEEN FUCKIN' WITH ME ~ AND ROB TOO...
NEVER KNEW THERE WAS SUCH A THING AS A CHRISTIAN GANGSTER. AND THIS ASSHOLE RIDES AROUND, BRANDISHING A SHOTGUN...
YIKES!
YEAH, AND I THINK THAT HE MIGHT BE THIS CLIFF GUY, BUT I'M NOT SURE... COULD BE SOME GUY HELPIN' OUT EARL...
OR, JUST SOME CRAZY FUCKER!
WELL, I'LL ASK AROUND... SOME-ONE MIGHT KNOW WHO THIS MYSTERY MAN IS...
GREAT. BE CAREFUL!
BIG-TIME WRITER NOW, EH? NO MORE COMICS?
NAH, I STILL DO THOSE, BUT I MAKE MONEY WRITING MOVIE REVIEWS.
I HEARD THAT! WELL, I'LL BE SEEING YA, LOUIE.
SEE YA... THANKS.

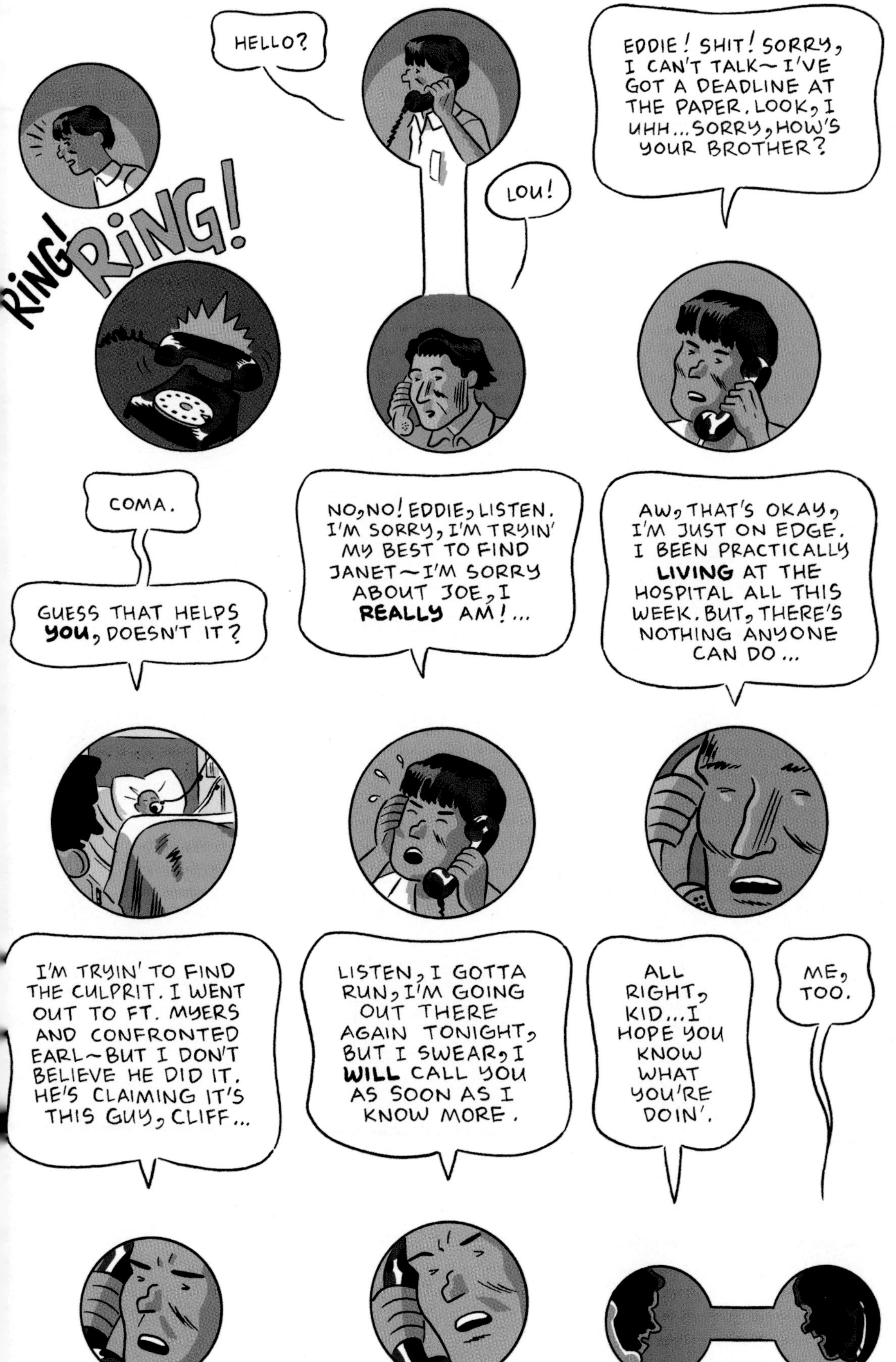
RING! RING!
HELLO?
LOU!
EDDIE! SHIT! SORRY, I CAN'T TALK~I'VE GOT A DEADLINE AT THE PAPER. LOOK, I UHH... SORRY, HOW'S YOUR BROTHER?
COMA.
GUESS THAT HELPS **YOU**, DOESN'T IT?
NO, NO! EDDIE, LISTEN. I'M SORRY, I'M TRYIN' MY BEST TO FIND JANET~I'M SORRY ABOUT JOE, I **REALLY** AM!...
AW, THAT'S OKAY, I'M JUST ON EDGE. I BEEN PRACTICALLY **LIVING** AT THE HOSPITAL ALL THIS WEEK. BUT, THERE'S NOTHING ANYONE CAN DO...
I'M TRYIN' TO FIND THE CULPRIT. I WENT OUT TO FT. MYERS AND CONFRONTED EARL~BUT I DON'T BELIEVE HE DID IT. HE'S CLAIMING IT'S THIS GUY, CLIFF...
LISTEN, I GOTTA RUN, I'M GOING OUT THERE AGAIN TONIGHT, BUT I SWEAR, I **WILL** CALL YOU AS SOON AS I KNOW MORE.
ALL RIGHT, KID... I HOPE YOU KNOW WHAT YOU'RE DOIN'.
ME, TOO.

12

WITH MY FILM REVIEW AND COMIC STRIP COMPLETE, I JUMP INTO MY CAR AND HEAD DOWN ALLIGATOR ALLEY ONCE AGAIN... I NEEDED TO CHECK IN ON WHAT OL' EARL WAS UP TO IN FT. MYERS. I HAD A FRIEND WHO LIVED THERE, WHO'D BEEN KEEPING TABS ON HIM FOR ME WHILE I'D BEEN AWAY... HE ENDED UP HAVING PLENTY OF MYSTERIOUS BEHAVIOR TO REPORT...

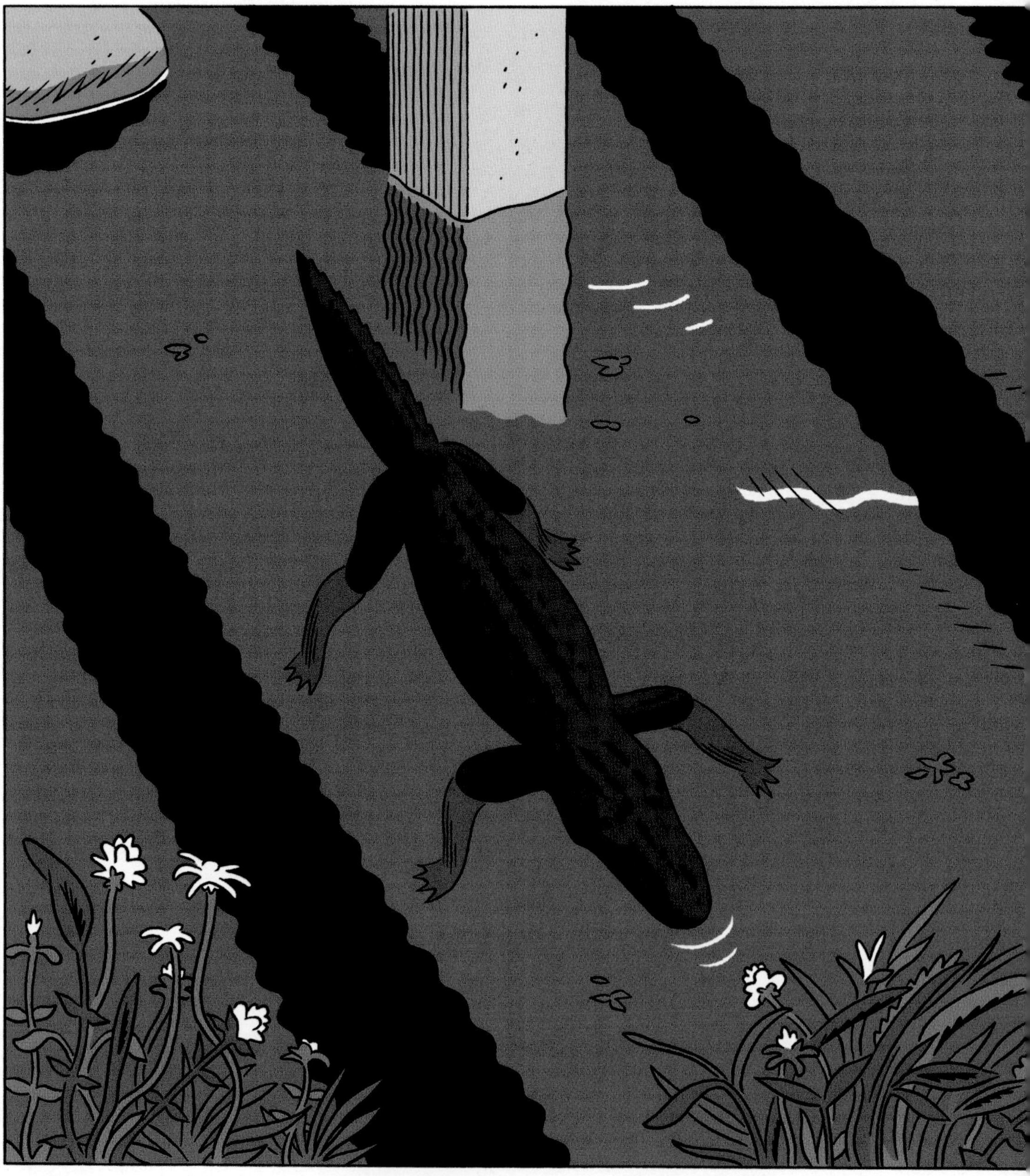

SO, I BEEN GOIN' BY EARL'S PUB EVERYDAY, RIGHT? FIRST COUPLE-A-DAYS, BORING... NUTHIN'...

BUT ON THE THIRD DAY, I SAW HIM COMING OUT OF HIS PUB WITH A BIG BOX OF BOTTLES. BOOZE, I'D ASSUME, RIGHT?

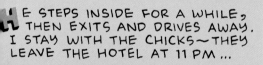

SO HE PUTS THIS BOX IN THE BACK OF HIS TRUCK AND TAKES OFF DOWN THE ROAD...

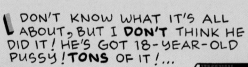

I FOLLOW HIM TO THIS HOTEL, WHERE HE HANDS THE BOOZE OVER TO FOUR BLONDE GIRLS...

HE STEPS INSIDE FOR A WHILE, THEN EXITS AND DRIVES AWAY. I STAY WITH THE CHICKS~THEY LEAVE THE HOTEL AT 11 PM...

I DON'T KNOW WHAT IT'S ALL ABOUT, BUT I **DON'T** THINK HE DID IT! HE'S GOT 18-YEAR-OLD PUSSY! **TONS** OF IT!...

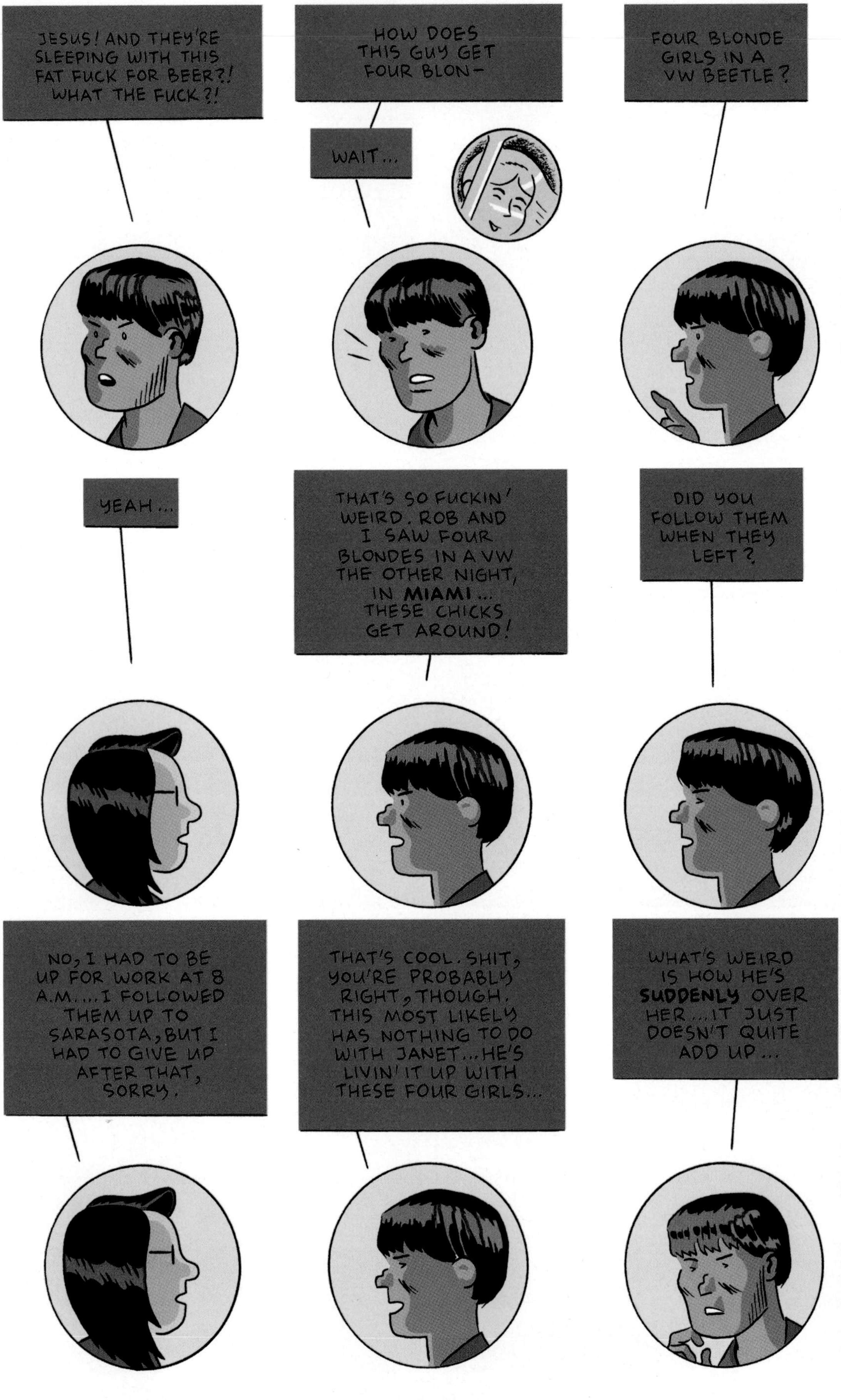
JESUS! AND THEY'RE SLEEPING WITH THIS FAT FUCK FOR BEER?! WHAT THE FUCK?!
HOW DOES THIS GUY GET FOUR BLON–
WAIT...
FOUR BLONDE GIRLS IN A VW BEETLE?
YEAH...
THAT'S SO FUCKIN' WEIRD. ROB AND I SAW FOUR BLONDES IN A VW THE OTHER NIGHT, IN MIAMI... THESE CHICKS GET AROUND!
DID YOU FOLLOW THEM WHEN THEY LEFT?
NO, I HAD TO BE UP FOR WORK AT 8 A.M.... I FOLLOWED THEM UP TO SARASOTA, BUT I HAD TO GIVE UP AFTER THAT, SORRY.
THAT'S COOL. SHIT, YOU'RE PROBABLY RIGHT, THOUGH. THIS MOST LIKELY HAS NOTHING TO DO WITH JANET... HE'S LIVIN' IT UP WITH THESE FOUR GIRLS...
WHAT'S WEIRD IS HOW HE'S SUDDENLY OVER HER... IT JUST DOESN'T QUITE ADD UP...

TAKE OFF FOR MIAMI AGAIN. IT DIDN'T MAKE SENSE...EARL WAS HAVING ORGIES WITH GIRLS EVEN YOUNGER THAN JANET~PAYING THEM WITH BOOZE~ AND JANET WAS SUPPOSED TO HAVE BEEN KIDNAPPED BY HER OTHER EX, CLIFF... WHO LIVED IN TEXAS?...I COULDN'T FIGURE **THAT** ONE OUT...

SNAPPED ON THE STEREO TO GET MY MIND OFF THINGS ON THE RIDE HOME. THEY WERE PLAYING **THE B-52s' CHANNEL Z**...THAT **COSMIC THING** ALBUM WAS BLOWIN' UP~ALMOST EVERY SONG ON THAT RECORD WAS A HIT...I TURNED THE VOLUME WAY UP...

GETTIN' NUTHIN' BUT STATIC!

ON EITHER SIDE OF ME, ALL I COULD SEE WERE SILHOUETTES OF PALM TREES AND SWAMP...SWAMP, SWAMP, SWAMP. IT WAS HUMID AS HELL, BUT HAVING THE WINDOWS DOWN COOLED IT FROM 90 TO 80 DEGREES.

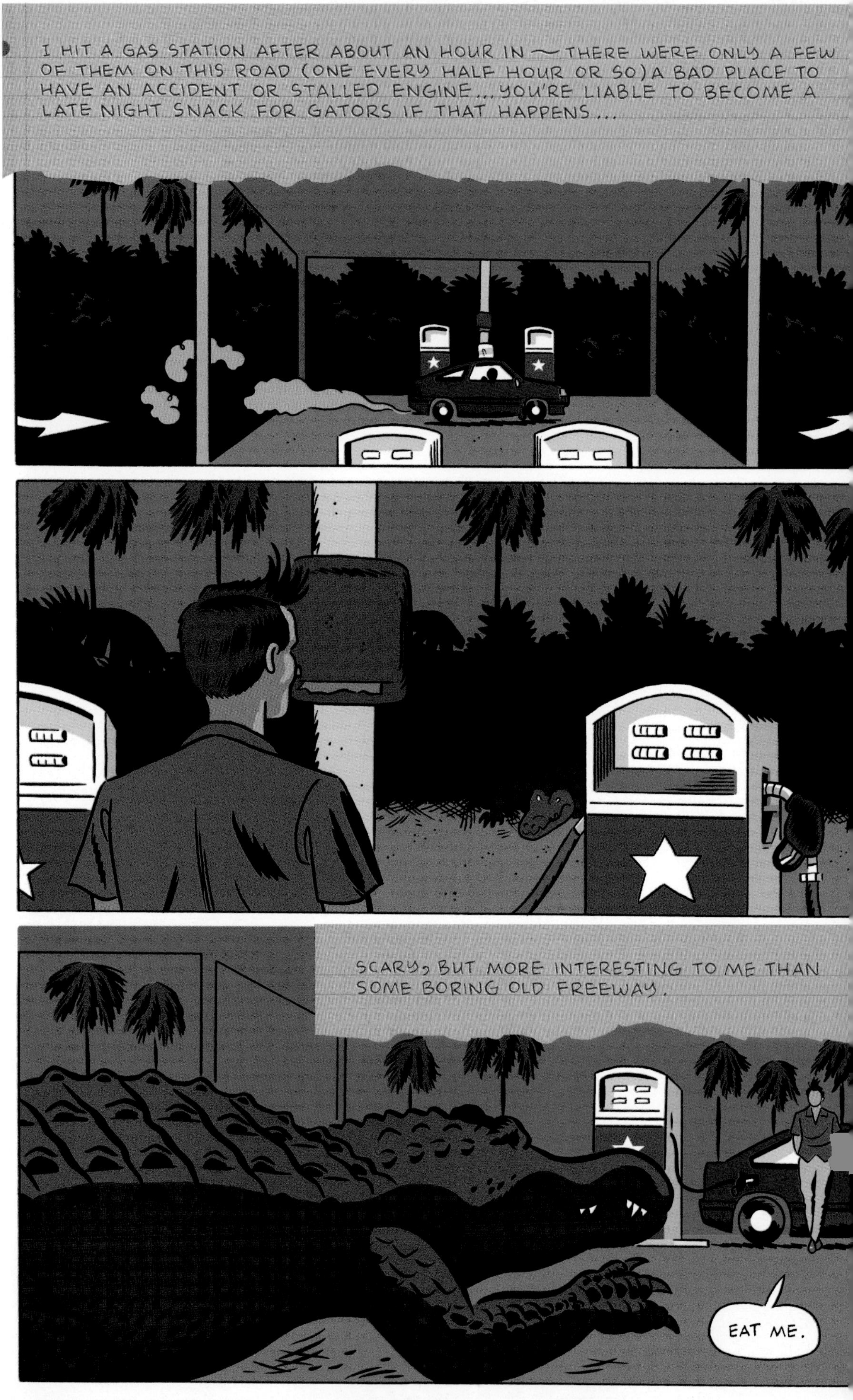
I HIT A GAS STATION AFTER ABOUT AN HOUR IN — THERE WERE ONLY A FEW OF THEM ON THIS ROAD (ONE EVERY HALF HOUR OR SO) A BAD PLACE TO HAVE AN ACCIDENT OR STALLED ENGINE... YOU'RE LIABLE TO BECOME A LATE NIGHT SNACK FOR GATORS IF THAT HAPPENS...
SCARY, BUT MORE INTERESTING TO ME THAN SOME BORING OLD FREEWAY.
EAT ME.

13

I FINALLY GOT TO BED BY ONE O'CLOCK THAT MORNING... BUT JUST AS I WAS DRIFTING OFF, I WAS **RUDELY** AWAKENED BY A SERPENT-LIKE VOICE...

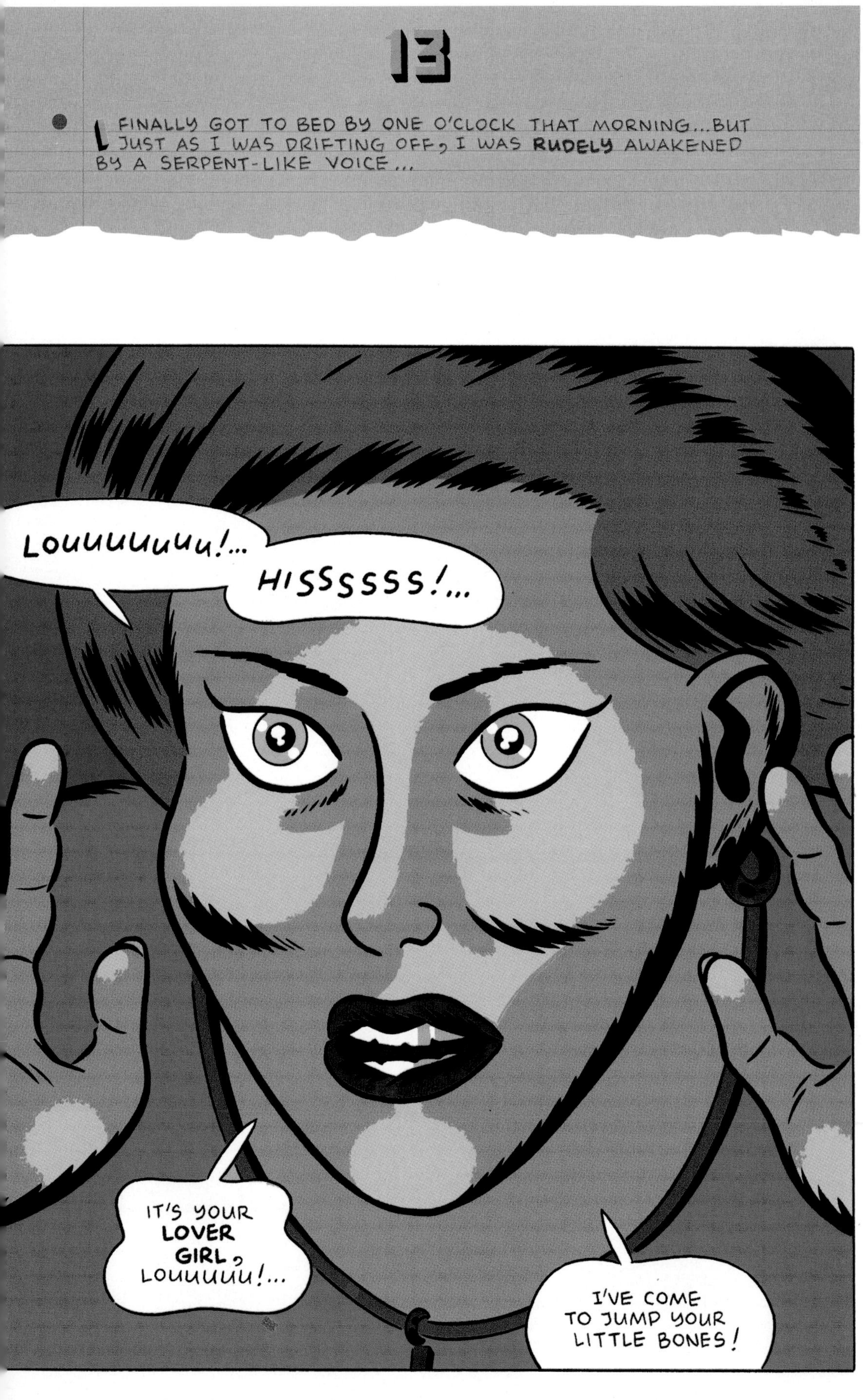

LOUUUUUUU!...
HISSSSSS!...
IT'S YOUR **LOVER GIRL**, LOUUUUU!...
I'VE COME TO JUMP YOUR LITTLE BONES!

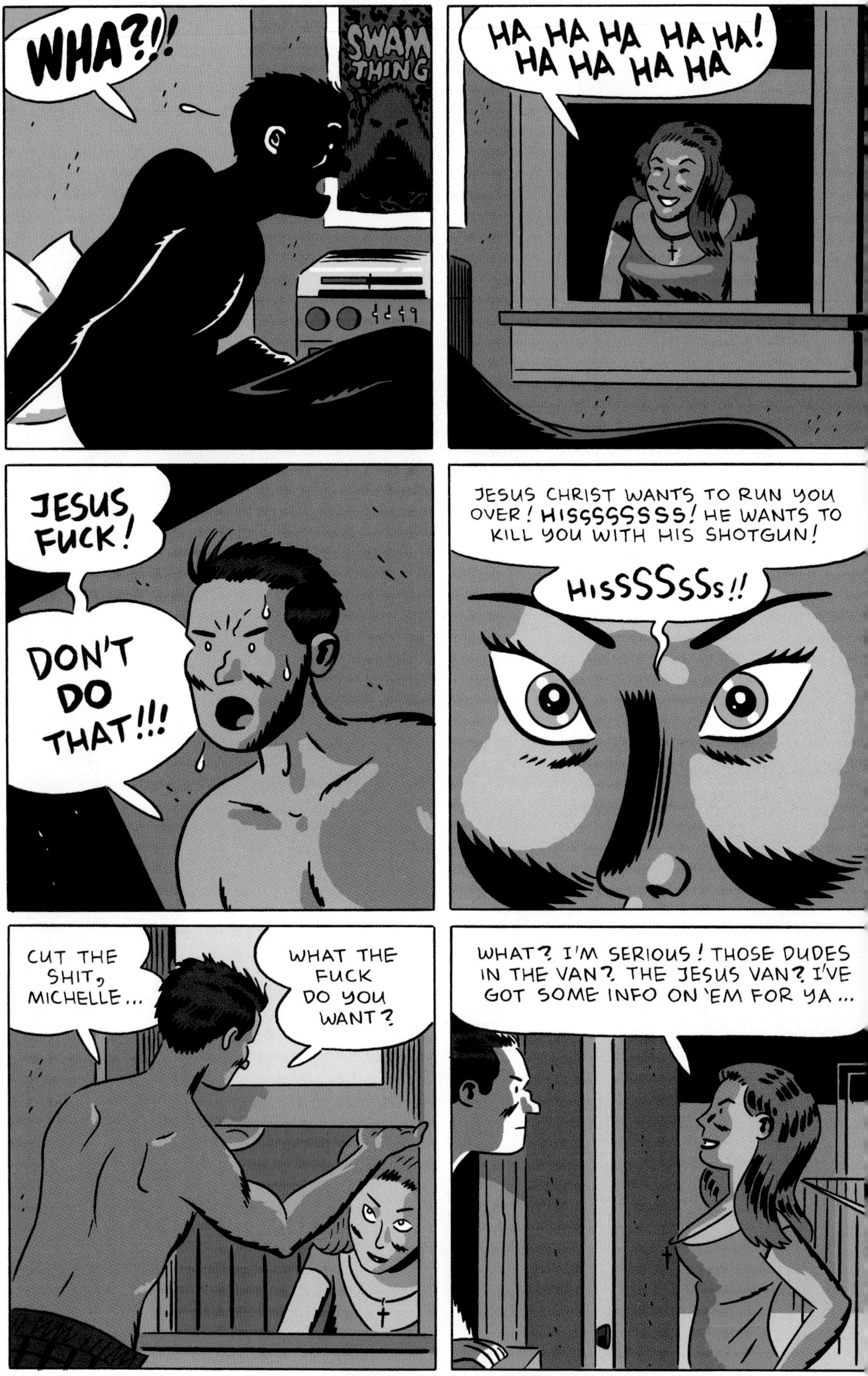
WHA?!!
SWAMP THING
HA HA HA HA HA!
HA HA HA HA
JESUS, FUCK!
DON'T DO THAT!!!
JESUS CHRIST WANTS TO RUN YOU OVER! HISSSSSSSS! HE WANTS TO KILL YOU WITH HIS SHOTGUN!
HisSSSsSs!!
CUT THE SHIT, MICHELLE...
WHAT THE FUCK DO YOU WANT?
WHAT? I'M SERIOUS! THOSE DUDES IN THE VAN? THE JESUS VAN? I'VE GOT SOME INFO ON 'EM FOR YA...

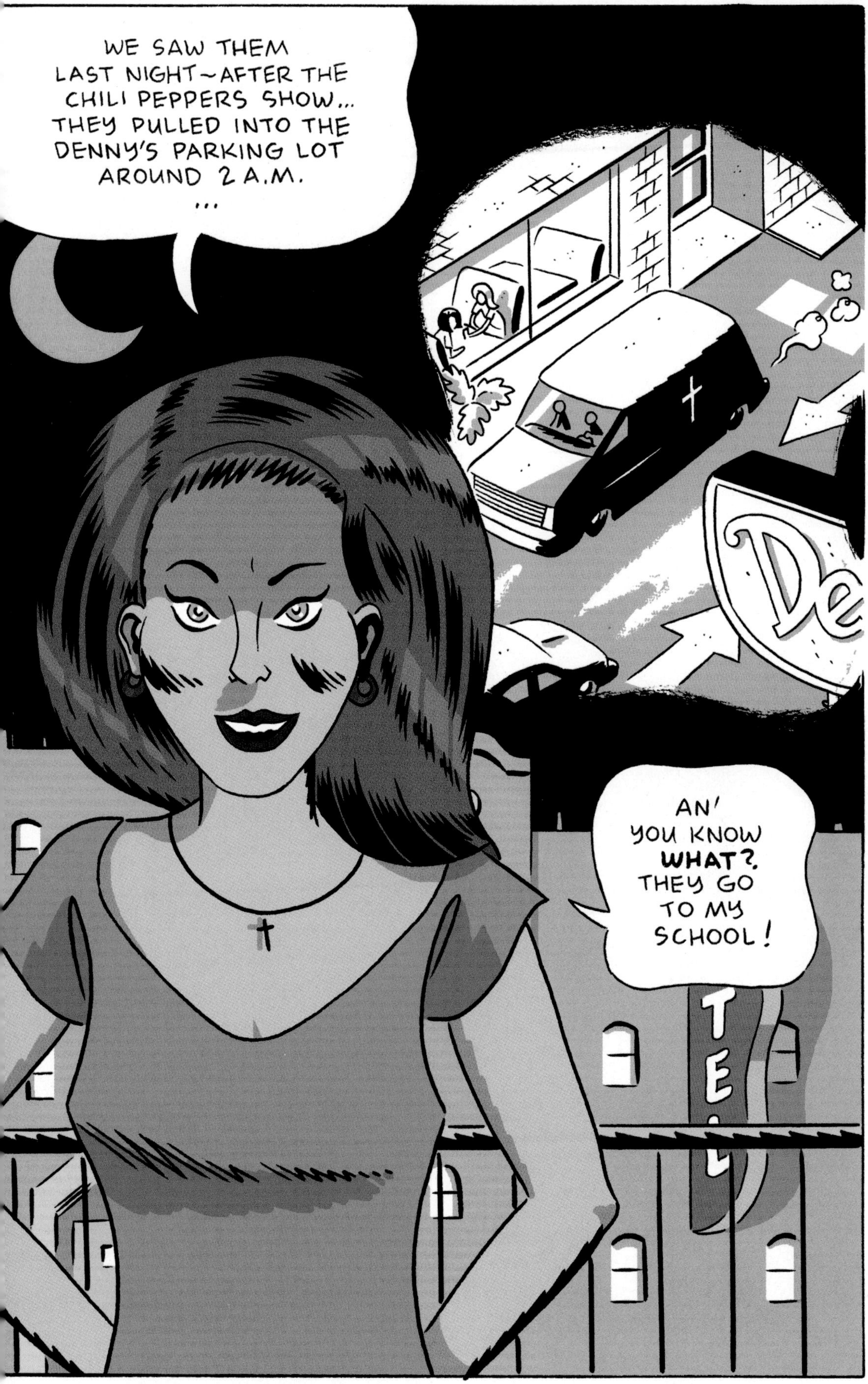
WE SAW THEM LAST NIGHT~AFTER THE CHILI PEPPERS SHOW... THEY PULLED INTO THE DENNY'S PARKING LOT AROUND 2 A.M. ...
AN' YOU KNOW **WHAT?** THEY GO TO MY SCHOOL!
TEL

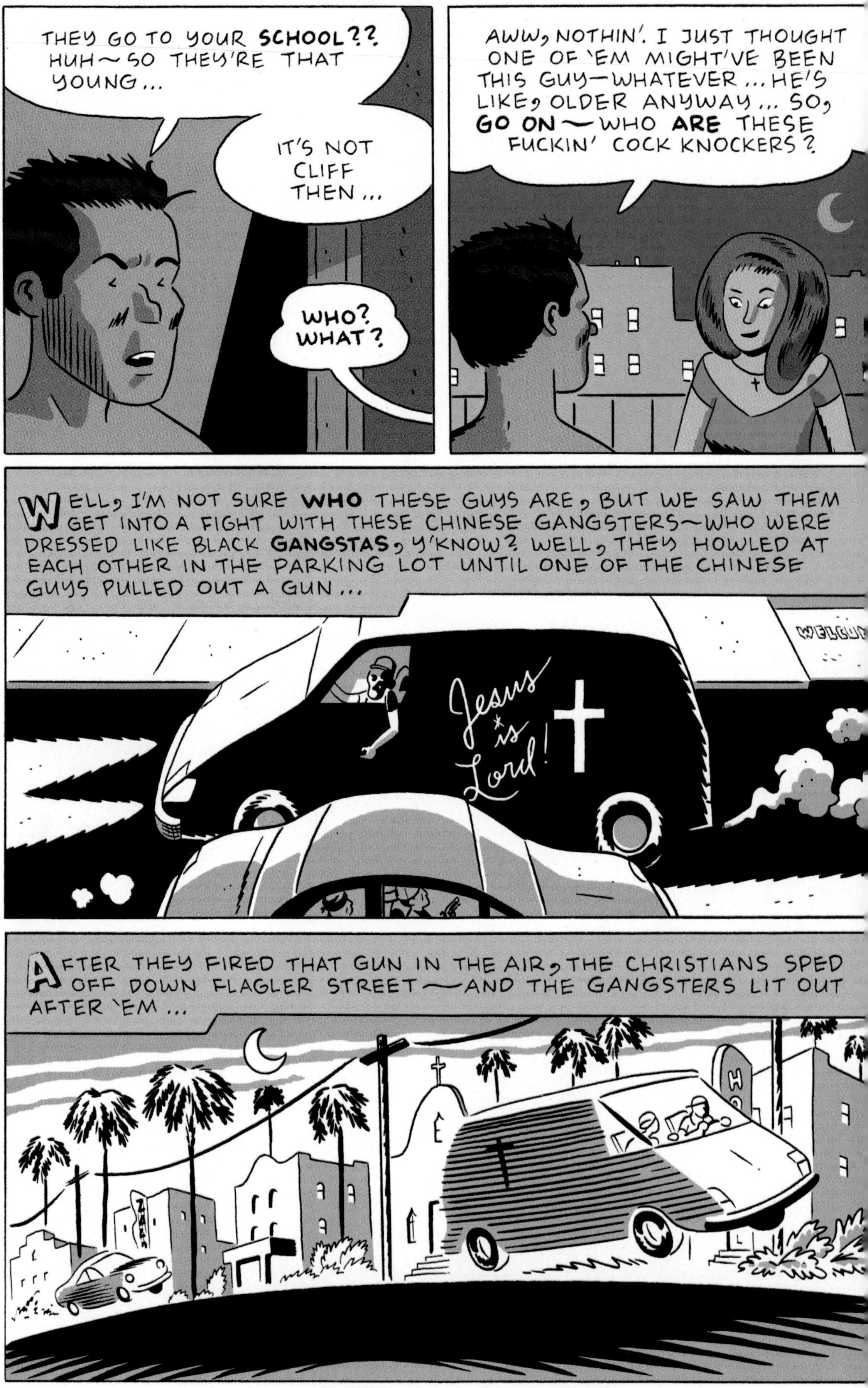

THEY GO TO YOUR SCHOOL?? HUH~SO THEY'RE THAT YOUNG...
IT'S NOT CLIFF THEN...
WHO? WHAT?
AWW, NOTHIN'. I JUST THOUGHT ONE OF 'EM MIGHT'VE BEEN THIS GUY—WHATEVER... HE'S LIKE, OLDER ANYWAY... SO, GO ON~WHO ARE THESE FUCKIN' COCK KNOCKERS?
WELL, I'M NOT SURE WHO THESE GUYS ARE, BUT WE SAW THEM GET INTO A FIGHT WITH THESE CHINESE GANGSTERS~WHO WERE DRESSED LIKE BLACK GANGSTAS, Y'KNOW? WELL, THEY HOWLED AT EACH OTHER IN THE PARKING LOT UNTIL ONE OF THE CHINESE GUYS PULLED OUT A GUN...
Jesus is Lord!
AFTER THEY FIRED THAT GUN IN THE AIR, THE CHRISTIANS SPED OFF DOWN FLAGLER STREET—AND THE GANGSTERS LIT OUT AFTER 'EM...

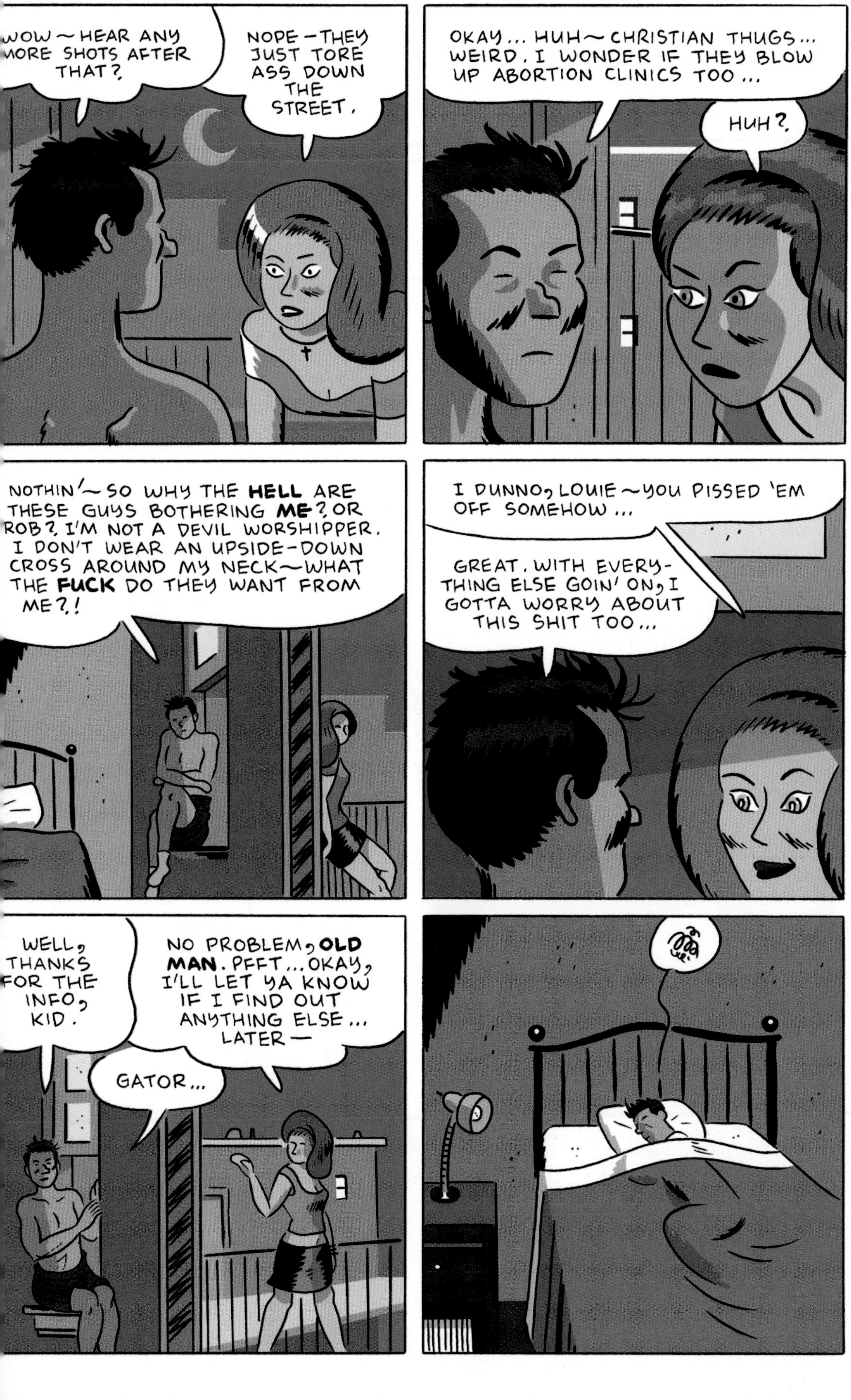
WOW ~ HEAR ANY MORE SHOTS AFTER THAT?
NOPE — THEY JUST TORE ASS DOWN THE STREET.
OKAY... HUH ~ CHRISTIAN THUGS... WEIRD. I WONDER IF THEY BLOW UP ABORTION CLINICS TOO...
HUH?
NOTHIN' ~ SO WHY THE **HELL** ARE THESE GUYS BOTHERING **ME**? OR ROB? I'M NOT A DEVIL WORSHIPPER. I DON'T WEAR AN UPSIDE-DOWN CROSS AROUND MY NECK ~ WHAT THE **FUCK** DO THEY WANT FROM ME?!
I DUNNO, LOUIE ~ YOU PISSED 'EM OFF SOMEHOW...
GREAT. WITH EVERYTHING ELSE GOIN' ON, I GOTTA WORRY ABOUT THIS SHIT TOO...
WELL, THANKS FOR THE INFO, KID.
NO PROBLEM, **OLD MAN**. PFFT... OKAY, I'LL LET YA KNOW IF I FIND OUT ANYTHING ELSE... LATER —
GATOR...

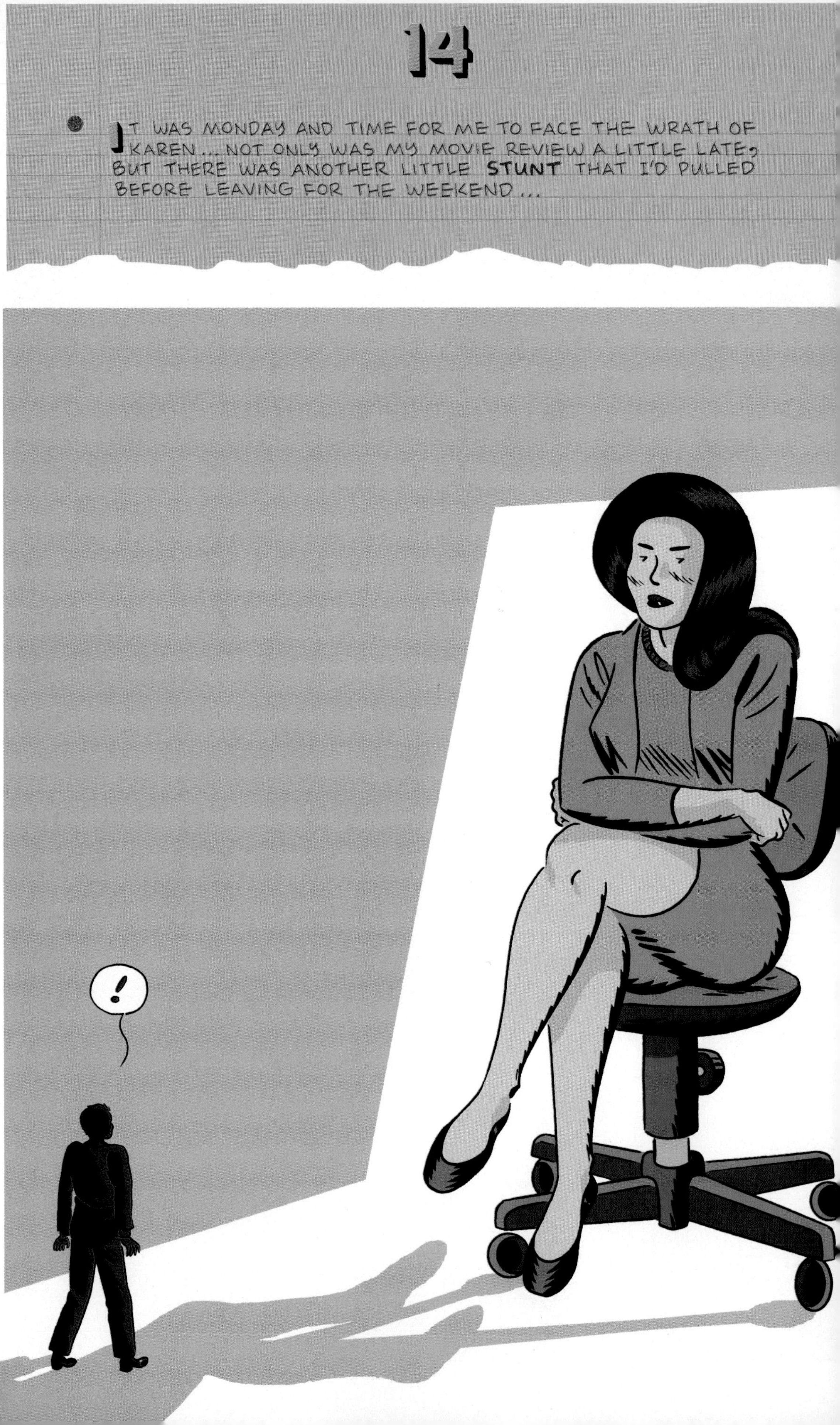
14
IT WAS MONDAY AND TIME FOR ME TO FACE THE WRATH OF KAREN... NOT ONLY WAS MY MOVIE REVIEW A LITTLE LATE, BUT THERE WAS ANOTHER LITTLE **STUNT** THAT I'D PULLED BEFORE LEAVING FOR THE WEEKEND...
!

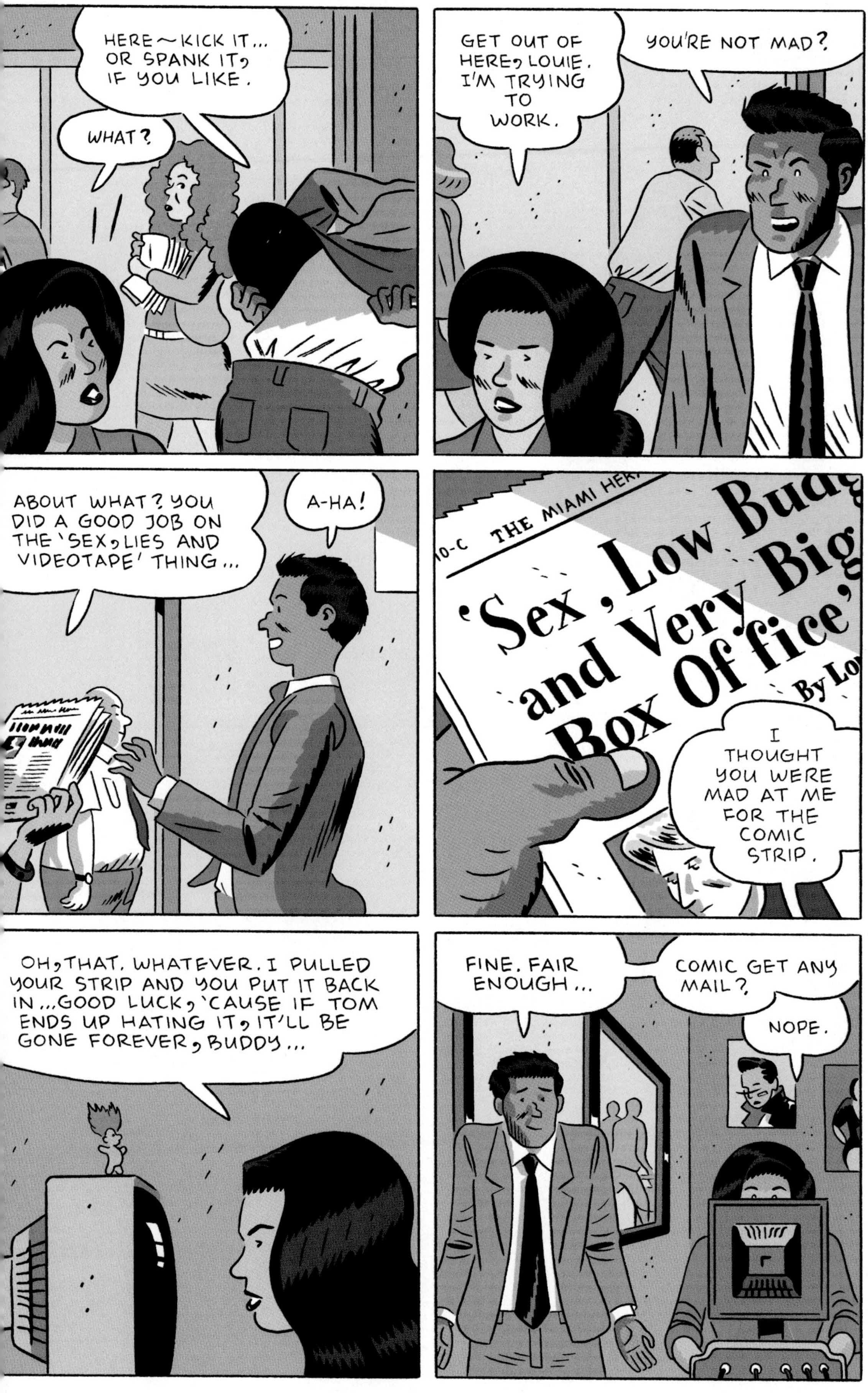
HERE ~ KICK IT... OR SPANK IT, IF YOU LIKE.
WHAT?
GET OUT OF HERE, LOUIE. I'M TRYING TO WORK.
YOU'RE NOT MAD?
ABOUT WHAT? YOU DID A GOOD JOB ON THE 'SEX, LIES AND VIDEOTAPE' THING...
A-HA!
10-C THE MIAMI HER
'Sex, Low Bud
and Very Big
Box Office'
By Lo
I THOUGHT YOU WERE MAD AT ME FOR THE COMIC STRIP.
OH, THAT. WHATEVER. I PULLED YOUR STRIP AND YOU PUT IT BACK IN... GOOD LUCK, 'CAUSE IF TOM ENDS UP HATING IT, IT'LL BE GONE FOREVER, BUDDY...
FINE. FAIR ENOUGH...
COMIC GET ANY MAIL?
NOPE.

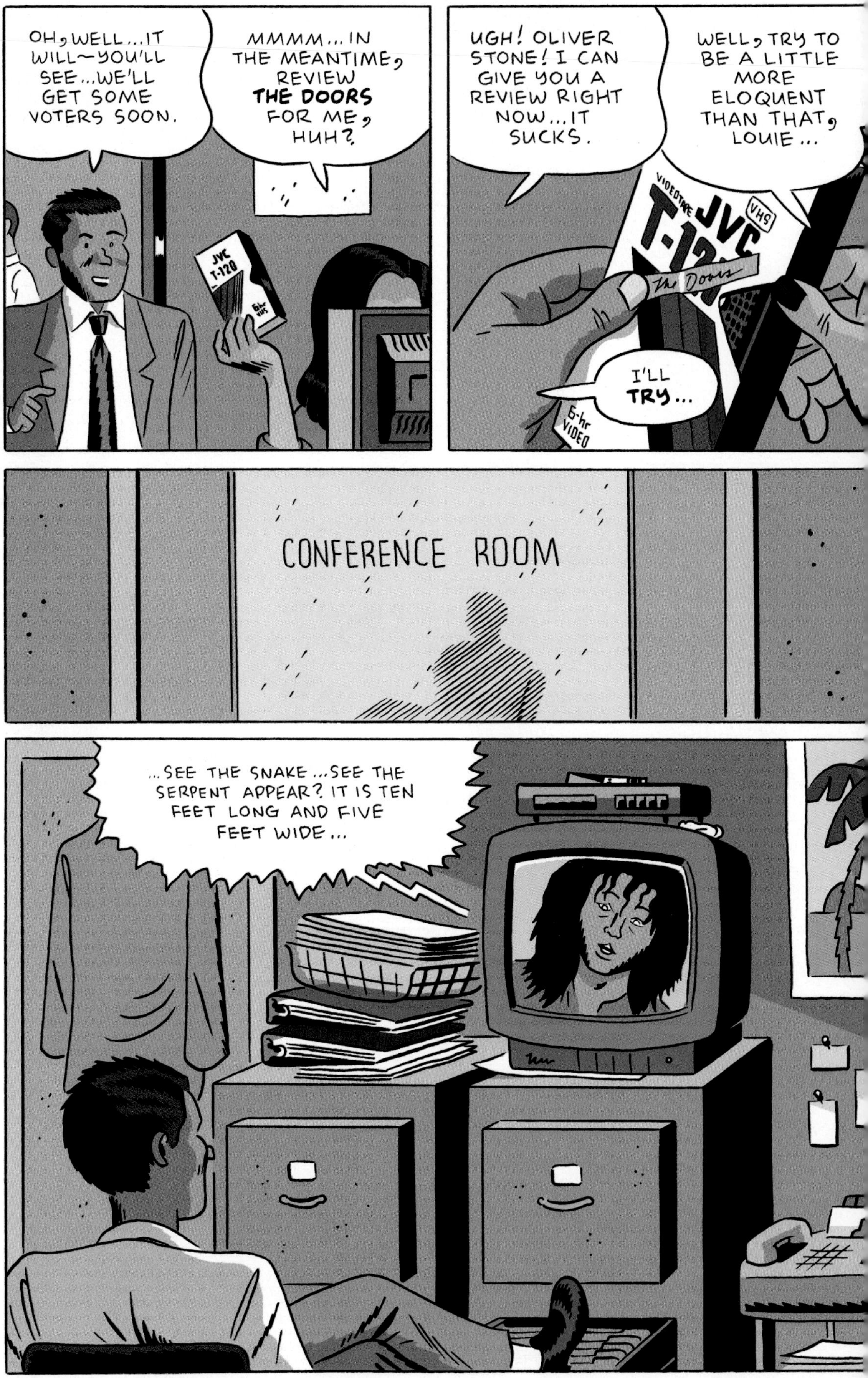
OH, WELL...IT WILL~YOU'LL SEE...WE'LL GET SOME VOTERS SOON.
MMMM...IN THE MEANTIME, REVIEW **THE DOORS** FOR ME, HUH?
JVC T-120 6-hr VHS
UGH! OLIVER STONE! I CAN GIVE YOU A REVIEW RIGHT NOW...IT SUCKS.
WELL, TRY TO BE A LITTLE MORE ELOQUENT THAN THAT, LOUIE...
VIDEOTAPE JVC T-120 VHS
The Doors
6-hr VIDEO
I'LL **TRY**...
CONFERENCE ROOM
...SEE THE SNAKE...SEE THE SERPENT APPEAR? IT IS TEN FEET LONG AND FIVE FEET WIDE...

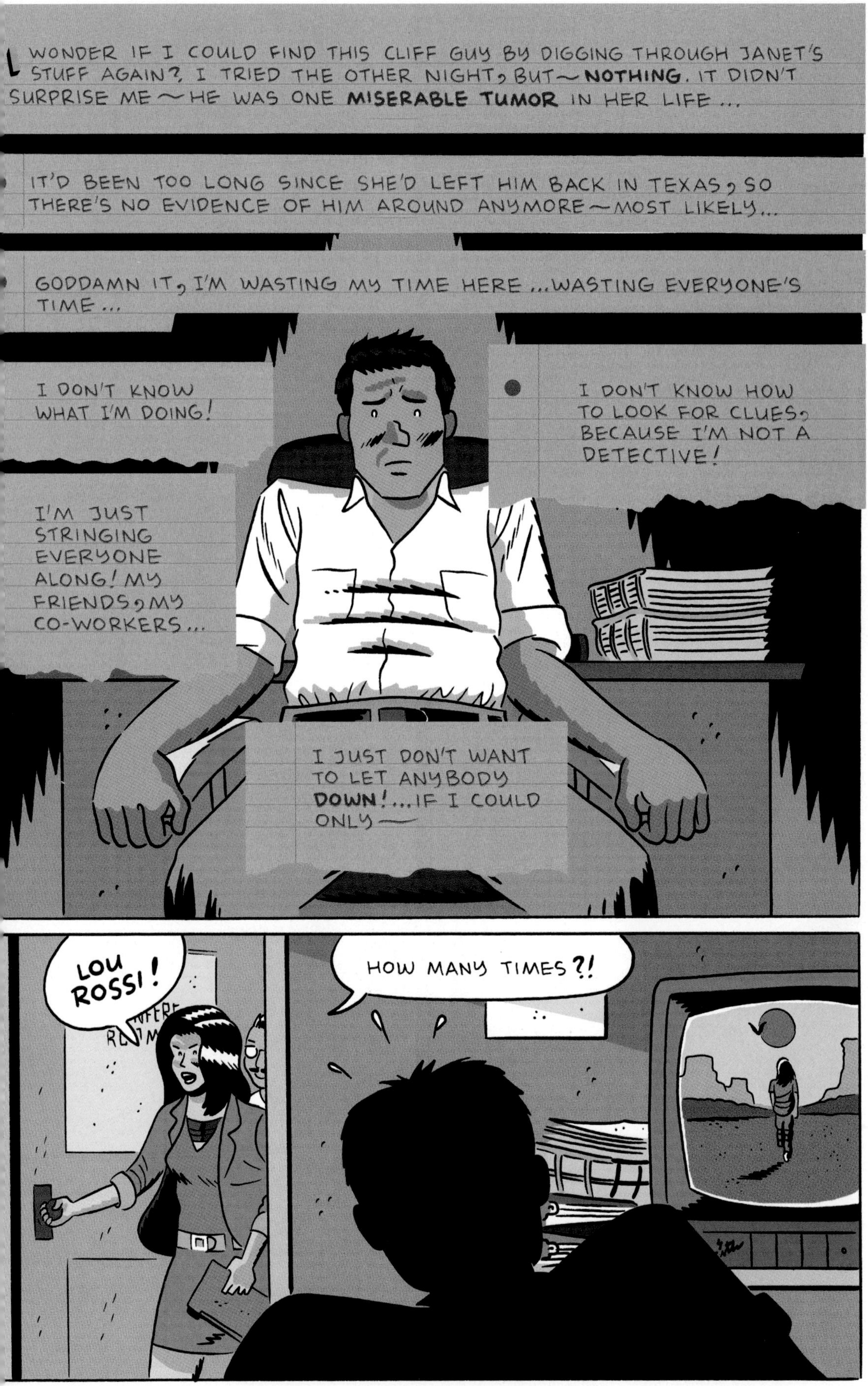

I WONDER IF I COULD FIND THIS CLIFF GUY BY DIGGING THROUGH JANET'S STUFF AGAIN? I TRIED THE OTHER NIGHT, BUT~ **NOTHING**. IT DIDN'T SURPRISE ME ~ HE WAS ONE **MISERABLE TUMOR** IN HER LIFE...
IT'D BEEN TOO LONG SINCE SHE'D LEFT HIM BACK IN TEXAS, SO THERE'S NO EVIDENCE OF HIM AROUND ANYMORE~ MOST LIKELY...
GODDAMN IT, I'M WASTING MY TIME HERE...WASTING EVERYONE'S TIME...
I DON'T KNOW WHAT I'M DOING!
I DON'T KNOW HOW TO LOOK FOR CLUES, BECAUSE I'M NOT A DETECTIVE!
I'M JUST STRINGING EVERYONE ALONG! MY FRIENDS, MY CO-WORKERS...
I JUST DON'T WANT TO LET ANYBODY **DOWN**!...IF I COULD ONLY—
LOU ROSSI!
HOW MANY TIMES?!

15

A FEW DAYS LATER I STROLLED BACK INTO THE OFFICE CARRYING MY REVIEW OF **THE DOORS** FOR KAREN... AND SHE HAD SOME NEWS FOR **ME** ON MY COMIC STRIP READERS CONTEST...

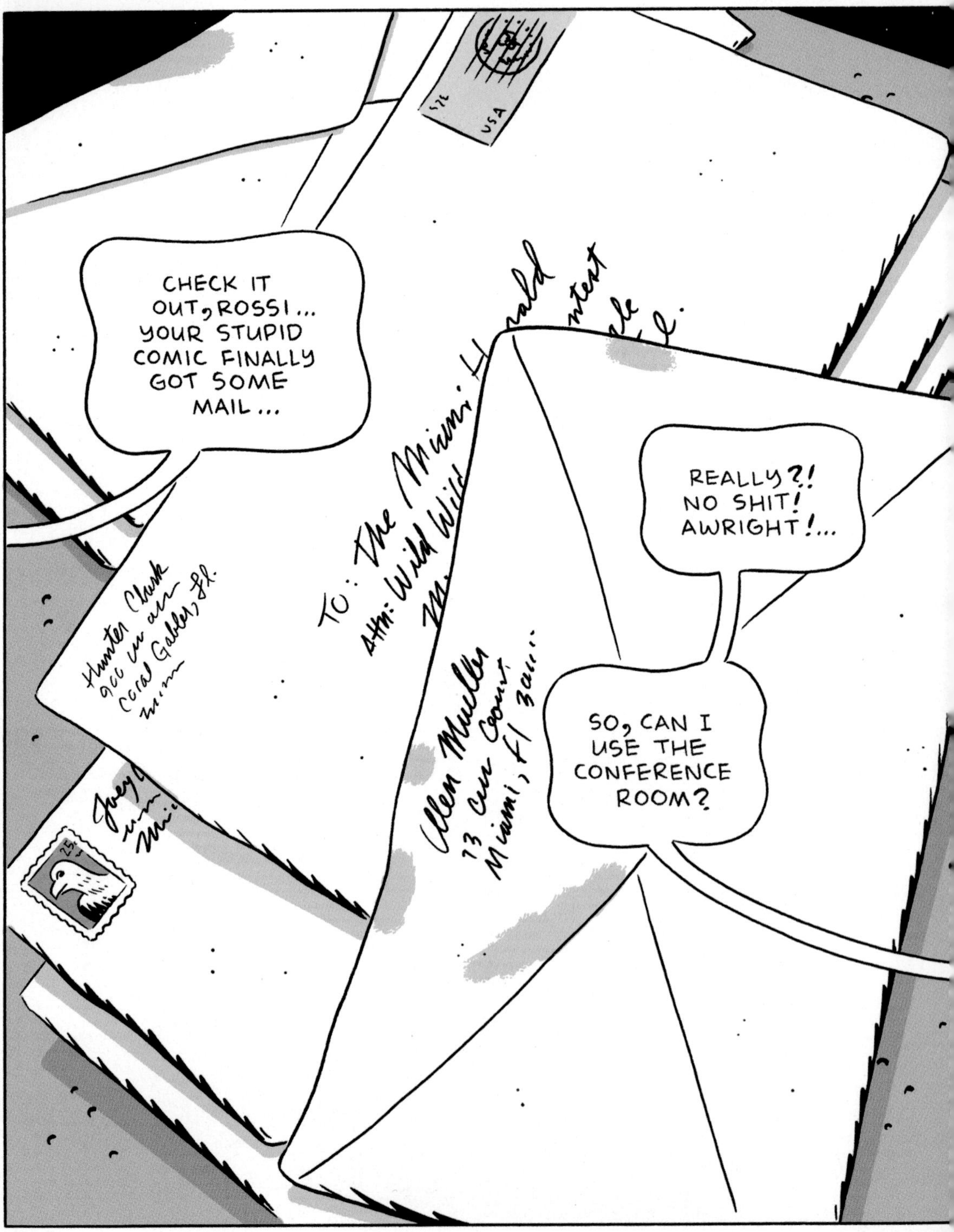
CHECK IT OUT, ROSSI... YOUR STUPID COMIC FINALLY GOT SOME MAIL...
REALLY?! NO SHIT! AWRIGHT!...
SO, CAN I USE THE CONFERENCE ROOM?

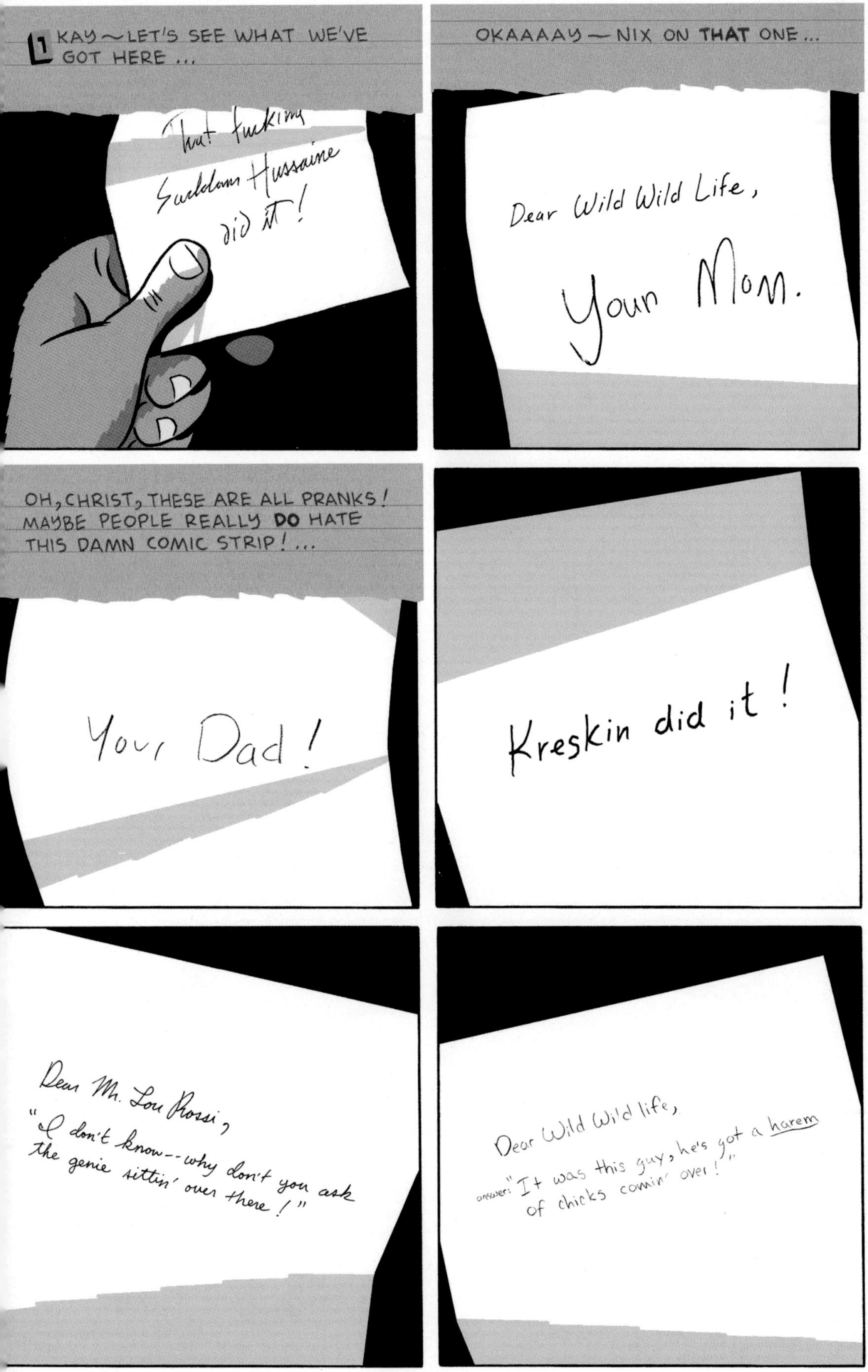

KAY~LET'S SEE WHAT WE'VE GOT HERE ...
That fucking Saddam Hussaine did it!
OKAAAAY—NIX ON THAT ONE...
Dear Wild Wild Life,
Your Mom.
OH, CHRIST, THESE ARE ALL PRANKS! MAYBE PEOPLE REALLY DO HATE THIS DAMN COMIC STRIP! ...
Your Dad!
Kreskin did it!
Dear Mr. Lou Rossi,
"I don't know--why don't you ask the genie sittin' over there!"
Dear Wild Wild life,
answer: "It was this guy, he's got a harem of chicks comin' over!"

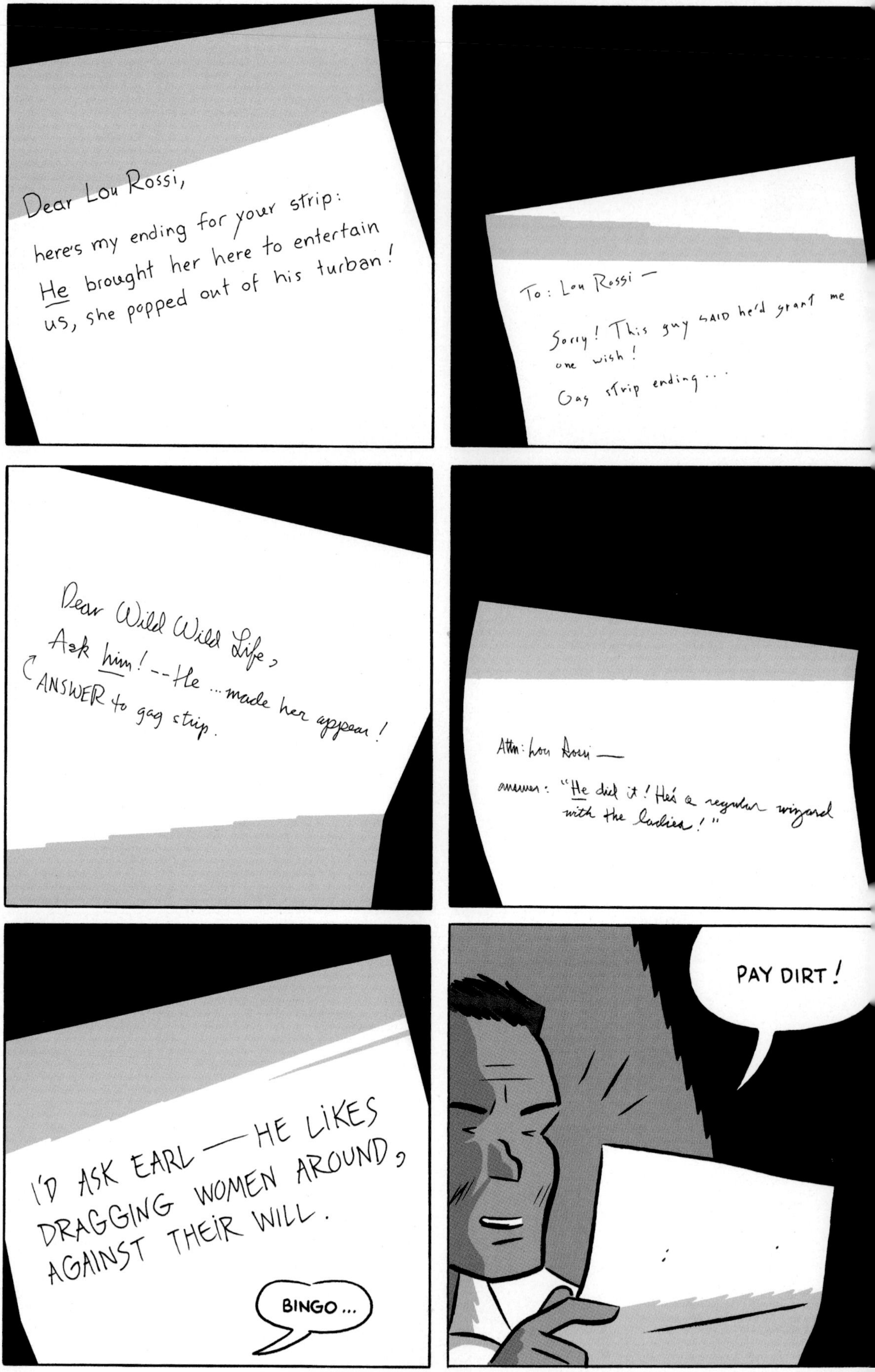
Dear Lou Rossi,
here's my ending for your strip:
He brought her here to entertain us, she popped out of his turban!
To: Lou Rossi —
Sorry! This guy SAID he'd grant me one wish!
Gag strip ending...
Dear Wild Wild Life,
Ask him! -- He ...made her appear!
ANSWER to gag strip.
Attn: Lou Rossi —
answer: "He did it! He's a regular wizard with the ladies!"
I'D ASK EARL — HE LIKES DRAGGING WOMEN AROUND, AGAINST THEIR WILL.
BINGO...
PAY DIRT!

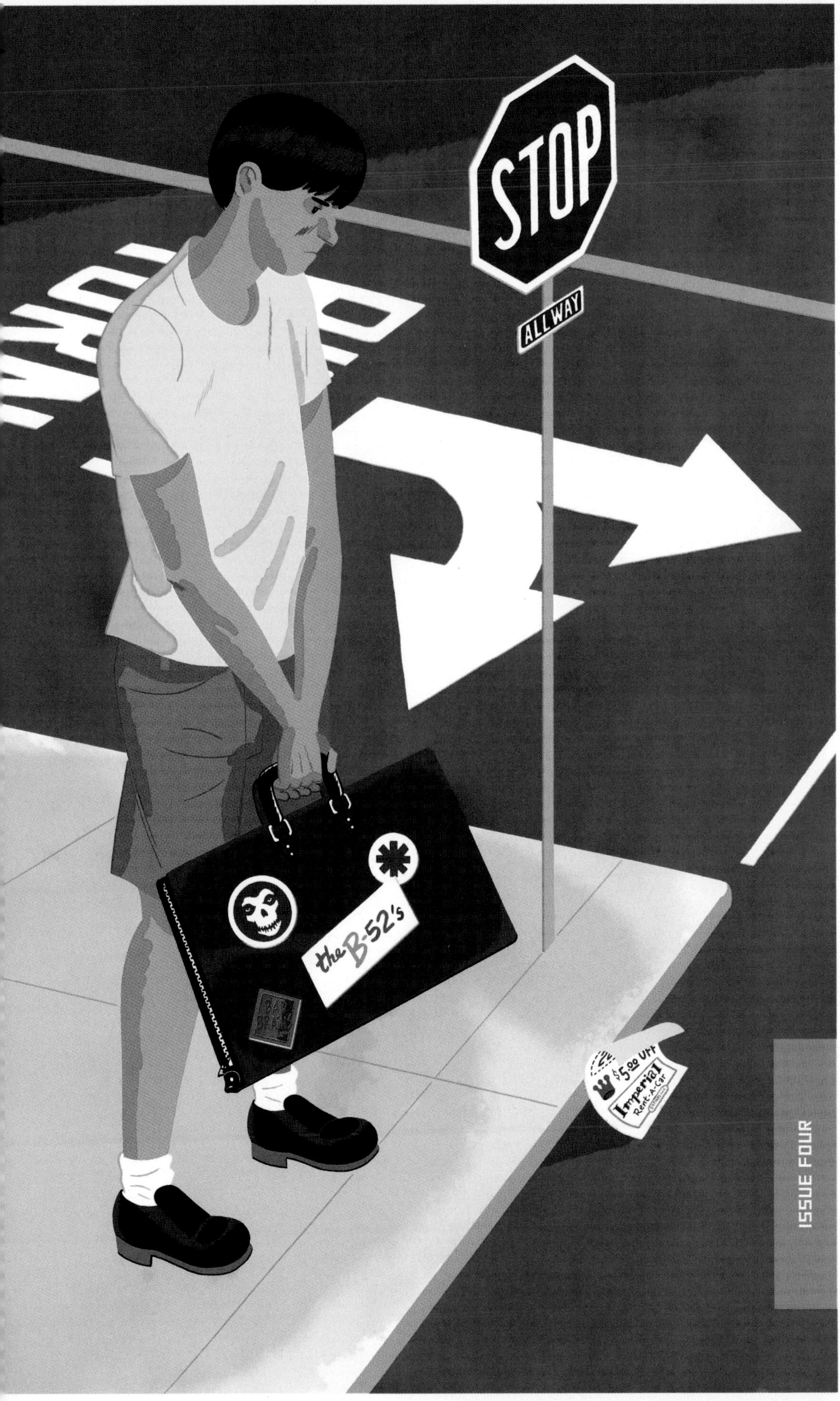
STOP
ALL WAY
the B-52's
Imperial
Rent-A-Car
ISSUE FOUR

16

HOLY SHIT... SHE **READ** IT! OR SOMEONE IN-THE-KNOW READ IT! THIS IS WORKING! BUT, SHOULD I **PRINT** IT? IF WE **DID**, IT **COULD** SCARE HIM... EXPOSE HIM TO THE PUBLIC! AND... MAYBE... HE'D LET HER GO? ...**NOW** THAT **HE** KNEW THAT **I** KNEW AND THAT THE **HERALD** KNEW! ...IT COULD SCARE HIM TO THINK THAT THE PRESS WAS ON TO HIS SCHEME... WHICH, WOULD BE ONE STEP CLOSER TO THE **POLICE KNOWING**?...

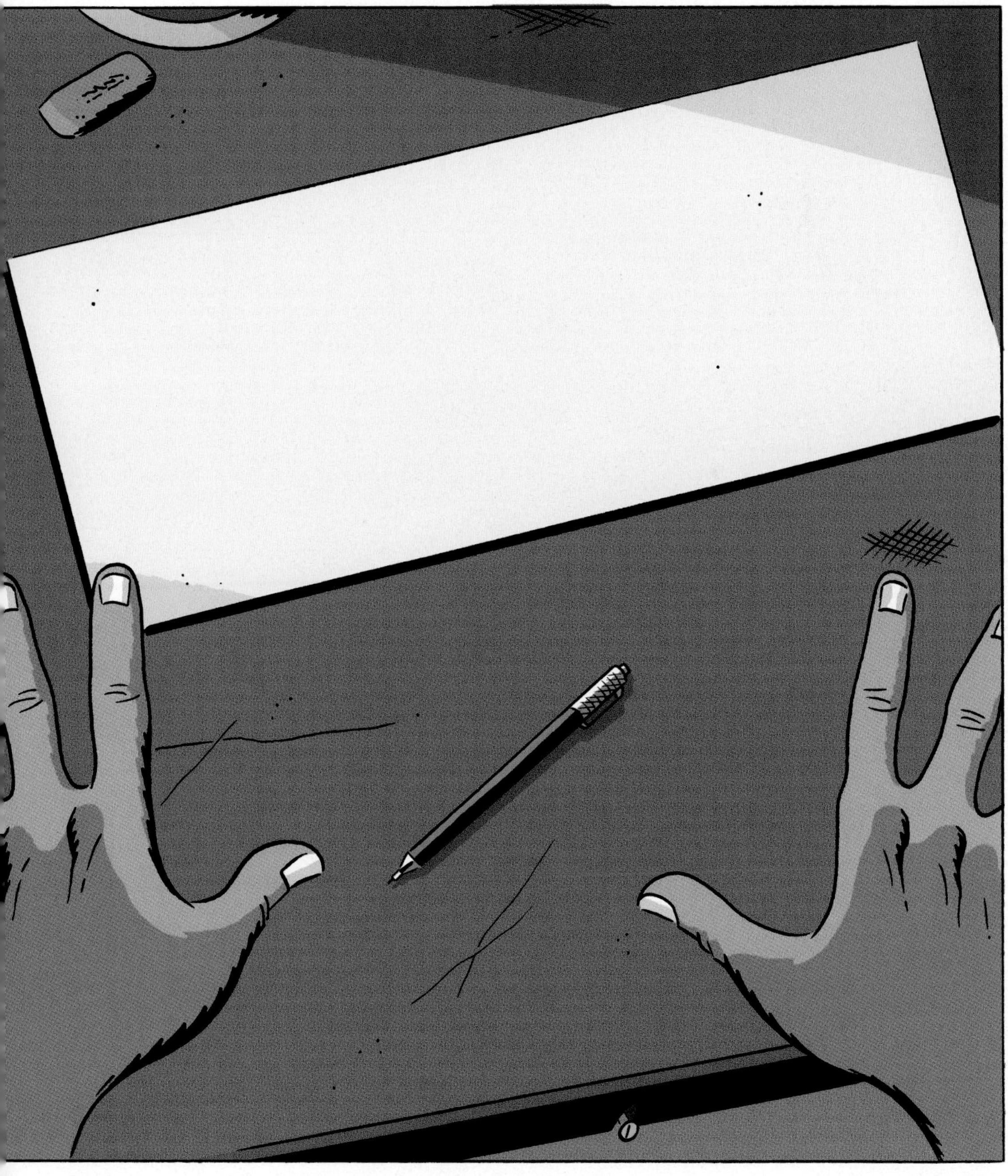

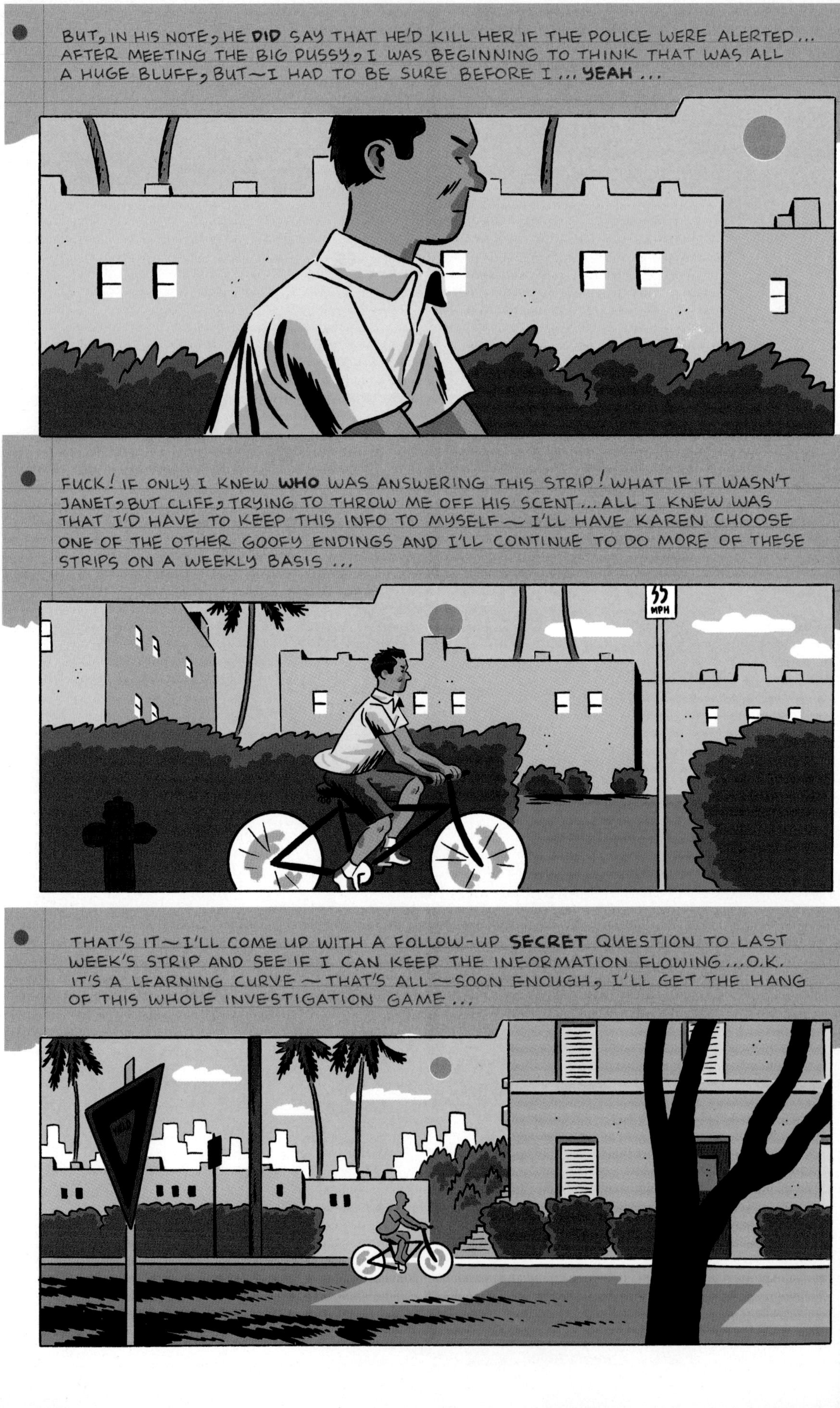
BUT, IN HIS NOTE, HE DID SAY THAT HE'D KILL HER IF THE POLICE WERE ALERTED... AFTER MEETING THE BIG PUSSY, I WAS BEGINNING TO THINK THAT WAS ALL A HUGE BLUFF, BUT—I HAD TO BE SURE BEFORE I... YEAH...
FUCK! IF ONLY I KNEW WHO WAS ANSWERING THIS STRIP! WHAT IF IT WASN'T JANET, BUT CLIFF, TRYING TO THROW ME OFF HIS SCENT... ALL I KNEW WAS THAT I'D HAVE TO KEEP THIS INFO TO MYSELF—I'LL HAVE KAREN CHOOSE ONE OF THE OTHER GOOFY ENDINGS AND I'LL CONTINUE TO DO MORE OF THESE STRIPS ON A WEEKLY BASIS...
55 MPH
THAT'S IT—I'LL COME UP WITH A FOLLOW-UP SECRET QUESTION TO LAST WEEK'S STRIP AND SEE IF I CAN KEEP THE INFORMATION FLOWING... O.K. IT'S A LEARNING CURVE—THAT'S ALL—SOON ENOUGH, I'LL GET THE HANG OF THIS WHOLE INVESTIGATION GAME...

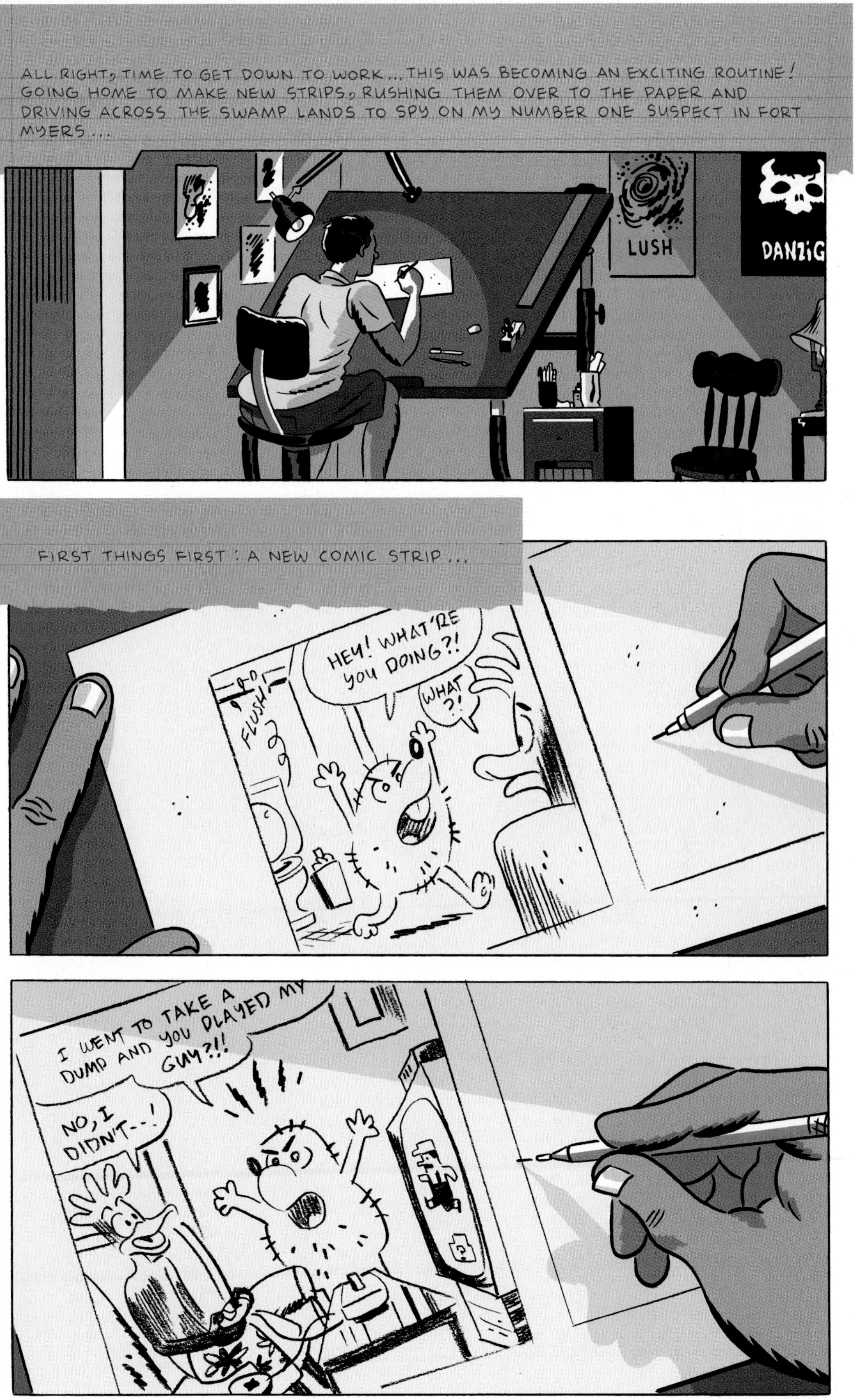
ALL RIGHT, TIME TO GET DOWN TO WORK... THIS WAS BECOMING AN EXCITING ROUTINE! GOING HOME TO MAKE NEW STRIPS, RUSHING THEM OVER TO THE PAPER AND DRIVING ACROSS THE SWAMP LANDS TO SPY ON MY NUMBER ONE SUSPECT IN FORT MYERS...
LUSH
DANZIG
FIRST THINGS FIRST: A NEW COMIC STRIP...
FLUSH
HEY! WHAT'RE YOU DOING?!
WHAT ?!
I WENT TO TAKE A DUMP AND YOU PLAYED MY GUY?!!
NO, I DIDN'T--!

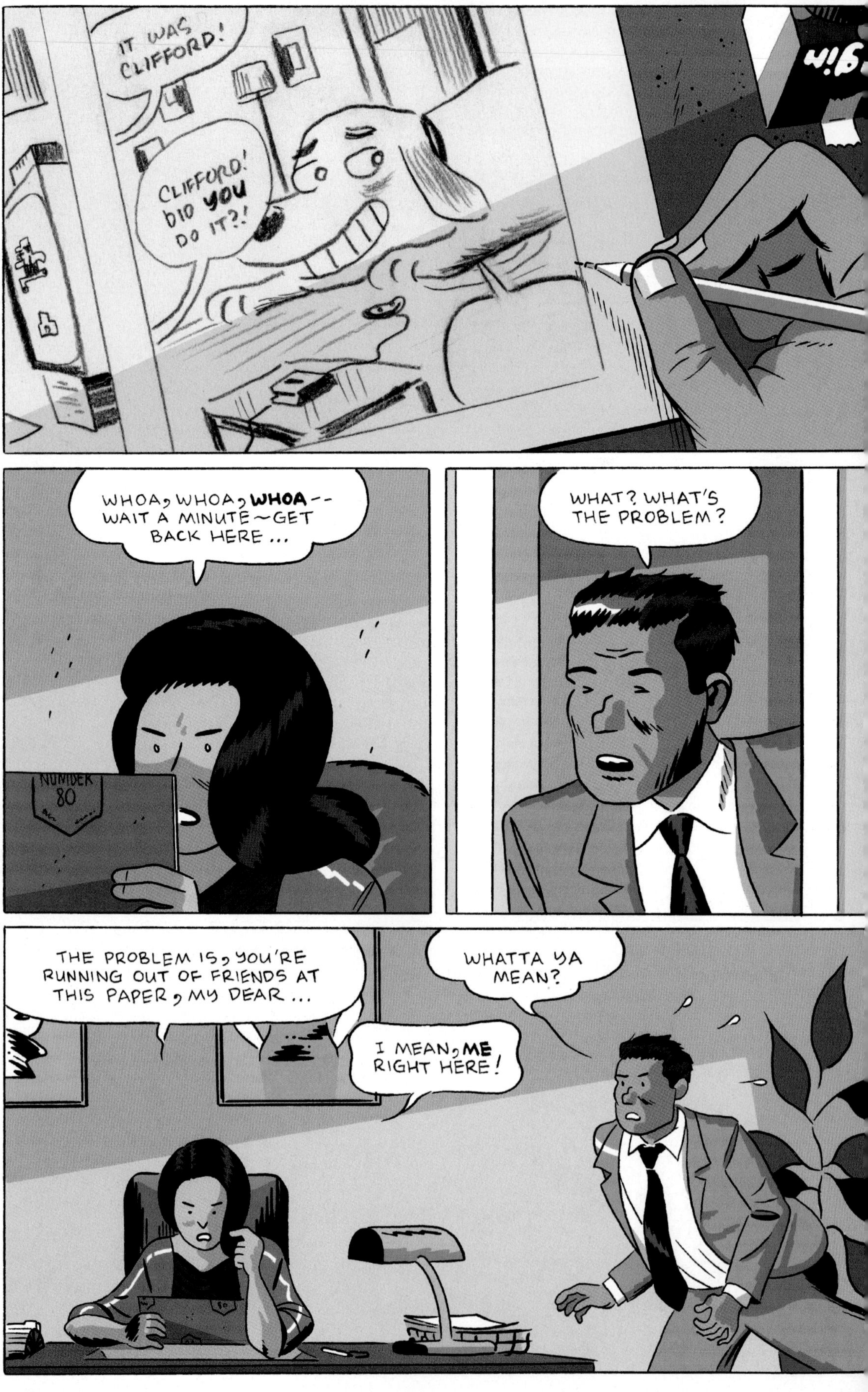
IT WAS CLIFFORD!
CLIFFORD! DID YOU DO IT?!
WHOA, WHOA, **WHOA**--WAIT A MINUTE~GET BACK HERE...
NUMBER 80
WHAT? WHAT'S THE PROBLEM?
THE PROBLEM IS, YOU'RE RUNNING OUT OF FRIENDS AT THIS PAPER, MY DEAR...
WHATTA YA MEAN?
I MEAN, **ME** RIGHT HERE!

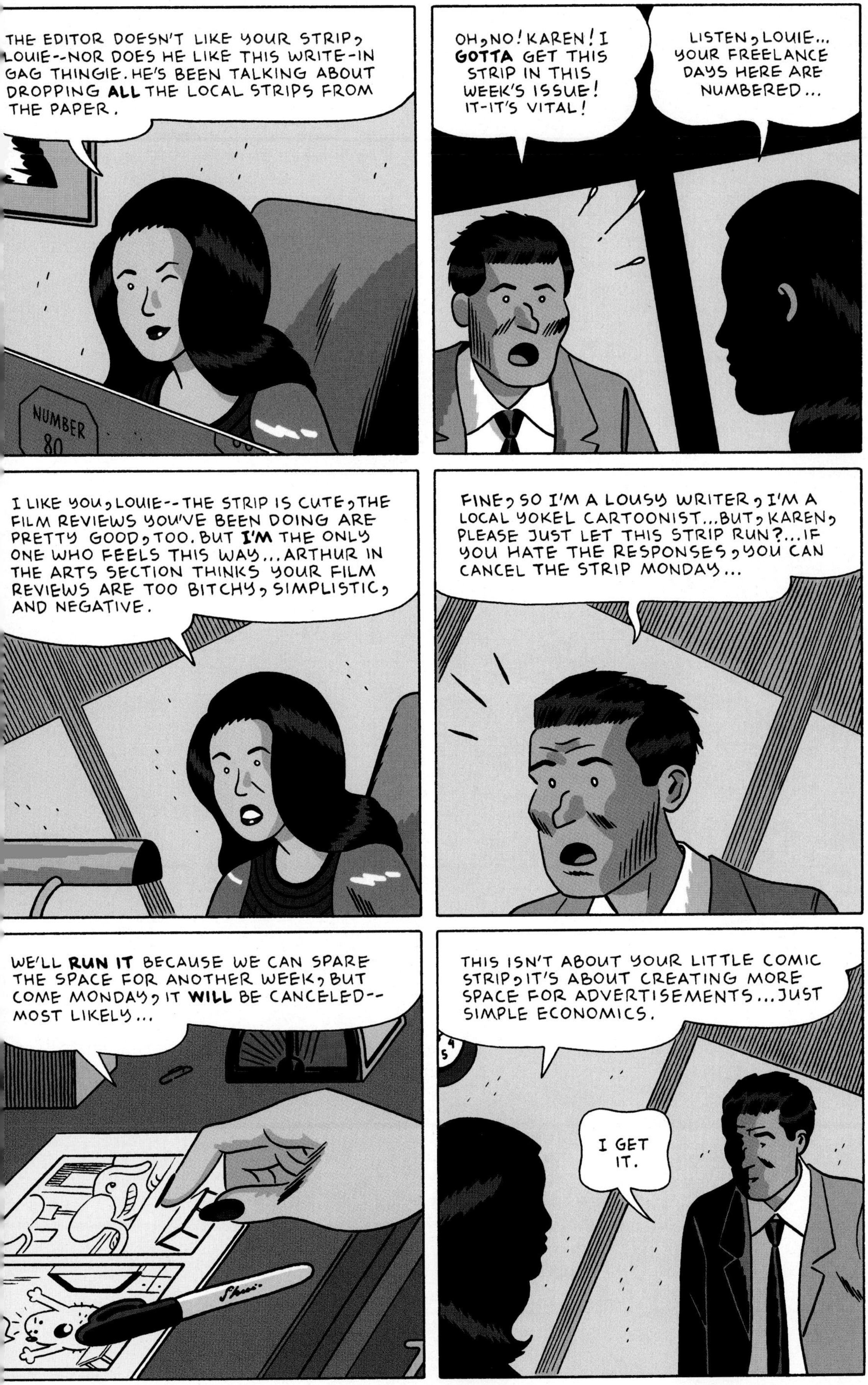
THE EDITOR DOESN'T LIKE YOUR STRIP, LOUIE--NOR DOES HE LIKE THIS WRITE-IN GAG THINGIE. HE'S BEEN TALKING ABOUT DROPPING **ALL** THE LOCAL STRIPS FROM THE PAPER.
NUMBER 80
OH, NO! KAREN! I **GOTTA** GET THIS STRIP IN THIS WEEK'S ISSUE! IT-IT'S VITAL!
LISTEN, LOUIE... YOUR FREELANCE DAYS HERE ARE NUMBERED...
I LIKE YOU, LOUIE--THE STRIP IS CUTE, THE FILM REVIEWS YOU'VE BEEN DOING ARE PRETTY GOOD, TOO. BUT **I'M** THE ONLY ONE WHO FEELS THIS WAY... ARTHUR IN THE ARTS SECTION THINKS YOUR FILM REVIEWS ARE TOO BITCHY, SIMPLISTIC, AND NEGATIVE.
FINE, SO I'M A LOUSY WRITER, I'M A LOCAL YOKEL CARTOONIST... BUT, KAREN, PLEASE JUST LET THIS STRIP RUN?... IF YOU HATE THE RESPONSES, YOU CAN CANCEL THE STRIP MONDAY...
WE'LL **RUN IT** BECAUSE WE CAN SPARE THE SPACE FOR ANOTHER WEEK, BUT COME MONDAY, IT **WILL** BE CANCELED--MOST LIKELY...
THIS ISN'T ABOUT YOUR LITTLE COMIC STRIP, IT'S ABOUT CREATING MORE SPACE FOR ADVERTISEMENTS... JUST SIMPLE ECONOMICS.
I GET IT.

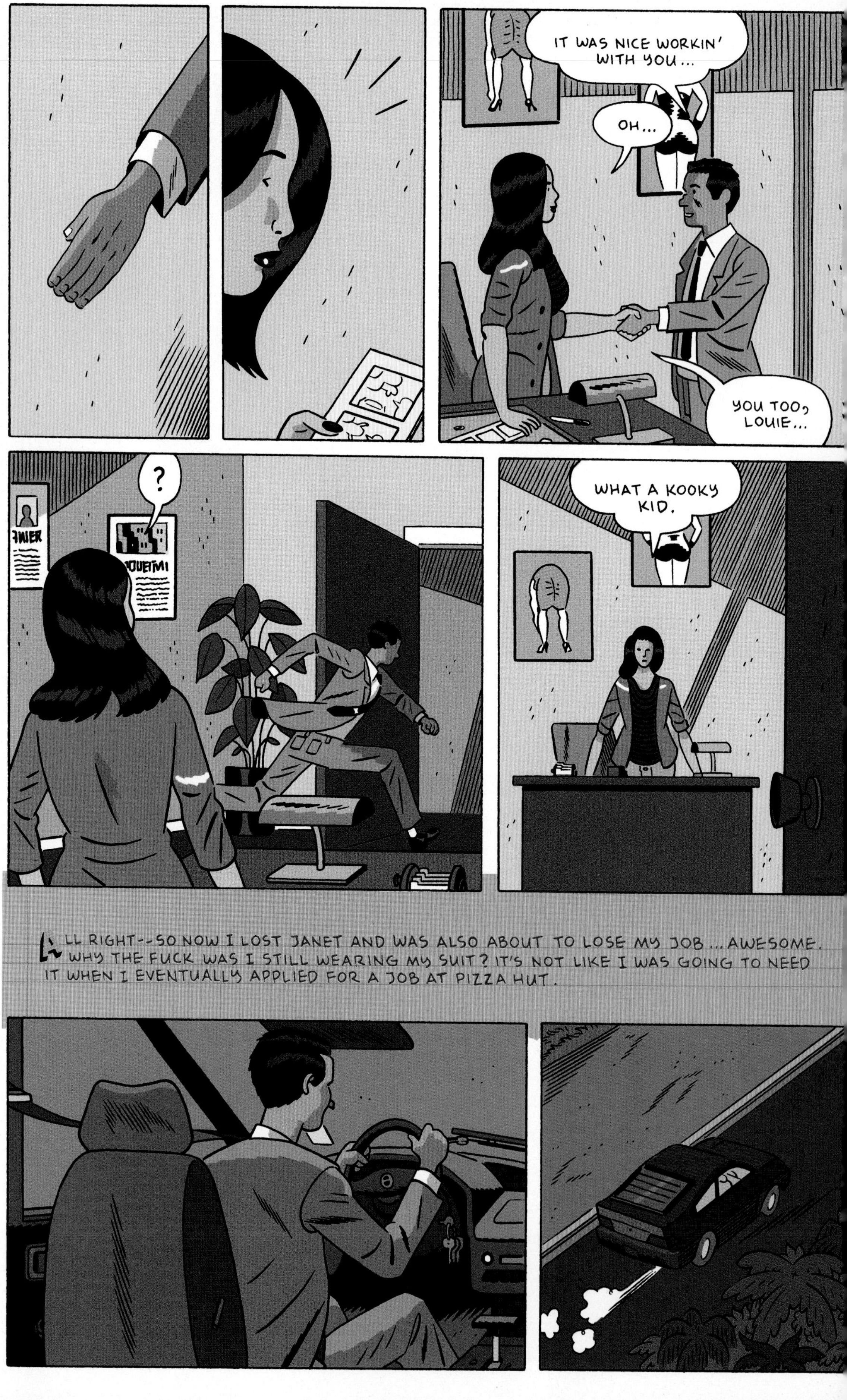

IT WAS NICE WORKIN' WITH YOU...
OH...
YOU TOO, LOUIE...
?
WHAT A KOOKY KID.
ALL RIGHT--SO NOW I LOST JANET AND WAS ALSO ABOUT TO LOSE MY JOB... AWESOME. WHY THE FUCK WAS I STILL WEARING MY SUIT? IT'S NOT LIKE I WAS GOING TO NEED IT WHEN I EVENTUALLY APPLIED FOR A JOB AT PIZZA HUT.

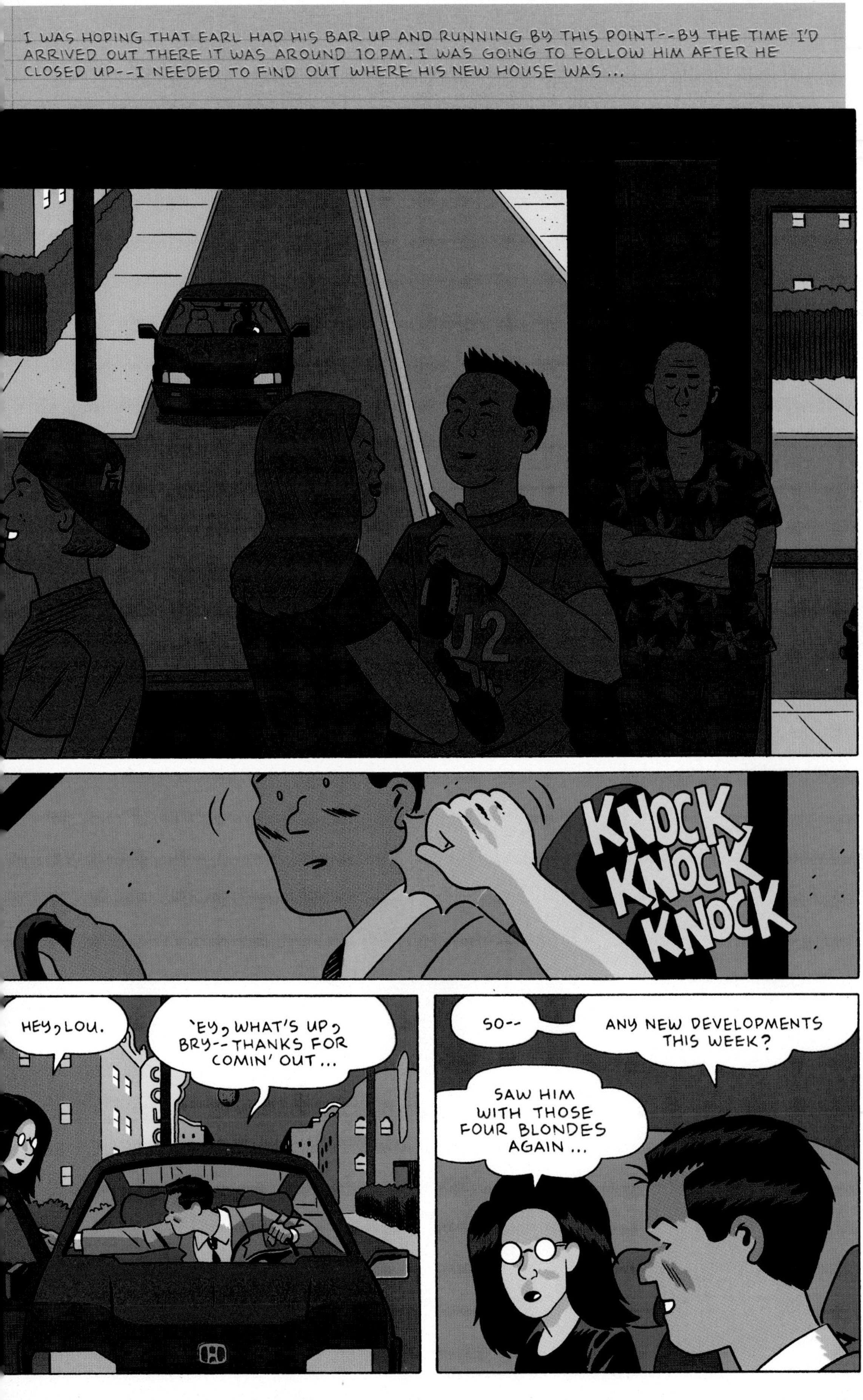
I WAS HOPING THAT EARL HAD HIS BAR UP AND RUNNING BY THIS POINT--BY THE TIME I'D ARRIVED OUT THERE IT WAS AROUND 10 PM. I WAS GOING TO FOLLOW HIM AFTER HE CLOSED UP--I NEEDED TO FIND OUT WHERE HIS NEW HOUSE WAS...
KNOCK KNOCK KNOCK
HEY, LOU.
'EY, WHAT'S UP, BRY--THANKS FOR COMIN' OUT...
SO--
ANY NEW DEVELOPMENTS THIS WEEK?
SAW HIM WITH THOSE FOUR BLONDES AGAIN...

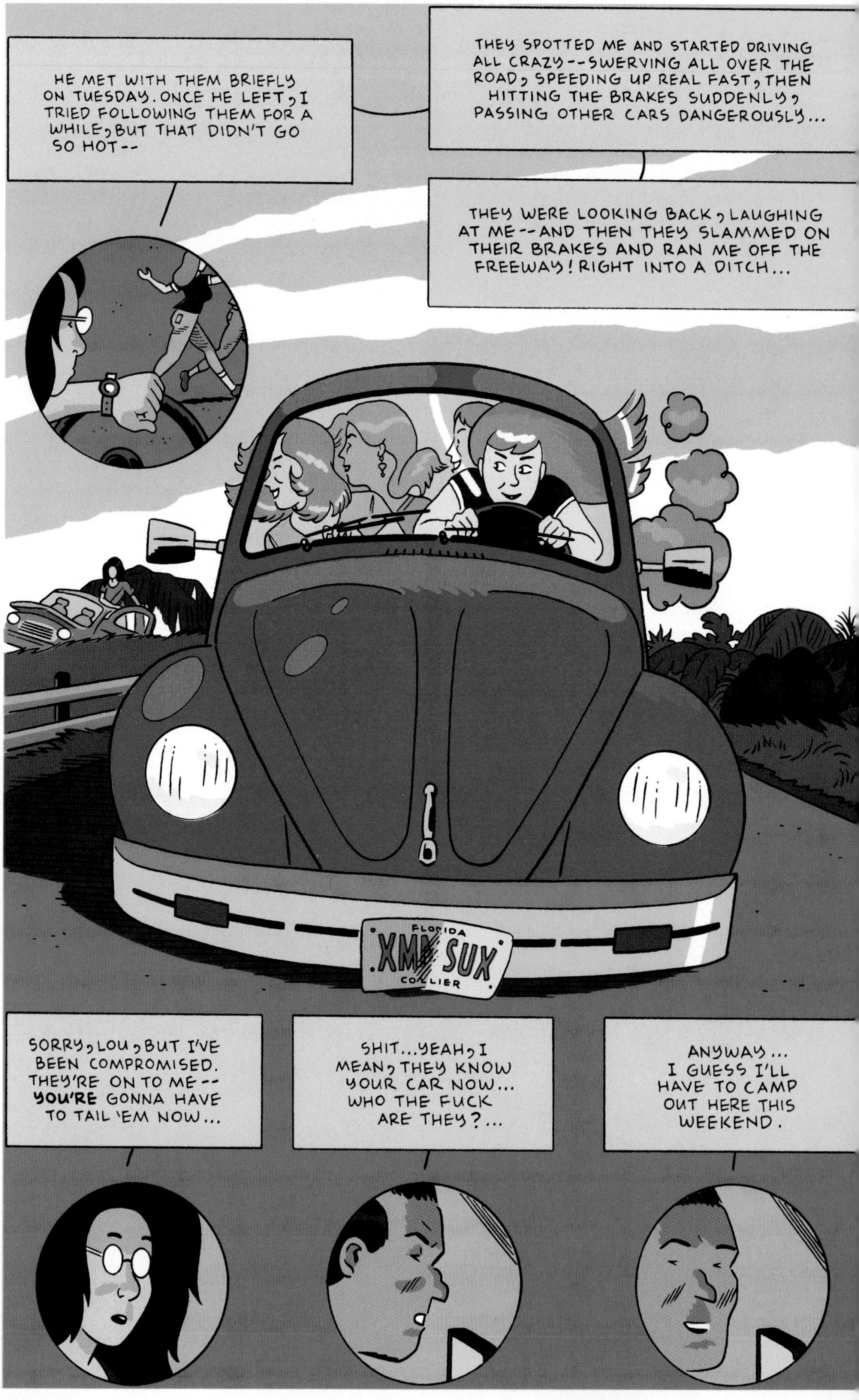
HE MET WITH THEM BRIEFLY ON TUESDAY. ONCE HE LEFT, I TRIED FOLLOWING THEM FOR A WHILE, BUT THAT DIDN'T GO SO HOT--
THEY SPOTTED ME AND STARTED DRIVING ALL CRAZY--SWERVING ALL OVER THE ROAD, SPEEDING UP REAL FAST, THEN HITTING THE BRAKES SUDDENLY, PASSING OTHER CARS DANGEROUSLY...
THEY WERE LOOKING BACK, LAUGHING AT ME--AND THEN THEY SLAMMED ON THEIR BRAKES AND RAN ME OFF THE FREEWAY! RIGHT INTO A DITCH...
FLORIDA
SUX
COLLIER
SORRY, LOU, BUT I'VE BEEN COMPROMISED. THEY'RE ON TO ME-- **YOU'RE** GONNA HAVE TO TAIL 'EM NOW...
SHIT...YEAH, I MEAN, THEY KNOW YOUR CAR NOW... WHO THE FUCK ARE THEY?...
ANYWAY... I GUESS I'LL HAVE TO CAMP OUT HERE THIS WEEKEND.

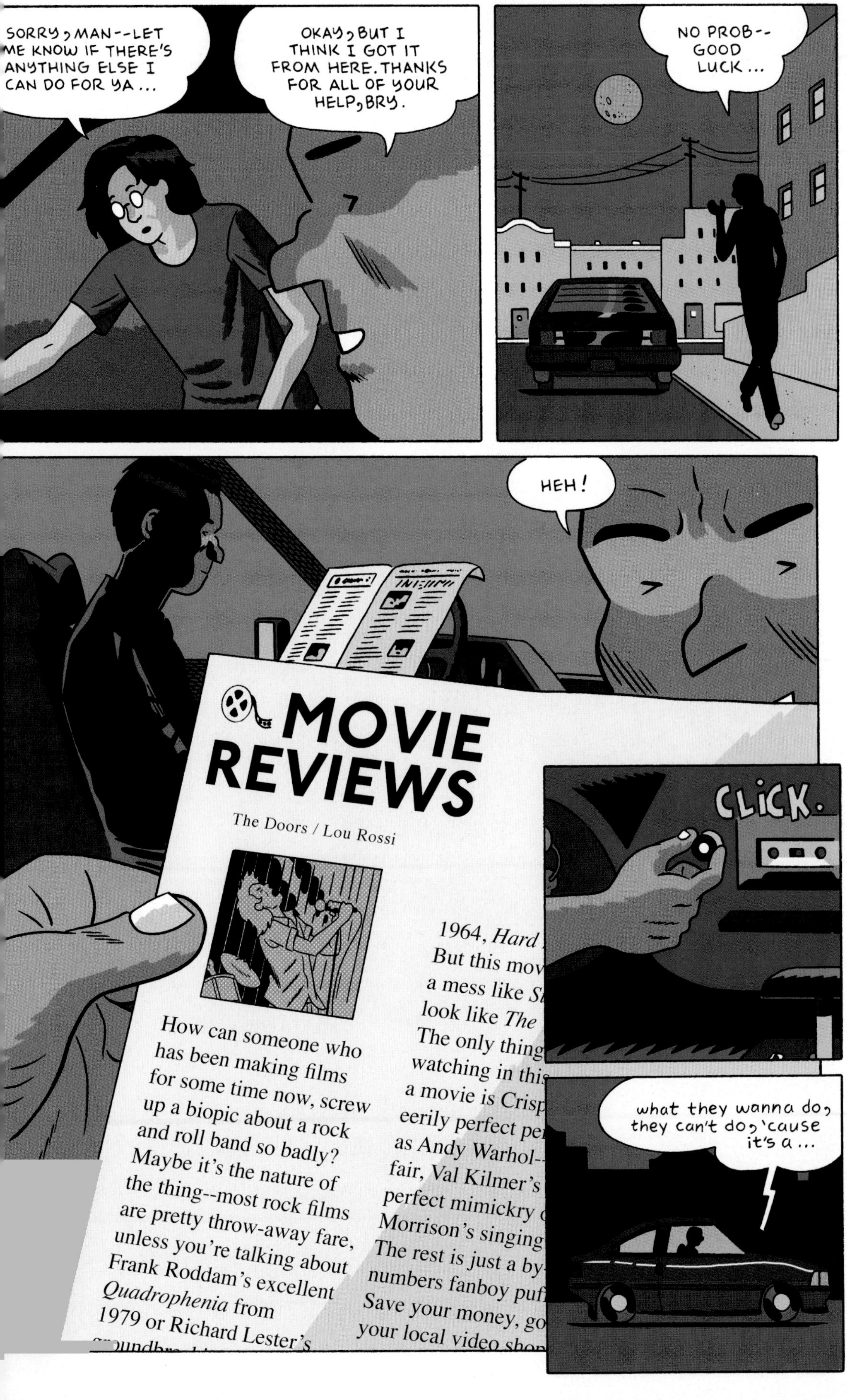

SORRY, MAN--LET ME KNOW IF THERE'S ANYTHING ELSE I CAN DO FOR YA...
OKAY, BUT I THINK I GOT IT FROM HERE. THANKS FOR ALL OF YOUR HELP, BRY.
NO PROB--GOOD LUCK...
HEH!
MOVIE REVIEWS
The Doors / Lou Rossi
How can someone who has been making films for some time now, screw up a biopic about a rock and roll band so badly? Maybe it's the nature of the thing--most rock films are pretty throw-away fare, unless you're talking about Frank Roddam's excellent Quadrophenia from 1979 or Richard Lester's
1964, Hard
But this mov
a mess like S
look like The
The only thing
watching in this
a movie is Crisp
eerily perfect pe
as Andy Warhol--
fair, Val Kilmer's
perfect mimickry o
Morrison's singing
The rest is just a by-
numbers fanboy puf
Save your money, go
your local video shop
CLICK.
what they wanna do, they can't do, 'cause it's a...

17

2 A.M.

FINALLY--THE PARTY'S OVER ... THERE WAS THE ASSHOLE, CLOSING UP SHOP AND HEADING FOR HOME ... TIME FOR ME TO GO TO WORK ...

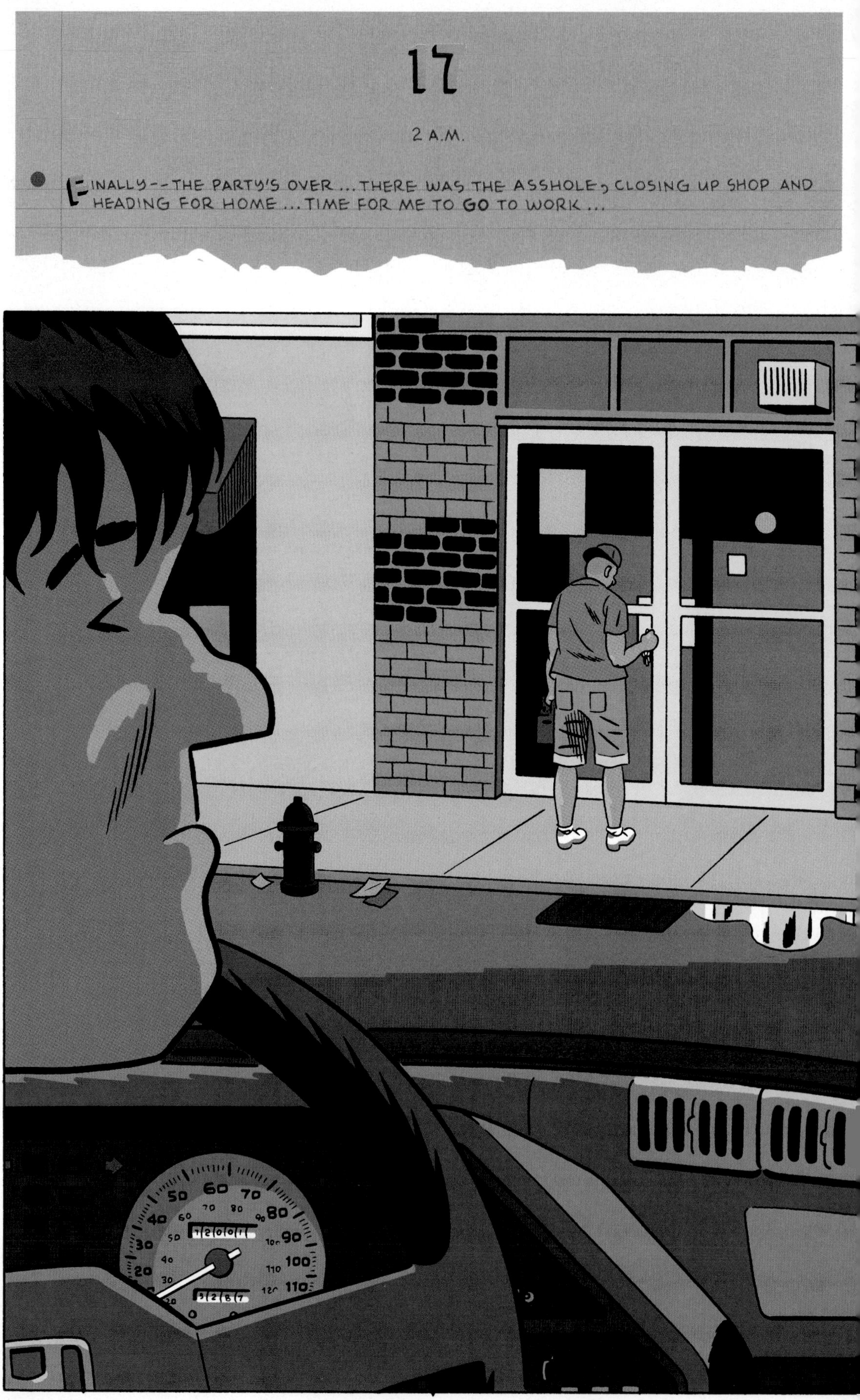

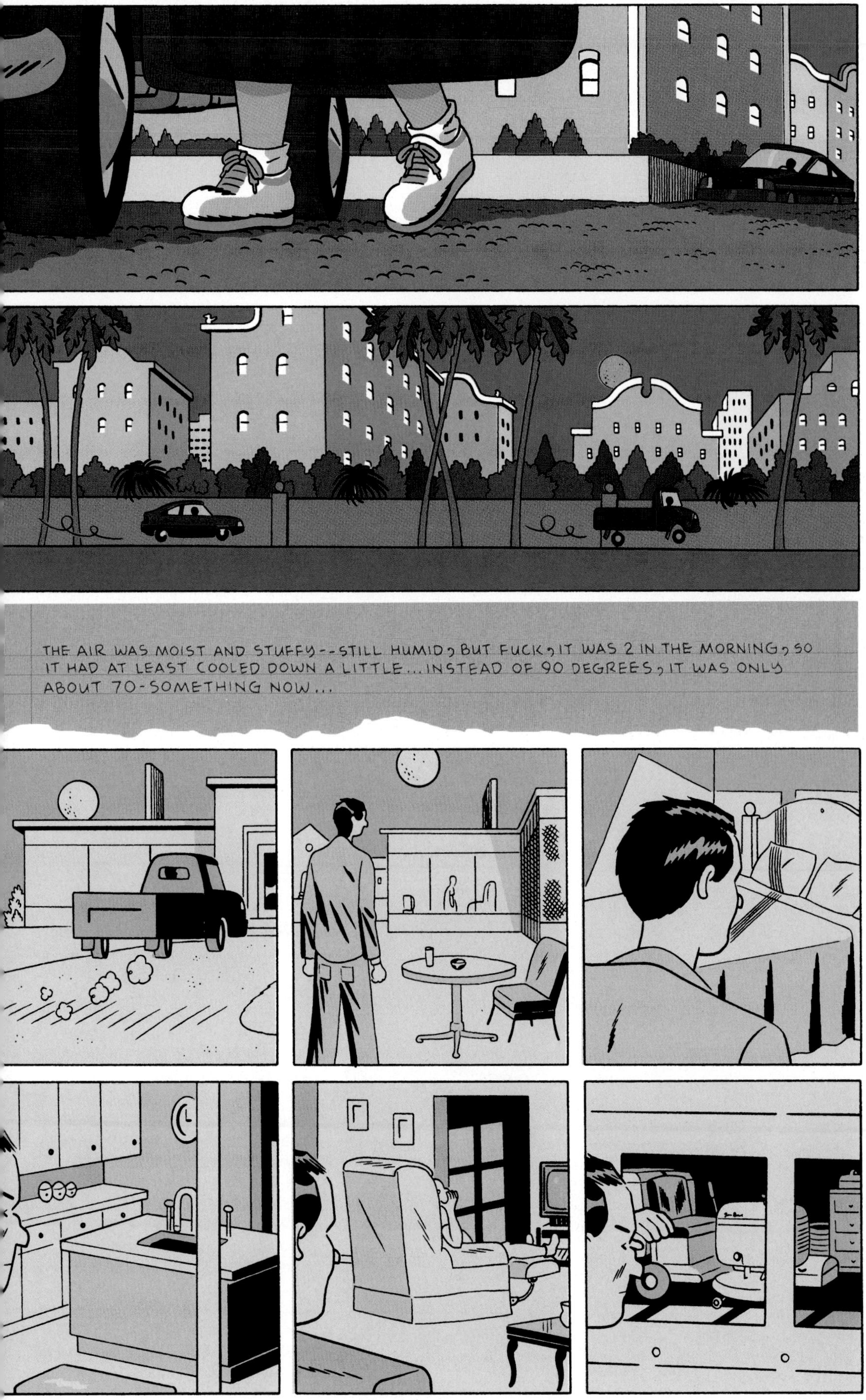
THE AIR WAS MOIST AND STUFFY--STILL HUMID, BUT FUCK, IT WAS 2 IN THE MORNING, SO IT HAD AT LEAST COOLED DOWN A LITTLE...INSTEAD OF 90 DEGREES, IT WAS ONLY ABOUT 70-SOMETHING NOW...

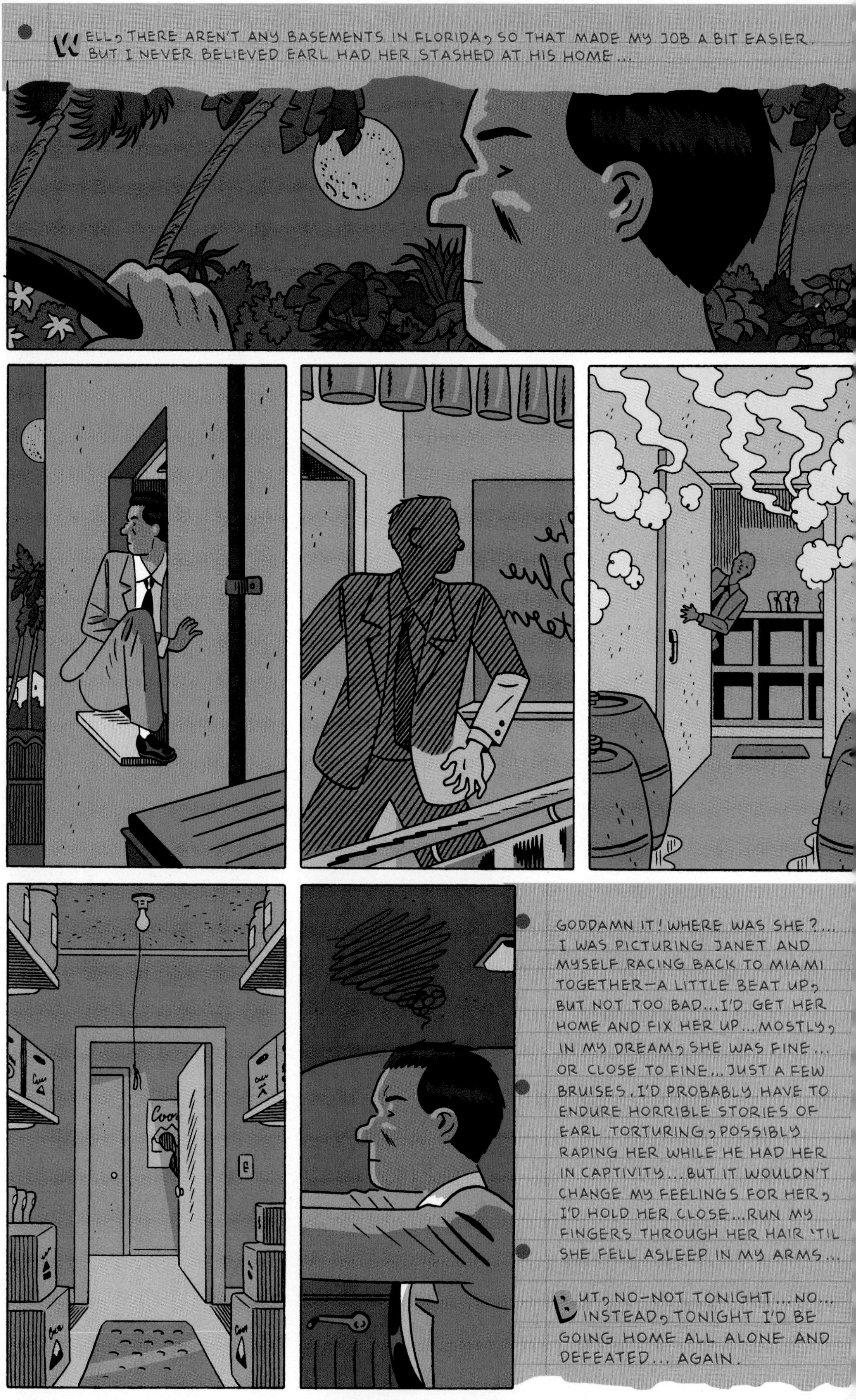
WELL, THERE AREN'T ANY BASEMENTS IN FLORIDA, SO THAT MADE MY JOB A BIT EASIER. BUT I NEVER BELIEVED EARL HAD HER STASHED AT HIS HOME...
GODDAMN IT! WHERE WAS SHE?... I WAS PICTURING JANET AND MYSELF RACING BACK TO MIAMI TOGETHER—A LITTLE BEAT UP, BUT NOT TOO BAD... I'D GET HER HOME AND FIX HER UP... MOSTLY, IN MY DREAM, SHE WAS FINE... OR CLOSE TO FINE... JUST A FEW BRUISES. I'D PROBABLY HAVE TO ENDURE HORRIBLE STORIES OF EARL TORTURING, POSSIBLY RAPING HER WHILE HE HAD HER IN CAPTIVITY... BUT IT WOULDN'T CHANGE MY FEELINGS FOR HER, I'D HOLD HER CLOSE... RUN MY FINGERS THROUGH HER HAIR 'TIL SHE FELL ASLEEP IN MY ARMS...
BUT, NO—NOT TONIGHT... NO... INSTEAD, TONIGHT I'D BE GOING HOME ALL ALONE AND DEFEATED... AGAIN.

18

SATURDAY
10 P.M.

TONIGHT WAS THE NIGHT... ROB AND I **HAD** TO PAY A VISIT TO THE FOUR BLONDE CHICKS IN THE VW... THEY MUST'VE BEEN THE ONES HOLDING JANET...

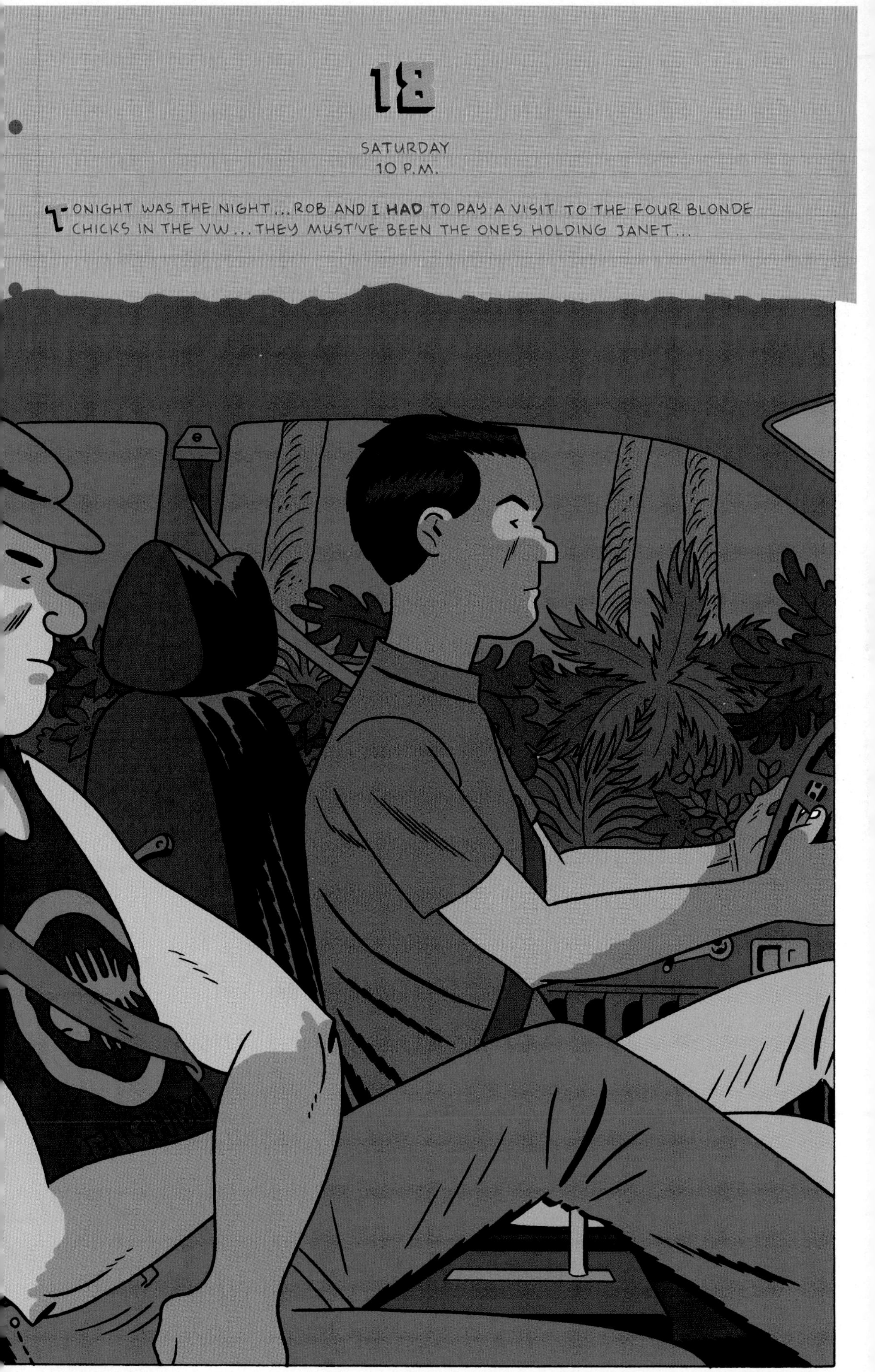

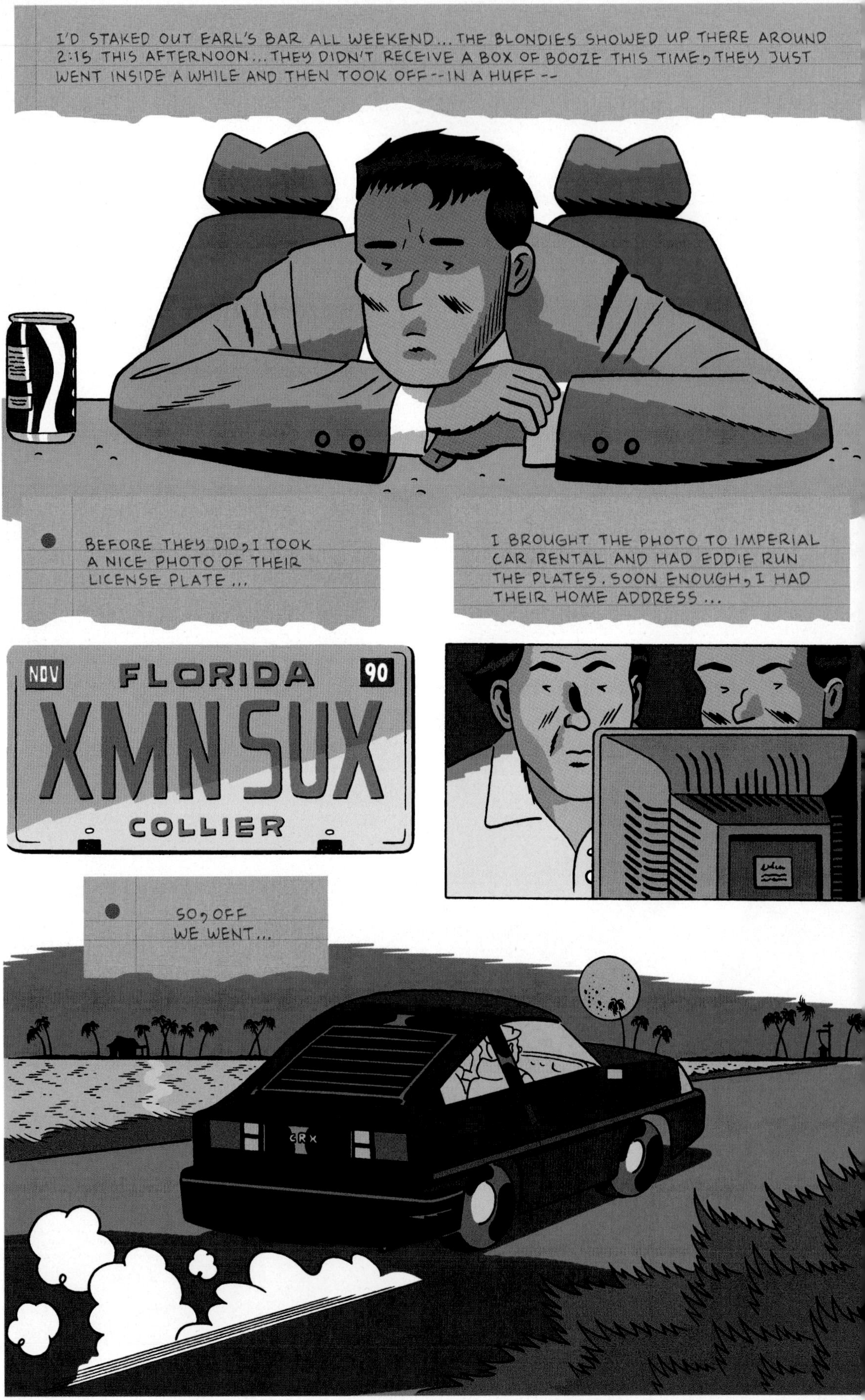
I'D STAKED OUT EARL'S BAR ALL WEEKEND... THE BLONDIES SHOWED UP THERE AROUND 2:15 THIS AFTERNOON... THEY DIDN'T RECEIVE A BOX OF BOOZE THIS TIME, THEY JUST WENT INSIDE A WHILE AND THEN TOOK OFF--IN A HUFF--
BEFORE THEY DID, I TOOK A NICE PHOTO OF THEIR LICENSE PLATE...
I BROUGHT THE PHOTO TO IMPERIAL CAR RENTAL AND HAD EDDIE RUN THE PLATES. SOON ENOUGH, I HAD THEIR HOME ADDRESS...
NOV
FLORIDA
90
XMN SUX
COLLIER
SO, OFF WE WENT...
CRX

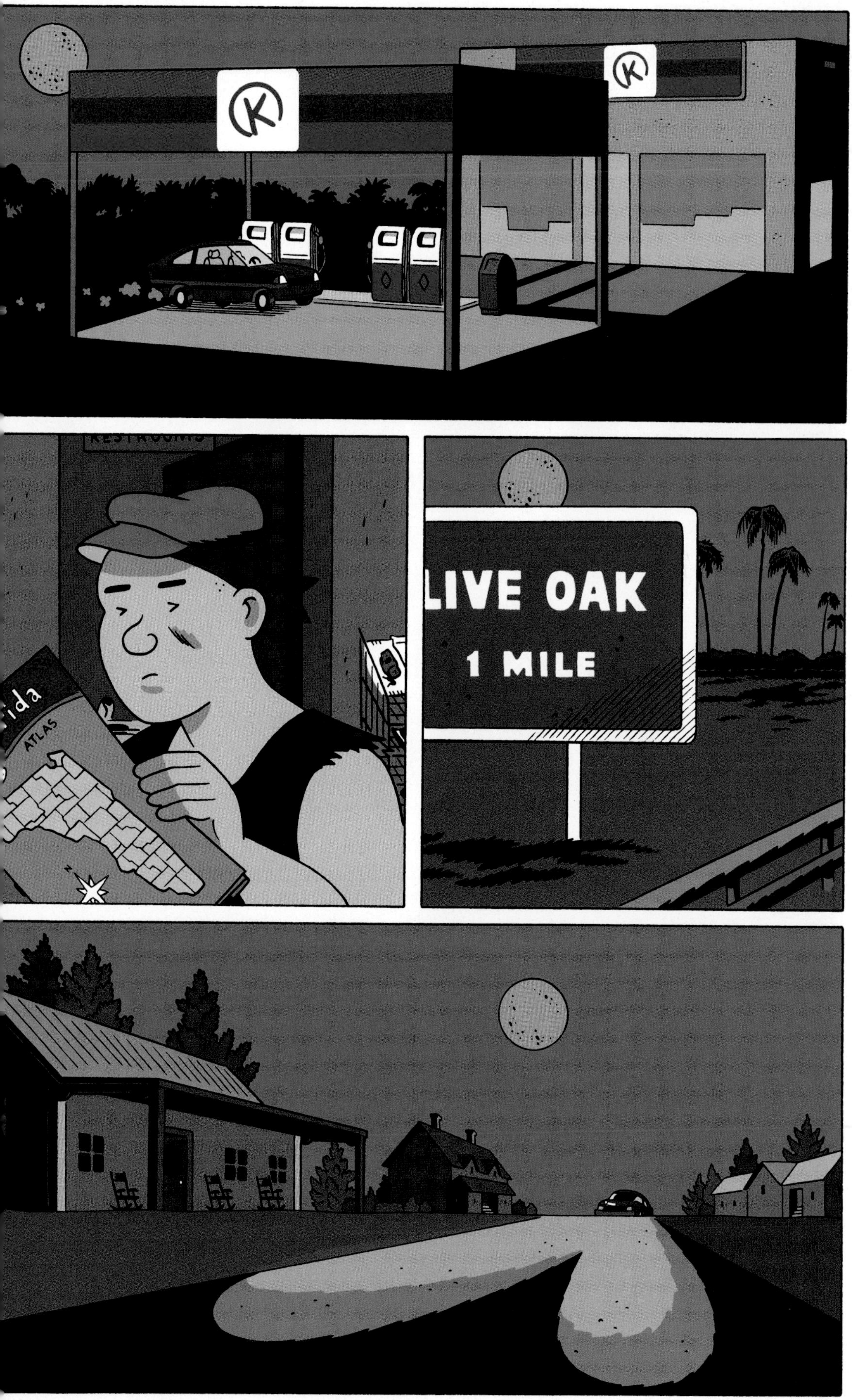
RESTROOMS
ATLAS
LIVE OAK
1 MILE

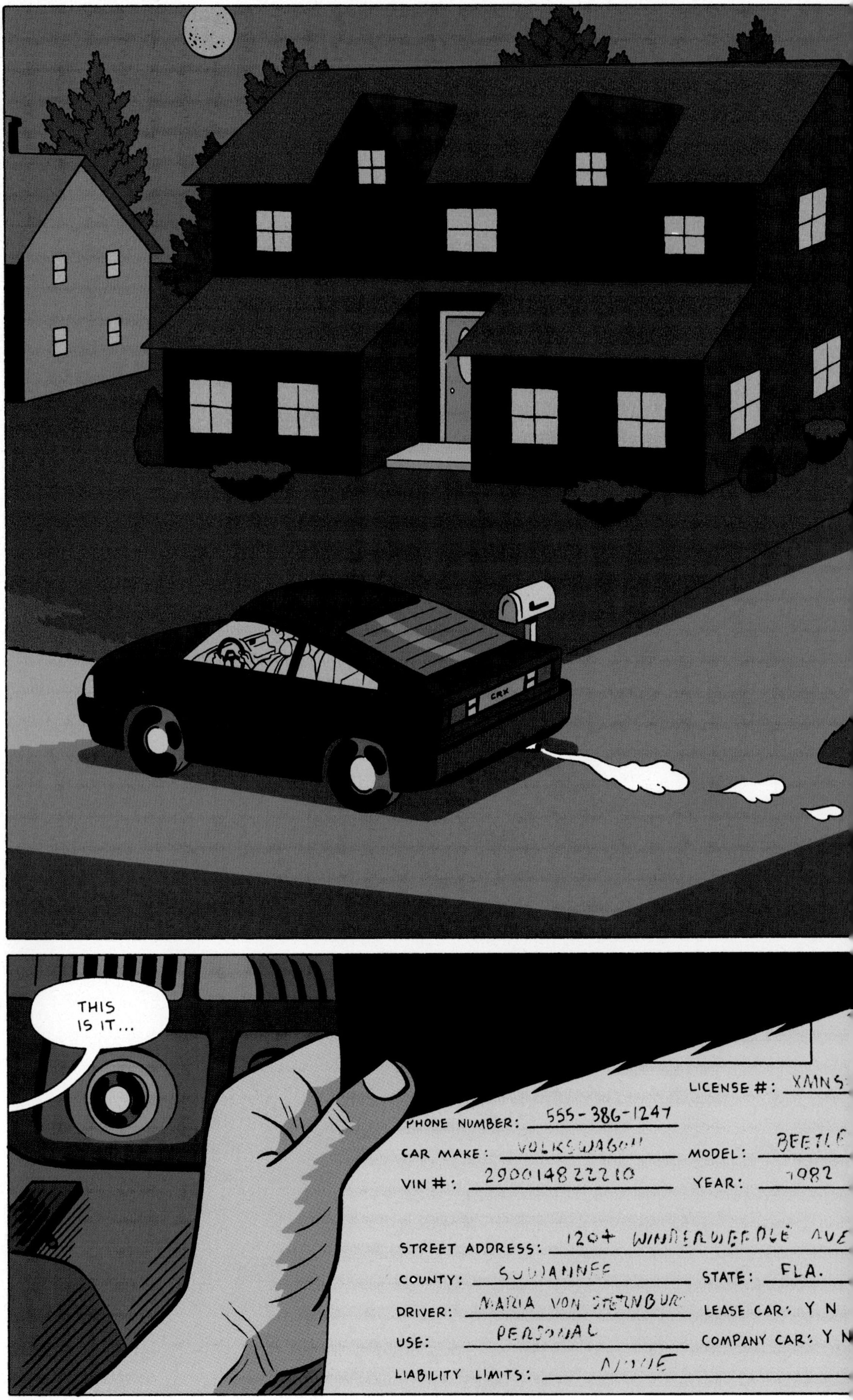
CRX
THIS IS IT...
LICENSE #:
PHONE NUMBER: 555-386-1247
CAR MAKE:
MODEL:
VIN #: 290014822210
YEAR:
STREET ADDRESS:
COUNTY:
STATE: FLA.
DRIVER:
LEASE CAR: Y N
USE: PERSONAL
COMPANY CAR: Y
LIABILITY LIMITS:

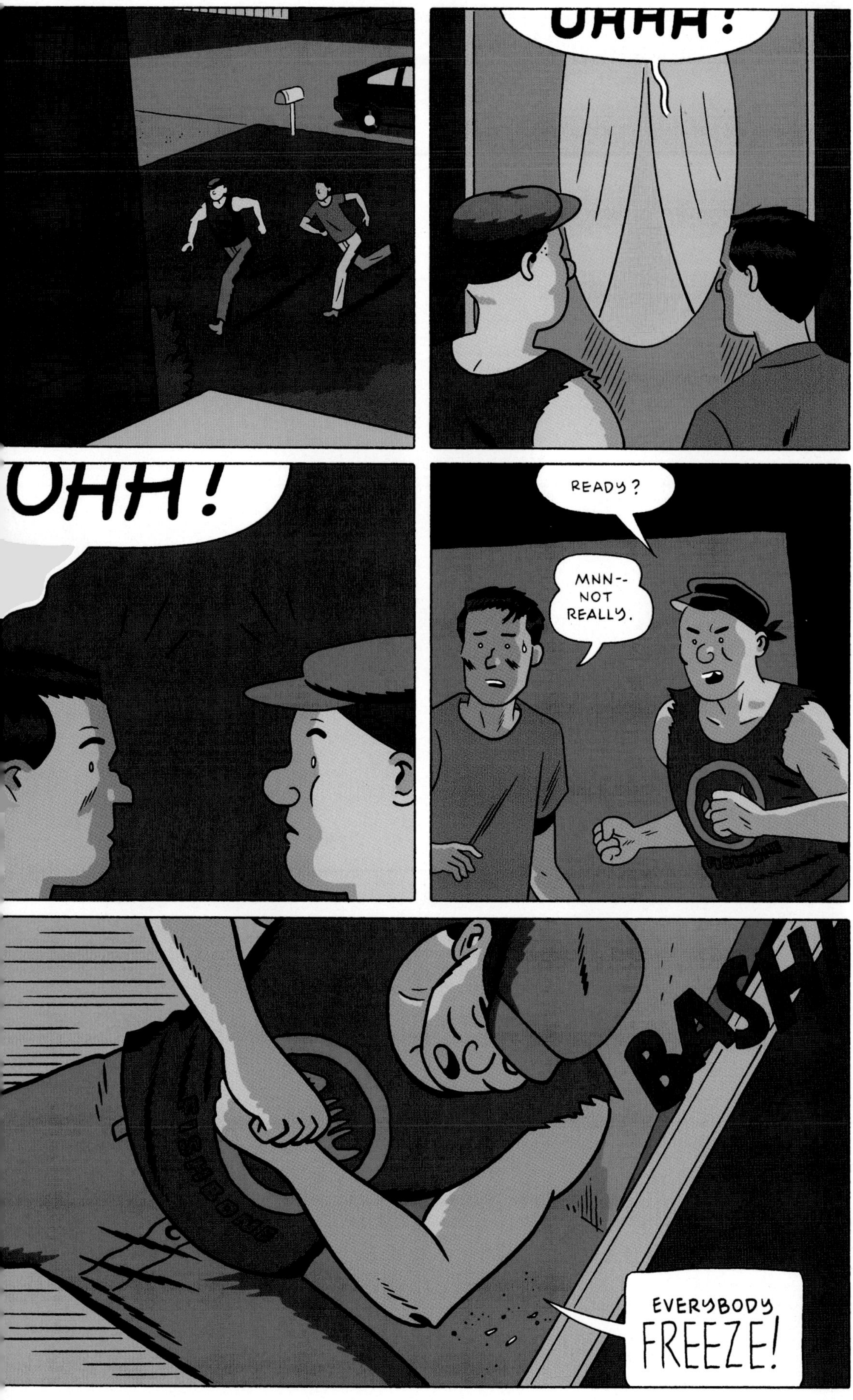

OHHH!
OHH!
READY?
MNN-- NOT REALLY.
BASH
EVERYBODY FREEZE!

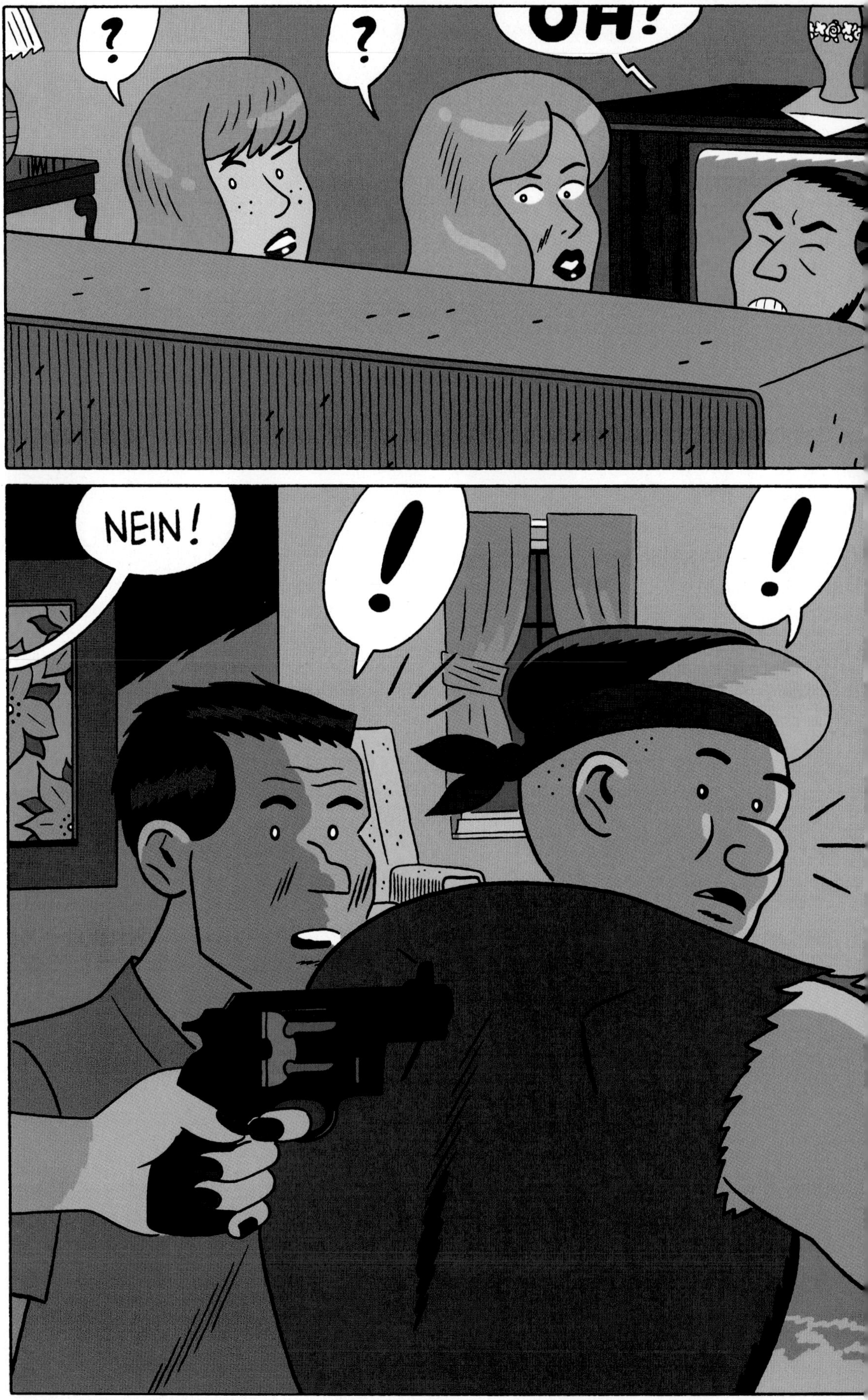
?
?
OH!
NEIN!
!
!

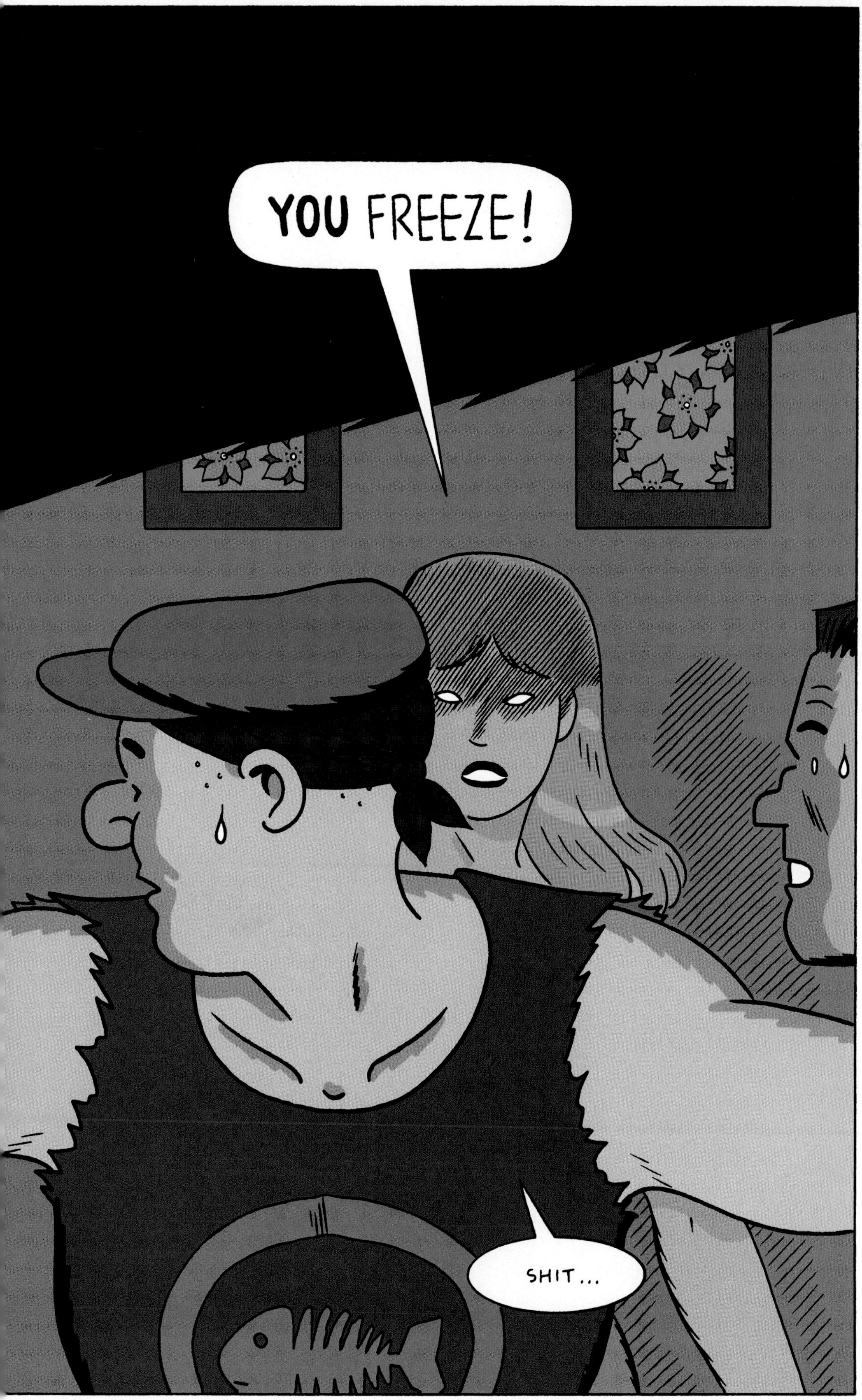
YOU FREEZE!
SHIT...

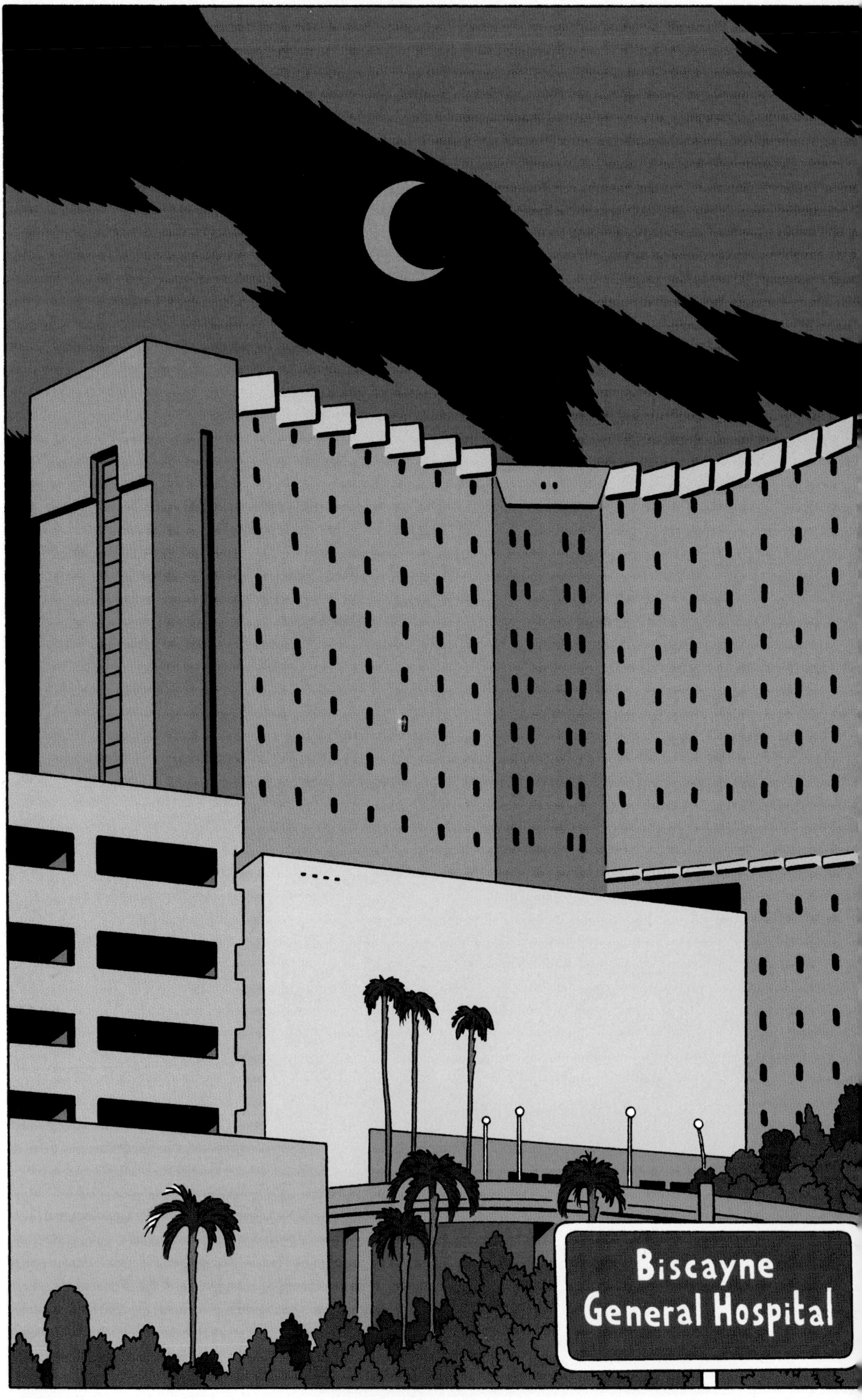
Biscayne
General Hospital

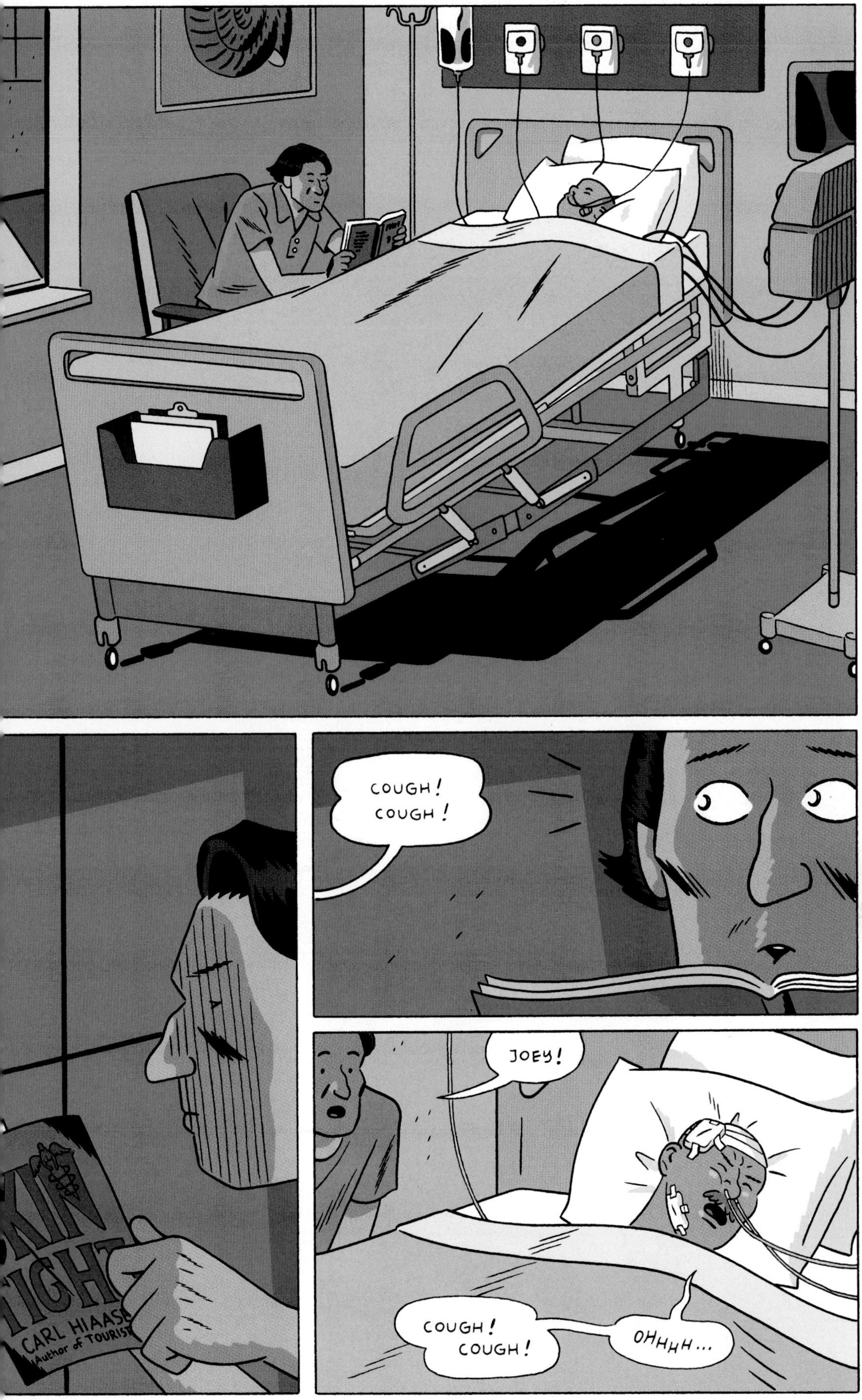
COUGH! COUGH!
JOEY!
COUGH! COUGH!
OHHHH...

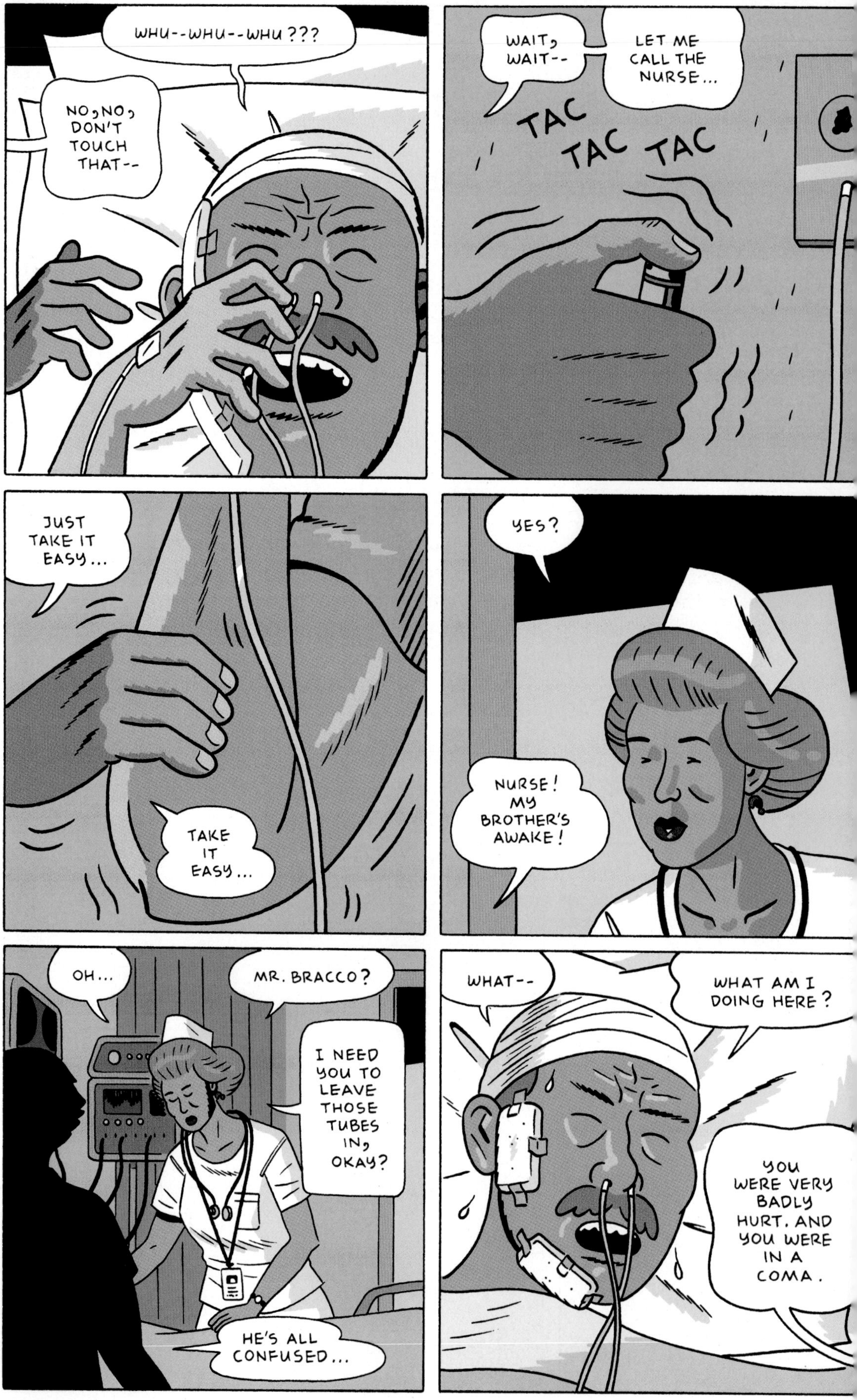
WHU--WHU--WHU???
NO, NO, DON'T TOUCH THAT--
WAIT, WAIT--
LET ME CALL THE NURSE...
TAC TAC TAC
JUST TAKE IT EASY...
TAKE IT EASY...
YES?
NURSE! MY BROTHER'S AWAKE!
OH...
MR. BRACCO?
I NEED YOU TO LEAVE THOSE TUBES IN, OKAY?
HE'S ALL CONFUSED...
WHAT--
WHAT AM I DOING HERE?
YOU WERE VERY BADLY HURT. AND YOU WERE IN A COMA.

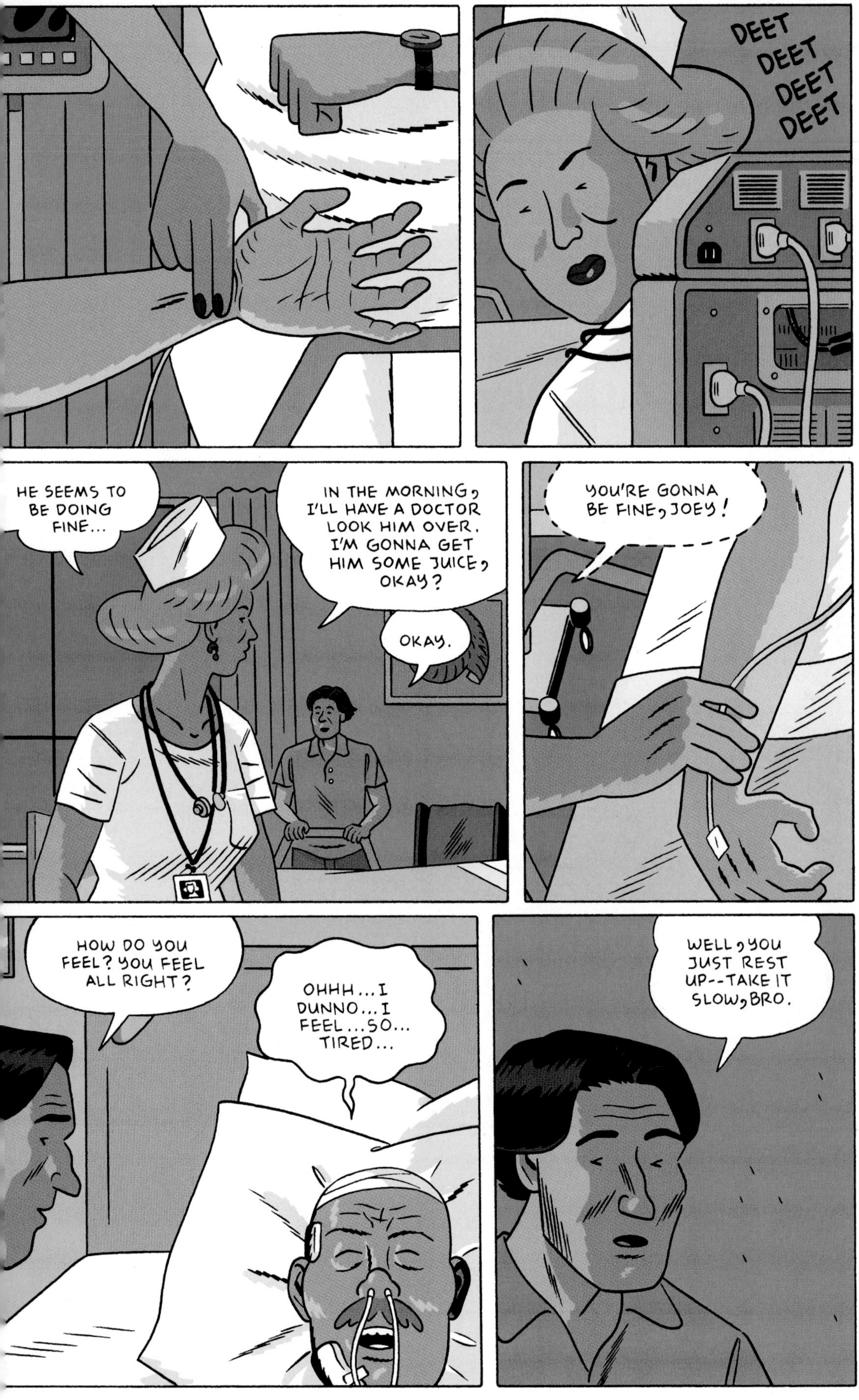
DEET DEET DEET DEET
HE SEEMS TO BE DOING FINE...
IN THE MORNING, I'LL HAVE A DOCTOR LOOK HIM OVER. I'M GONNA GET HIM SOME JUICE, OKAY?
OKAY.
YOU'RE GONNA BE FINE, JOEY!
HOW DO YOU FEEL? YOU FEEL ALL RIGHT?
OHHH...I DUNNO...I FEEL...SO... TIRED...
WELL, YOU JUST REST UP--TAKE IT SLOW, BRO.

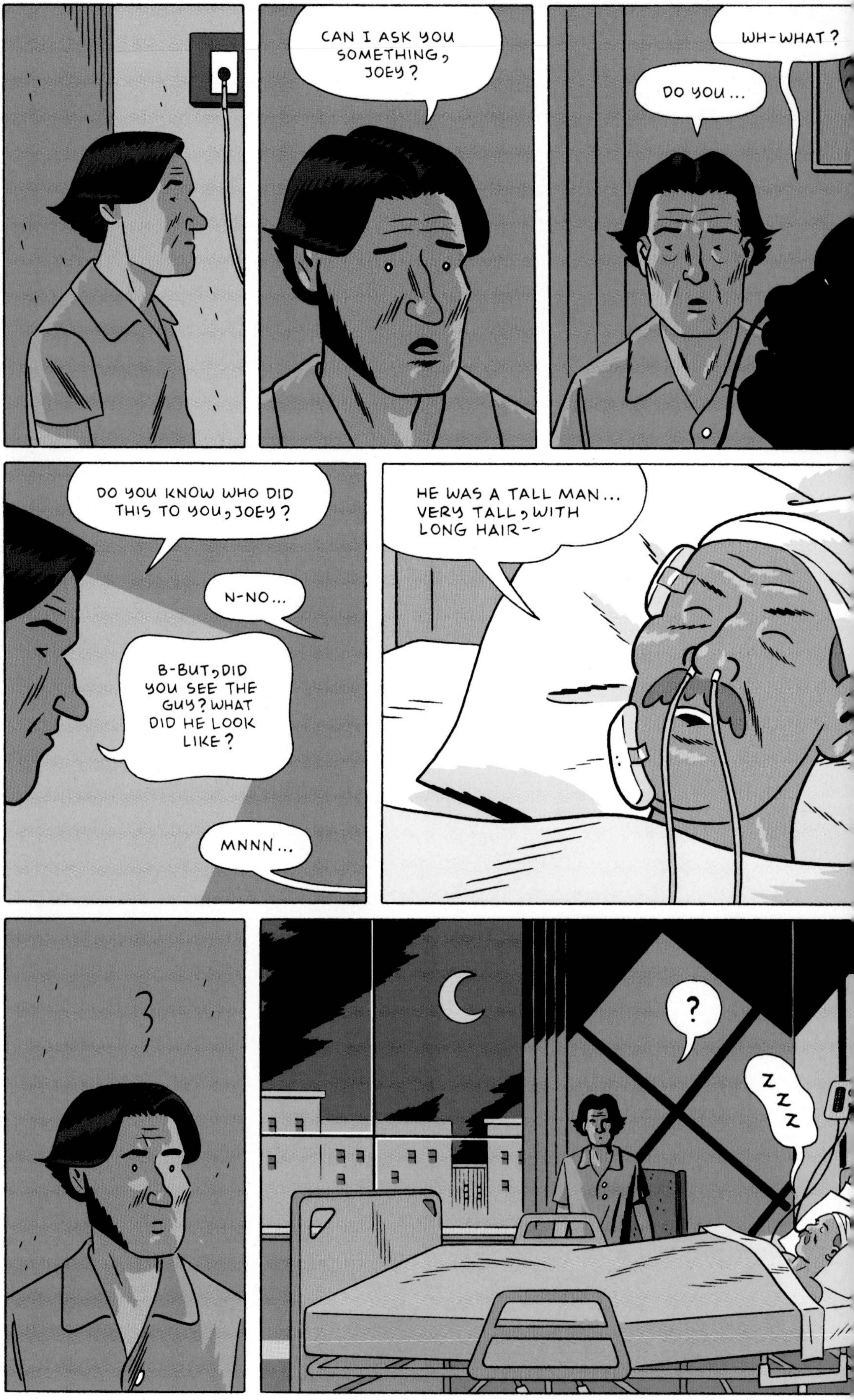
CAN I ASK YOU SOMETHING, JOEY?
DO YOU...
WH-WHAT?
DO YOU KNOW WHO DID THIS TO YOU, JOEY?
N-NO...
B-BUT, DID YOU SEE THE GUY? WHAT DID HE LOOK LIKE?
MNNN...
HE WAS A TALL MAN... VERY TALL, WITH LONG HAIR--
?
Z Z Z

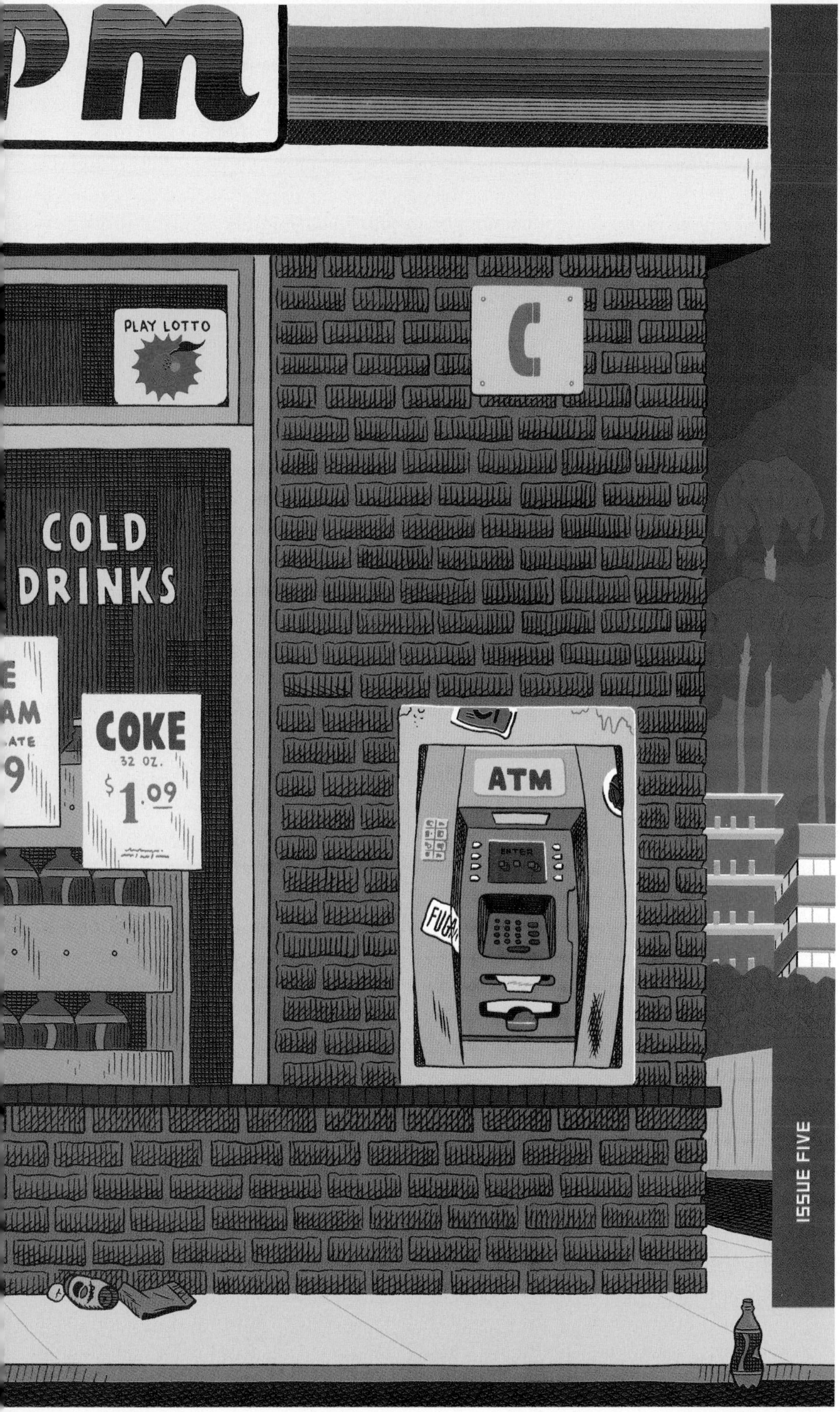
pm
PLAY LOTTO
COLD
DRINKS
COKE
32 OZ.
$1.09
ATM
ENTER
ISSUE FIVE

19

5:30 P.M.

THREE WEEKS BACK...

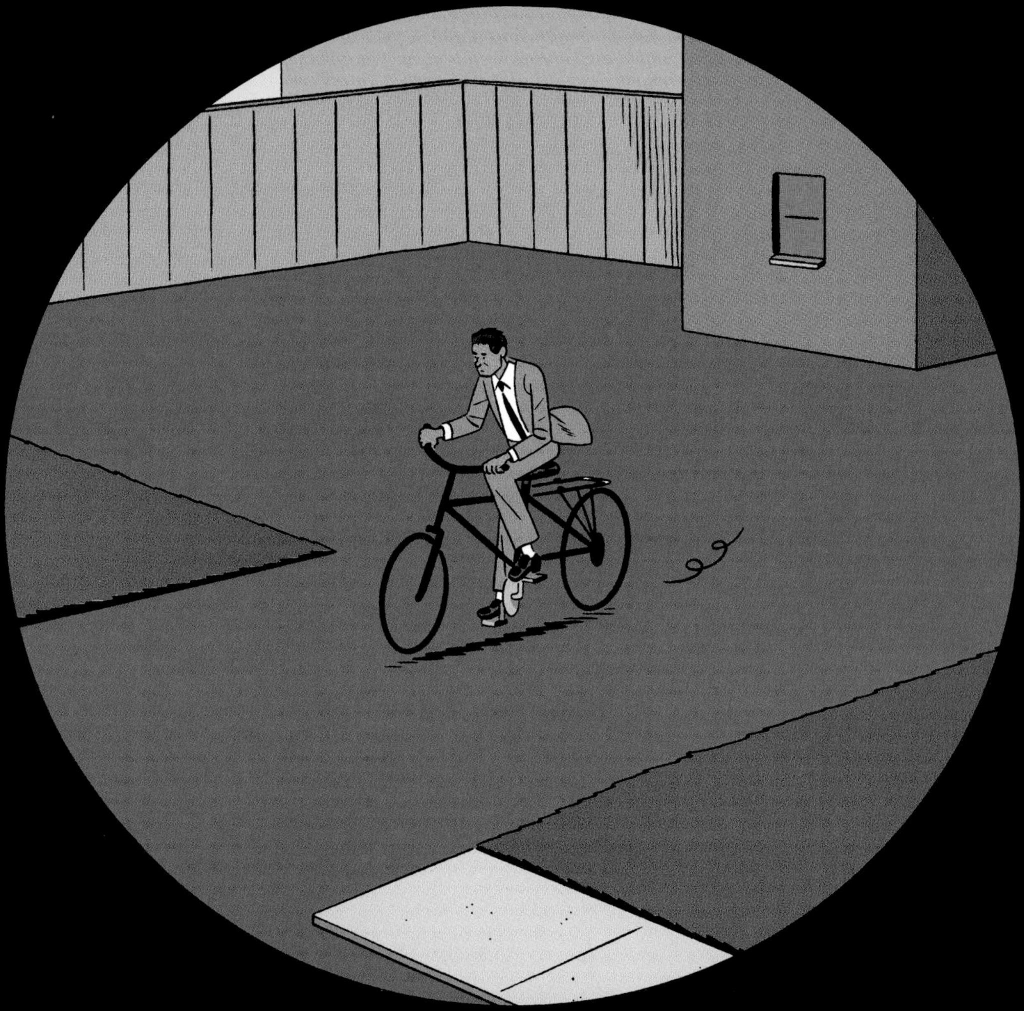

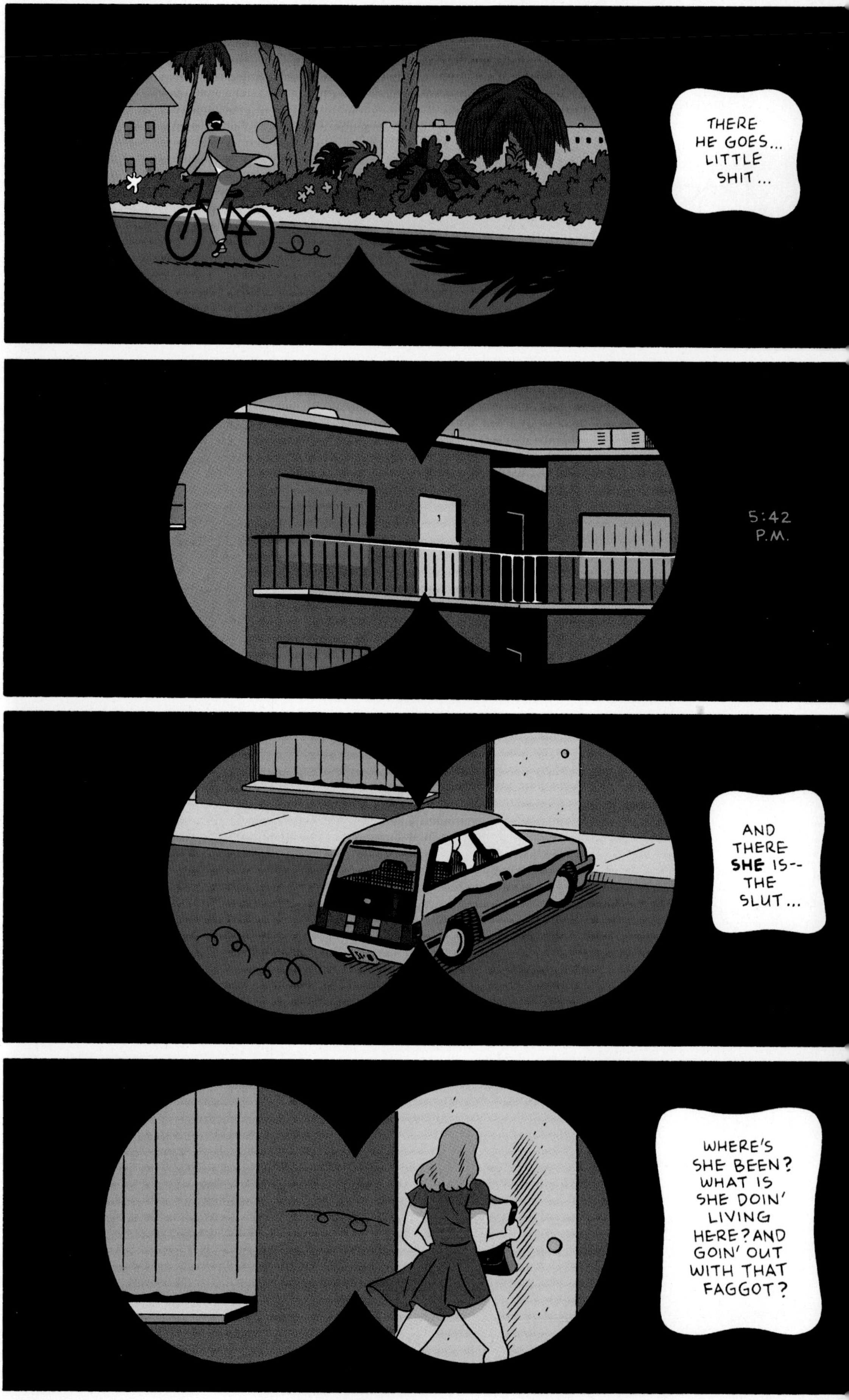
THERE HE GOES... LITTLE SHIT...
5:42 P.M.
AND THERE SHE IS-- THE SLUT...
WHERE'S SHE BEEN? WHAT IS SHE DOIN' LIVING HERE? AND GOIN' OUT WITH THAT FAGGOT?

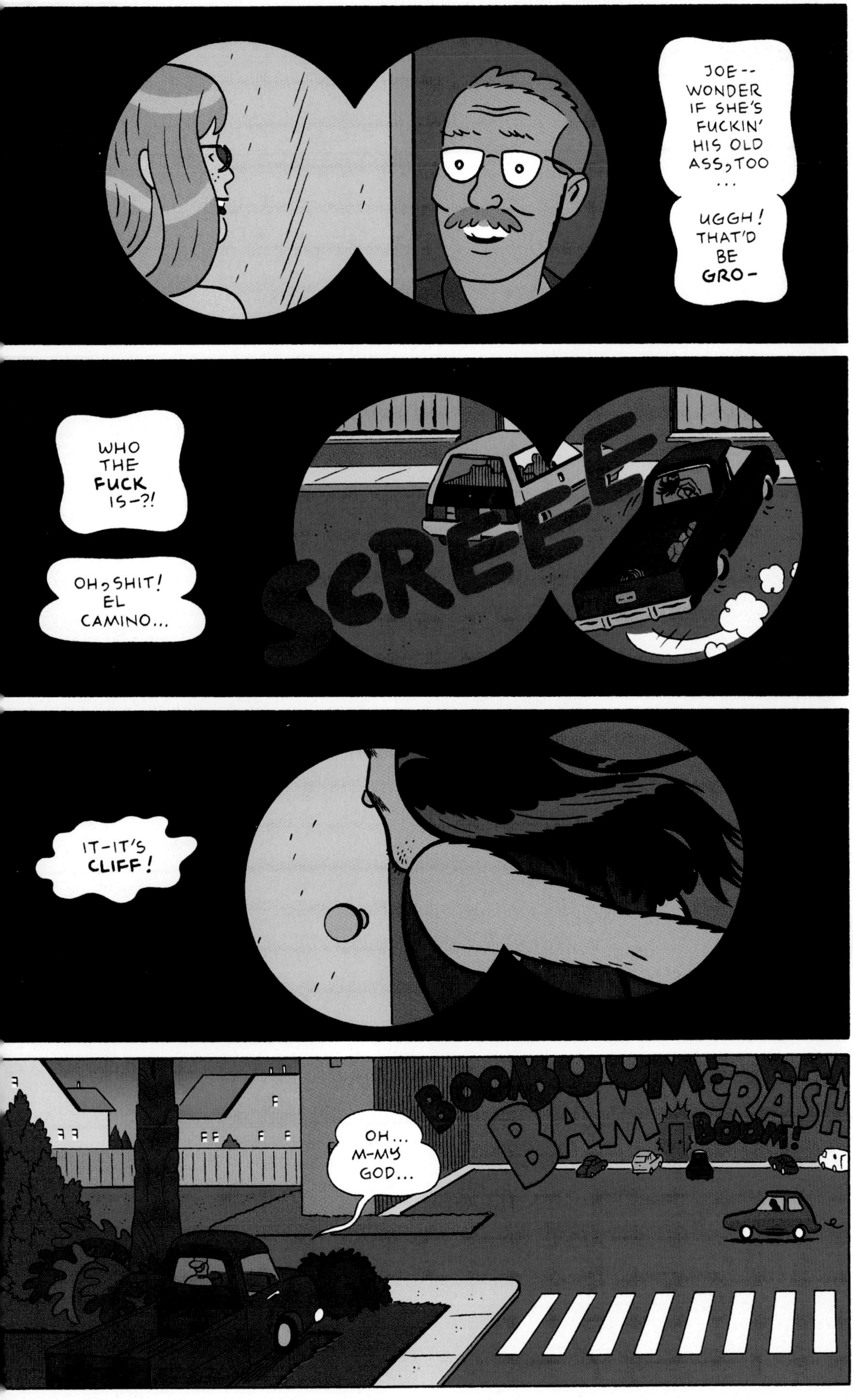
JOE-- WONDER IF SHE'S FUCKIN' HIS OLD ASS, TOO ...
UGGH! THAT'D BE GRO-
WHO THE FUCK IS-?!
SCREEE
OH, SHIT! EL CAMINO...
IT-IT'S CLIFF!
BOOM BOOM BAM CRASH BAM BOOM!
OH... M-MY GOD...

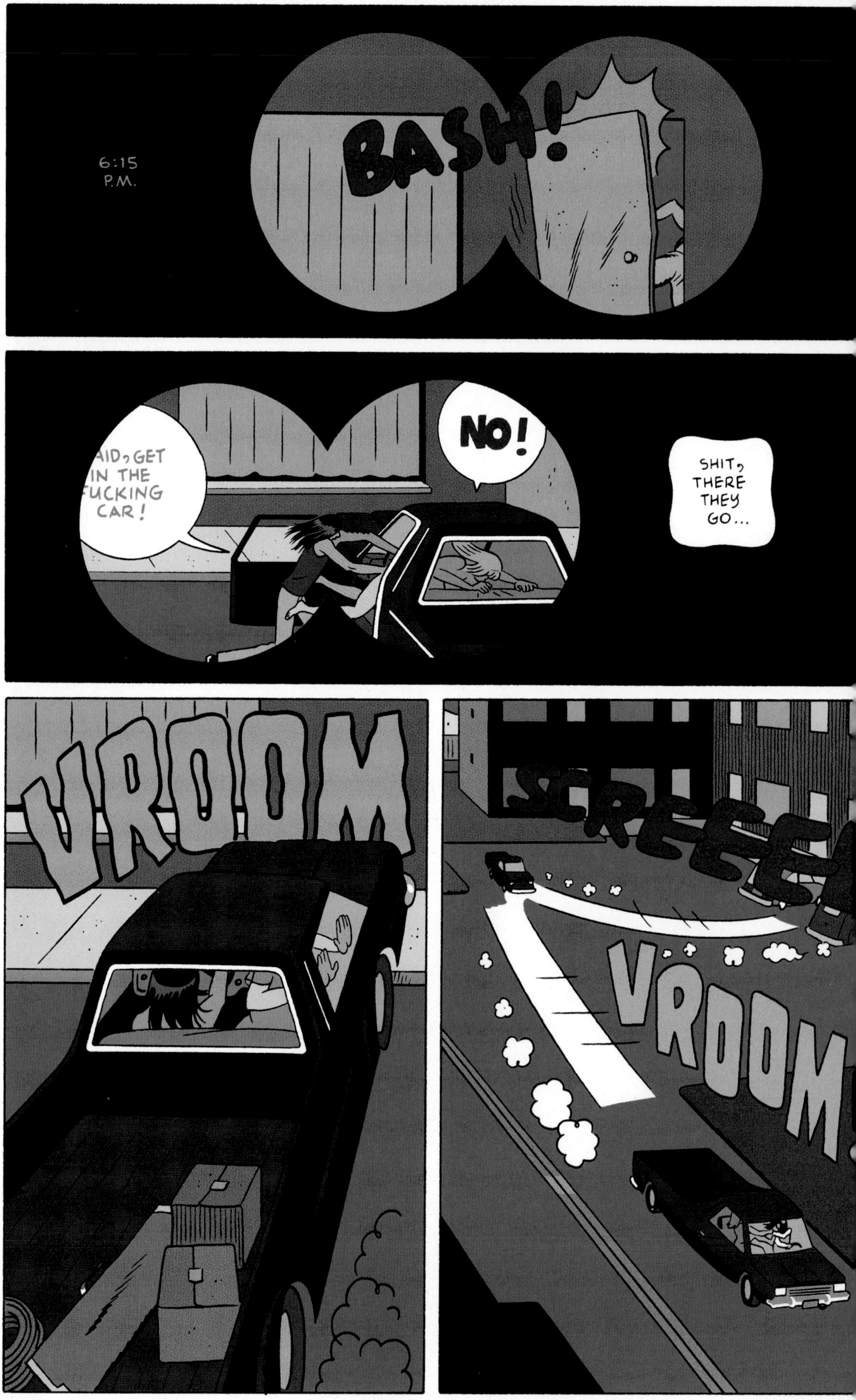
6:15 P.M.
BASH!
AID, GET IN THE FUCKING CAR!
NO!
SHIT, THERE THEY GO...
VROOM
SCREEEE
VROOM

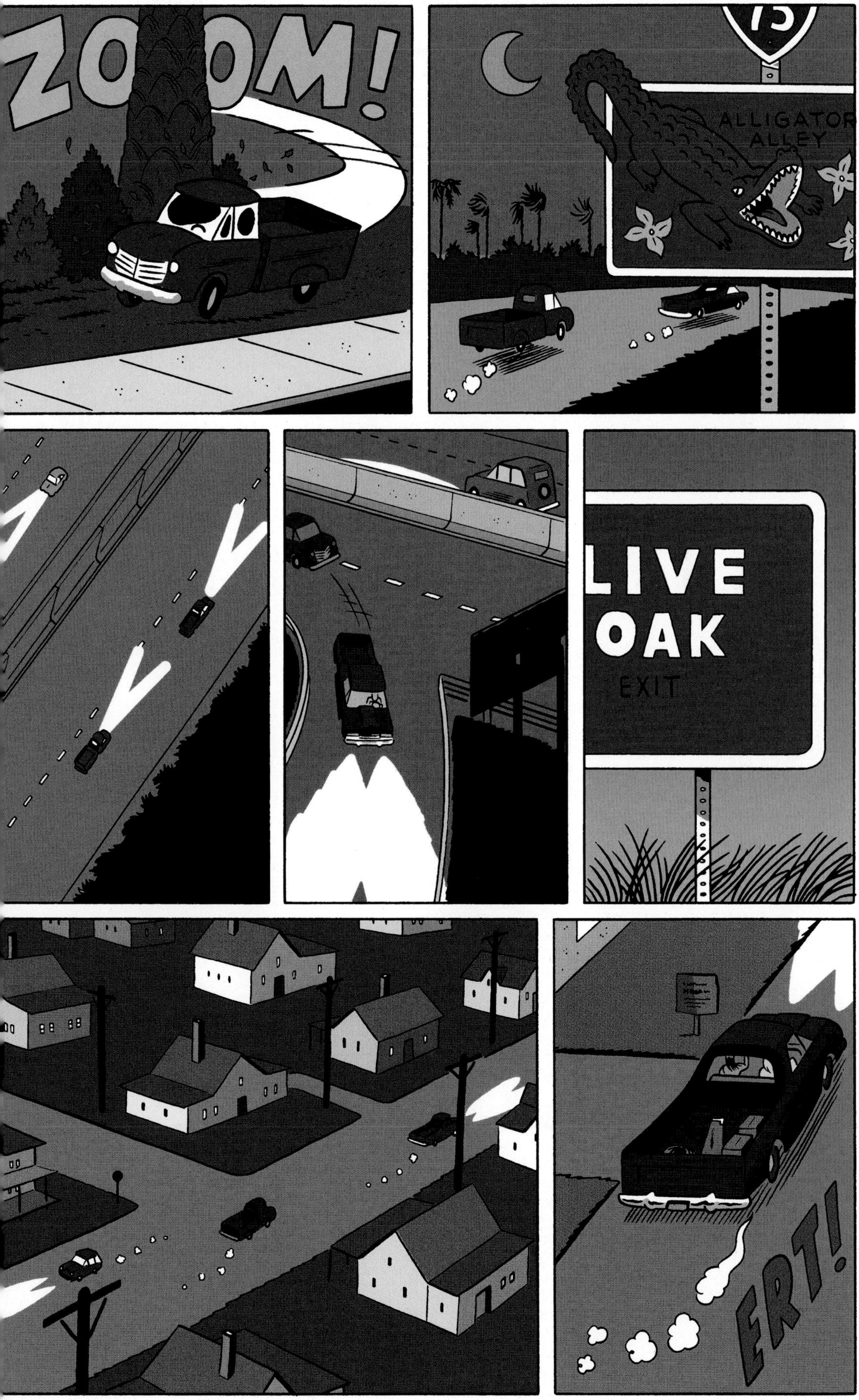
ZOOM!
15
ALLIGATOR
ALLEY
LIVE
OAK
EXIT
ERT!

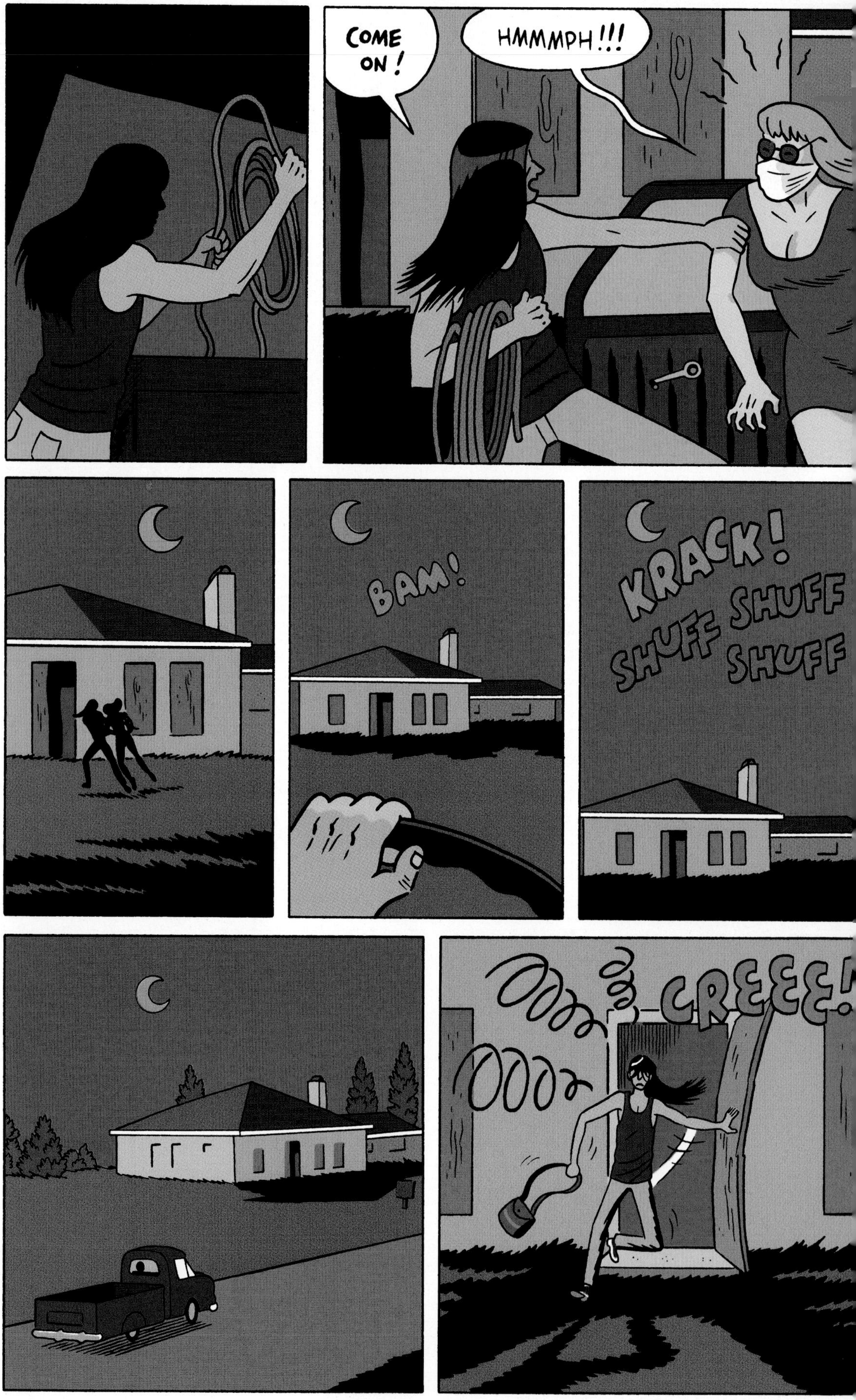
COME ON!
HMMMPH!!!
BAM!
KRACK!
SHUFF SHUFF
SHUFF
CREEE!

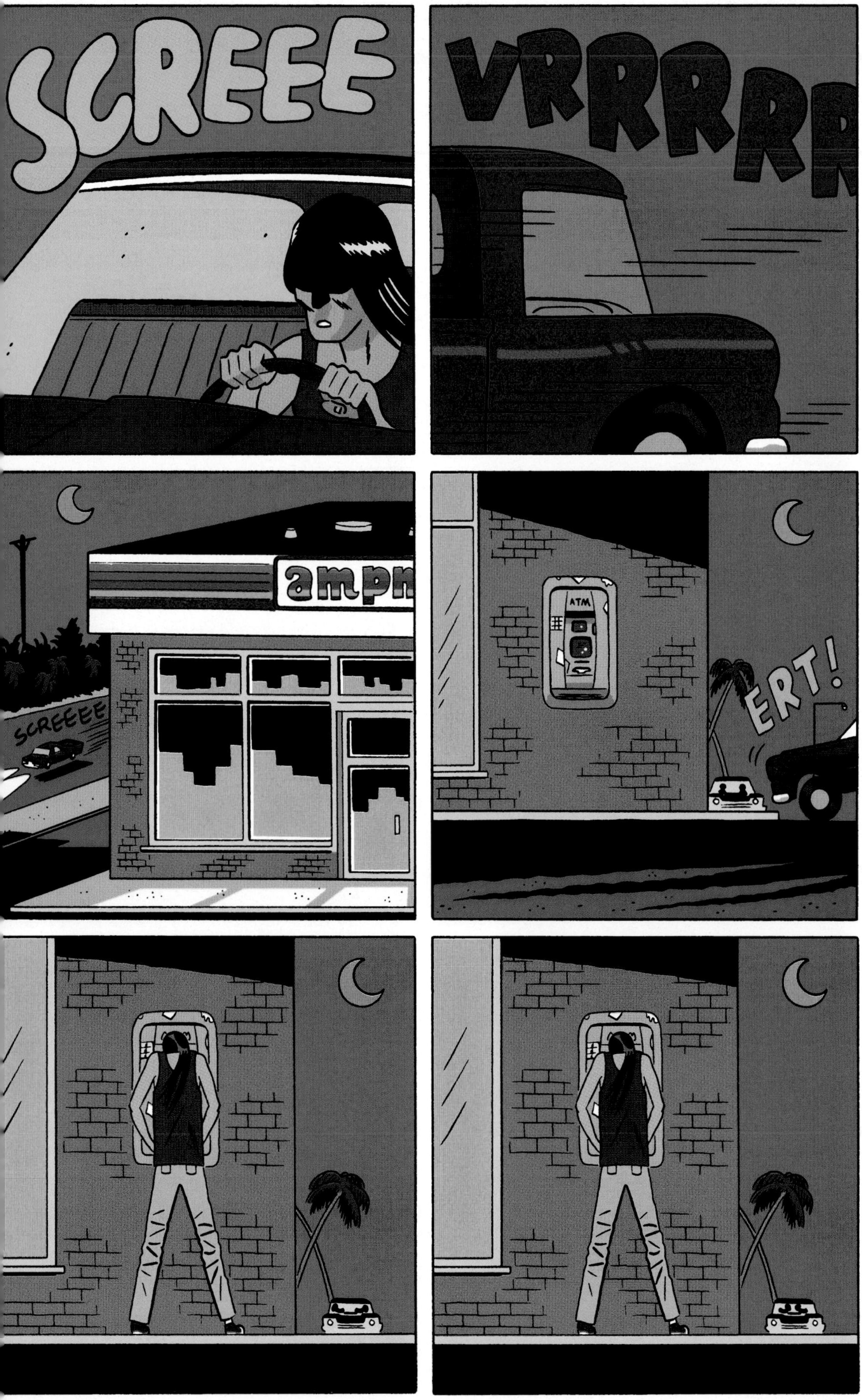
SCREEE
VRRRRRR
ampm
SCREEEE
ATM
ERT!

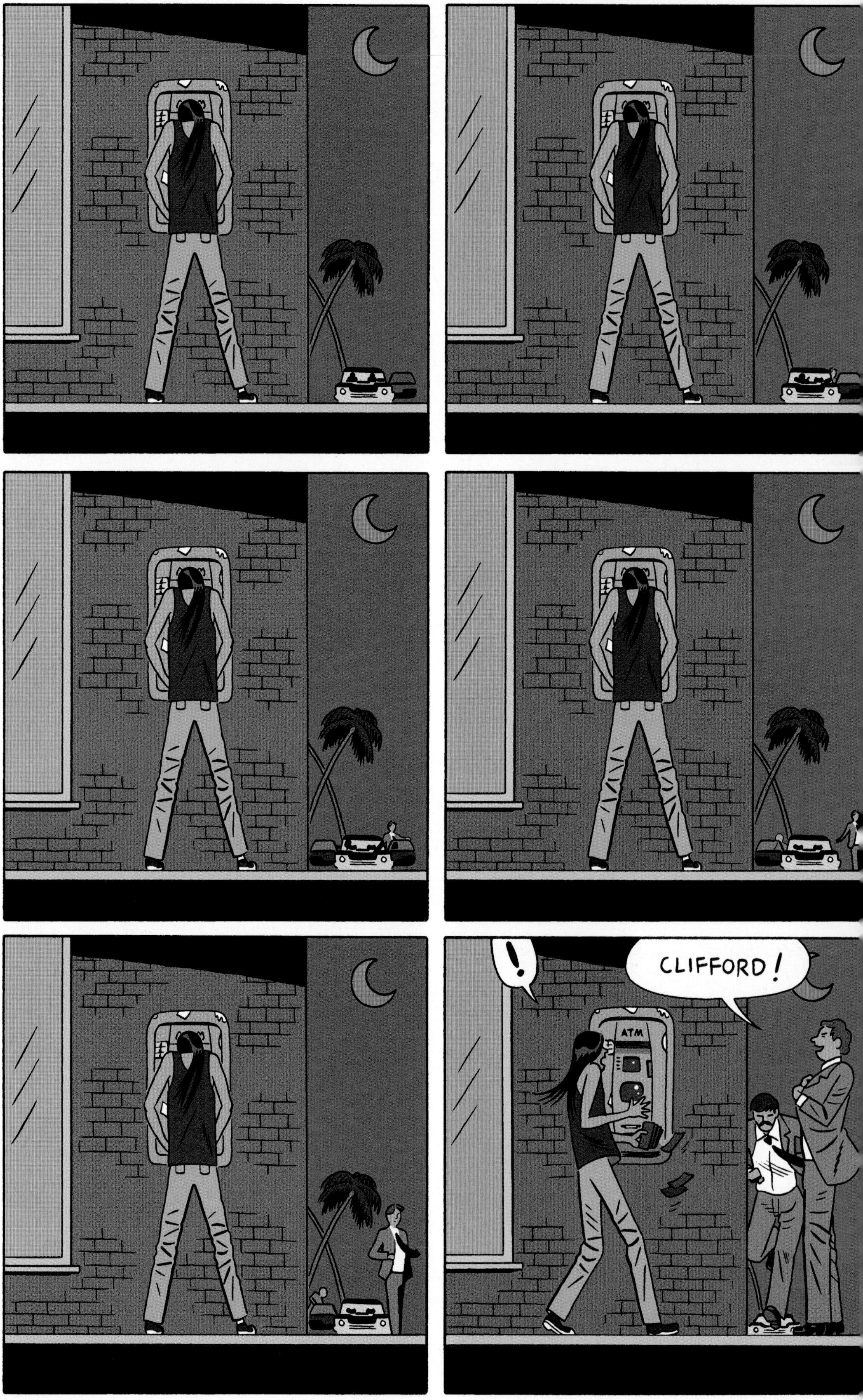
!
CLIFFORD!
ATM

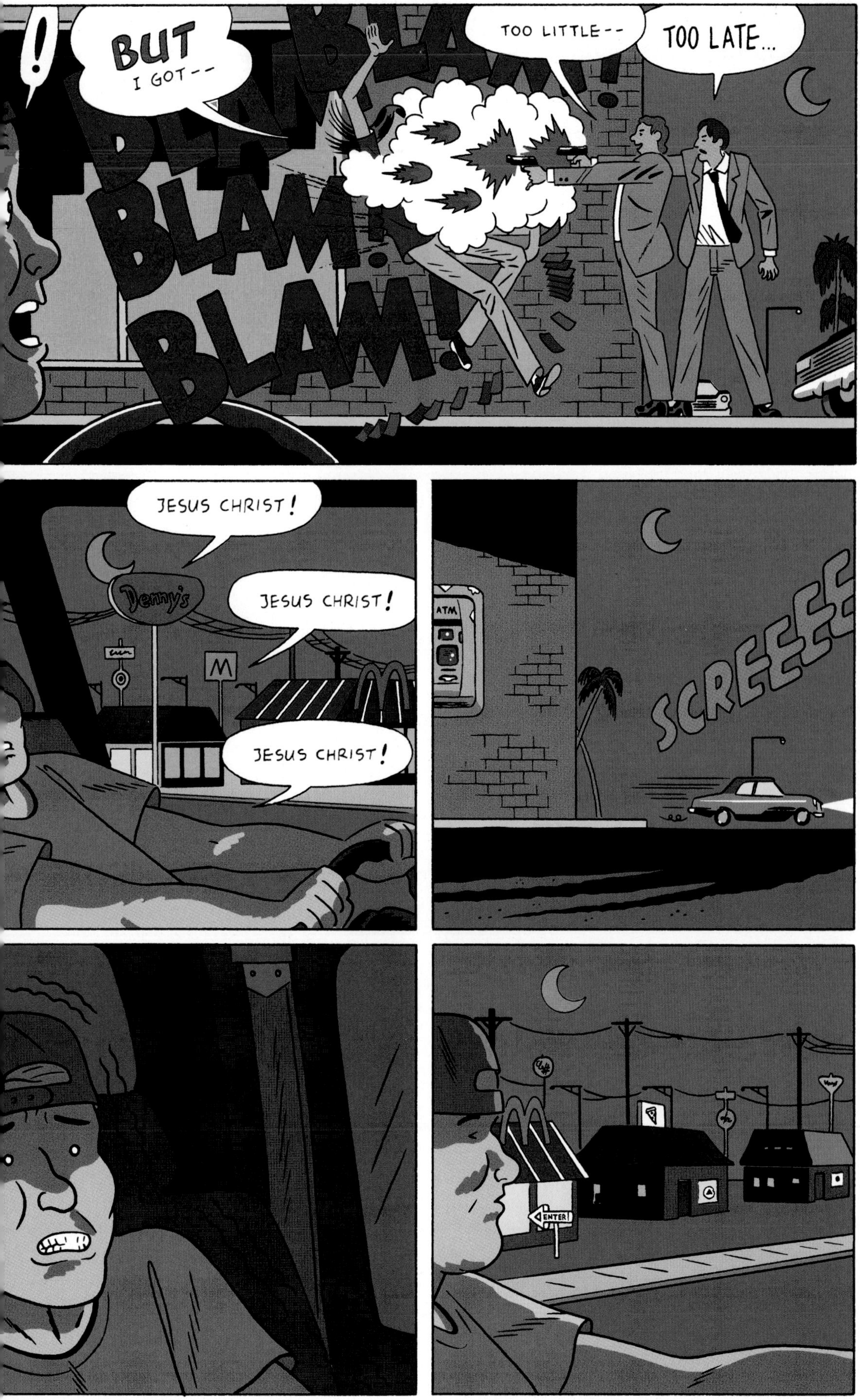
!
BUT I GOT--
BLAM! BLAM! BLAM! BLAM!
TOO LITTLE--
TOO LATE...
JESUS CHRIST!
JESUS CHRIST!
JESUS CHRIST!
Denny's
ATM
SCREEEE
ENTER!

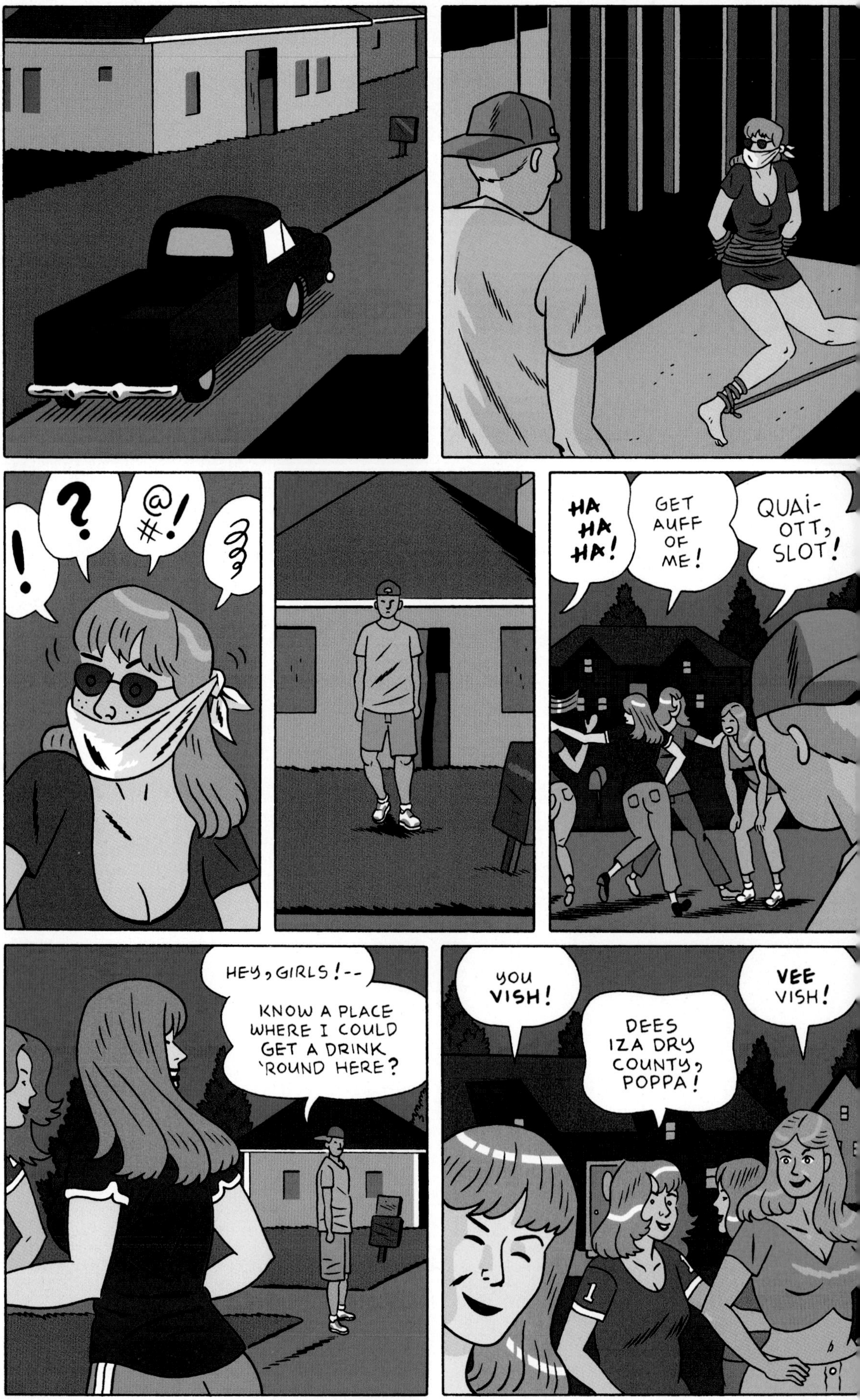
!
?
@#!
HA HA HA!
GET AUFF OF ME!
QUAI-OTT, SLOT!
HEY, GIRLS!--
KNOW A PLACE WHERE I COULD GET A DRINK 'ROUND HERE?
YOU VISH!
DEES IZA DRY COUNTY, POPPA!
VEE VISH!

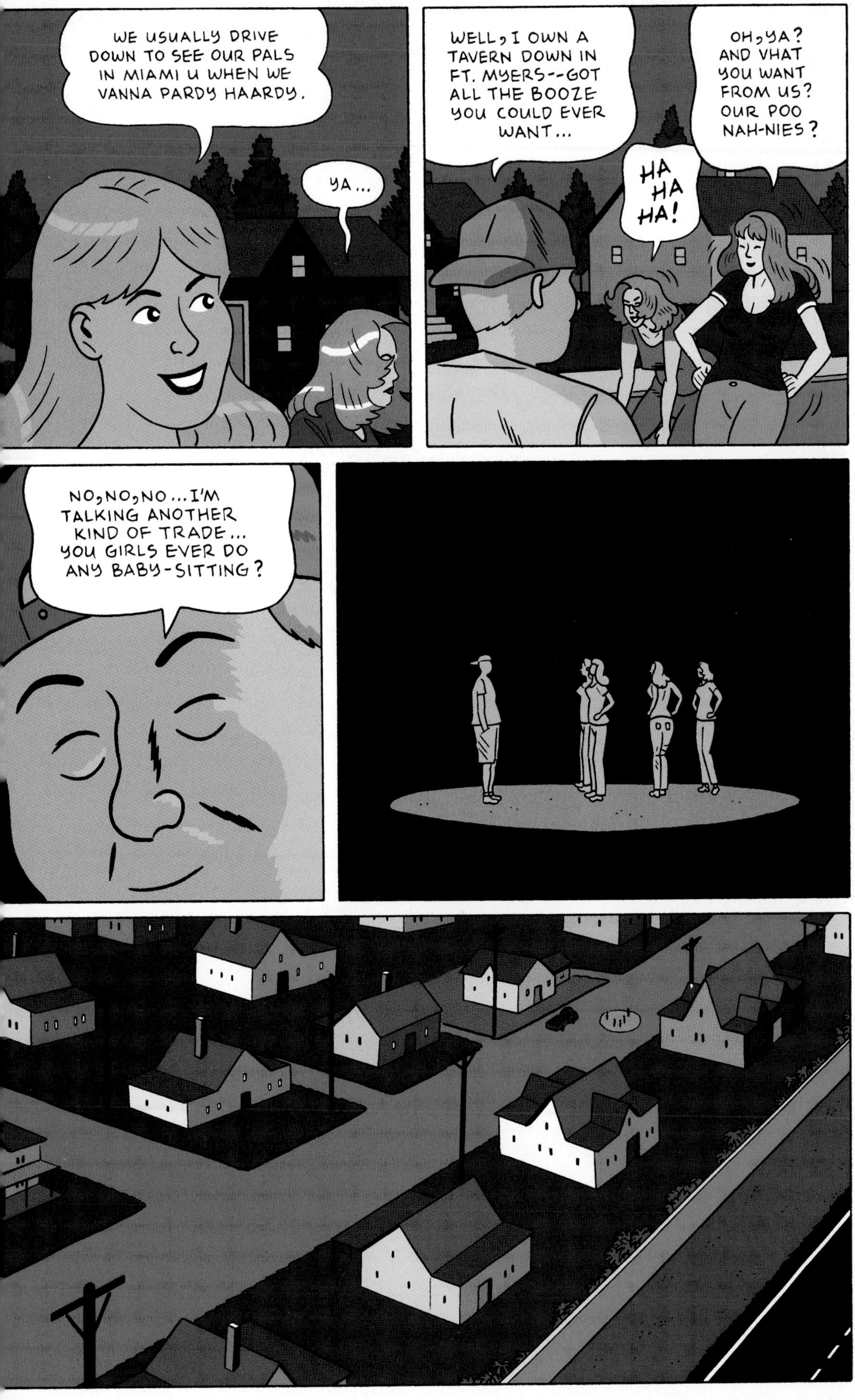
WE USUALLY DRIVE DOWN TO SEE OUR PALS IN MIAMI U WHEN WE VANNA PARDY HAARDY.
YA...
WELL, I OWN A TAVERN DOWN IN FT. MYERS--GOT ALL THE BOOZE YOU COULD EVER WANT...
OH, YA? AND VHAT YOU WANT FROM US? OUR POO NAH-NIES?
HA HA HA!
NO, NO, NO... I'M TALKING ANOTHER KIND OF TRADE... YOU GIRLS EVER DO ANY BABY-SITTING?

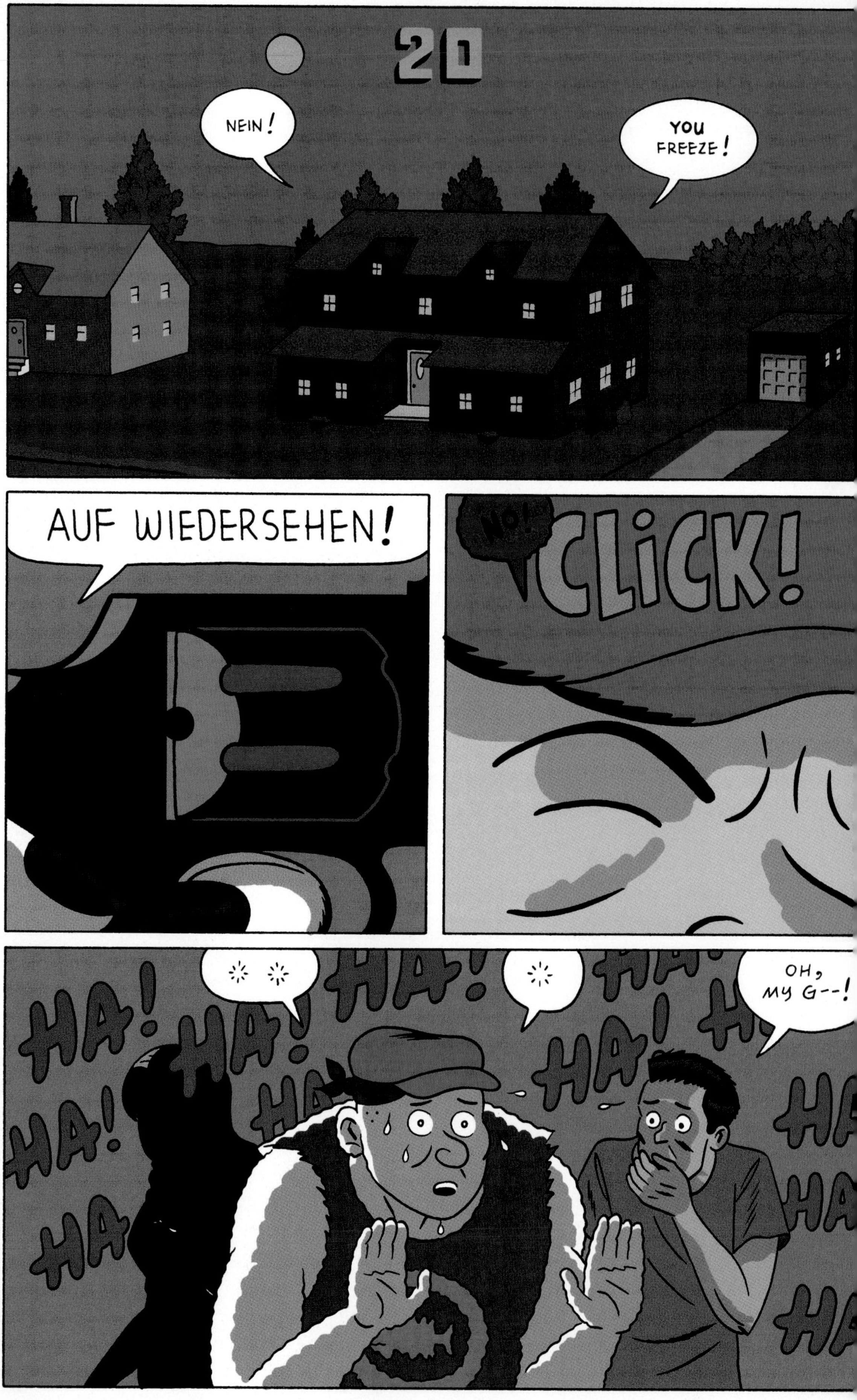
20
NEIN!
YOU FREEZE!
AUF WIEDERSEHEN!
NO!
CLICK!
HA! HA! HA! HA! HA! HA! HA! HA! HA!
OH, MY G--!

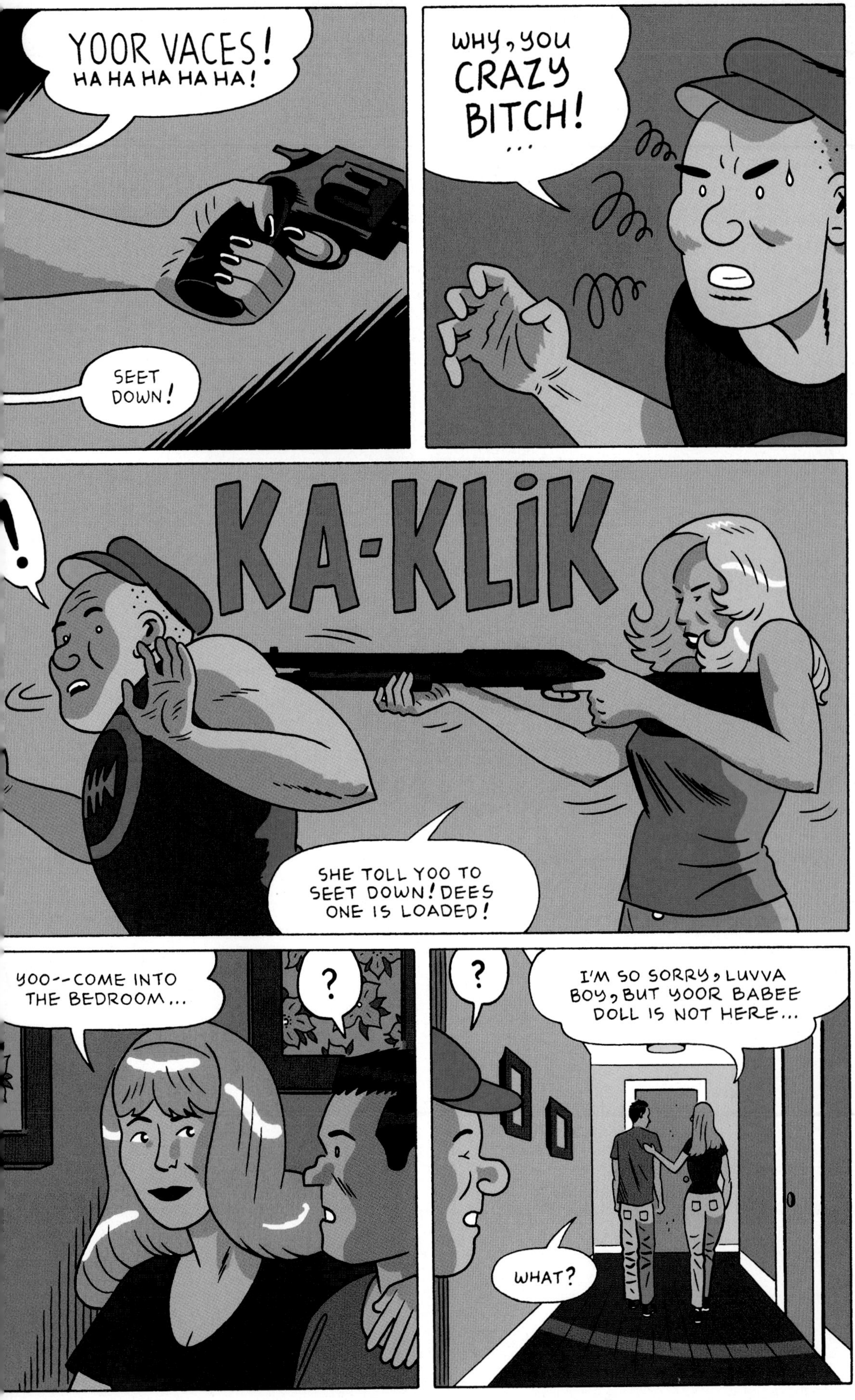
YOOR VACES! HA HA HA HA HA!
SEET DOWN!
WHY, YOU CRAZY BITCH! ...
!
KA-KLIK
SHE TOLL YOO TO SEET DOWN! DEES ONE IS LOADED!
YOO--COME INTO THE BEDROOM...
?
?
I'M SO SORRY, LUVVA BOY, BUT YOOR BABEE DOLL IS NOT HERE...
WHAT?

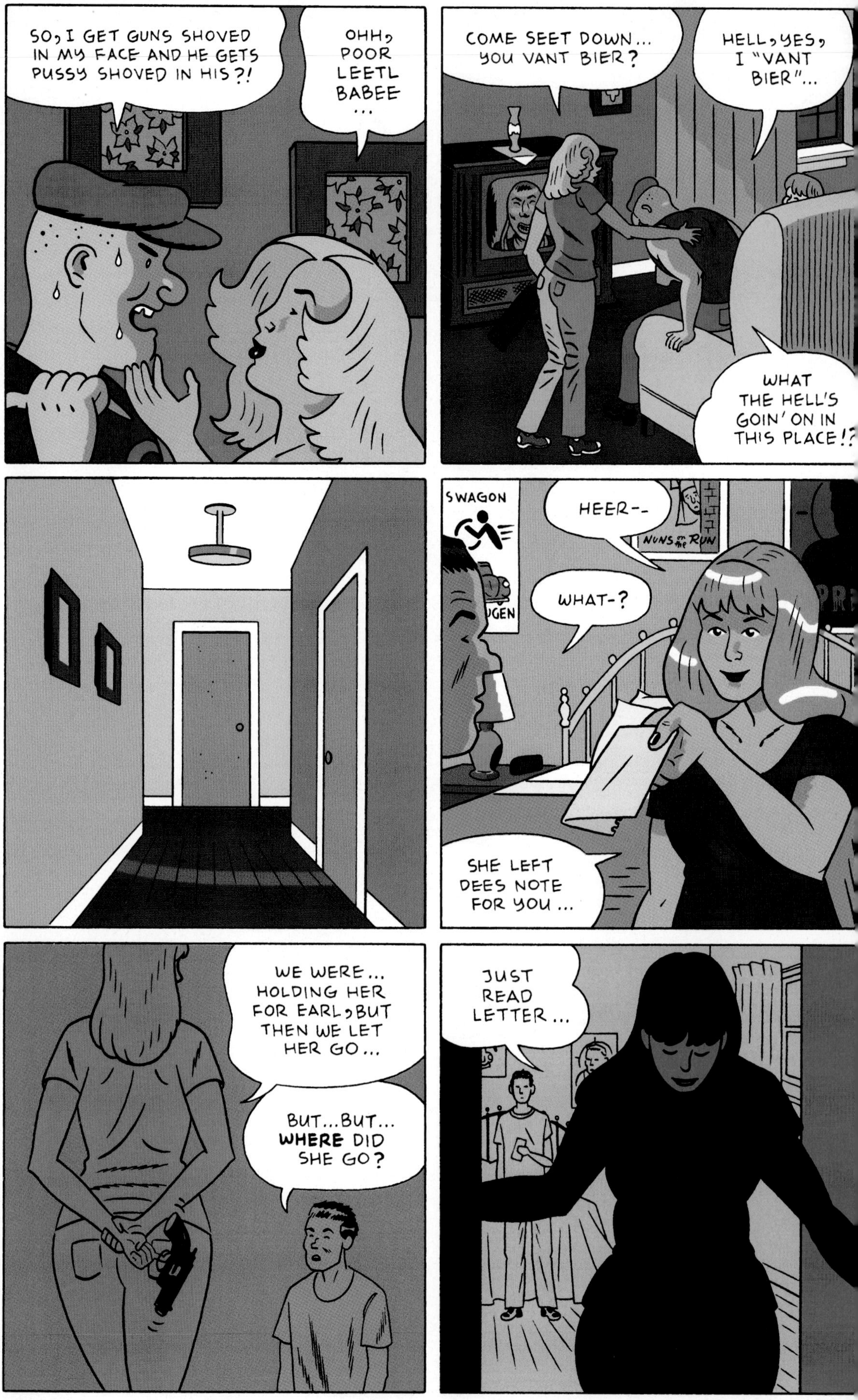
SO, I GET GUNS SHOVED IN MY FACE AND HE GETS PUSSY SHOVED IN HIS?!
OHH, POOR LEETL BABEE...
COME SEET DOWN... YOU VANT BIER?
HELL, YES, I "VANT BIER"...
WHAT THE HELL'S GOIN' ON IN THIS PLACE!?
SWAGON
NUNS ON THE RUN
HEER--
WHAT-?
SHE LEFT DEES NOTE FOR YOU...
WE WERE... HOLDING HER FOR EARL, BUT THEN WE LET HER GO...
BUT...BUT... **WHERE** DID SHE GO?
JUST READ LETTER...

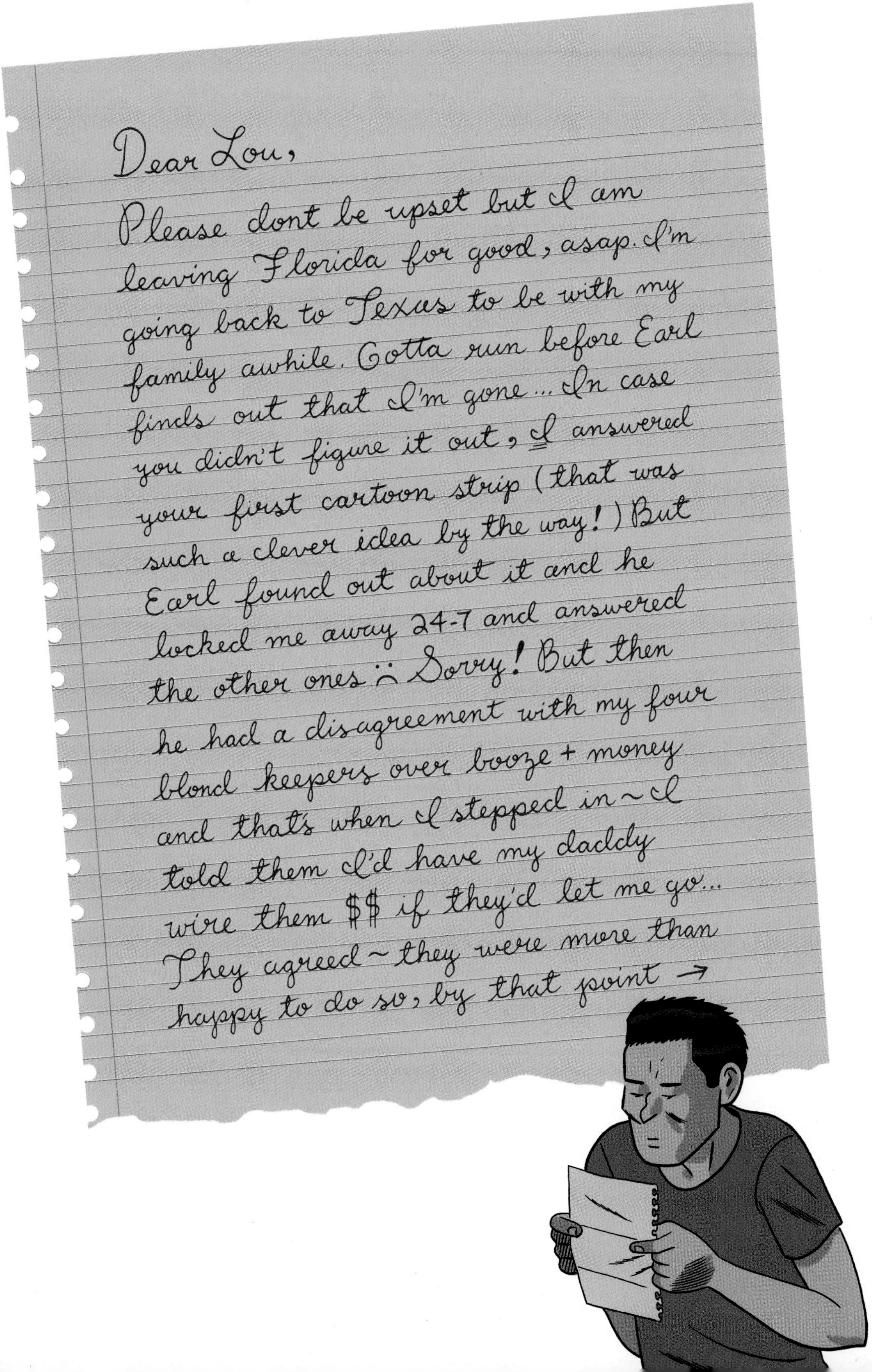
Dear Lou,
Please dont be upset but I am
leaving Florida for good, asap. I'm
going back to Texas to be with my
family awhile. Gotta run before Earl
finds out that I'm gone... In case
you didn't figure it out, I answered
your first cartoon strip (that was
such a clever idea by the way!) But
Earl found out about it and he
locked me away 24-7 and answered
the other ones ☹ Sorry! But then
he had a disagreement with my four
blond keepers over booze + money
and that's when I stepped in ~ I
told them I'd have my daddy
wire them $$ if they'd let me go...
They agreed ~ they were more than
happy to do so, by that point →

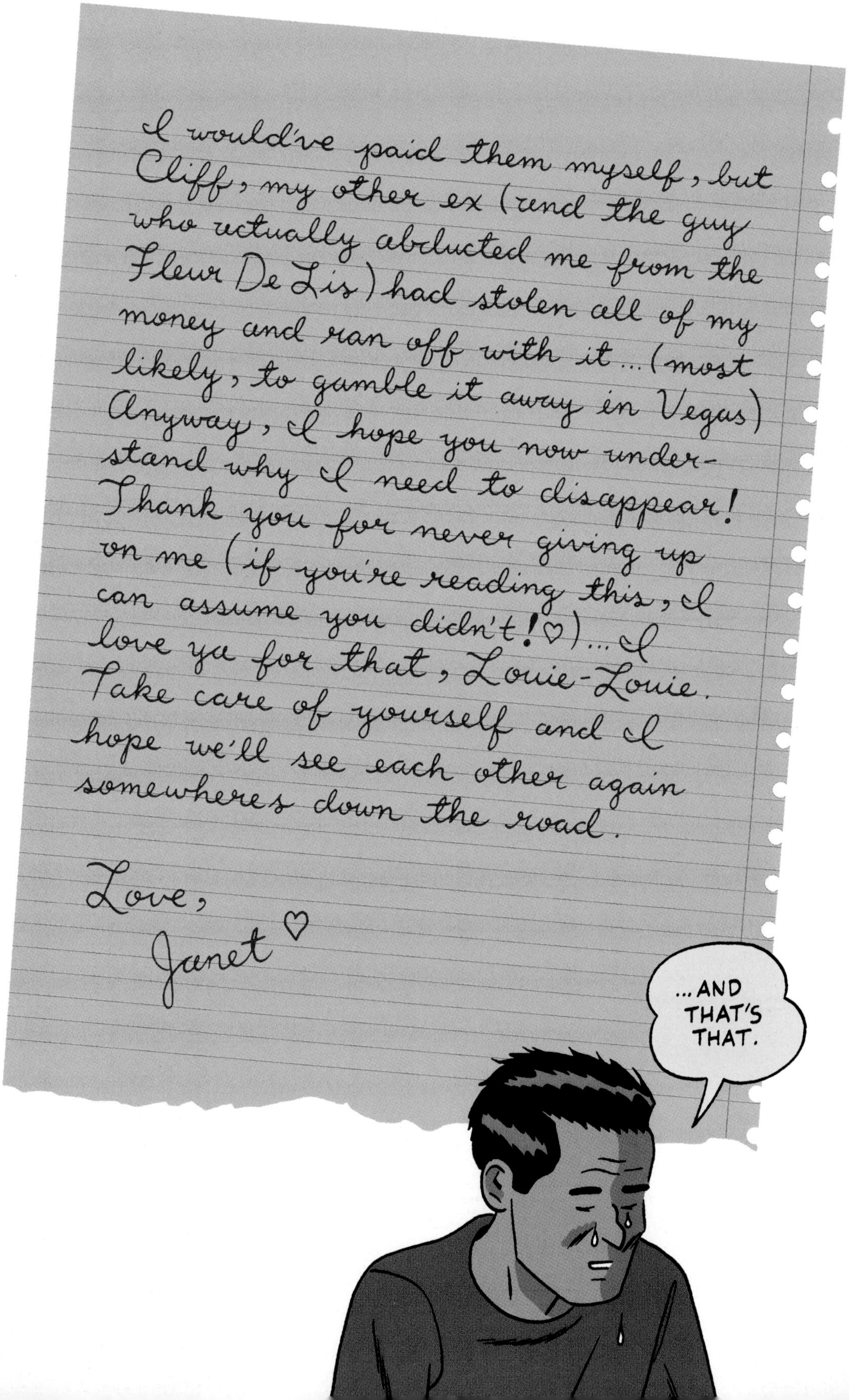

I would've paid them myself, but Cliff, my other ex (and the guy who actually abducted me from the Fleur De Lis) had stolen all of my money and ran off with it... (most likely, to gamble it away in Vegas) Anyway, I hope you now understand why I need to disappear! Thank you for never giving up on me (if you're reading this, I can assume you didn't!♡)... I love ya for that, Louie-Louie. Take care of yourself and I hope we'll see each other again somewheres down the road.

Love,
Janet ♡

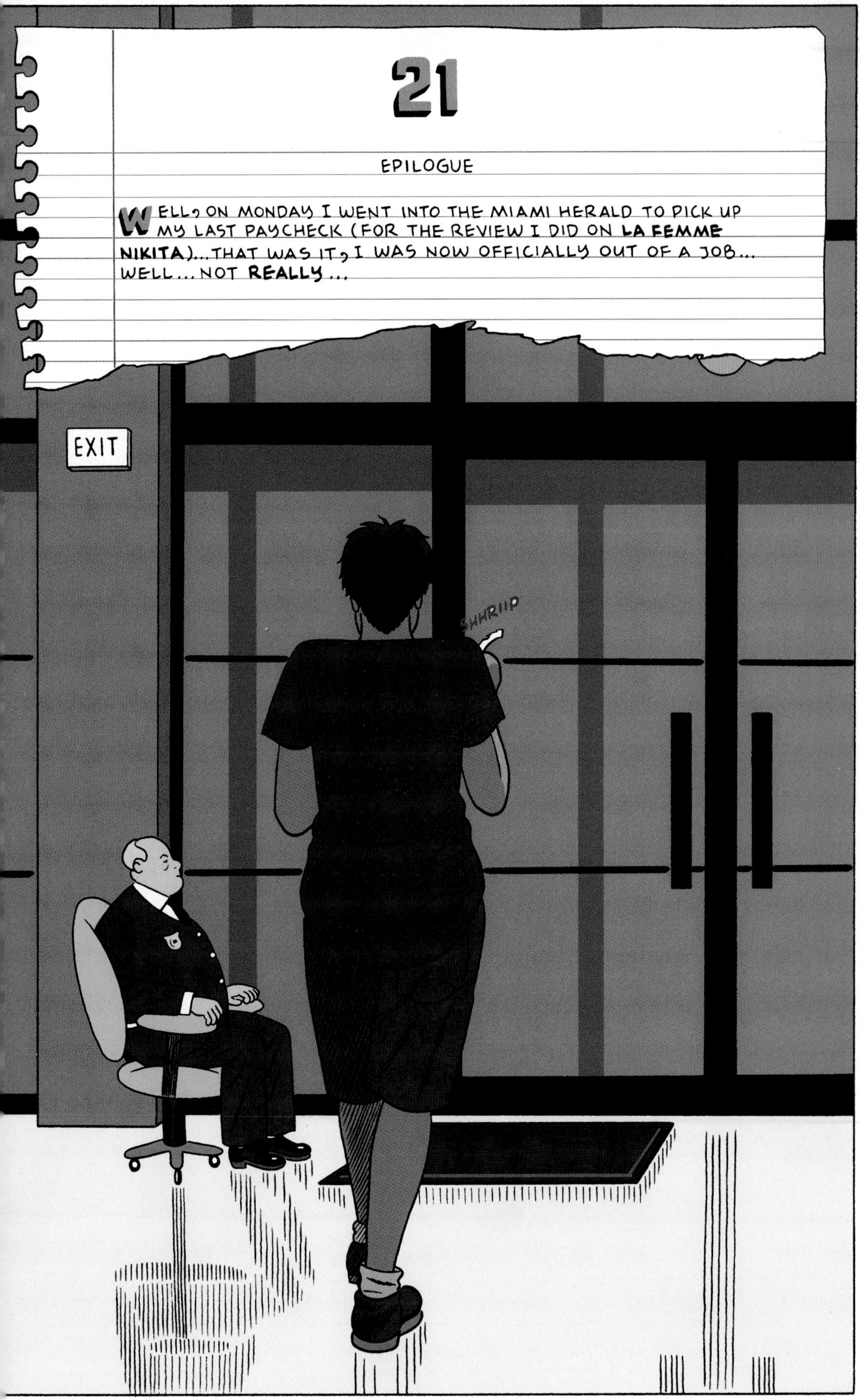
21
EPILOGUE
WELL, ON MONDAY I WENT INTO THE MIAMI HERALD TO PICK UP MY LAST PAYCHECK (FOR THE REVIEW I DID ON **LA FEMME NIKITA**)... THAT WAS IT, I WAS NOW OFFICIALLY OUT OF A JOB... WELL... NOT **REALLY**...
EXIT
SHHRIIP

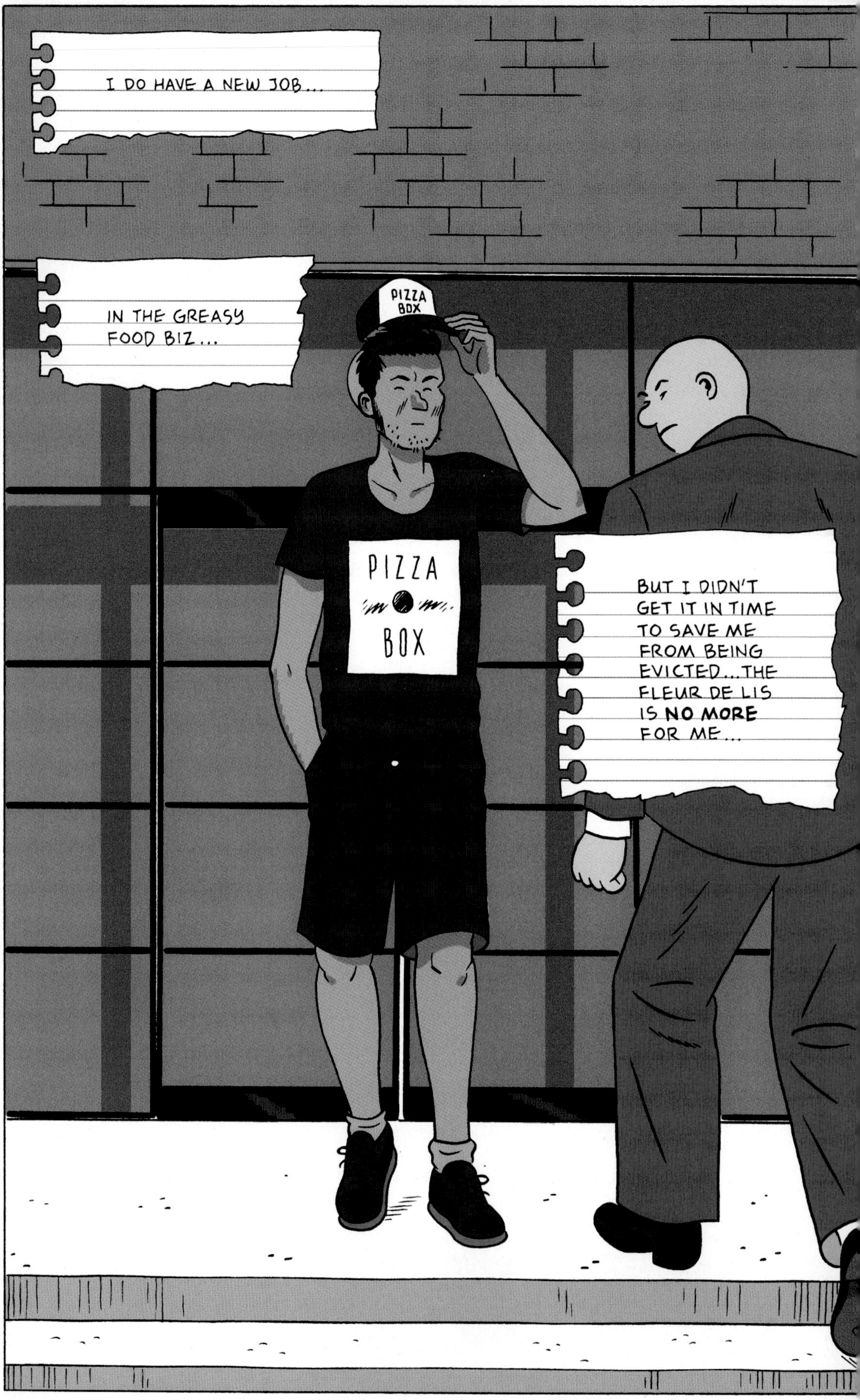
I DO HAVE A NEW JOB...
IN THE GREASY FOOD BIZ...
PIZZA BOX
PIZZA BOX
BUT I DIDN'T GET IT IN TIME TO SAVE ME FROM BEING EVICTED...THE FLEUR DE LIS IS **NO MORE** FOR ME...

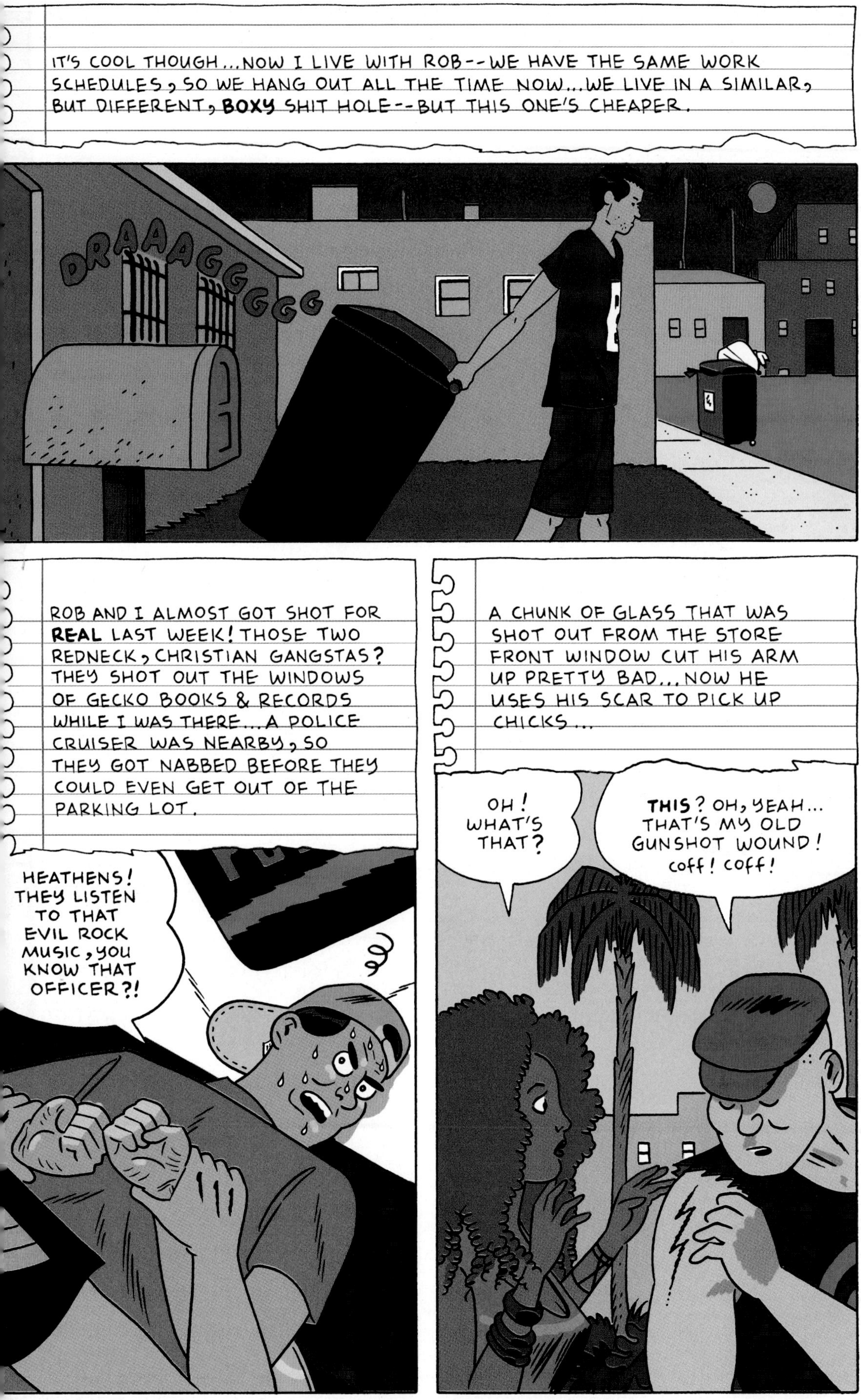
IT'S COOL THOUGH... NOW I LIVE WITH ROB--WE HAVE THE SAME WORK SCHEDULES, SO WE HANG OUT ALL THE TIME NOW... WE LIVE IN A SIMILAR, BUT DIFFERENT, **BOXY** SHIT HOLE--BUT THIS ONE'S CHEAPER.
DRAAAGGGGGG
ROB AND I ALMOST GOT SHOT FOR **REAL** LAST WEEK! THOSE TWO REDNECK, CHRISTIAN GANGSTAS? THEY SHOT OUT THE WINDOWS OF GECKO BOOKS & RECORDS WHILE I WAS THERE... A POLICE CRUISER WAS NEARBY, SO THEY GOT NABBED BEFORE THEY COULD EVEN GET OUT OF THE PARKING LOT.
HEATHENS! THEY LISTEN TO THAT EVIL ROCK MUSIC, YOU KNOW THAT OFFICER?!
A CHUNK OF GLASS THAT WAS SHOT OUT FROM THE STORE FRONT WINDOW CUT HIS ARM UP PRETTY BAD... NOW HE USES HIS SCAR TO PICK UP CHICKS...
OH! WHAT'S THAT?
THIS? OH, YEAH... THAT'S MY OLD GUNSHOT WOUND! COFF! COFF!

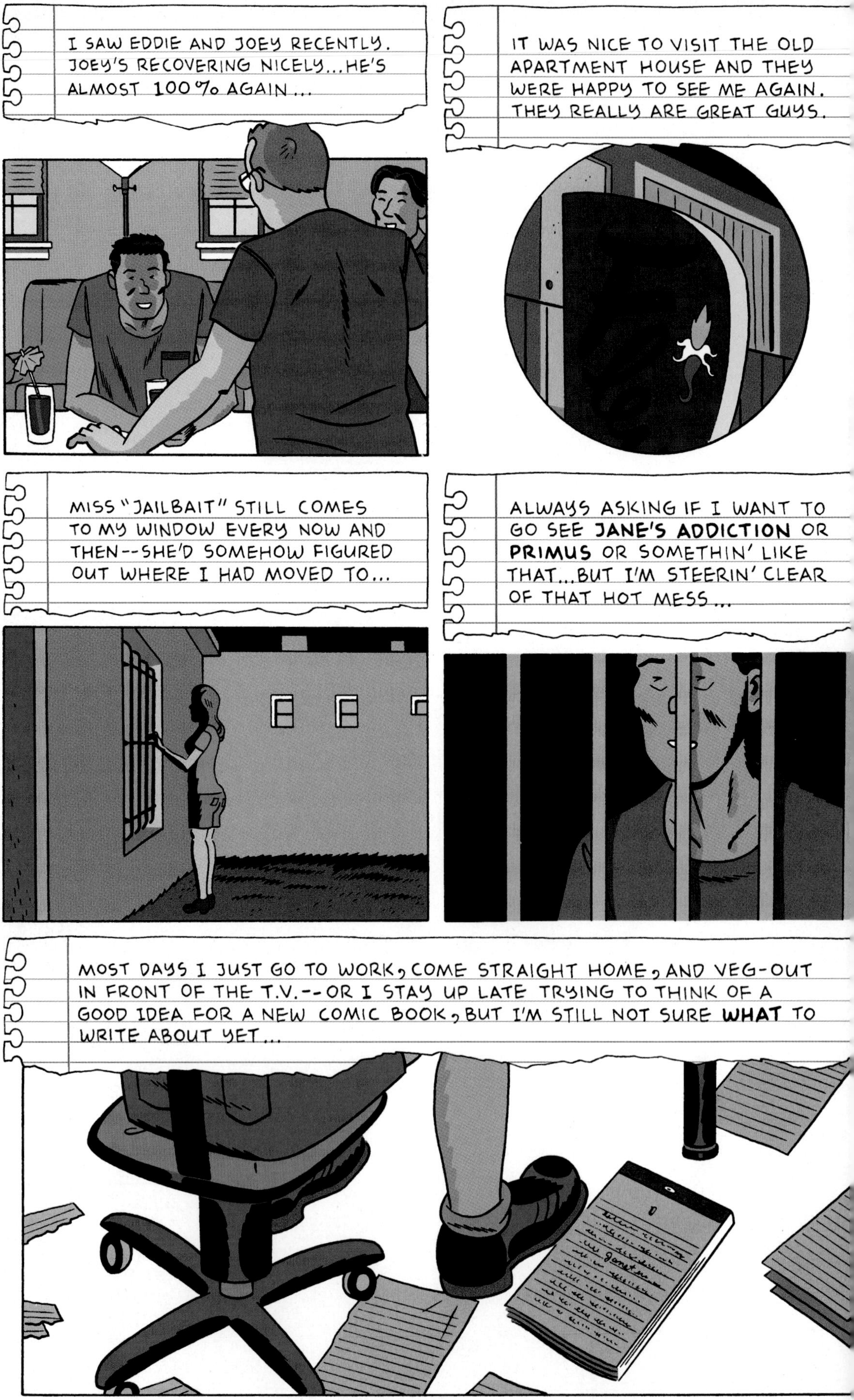
I SAW EDDIE AND JOEY RECENTLY. JOEY'S RECOVERING NICELY...HE'S ALMOST 100% AGAIN...
IT WAS NICE TO VISIT THE OLD APARTMENT HOUSE AND THEY WERE HAPPY TO SEE ME AGAIN. THEY REALLY ARE GREAT GUYS.
MISS "JAILBAIT" STILL COMES TO MY WINDOW EVERY NOW AND THEN--SHE'D SOMEHOW FIGURED OUT WHERE I HAD MOVED TO...
ALWAYS ASKING IF I WANT TO GO SEE **JANE'S ADDICTION** OR **PRIMUS** OR SOMETHIN' LIKE THAT...BUT I'M STEERIN' CLEAR OF THAT HOT MESS...
MOST DAYS I JUST GO TO WORK, COME STRAIGHT HOME, AND VEG-OUT IN FRONT OF THE T.V.--OR I STAY UP LATE TRYING TO THINK OF A GOOD IDEA FOR A NEW COMIC BOOK, BUT I'M STILL NOT SURE **WHAT** TO WRITE ABOUT YET...

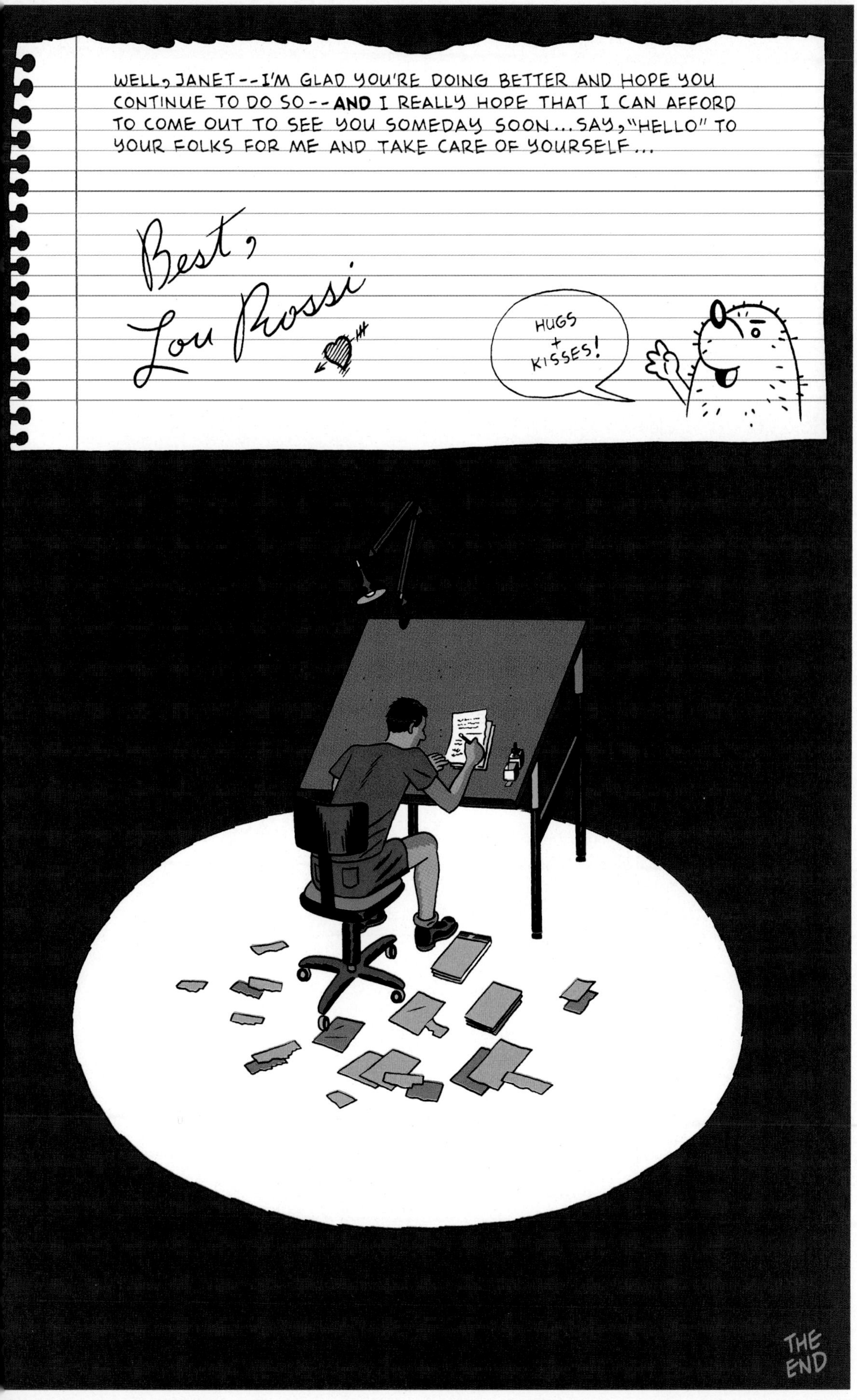
WELL, JANET--I'M GLAD YOU'RE DOING BETTER AND HOPE YOU CONTINUE TO DO SO--**AND** I REALLY HOPE THAT I CAN AFFORD TO COME OUT TO SEE YOU SOMEDAY SOON... SAY, "HELLO" TO YOUR FOLKS FOR ME AND TAKE CARE OF YOURSELF...
Best,
Lou Rossi
HUGS + KISSES!
THE END

CATCH UP ON ALL OF THE EXCITING IMAGE COMICS O

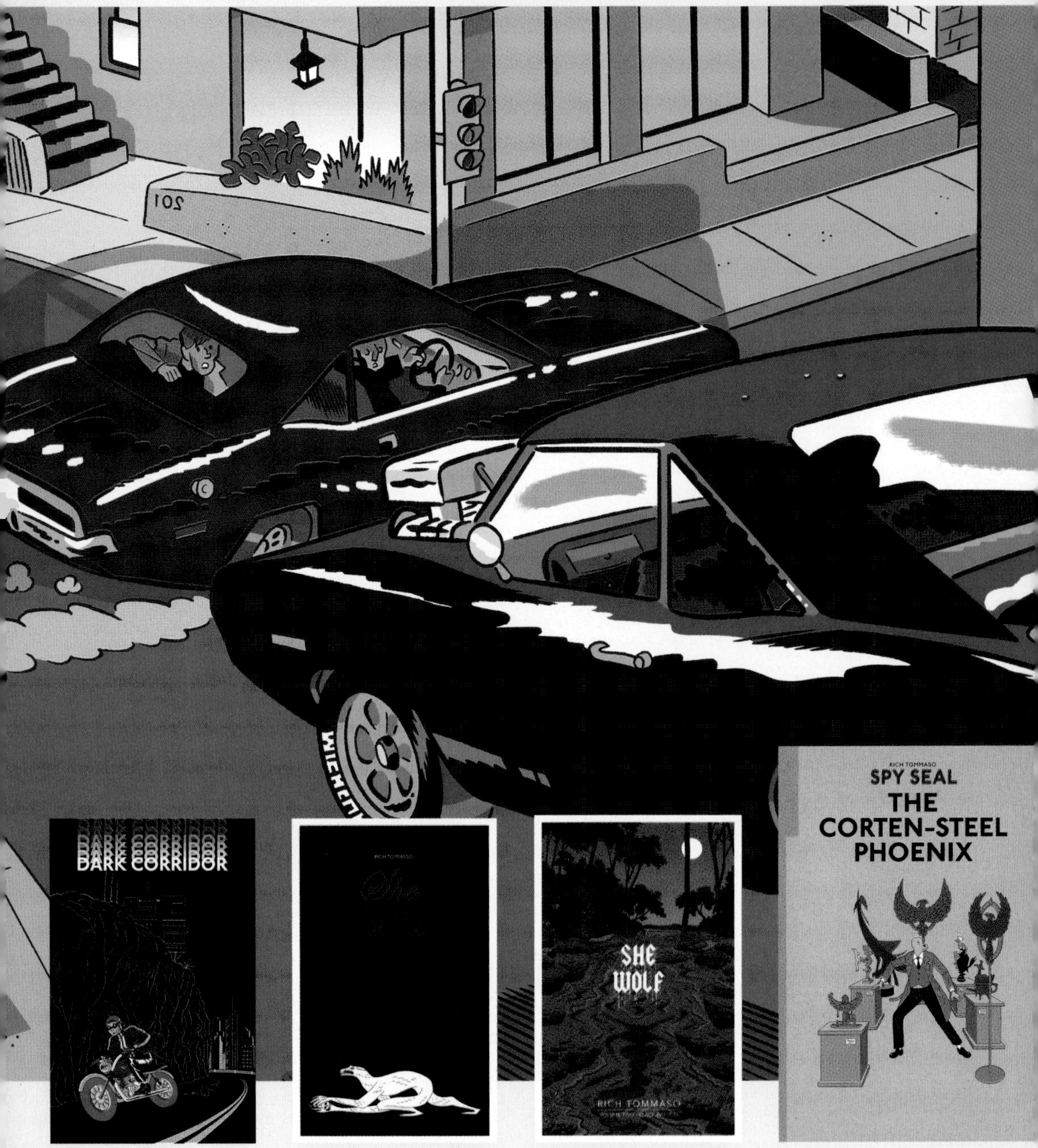

201
DARK CORRIDOR
RICH TOMMASO
SHE WOLF
RICH TOMMASO
SPY SEAL
THE CORTEN-STEEL PHOENIX

This trade conatains the entire run of Rich's first series for Image Comics. A rapidfire, fast paced crime adventure, filled with a variety of hard boiled criminal figures. Set in the fictional city of Red Circle, a place overrun with crime and corruption.

Collects Issues #1-7
$14.99

Read the origin of Rich's werewolf saga that begins with Gabby Catella, Lizzie's older sister. She discovers her transformative powers and struggles to understand and control those evil powers before they can rule and possibly *ruin* her life.

Collects Issues #1-4
$9.99

She Wolf 2 follows Liz Catella and our former monster heroes into the underworld wherein there exist monsters even scarier than themselves! Does this sequel dispell the theory that sequels can't live up to their predecessors? Tune in and find out.

Collects Issues #5-8
$12.99

The first in a new, long-running series c
Tintin-like books about a young seal an
his adventures into the world of spies!
this first volume we see Malcolm Warn
(aka Spy Seal) stumble into his position
as secret agent for Britain's MI-6 divisic
His first mission takes him to various e
otic places across the globe, as he hunt
down the elusive "Phoenix"!

Collects Issues #1-4
$12.99

RICH TOMMASO

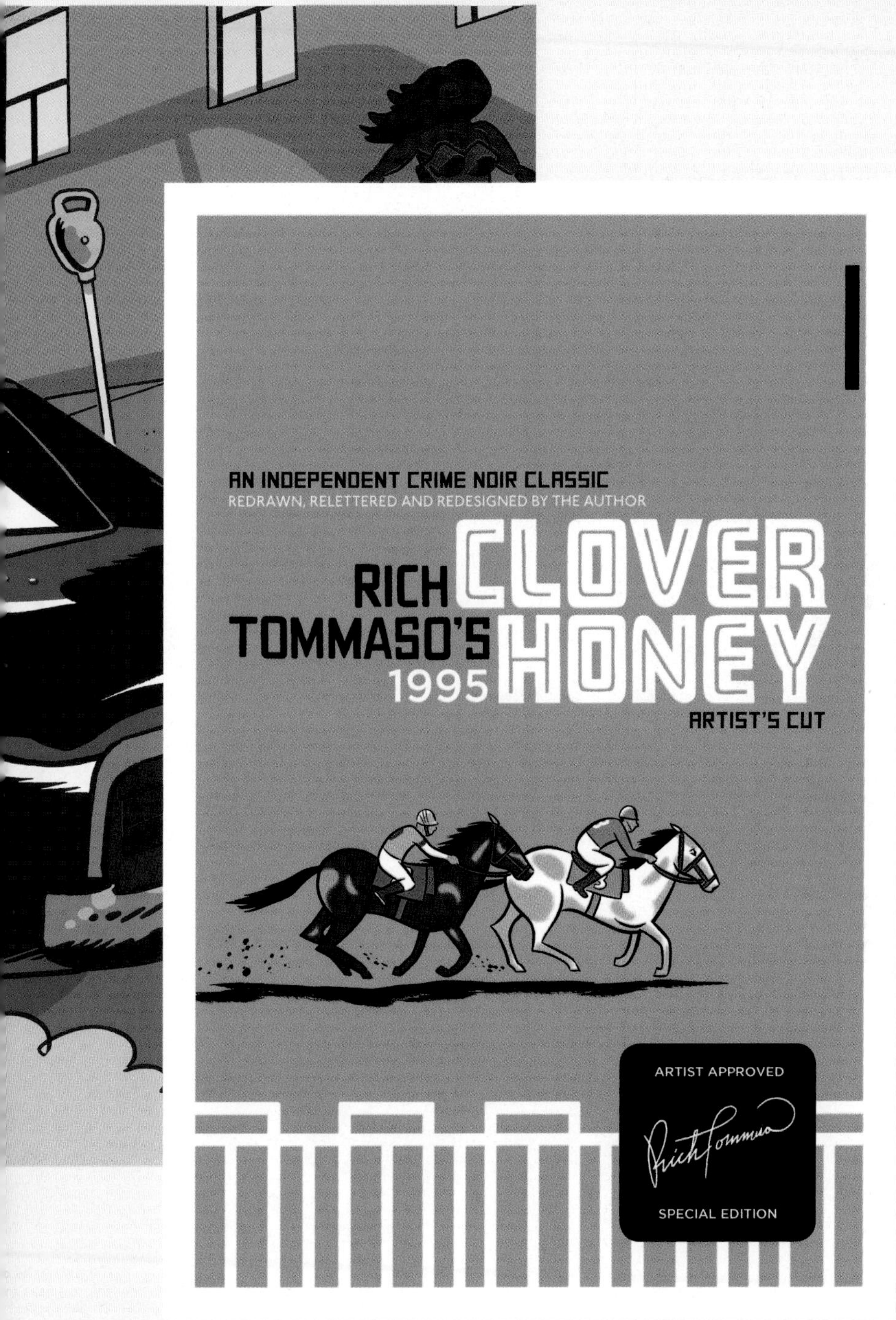

AN INDEPENDENT CRIME NOIR CLASSIC
REDRAWN, RELETTERED AND REDESIGNED BY THE AUTHOR
RICH TOMMASO'S
CLOVER HONEY
1995
ARTIST'S CUT
ARTIST APPROVED
Rich Tommaso
SPECIAL EDITION

NEW RELEASE! Out in stores now: The CLOVER HONEY SPECIAL EDITION reprint! 136 pages, $12.99, Rated M Mature

"we aim to please" - rich tommaso, artist / writer / night manager

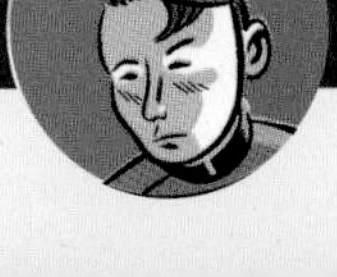

ORIGINS OF DRY COUNTY

This book went through many iterations. At first it was about a guy named Lou who was skipping town, leaving Miami Beach, to extricate himself from a fellow drug dealer who had overdosed at the story's opening. That book was called, ReBound. Below (left) is a facsimile of the original cover art.

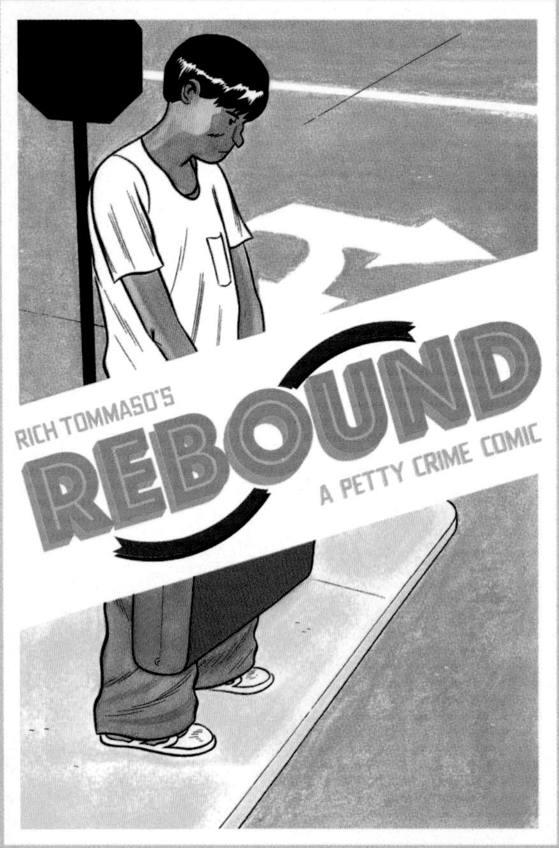
RICH TOMMASO'S
REBOUND
A PETTY CRIME COMIC

ORIGINAL COVER, 2001. (*Left*) I'd hand painted the background art on 3-ply Bristol board and painted the logos on a separate piece of Bristol board. This is a Photoshop facsimile shown here. The original is long gone for this. It says, "comic" but I later decided to do this as a graphic novel. It was to be my first self-published book under an imprint I had come up with called ***Recoil Books***. This novel was torn to pieces after having drawn 75 pages. I foolishly tried to draw the book, one panel at a time, each panel the size of 8 1/2 X 11". This led to a very time-consuming book to make. In one year, I had only managed to draw 75 panels--***and*** I was married to the idea that each page would be a 9-panel grid.

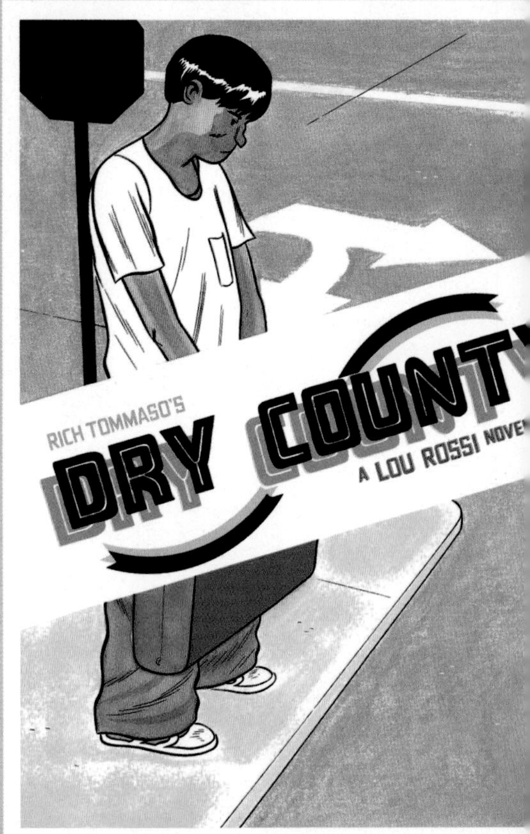
RICH TOMMASO'S
DRY COUNTY
A LOU ROSSI NOVE

DRY COUNTY COVER, 2009. (*Right*) This was the first cover art design for the new, DRY COUNTY version of the story (the crime story you've just read). This was supposed to be--again--the cover for a graphic novel format book. In 2018, it became the cover for DRY COUNTY, issue five, which I completely re-inked and colored for the Image serialization. I believe the inspiration for this cover came from Chip Kidd's book design for the new, 1990s line of Elmore Leonard novels.

SECOND DRAFT PAGES

As the first-draft pages were torn up, I only have the second draft to show here--from the early version I'd started working on in 2009. My tactic then was the complete opposite of my first approach in 2001--this time I tried to see if I could draw the entire novel in one to two months. That plan was abandoned pretty fast. These pages are a few of the results from that experiment--I drew four of these pages a day--and gave up on this frequency in less than a week.

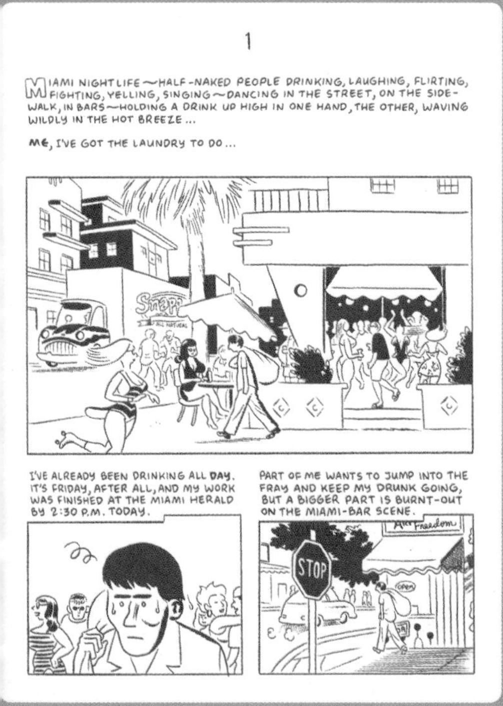
1
MIAMI NIGHTLIFE — HALF-NAKED PEOPLE DRINKING, LAUGHING, FLIRTING, FIGHTING, YELLING, SINGING — DANCING IN THE STREET, ON THE SIDE-WALK, IN BARS — HOLDING A DRINK UP HIGH IN ONE HAND, THE OTHER, WAVING WILDLY IN THE HOT BREEZE...
ME, I'VE GOT THE LAUNDRY TO DO...
I'VE ALREADY BEEN DRINKING ALL DAY. IT'S FRIDAY, AFTER ALL, AND MY WORK WAS FINISHED AT THE MIAMI HERALD BY 2:30 P.M. TODAY.
PART OF ME WANTS TO JUMP INTO THE FRAY AND KEEP MY DRUNK GOING, BUT A BIGGER PART IS BURNT-OUT ON THE MIAMI-BAR SCENE.
STOP

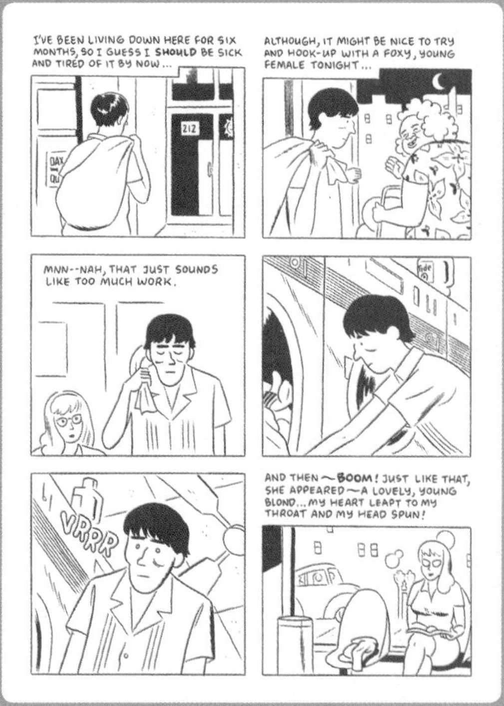
I'VE BEEN LIVING DOWN HERE FOR SIX MONTHS, SO I GUESS I SHOULD BE SICK AND TIRED OF IT BY NOW...
212
ALTHOUGH, IT MIGHT BE NICE TO TRY AND HOOK-UP WITH A FOXY, YOUNG FEMALE TONIGHT...
MNN--NAH, THAT JUST SOUNDS LIKE TOO MUCH WORK.
VRRR
AND THEN — BOOM! JUST LIKE THAT, SHE APPEARED — A LOVELY, YOUNG BLOND... MY HEART LEAPT TO MY THROAT AND MY HEAD SPUN!

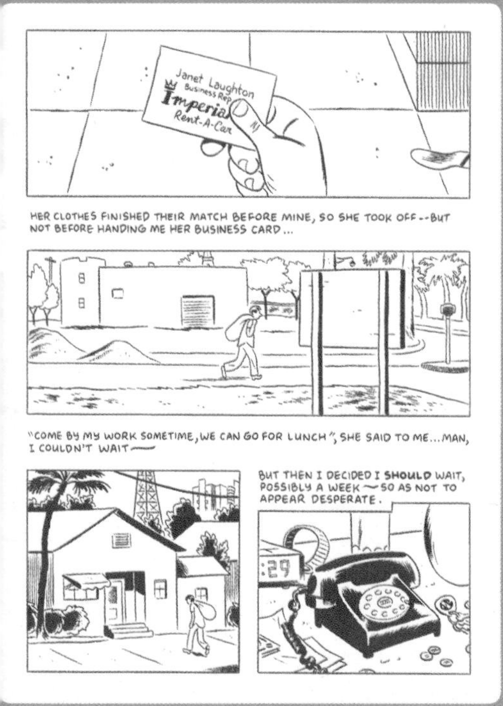
Janet Laughton
Business Rep
Imperial
Rent-A-Car
HER CLOTHES FINISHED THEIR MATCH BEFORE MINE, SO SHE TOOK OFF -- BUT NOT BEFORE HANDING ME HER BUSINESS CARD...
"COME BY MY WORK SOMETIME, WE CAN GO FOR LUNCH", SHE SAID TO ME... MAN, I COULDN'T WAIT —
BUT THEN I DECIDED I SHOULD WAIT, POSSIBLY A WEEK — SO AS NOT TO APPEAR DESPERATE.

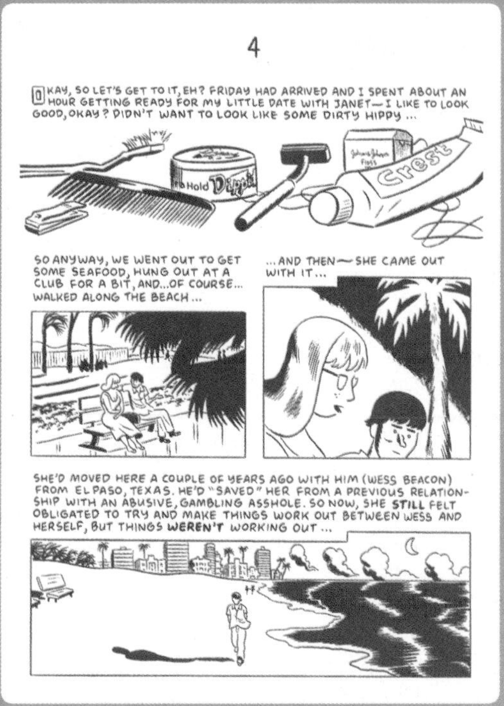
4
OKAY, SO LET'S GET TO IT, EH? FRIDAY HAD ARRIVED AND I SPENT ABOUT AN HOUR GETTING READY FOR MY LITTLE DATE WITH JANET — I LIKE TO LOOK GOOD, OKAY? DIDN'T WANT TO LOOK LIKE SOME DIRTY HIPPY...
Crest
SO ANYWAY, WE WENT OUT TO GET SOME SEAFOOD, HUNG OUT AT A CLUB FOR A BIT, AND... OF COURSE... WALKED ALONG THE BEACH...
...AND THEN — SHE CAME OUT WITH IT...
SHE'D MOVED HERE A COUPLE OF YEARS AGO WITH HIM (WESS BEACON) FROM EL PASO, TEXAS. HE'D "SAVED" HER FROM A PREVIOUS RELATION-SHIP WITH AN ABUSIVE, GAMBLING ASSHOLE. SO NOW, SHE STILL FELT OBLIGATED TO TRY AND MAKE THINGS WORK OUT BETWEEN WESS AND HERSELF, BUT THINGS WEREN'T WORKING OUT...

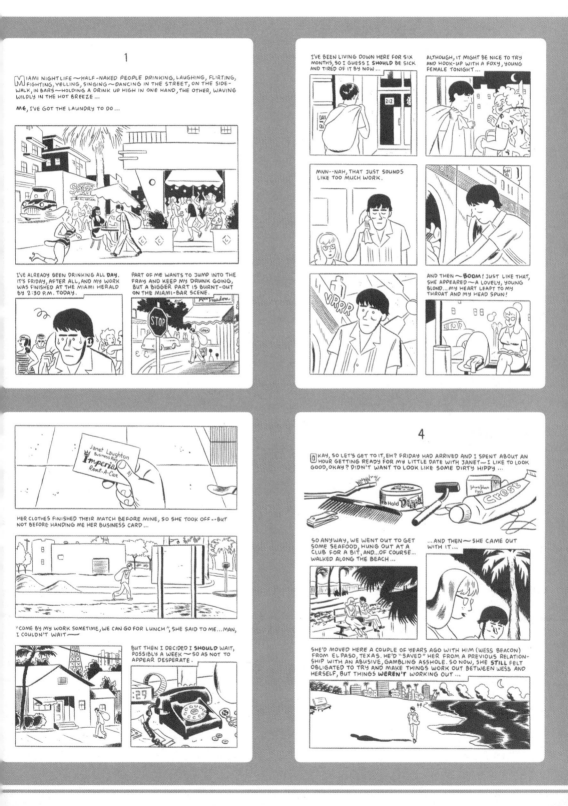

CREATING LOU ROSSI

Here's a crazy sketch page with me going crazy trying to come up with a look and a name for our lazy-eyed, Generation X anti-hero. Something lightly Italian (as he's based on myself and my late brother, Louis). At the bottom right corner, you can see I scratched out what would actually become his name in the end.

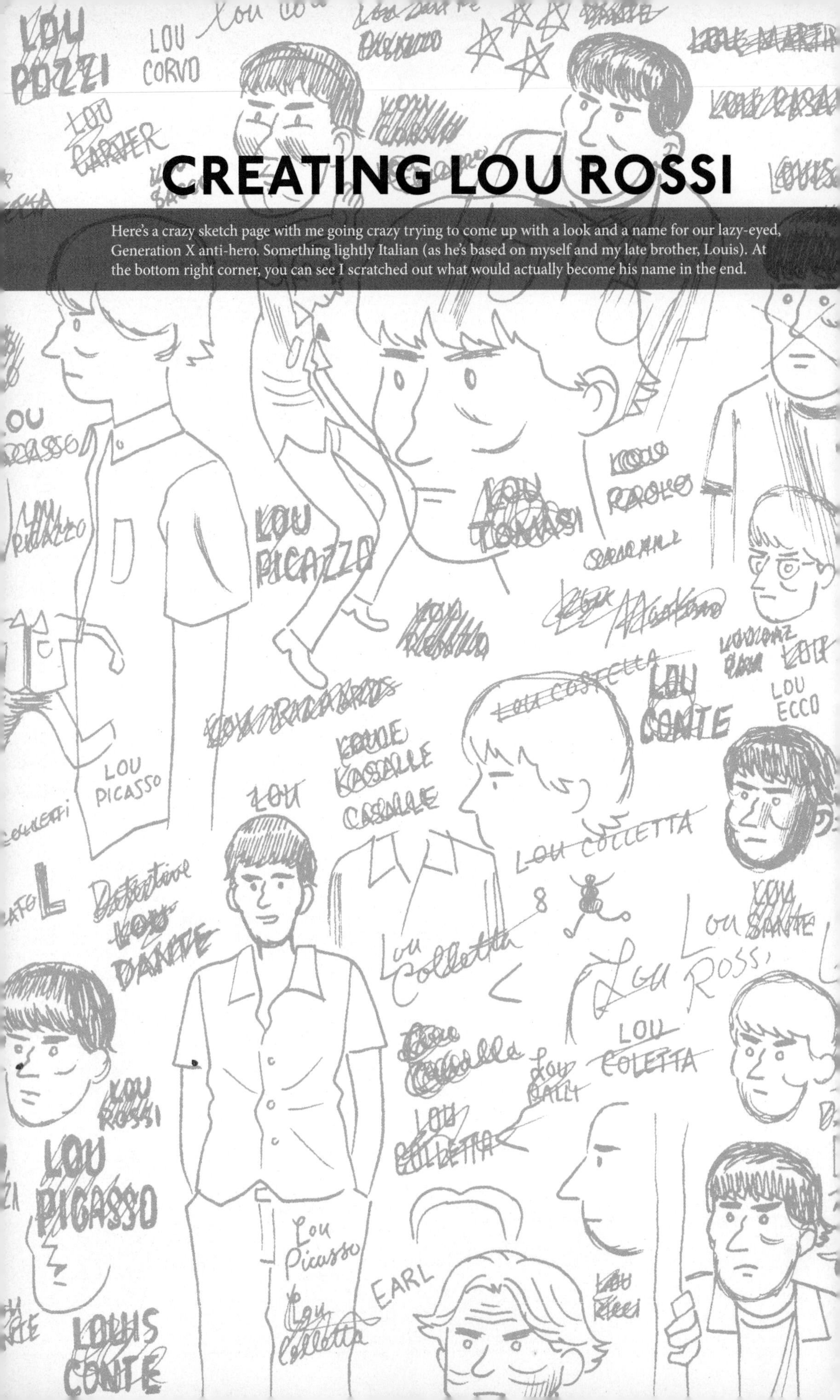

LOU POZZI
LOU CORVO
LOU CARTER
LOU PICASSO
LOU PICAZZO
LOU TOMASI
LOU PICASSO
LOU COSTELLA
LOU CONTE
LOU ECCO
LOU COLLETTA
Detective LOU DANTE
Lou Colletta
Lou Rossi
LOU COLETTA
LOU ROSSI
LOU PICASSO
Lou Picasso
EARL
Lou Colletta
LOUIS CONTE
LOU RICCI